THE Physician's Daughter

Martha Conway has been nominated for an Edgar Award and won the North American Book Award for Best Historical Fiction. She teaches creative writing for Stanford University's Continuing Studies Program. Born in Cleveland, Ohio, she is one of seven sisters. She now lives in San Francisco with her family.

Also by Martha Conway

The Floating Theatre (also known as
The Underground River in the USA)
Thieving Forest
Sugarland
12 Bliss Street

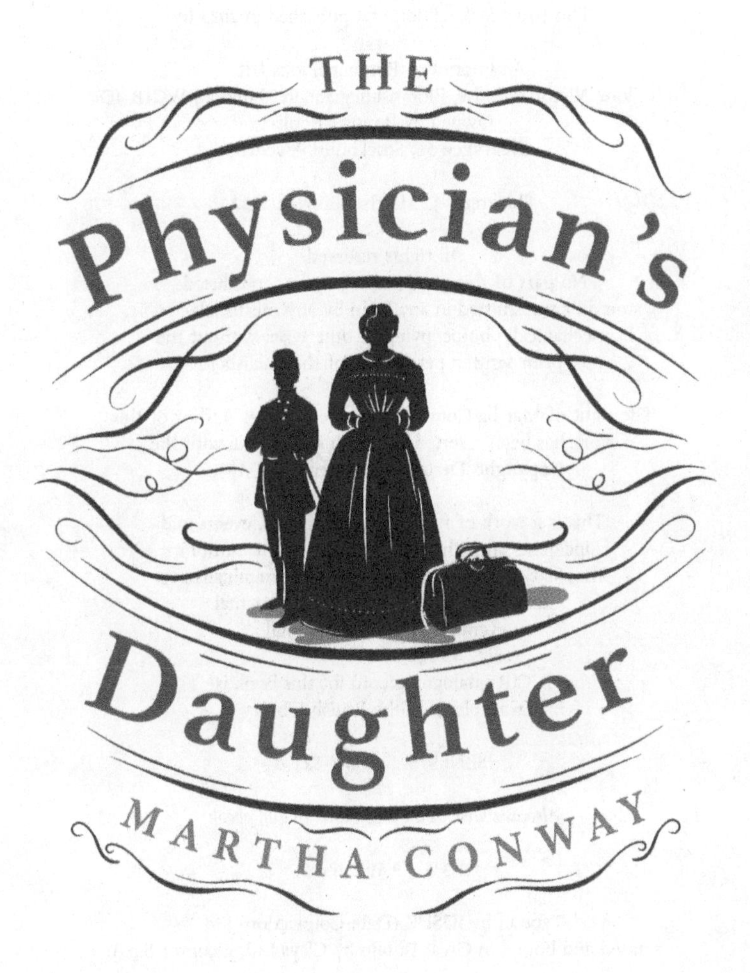

ZAFFRE

First published in the UK in 2022
This paperback edition first published in 2023 by
ZAFFRE
An imprint of Bonnier Books UK
4th Floor, Victoria House, Bloomsbury Square, London, WC1B 4DA
Owned by Bonnier Books
Sveavägen 56, Stockholm, Sweden

Copyright © Martha Conway, 2022

All rights reserved.
No part of this publication may be reproduced,
stored or transmitted in any form by any means, electronic,
mechanical, photocopying or otherwise, without the
prior written permission of the publisher.

The right of Martha Conway to be identified as Author of this
work has been asserted by her in accordance with the
Copyright, Designs and Patents Act, 1988.

This is a work of fiction. Names, places, events and
incidents are either the products of the author's
imagination or used fictitiously. Any resemblance to
actual persons, living or dead, or actual
events is purely coincidental.

A CIP catalogue record for this book is
available from the British Library.

ISBN: 978–1–83877–821–7

Also available as an ebook and an audiobook

1 3 5 7 9 10 8 6 4 2

Typeset by IDSUK (Data Connection) Ltd
Printed and bound in Great Britain by Clays Ltd, Elcograf S.p.A.

Zaffre is an imprint of Bonnier Books UK
www.bonnierbooks.co.uk

For Richard, John Henry, and Lily

PART 1

CHAPTER ONE

'Hysteria is often excited in women by indigestion.'
(*On Diseases Peculiar to Women*,
Dr. Hugh Lenox Hodge, 1860)

June 1865, Lark's Eye, Massachusetts

Vita was sitting on the front stairs in a shaft of sunlight reading *On Diseases Peculiar to Women* when they carried the Boston man into her house.

Her mother and sister had gone to visit Aunt Norbert in town, and Vita was waiting for her father to emerge from his office, which was directly across from the staircase. She knew he was in there although for the last thirty minutes – she squinted at the watch pinned upside down to the shoulder of her dress – she'd heard nothing, not even the shush of a newspaper page turning.

'What does he do in there all day?' Vita asked Sweetie, her brother's parakeet, perched on her shoulder. Sweetie repositioned her claws and butted her soft pale head against Vita's ear – the triangular fossa. *Triangular fossa, scapha, auricular lobule,* Vita recited to herself. Parts of the outer ear.

The book's pages were mostly uncut since it had only arrived yesterday, from England; everything was still slow because of the war. In one hand Vita wielded a silver letter opener like a surgeon's knife, slicing the crisp, cream-colored pages to reveal row after row of dark print like so many ants marching from one idea to the next. But her neck was getting sore, and the light from the landing window dropped to almost nothing whenever a cloud passed over the sun. She was about to give up her vigil when she heard the sound of carriage wheels on the gravel drive, and then a man shouting:

'Dr. Tenney! Dr. Tenney!'

A minute later the front door banged open and two men came into the house carrying a third man by the armpits and ankles. As Vita stood up, Sweetie flew off her shoulder to the fixed safety of the newel post.

'Dr. Tenney!'

Maneuvering, the men knocked over the little oak table with its double-wick lamp. Now there was glass on the floor.

'Dar?' Vita called. Like her brother and sister, Vita always called her father Dar and her mother Mitty – her older brother Freddy's attempt at saying their names, Arthur and Marie, when he was a baby.

Her father opened his door and stood in the doorway, unshaven and wearing the same gray waistcoat he'd been wearing for three weeks straight. For some reason he looked at Vita first.

'Stop that shouting.'

Sherman Tillings, who owned the saddlery and the public stable and had a wife named Thankful, was at the injured man's head; Vita didn't recognize the other man.

'We was just changing horses for the Boston coach,' Mr. Tillings explained. 'He collapsed on the porch, didn't say a word. Where can we set him?'

Her father directed them to the long sofa against the windows in his office, where the light was best.

'Not one word,' Mr. Tillings went on, lowering the man onto the green velvet upholstery. 'A Boston man. You see where his forehead is swelling? Cracked the rail when he fell.'

The man's face – closed eyes, open mouth – had a waxy tinge, like skin on hot milk. Was he breathing? Vita, who had seen many an injured man brought into their house, stared at his chest but couldn't make out a rise and fall.

'Shall I fetch a blanket?' she asked. It's important to keep the extremities warm, her father always said. He sat down on the stool next to the sofa and put his ear to the man's mouth. Then he placed two fingers against his wrist.

'No pulse,' he announced.

He told Tillings to prop the fellow up while he opened a bottle of whiskey. Holding the bottle by the neck, he pushed back the man's head and poured a glug down his throat. 'To encourage the swallowing reflex.' But the man didn't swallow. Two uneven streams ran down either side of his beard.

'Get a hot poker, set it against his head, that'll shock him awake,' Tillings said.

'Or blow tobacco smoke into his mouth,' suggested the other man – the coach driver? – who was small and freckled with wiry red hair.

'Nonsense.' Her father began massaging the man's chest. 'But perhaps I can work up the heart.'

'Work it up?' Vita asked. The human heart, with its auricles and ventricles and valves, its precise oscillation, was, to her, a miracle of engineering. She had seen her father perform countless exceptional procedures – setting badly broken bones, draining pustulous head wounds, and once he made an incision into a man's bladder to extract a stone the size of a fig – but she had never seen him restart a stopped heart. Scientifically, it seemed impossible, but there was so much she didn't know. She stepped closer.

'I thought you were getting a blanket,' her father said.

When she came back into the room they were pushing the man forward and back, bending him at the waist as though he were a lever. They stopped long enough for Vita to spread the tartan blanket over his legs. The man's eyes were not altogether closed although he was clearly unseeing. He had a craggy round face with a cluster of white warts under one eye; whiskey drops glistened on his beard. She touched the top of his hand. It was still warm. Of course, she thought, it will take a while for blood in the body to cool.

The three men began again to pull him up and shake him, set him down, pull him up. Meanwhile her father was becoming angrier and angrier, as though the unlucky man was clinging to death just to vex him.

'Enough!' he said at last. 'He's clearly past saving.'

Mr. Tillings, his face solemn, stepped back and took off his hat. By now the Boston man's mouth was fully open, and his neck and shoulders seemed unnaturally still. For a moment, looking at him, Vita could almost understand it: how the body, with its layered, exact systems and its rhythmic machinery, might at any moment halt absolutely. Here was proof. However, the next moment the man, a stranger on her father's green sofa, didn't seem quite real.

'Rupture of the heart,' her father said with his usual authority. But how did he know?

After the men left – Vita could hear Mr. Tillings arguing with the coach driver about the man's belongings as they carried him out of the house – she watched her father pour himself a shot of the whiskey, drink it, and pour a second shot. He had a long thin nose with wide nostrils, which widened further into little round caves of distaste when he was annoyed.

They widened now. 'I'll just get on with my work, then,' he said, seeing that Vita was still standing there.

But this was her chance.

She looked around, steeling herself for her task. She hadn't been in her father's office for weeks; no one had. He wouldn't even let Gemma clean it. As children the room had always been off limits to them, which meant that whenever Dar was gone Vita and her brother Freddy would sneak in. Dar had a peculiar collection of what he called 'my curiosities,' which included ancient nested bleeding bowls, Roman instruments for pulling teeth, and a set of mandibles he'd gotten as a prize while studying medicine at Yale – a seagull, a porcupine, and a snake. Framed pictures of iridescent beetles hung on the walls like soldiers awaiting inspection, and he kept a two-tailed lizard in a jar of liquid on his desk.

Once Freddy bet Vita a penny that she wouldn't touch both tails of the lizard; she won the penny easily. Sometimes even without Freddy, if Dar was out, Vita pulled books from the bookshelves to read about the uses of quinine or how to reset a dislodged shoulder. She had always been healthy – no trouble sleeping, a good appetite, and although she was clumsy (her father was always scolding her for that), she never broke any bones. There were times she almost wished she had an affliction that she could diagnose. But at least she could read about them, and as a child – before the war – the more gruesome the illnesses were, the more she liked them.

Now the bookshelves were visibly covered with fine ashy dust. Vita half expected to find something horrible or secretive in here, something her father didn't want to be seen.

However, except for the stacks of yellowing newspapers piled up on the floor, the room seemed much the same. What struck her most was the smell, which was heavy and densely male: sweat and stale tobacco smoke and wool clothes that needed airing. She looked down at his set of mandibles and picked up her favorite, the snake. A bone as smooth as glass.

'And take that blanket with you as you go,' he said. 'Best to have Mrs. Oakum wash it.'

She put the snake mandible back on the painted tray with the others, turning it slightly so it faced the door.

'Dar,' she said, lifting the blanket and beginning to fold it. Her heart pumped out a couple of hard beats. 'I've discovered something. Well, I've known it for a long time. But it's important.'

She waited for him to look at her but he didn't. He slid his hand in his pocket and then took it back out.

She went on in a rush: 'I want to study medicine. I want to be a doctor, like you.'

'What's that?' He put his hand in his other pocket and pulled out a pouch of tobacco.

'A doctor. I want to study to become a doctor. I've looked into it, and there are colleges that I can apply to. That accept women, I mean. Medical colleges. One in Philadelphia and one in Boston.' Although she'd practiced this speech a hundred times, she found herself stumbling her way around the points she wanted to make. 'I could start in the fall. It wouldn't cost that much. If you let me.'

Dar set the tobacco pouch down on his desk and turned to lock his whiskey and shot glass into the cabinet behind him. He said, with his back to her, 'You want to help people, is that it?'

She hadn't thought about it that way. 'Well – yes. I suppose. That is, I've always been interested in biology and medicine. The art of healing.' One of his own pet phrases.

'The art of healing, I see. And you've decided to apply to medical college so you can do that?'

'Yes.'

'And you would like to attend this fall? This is what you're proposing?'

She nodded, but he still wasn't looking at her. 'I – yes. If I can. If they'll have me.'

For a shining, unreal moment she thought he would say all right then, go. His mood swings had become excessive in the last few months. For days at a time he ignored her, and then suddenly he berated her for nothing.

'Well then,' he said now, 'you're a fool.'

Her heart dropped. 'Why?'

He began to fill his pipe. 'Obviously you don't know the first thing about it. You can't just apply to medical college; first you must find a sponsor, a doctor who will mentor you so that you can gain practical experience. A preceptor, he's called. You assist him during the day, seeing patients and so on, and then you go home at night to study up on your own. Cheselden on the bones, Jones on the muscles, Vansweiten on humoral pathology. Also Haller, Quincy; I could name a dozen more. You must know these texts inside and out before you even begin to approach the college dean. He'll ask you, you know. You'll be required to submit to an interview, and he'll want to know what you've read and what you've memorized. It took me almost a year to learn enough just to be interviewed, and I was a fast reader.'

'I'm a fast reader,' Vita said.

'Anyway it's unnecessary. There are quite enough men in the world to serve as doctors. You'd only get in their way.'

She had thought of this argument. 'There may be women who are more comfortable seeing a woman – having a woman examine them.'

'Then they're being childish.' He bent to turn the snake mandible around so it faced his desk instead of the door. 'It's unnecessary,' he said again. 'You're eighteen years old now, and the war is over. The time has come for you to accept your station in life.'

She felt the heat rise in her face. 'My station in life? What station is that?'

'Vita. Lower your voice.'

Vita's voice was naturally low-pitched and loud – 'mannish,' her younger sister Amelia called it – and the slightest hint of emotion made it go even louder. It surprised people in part because Vita herself was so small; Amelia, at seventeen, was taller than Vita was at eighteen. Vita had her mother's thick black hair, whereas Amelia was blonde like Dar. The only thing that Vita shared with her father, as far as she could tell, was a bad temper. Though of course Dar never admitted he had a temper. He called his outbursts 'setting things to rights.'

'What is my station?' Vita repeated. She was still clutching the tartan blanket; one lopsided triangle had fallen outside the folds and she squished the errant piece up, trying to hide it. Her hands were shaking.

'You know very well. To marry, to have babies. Boys in particular. That's every woman's duty after a war. To replace the men we've lost.'

But here his voice faltered, and Vita felt something dark and raw pulse in the deepest part of herself. It had only been two months since they received the telegram about Freddy. Their horses still wore black ribbons in their manes.

'It's time you married. I've thought it out. You'll have a double wedding, with your sister. That will save on expense.'

'A double wedding? But, Dar, I'm not – I don't have anyone to marry, even if I wanted to. What I want is to follow in your footsteps.' Maybe appealing to his vanity would help? 'I want to be a doctor, like you. Like Freddy was going to.'

But at that he turned on her, suddenly furious. 'You think you can replace your brother?'

She felt the blood drain from her face. 'No! Nothing like that!'

'You hope to profit from our loss, like a turkey vulture?'

'Of course not! I only meant that I want to study medicine, like . . . like he would have.'

Her father was glaring at her now, his nostrils flaring. His cheeks, above his untrimmed beard, were an angry, mottled red. He yanked his door open and stood with his hand on the doorknob, pointedly waiting for her to leave. This conversation was over.

'No one can take the place of my son.'

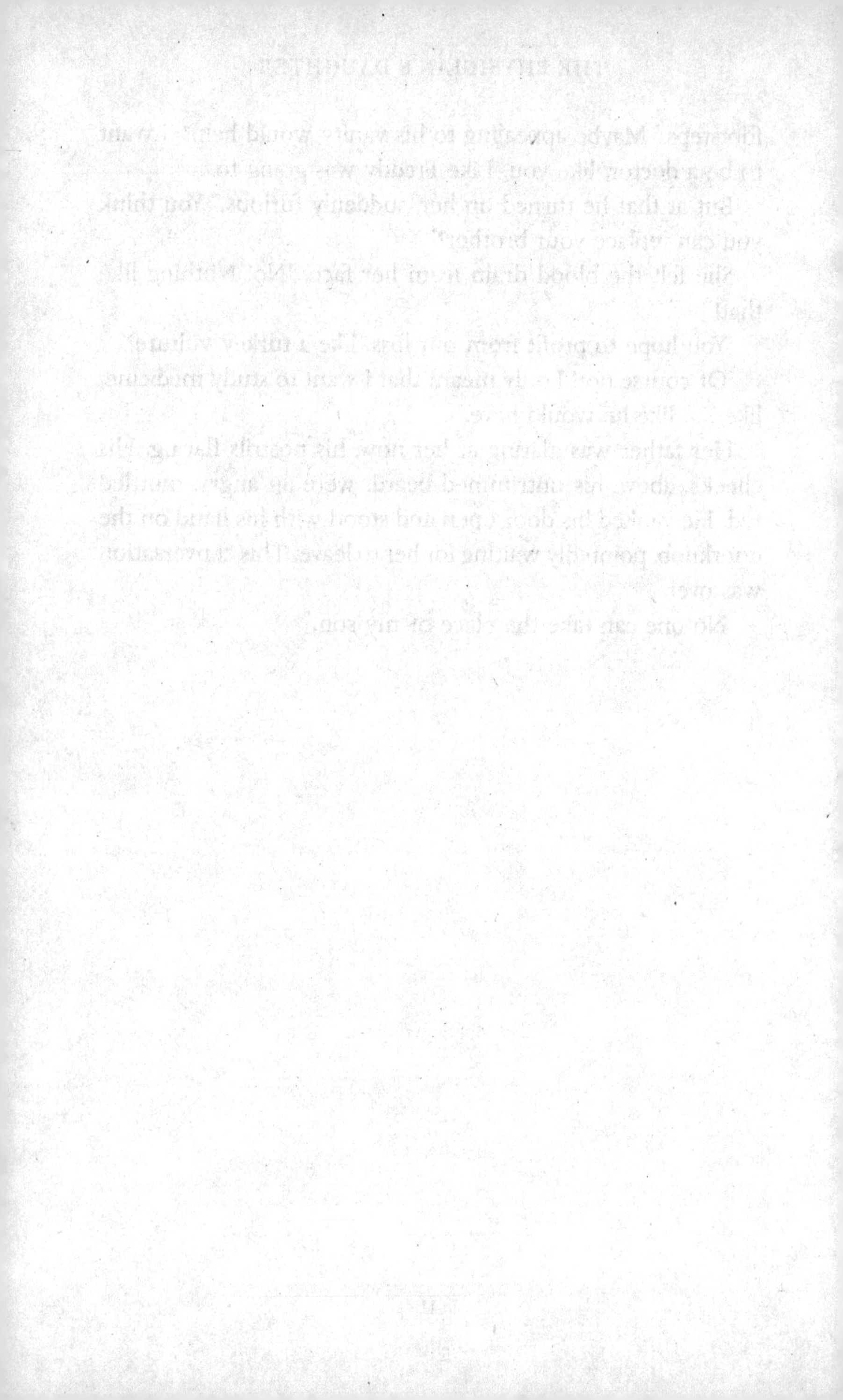

CHAPTER TWO

'If the groom attempts to kiss his bride any place other than the cheek or the hand, she should announce that nature calls her to the toilet. This will generally dampen his desire.'
(*Instruction and Advice for the Young Bride*, Mrs. Ruth Smythers, 1894)

Vita didn't want to take the place of her brother. She wanted, more than anything, for Freddy to still be alive.

At night she sometimes dreamed of him, but his voice was always different, or his hair, or he said things to her that he would never have said in real life. In her dreams he was blander, more complacent. He wasn't the prankster she knew as a child. Once he put molasses inside Amelia's boot and he got in real trouble for that since it was always gummy afterwards.

But he was a good brother too, usually letting her in on his games if she asked. He loved being outdoors; climbing trees and fishing, or just walking around the marshes. As a boy he kept little stones or sticks in his pockets that he said looked like animals – a cat, a sitting bear, a giraffe. He was forever bringing home injured birds or motherless kittens. While I'm away, he told Vita, you're in charge of my pets.

He was seventeen when he signed up with the 28th Regiment of Massachusetts. He survived the battles of Antietam, Fredericksburg, and Gettysburg, but at Hatcher's Run he took a bullet above the elbow and an infection set in. The company's assistant surgeon decided not to take off the arm, and ten days later Freddy died of gangrene.

On the morning the telegram arrived, a full week after peace had been signed and they'd all been rejoicing because they thought Freddy had made it safely through, Vita's insides seemed to crumble into ash. She was coming down the staircase reciting to herself the bones of the cranium – *frontal, parietal, temporal* – when she saw Mitty standing at the front door with a black-edged envelope in her hand. In that instant she knew.

How did they get through the first day? They must have eaten but Vita couldn't remember what they ate or even sitting at the dinner table. During the night she kept waking up and sobbing into her pillow, and in the morning she found a tiny goose feather in the wet pocket of her gum – the *gingiva*. She kept it as a memory of her initial grief, which throbbed less as the weeks passed but never went away.

Vita paced the length of her bedroom, digging her nails into the palms of her hands. Once Dar understands how serious I am, she thought, he'll come around. Won't he? She worried that, in his eyes at least, she had never been good enough. Sometimes he praised the work she had done for Freddy – a graph or an equation – and that was gratifying. Of course he thought Freddy had done it and praised him, not her, but she knew. Dar didn't think women were capable of 'logic and straight lines'; he'd said this more than once, even around Mitty, who once bested their old tutor on a point of geometry.

Mitty's face always flushed with emotion when he said this, but she didn't try to argue.

Why get into a quarrel, she said when Vita asked her about it. You can't change other people, you can only change yourself. Wise words, but not particularly helpful. Vita didn't need to change herself. It was the rest of the world that needed to change.

The sky darkened, and tree branches bent back and forth dramatically in the wind. She heard the front door open and close, and two voices floated up – Mitty and Amelia getting home just before the rain. Vita didn't go down to see them. Her bedroom was her sanctuary even though it was dark and messy and usually chilly, even in the spring. In the summer, after a humid rain, the walls smelled like raspberries. They lived in a three-story gray saltbox with inconveniently sloped ceilings, and most of the windows were clustered on the house's southern side (her bedroom faced north). Her father bought the house for its large front parlor, which became his office. All the other rooms were small and cramped, and the pantry made Vita think of an upright coffin.

Her earliest memory had the flavor of sawdust: she was four years old and having a tantrum in the back hall, which had been fitted out the week before with closets. What had she been so upset about? She couldn't remember. Her chubby legs didn't have enough room to kick properly without hitting a wall, and that made her angrier. She screamed and kicked and banged her fists as she lay there on her stomach. Carpentry dust rose from cracks in the floorboard, and every large breath – absolutely necessary for a prolonged, solid wail – brought with it a gritty taste.

'You'll get a splinter,' her mother had said, watching her from the doorway. And her father: 'Ignore her.'

Even at so young an age, Vita sensed that the place she lived was not the place she belonged.

She began to hunt around her bedroom for a pencil bigger than a cigar stub; when she was upset, she wrote lists. The room was cluttered with paper and books, notebooks filled with her observations, and piles of old science journals – her father had several subscriptions mailed to the house. Although there were the usual combs and hairpins on her dressing table, she also kept, in a mason jar lid, the remains of a dry June bug she had dissected.

At last she found a pencil in use as a bookmark (*On the Motion of the Heart and Blood in Animals*), and licked its end. The combination of the smooth lead and the rough end of shaved wood against her tongue always soothed her. She turned to a blank page in her notebook.

Who does he imagine I'll marry? she wrote.

She tried to think of all the men she knew who had survived – or never went off to – the war.

Clarence Witt: missing an arm

Tom Fuller: missing a leg

Andrew Meany: not right in the head

Blind; scarred; long gray hairs sprouting from their ears (that was Robinson Jameson, who was at least sixty years old) – they all had something. Vita was a scientist and had trained herself to be observant. Also dispassionate. Even so, by the end she felt tears in her eyes.

There was a knock at her door, and her sister Amelia walked in looking brushed and neat.

'Dar said you're in a temper. Did you quarrel again?'

Amelia was the beauty of the family with smooth blonde hair and a nose on the shorter side of Roman. Their mother called Vita handsome rather than pretty, praising her long neck and wide mouth – like a goose, Vita thought.

'Mitty sent this up for you,' Amelia said, handing her a piece of cake. 'Also, look at this. Aunt Norbert gave it to me.'

She held out a narrow pamphlet bound in pliable pasteboard. The title, in heavy black type, modeled the look of scientific tracts: *Instructions for the Young Bride*, and underneath, in type just as large: *By the Wife of a New England Reverend.*

Vita read the first sentence aloud:

> *'To the sensitive young woman who has had the benefits of a proper upbringing, the wedding day is, ironically, both the happiest and most terrifying day of her life.'*

'Is it satire, do you think?' Amelia asked.

Vita shoved a big bite of cake into her mouth and skimmed the rest of the paragraph.

'I don't think it's satire,' she said.

❁

As children, they were divided into types: Freddy was fun, Vita was smart, and Amelia was pretty. When she got older Amelia wanted to be sweet as well as pretty, so her type was amended, reluctantly – no one could decide if she was actually sweet or not. She cried when she saw a dead mouse or a dead sparrow or one of the barn cat's kittens dead on the lawn, but she laughed a little, too – she said from nerves.

Vita didn't care about being pretty *or* sweet. Unlike Amelia, she wasn't interested in husbands and weddings; she dreamed of a college classroom with dissecting equipment and long rubber aprons and a professor who wrote so rapidly on the board he snapped his chalk in half (she once read a version of this scenario in a story in *The Atlantic Monthly*). One morning, when Freddy was struggling to draw a diagram of the bones of the human hand – Dar sometimes gave him extra work to give him a leg up, as he put it, for studying medicine – Vita drew the diagram for him, and then she went on to diagram the bones of a leg and foot, as well. 'To give you a leg up,' she joked.

'Say, these are pretty good,' Freddy had said, looking at her neatly labeled drawings.

'I think so, too.'

'Makes me wonder if you're the one who should be a doctor.'

This being Freddy, she couldn't tell if he was joking or not.

'Really?'

Freddy had shrugged. 'Sure.'

A doctor!

The idea was like a new spice in a common dish – she wasn't sure at first if she liked it or not. She imagined herself as an adult carrying her father's black doctor's bag, the neat instruments inside held in place by cloth tape, the envelopes of colored powders tucked away in special pouches. Walking into a farmhouse or seeing people in her own home office; feeling foreheads and limp wrists; stirring medicine into a glass of water. A doctor. She hugged the possibility to herself, jealously guarding it, not wanting to be laughed at. She was small, and she was a woman. Maybe it was impossible. But she was good at schoolwork – more than good. She had an excellent memory and she grasped concepts quickly. She was healthy and could walk for miles or stay up all night if needed. Why not?

'Maybe I *will* be a doctor,' she said to Freddy a few weeks later. 'Maybe we could be doctors together.' He was the only one she ever mentioned this new, and increasingly exciting, dream to; although she did bring up the idea of going to college from time to time (her father ignored it).

'As long as you do most of the work,' Freddy had joked.

Her brother wasn't stupid or lazy, he just wasn't interested in books. He liked training animals, and on clear nights in every season he studied the stars. But that hardly mattered to Dar. From the moment Freddy was born, and probably even before, Dar had decided his son would be a doctor like him.

Amelia wasn't interested in books, either, until old Mr. Denton retired as their tutor and young Holland Granger came to take his place. Even before her sixteenth birthday Amelia began to put her hair up, whereas Vita still wore hers in a long braid that she usually slept in. Seven months after he started tutoring them, Holland resigned and proposed to Amelia. Their wedding was to be in September.

Their Aunt Norbert liked to say that Amelia was old for her age and Vita was young; it was not meant to be a compliment on either side. Holland couldn't fight in the war because he had a wandering eye, also his right leg was slightly shorter than his left. But none of that bothered Amelia. He was still handsome, especially if he was sitting and his eye was fixed on an object. Amelia sent away to Boston for special shoes she'd seen advertised, to minimize his limp.

'I wonder where Aunt Norbert got it,' Vita said, meaning the pamphlet. They were sitting side by side on Vita's window seat, paging through it.

'She told me it would *see me on my proper way*,' Amelia said, mimicking Aunt Norbert's sprawling tones. She was good at voices.

Vita laughed in spite of her foul mood. 'Did she.'

'She also told me she plans to give me money. For when I'm married.'

'Money?' This was a surprise. 'How much money?'

'House-buying money, she called it. She said she'd do the same for you when you get married.'

Did Dar know about this plan? Was that the reason for his baffling decision to marry her off? A double wedding, he'd said. Her heart burned when she thought of it.

'*While sex is at best revolting and at worst rather painful,*' she read aloud, '*it must be endured. Many women have found it useful to have thick cotton nightgowns which they don in a separate room, and which need not be removed during the sex act.*'

'But what *is* the sex act, I wonder,' Amelia asked.

'You don't know?'

'You do?'

'I have a book upstairs.' That was their classroom. 'Do you want to look at it?'

Amelia hesitated, and then shrugged in a way that meant yes. Vita felt a thread of cool air skimming her back from a crack in the windowpane behind her. Thick cotton nightgowns, she thought. Well, she wouldn't let old Robinson Jameson with his hairy ears touch her even so.

'Listen to this part,' Amelia said, turning the page.

> *'Most men are by nature rather perverted, and if given half a chance would engage in the most disgusting practices, such as mouthing the female body, and offering their own vile bodies to be mouthed in turn.'*

They looked at each other. 'What do you suppose that means?' Amelia asked.

Vita leaned forward to read the paragraph again. 'Haven't a clue.'

Vita, who thought of herself as a scientist, was naturally interested in sex – *marital relations*, as the reverend's wife put it.

Her first crush had been on the gardener's son, Nicky Hoag; a serious but friendly boy. He wore short gray pants and a little wool cap, and he helped his father deadhead the roses in the spring, press apples into cider in the fall, weed, wash the paving stones, and tend to anything else that needed tending to in their yard. Sometimes, when Vita went outside, Nicky showed her something interesting – a perfectly shaped wasps' nest in the V of two branches, or a spider web set so the sunlight made diamonds in it. Once, when he gave her a small misshapen apple, their hands touched; Vita felt a tingle go up her spine. For weeks afterward she relived that moment, and she kept the apple core until it began drawing ants.

She studied pictures of stamen and pistils; not proper intercourse, certainly, but at least reproduction. In terms of observation, it would have been better if they'd lived on a farm. Sometimes Vita stood at the window of their third-floor classroom looking down at the snake of road that went past Carver's farm, over the old stone bridge, and into town. She could see dots of sheep but not much else, and she used to daydream of following the road all the way out of the town, escaping Lark's Eye forever. No one else went up to the third floor much – Amelia and Freddy refused to set foot there if they didn't have a lesson, and Mrs. Oakum didn't care for the steep staircase.

It was the perfect place to hide a book.

Aristotle's Masterpiece, it was called – no relation to the philosopher. Mr. Palmer, who owned the only bookshop in town, clearly didn't look past the title, and moreover he was confused about who Aristotle was since Vita discovered the volume in the mathematics section in the shop's musty back room. She was fourteen when she brought it home, and the book, though incomprehensible in parts, was on the whole a revelation.

She read it secretly with Gemma, their housemaid and Vita's friend and co-conspirator. When Gemma came up to her room a few minutes later with a can of lamp oil, Vita prevailed on her to go up to the classroom to fetch it.

'It turns out Amelia is completely ignorant about everything,' Vita said.

'That's not true!'

Gemma had fair hair and hooded gray eyes, and like Amelia she was taller than Vita even though she was younger. She wore a thin, gray dress too short in the sleeves, and, after coming back with the book, she crossed her arms over her chest, trying to warm herself.

The rain had started pulsing hard against the window. Even in the summer the house could be cold during a rainstorm, and Dr. Tenney didn't believe in having fires lit in the upstairs rooms.

'Let's get under the quilt,' Vita said. 'You can tell Mrs. Oakum I asked you to help me find a book, and that wouldn't even be lying.'

They often used such stratagems. Vita had taught Gemma to read when Gemma was five and they'd been reading together ever since. At the time Gemma's mother had been the Tenneys' housemaid; eight years later, when her mother died of stomach cancer, Gemma took her place. Gemma learned everything quickly, from how to combine letters into words to how to repair broken crockery with a piece of thread. If she could squeeze out time she also helped Vita with her experiments up in the classroom. Gemma had long, thin fingers – the fingers of a botanist, Vita fancied, whereas her own were short and stubby.

When the three of them were settled in bed, Vita, in the middle, opened the book.

'"Of the Secret Parts in Women,"' she read aloud.

The external parts in women's privities are designed by Nature to cover the great orifice, Nature intending that orifice to receive the penis, or yard, in the act of coition.

'What's an orifice?' Amelia asked.

Gemma pointed to the illustration. 'The man's maypole goes in there.'

Amelia's face went pink. 'Does it hurt?'

Gemma shrugged herself a little further under the quilt. 'My cousin said only the first time. Trick is not to let the man go too fast.'

A branch of the fir tree began hitting the windowpane: Tap, scrape; tap, scrape. They were sitting up against the headboard, the blankets scrunched around them.

'Let's get to a good bit,' Vita said impatiently. She turned to a page that was grimy from being handled so many times.

The action of the clitoris in women is like that of the penis in men. It is the seat of the greatest pleasure during the act of copulation, and is therefore called the sweetness of love.

'Disgusting!' Amelia said, after she'd silently read the page through to the end.

Vita looked at her. 'Why?'

Amelia shut the book with a slam. Her neck, face, and ears were all an angry red. 'How can that . . . what he described . . . feel good? It sounds painful and perverted.'

'But haven't you ever felt a little thrill of excitement,' Vita asked, 'down there? Around Holland?'

Amelia was silent for a moment. Then she said, 'The author must be lying. I don't think that's how it happens. It can't.'

'Why not?'

'It sounds awkward, and . . . I just can't imagine it working.'

'It's true, though,' Vita told her.

'It can't be.'

'It is.'

Amelia shoved the book at her and jumped off the bed. Vita smiled to herself just a little; she had wanted to shock her. It was annoying how good Amelia pretended to be, and how that meant she got whatever she wanted. She was Dar's favorite now that Freddy was gone. Maybe she'd always been Dar's favorite. Whereas I'm thwarted at every turn, Vita thought.

'Well I don't believe you,' Amelia said.

CHAPTER THREE

'How comes it that a tall man is seldom wise?
By reason that the largeness of his body
proceeds from an excess of heat.'
(*Aristotle's Masterpiece*, Anonymous, 1717)

Jacob Culhane learned about his father's death in the middle of the war, nearly six months before he was captured and taken prisoner by the Confederate army. At the time his company was stationed in what proved to be the largest and nicest of all the camps they erected; it was built in a pine grove, laid out in streets, with plenty of shade trees and a clear stream running through it. The canvas hospital tent stood at one end and a stubbly field, with a farmhouse that had been burned down to its stones, stood at the other.

When ordered to the battlefront some five miles away, Jacob and his tent mate Matthew Ames, along with the rest of the infantry, marched with full canteens and haversacks containing three days' worth of rations: hard tack, salt pork, and a paper twist of speck sugar for their coffee. Jacob and Matthew had signed up on the same day in Cincinnati, and found they both had a liking for trout fishing and ship mechanics – Matthew was a ship carpenter, and Jacob had built up a business fitting steam engines to boats. They'd been fighting side by side now for almost two years.

As they marched down the road Matthew told Jacob about the latest letter from his wife and the mischief their four-year-old had gotten into, involving handfuls of flour and their housecat. It was a cool day in early September with golden leaves fluttering down to the dirt road and a smell of dry earth. Both Matthew and Jacob wore small wooden discs on strings around their neck, which Matthew had made for them a month ago. The discs – lopsided rectangles, really – were carved with their first initial and last name. Some men kept pieces of paper with their addresses in their pockets or pinned to their uniforms; they'd all seen too many corpses mutilated beyond recognition in battle, and if they died they wanted folks back home to know. Jacob could feel the scratch of wood under his shirt like a splinter, shifting slightly as he swung his arms. The trees on either side of the road had the look of women wearing dark, wrinkled skirts, and the wind blew up softly behind the marching men as if urging them on.

They got to the designated field, made camp, and ate dinner. Their division was tasked with holding back the southern advance, and Jacob's job was to help load canisters – a bag with a hundred bullets – into the cannons. When fired, the canister burst and bullets zoomed out in all directions. The sound was like a hundred angry, wayward bees.

The battle broke out at daybreak when a horde of Confederate soldiers rushed through the trees whooping and shooting, bending to reload, running again. They were viciously good shots although outnumbered and getting hit from two sides. From Jacob's position he could see them falling in heaps despite the fact they were firing as fast as they could, spraying a bee storm of lead and iron directly at his unit.

Jacob's ears rang from the noise, and the smoke and confusion seemed to herald the end of the world. But his division held their ground, and after a few hours the rebels retreated. That night Jacob and Matthew slept side by side on blankets under the stars, the air still choked with smoke and the smell of battle: metallic, but also human – blood and flesh and excrement. The next day, advancing again, the rebels gained some ground. In this way three days were spent; basically, as far as Jacob could tell, fighting over one ditch.

The fact that the ditch led to a field and the field to a road and the road to a town wasn't lost on him, but nor was the fact that scores of men were dying to protect one small rise of mud. All this because six southern states had seceded from the United States after the election of Abraham Lincoln. Four more states soon followed, and northern newspapers began running headlines like 'Save the Union!' or 'Crush the Rebellion!' When southern troops fired on federal soldiers in Fort Sumter in April, the war officially began. Jacob didn't feel any particular connection to the southern states, but ever since the day he saw slaves being auctioned on the block in St. Louis he was revolted by slavery – not the idea of it, the inhumane fact of it. Shackled black men were made to stand on blocks too narrow for their feet, and whipped when they fell, and given no water. And that was just the treatment Jacob had seen for himself. How could a country tolerate slavery in one half and condemn it in the other? It felt like a mind shattering and splitting, only it was the whole country. The war lasted longer and was more brutal than anyone ever expected.

On their third day defending the field, Jacob was crouching in the dirt loading more bullets into a canister when he saw Matthew fall. He was only a few yards away and it looked to him at first as though his friend had simply stumbled. But as Jacob scrambled over to help he saw a spray of blood shooting from Matthew's neck. He covered the wound with his grimy hands, searching for a piece of cloth, a hat, anything, to staunch the flow, but it was too late. Matthew died staring off to the side with a surprised look on his face, his neck and chest wet with bright red blood.

There was no time to mourn him; Jacob had to get back to the cannon or more Union men would be killed. That, he decided later, was the moment his mind clicked off. Altogether clicked off, like a piece of machinery drained of fuel and cutting out. He filled a bullet bag and loaded the cannon. He was no longer a man, no longer human, although his eyes were wet with tears. He filled a bullet bag, loaded it, filled another. Someone else dragged Matthew's body away.

When his unit was finally relieved and they marched the five miles back to their large, shady camp, Jacob was too exhausted even to eat. He carried in his pocket Matthew's carved identification tag to send to his wife, *M. Ames*, the M slanted slightly away from his family name. The wood, a jagged piece of oak stripped of its bark and rubbed with linseed oil, felt as light as a fingernail. He couldn't begin to think what to write to Matthew's wife. But before he could do anything, he found a letter addressed to him waiting in his tent.

Lark's Eye, Massachusetts
September 2, 1863

Mr. Jacob Culhane
Dear Sir,

It saddens me that I must inform you in this way, by letter, of your father's recent death. I attended him in his final illness, which lasted just under three months. I can only offer the solace – and I hope it is solace – that he did not much suffer in the end. As you are off performing your duty to our great nation in this our time of trouble, Reverend Chenowith has undertaken the responsibility of your father's last service and burial.

I am deeply sorry for your loss. I pray for your health and safety in these difficult times, and I look forward to seeing you again in Lark's Eye when this terrible conflict is over.

Most Sincerely Yours,
Dr. Arthur Tenney

Jacob had run away from Lark's Eye after his mother died when he was fourteen, and he hadn't set eyes on his father – a bully and a drunk – even once since that day. He held Dr. Tenney's letter in trembling fingers – trembling from fatigue, he'd thought at the time. He re-folded the paper along its creases and waited to feel something, but inside he was spent. Emptied out. All he wanted to do was close his eyes and be somewhere else.

Six months later this wish was granted when he was captured and taken to Andersonville prison camp. An irony that wasn't lost on him.

Now, almost two years after he'd received the letter about his father's death, Jacob found himself returning to Lark's Eye in an open wagon with four other soldiers who, like himself, had somehow survived the war.

It was June. The peace had been signed in April, and Jacob had been released from Andersonville on the first of May. His plan was to sell his father's farm and then never set eyes on Lark's Eye again. It was nearly noon and he was hungry, but then again he was always hungry. The problem was he couldn't eat much at any one sitting – the effect of near-starvation and bodily neglect during his months at the prison camp.

Nathan Hay, who joined the wagon in West Virginia, wasn't as thin as Jacob but he had a stump instead of a right hand; and Willie Hawkins, asleep beside him, was missing a leg. Hiram and Johnny Dickerson – brothers who were traveling all the way up to their farm in Barnet, Vermont – featured one working eye between them.

Jacob could hear the American flag that was pinned to the back of the wagon snapping in the wind. They'd started in Kentucky six days ago and yesterday had crossed into Massachusetts after trundling through Ohio, Pennsylvania, and Connecticut. The wagon driver was an older man who'd been hired by the army to take veterans home; a tedious job, Jacob couldn't help thinking. Those soldiers who could went by train, but there were still plenty of little towns that the railroads didn't get near to. Lark's Eye was only about three miles from a train station, but after so much confinement in prison, Jacob preferred the open ride. Besides, he was in no hurry to get there.

He was sitting with his back against the box sill, facing forward so he could see what was coming. He'd just begun to pick out familiar landmarks – Briggs Marsh, Long Pond, the gravelly road that led to Tinkertown – when he noticed some boys up ahead in the distance. They were kneeling at the edge of the field, examining something. Suddenly they lunged back and there was an ear-splitting series of cracks. The wagon horse startled at the noise, thrashed her head around, and reared up.

A switch flicked on in Jacob's head. Horses were galloping all around him. Smoke filled the air. The enemy was closing in.

'March and draw pistols!' his commander was shouting.

The sharp, sputtering sound of the infantry volley was deafening. There was no time to reload.

The wagon horse came down at a slant and the wagon toppled over, spilling all of the men out onto the road. A thunderous snap sounded as one of the axles broke. Jacob crawled off to the edge of the field, trying to find cover. Bullets were flying but he had no gun. Where was his gun?

'Some help, here! Aaron's pinned!' Nathan Hay was trying to pull the wagon driver out from under a cracked wheel with his one good hand. He looked over at Jacob. But Jacob could only stare back, unable to move.

'Here, I've got him.' Willie Hawkins, who had an army-issued wooden leg but two good hands, helped pull the driver free. Meanwhile the horse was galloping off, trailing the split wooden shaft behind her. The noise – firecrackers, not artillery – had crackled to a stop. Jacob was shaking all over.

'That's all right now, it's done,' Hiram Dickerson told him, helping him to his feet. 'Only boys setting off firecrackers. That's all.'

Jacob, coming to his senses – he was in Massachusetts, the battles were over – felt a deep shame rise up, and his face burned hot. 'I'm sorry, I . . .' He couldn't find the words to excuse himself. These men had been through what he'd been through. Maybe worse. But they didn't hesitate, or find themselves lost.

But Hiram only nodded. 'Don't worry, son.' They watched the driver take a few steps on the dirt road to test his ankle. He nodded, *It's fine.* 'Looks like we got away with just some cuts and bruises all around,' Hiram said. 'But we'll need to get the horse.'

'I'll do it,' Jacob offered, ashamed of his frozen inaction, and hoping that at the same time he could walk off his shakes.

The horse was standing near a scrawny pine tree, tired out probably from lugging the shaft behind her. The boys who lit the firecrackers had all scampered off once they saw what they had started. As Jacob neared the horse her tail twitched nervously. He put a hand on her neck. It was sweaty and hot.

'That's all right, girl,' he said. Gradually, his heartbeat slowed. He took the horse by the bridle and got hold of the reins. Her eyes still had a wild, scared look to them, and he wished he had a piece of apple or a carrot to give her. 'It'll be all right.'

Jacob volunteered to walk the rest of the way to Lark's Eye to see if the local blacksmith would come help with the wagon. 'It's my stop anyway,' he said, trying to smile.

The road rose gently, and the sloping dunes to his right hid the water. Jacob could still remember the gritty feel of sand in his ears on windy days. As he approached the town a strange feeling came over him: nostalgia, but also a kind of displacement. The sight of the slanted town sign with its black outline of a lark was familiar but also unreal. *Welcome to Lark's Eye.* A sense of enclosure, of being trapped as a child, came back to him. But you're a free man now, he reminded himself. And there's no bullying father taking his belt to you.

In town everything looked the same but dustier. The old sail loft and the cotton mill were both shuttered – he wondered where the men worked now – but he could hear voices inside Tillings' Stables, so that was still open. The old sea captain's mansion, which used to be visible from where he stood, had apparently been torn down, and the town green was deserted. A New England whaling village past its prime; that was Lark's Eye. No industry to speak of anymore, no whaling, no boatbuilding, and its scrubby land had always been almost hopeless for farming.

After he spoke to the blacksmith, Jacob sat down on a bench in the town green to rest and collect his thoughts. It was still a pretty village, with square brick buildings fronting the green and a bandstand where a vendor sometimes sold ice cream in paper cups on summer evenings. Why had the town been named Lark's Eye? He couldn't remember. A lark, his mother once told him, could be either lucky or unlucky. If a lark casts its eye upon someone who is ill then that person will recover. But if the lark turns its head away, they will not. This is why some people carry larks into sick rooms, she told him. To give the ill hope. Because when does a bird ever look straight at a person?

When she died, his mother – like his father – had died with only the town doctor beside her, Dr. Tenney. Dr. Tenney had delivered a stillborn son to her, and afterwards couldn't revive her. Jacob and his younger sister Gracie – his brother Benjy had died of diphtheria the winter before – had spent the hours of his mother's labor crouching in the crawl space beneath the farmhouse. It stank of sheep excrement and soiled wool, but it felt safer than being up in the house where the close sound of their mother's pained cries was unbearable. Of course it was worse – much worse – when the muffled cries stopped altogether. His father, as usual, had been outside drinking.

Their family scratched out a living farming and raising sheep. Every one of them worked hard every day – even Gracie, who started scrubbing the sheep dung from his father's boots when she was four. Their poor excuse of a farmhouse had been built against a hill, with the lower end of it on stumpy stilts; fenced, the partial crawl space became the sheep cove in winter. On bitterly cold nights Jacob used to bring the lambs up to the house to warm them by the fire. If their mothers died, he fed them cows' milk, holding their little muzzles into a bowl until they learned the mechanics of drinking. They pushed his hand with their wet, pink noses, and sometimes let him pet their craggy wool.

But by now of course the sheep were all gone. Only the land was worth something; what, he didn't know. He would make an appointment with a banker tomorrow. In the meantime he wanted to find a room in town. Even if the farmhouse was still inhabitable, which he doubted, he didn't want to stay there. Too many bad memories. Too many ghosts.

I seem to collect them, he thought.

'You related to old Mr. Grant Culhane, over out near Tinkertown?' the woman who ran the boarding house, Mrs. Linden, asked him. When Jacob told her he was Grant Culhane's son, she pulled a pair of spectacles from her apron pocket to inspect him. 'I see a scant likeness,' she decided.

Supper was at six every night, breakfast at seven, and candles were included in the weekly rate. From the window of his room Jacob could see the spire of the First Parish Church, where his father, his mother, and his brother Benjy were all buried; his little sister Gracie was buried next to her husband in Illinois. She died when she was only seventeen, in childbirth like their mother.

His bedroom was small and smelled strongly of wood varnish. Besides the narrow bed, there was a washstand, an oak wardrobe with a pair of pineapples carved on the paneled doors, and a small desk with a rush-seated chair pushed up against it. The mirror over the washstand was so small Jacob could only see half his face at a time.

After washing his hands and face and rolling up his cuffs, he pulled a rolled-up plan from his haversack. He laid it out on the desk and used two stones he carried with him for this purpose as paperweights, one on either corner. The plan was his friend Caleb's plan for a barrel that wouldn't leak oil. For the past three months Jacob took some time almost every day to darken the lines with a pencil, or to rub out any smudges he'd inadvertently made while rolling and unrolling it. The yellowed paper was grimy and soft at the edges, with a tear as slight as a thread end at the top. Beneath Caleb's sketches of a barrel and variously shaped staves there was a chemical formula half worked out, lots of *X*s and equal signs. And in the corner, Caleb's slanted initials inside a square: *CL*.

Caleb Locke. He had taken Jacob under his wing at prison camp; he had saved Jacob's life. When Jacob arrived at Andersonville, Caleb invited him to share the tent that he and four other men – the Five Knights, they called themselves – had cobbled together out of pine branches and knotted rags. One of the men had died the previous day from pneumonia, and they were looking to replace him.

'Why me?' he'd asked Caleb later. They'd never met before; they were strangers. The answer was simple and practical: 'You had a blanket. We needed a man with a blanket.' They used it, along with two other blankets, to cover their stick and twig structure. There were no formal tents at Andersonville; you had to build your own shelter somehow, or sleep on the ground.

Jacob unrolled a second, clean sheet of paper that he'd been carrying with him since he left Kentucky, and laid it over Caleb's plan. Then he anchored the two sheets with the stone paperweights and began tracing the original drawing.

All that remained of Caleb now was this formula, which Jacob couldn't altogether understand, and which Caleb himself had said wasn't quite right. I owe it to him to see it's done properly, Jacob told himself. He would make a fresh copy that he could show to investors, and then build a business out of it. Locke and Culhane, he would call it, though there was no Locke anymore.

Gradually, bending over the paper, Jacob began to feel useful again. When the bell rang for supper, he looked over his work with pride. He rolled the two sheets up together and bound them with twine, and as he went down the stairs he tried to guess at what was for supper. Fried potatoes? Eggs in cream? His sense of smell was not what it once was.

It was fish. Lark's Eye was a fishing village after all. Even after the whales and whaling ships disappeared, there was still, apparently, fish.

The meal was neither well-cooked nor plentiful, but Jacob had no complaints – compared to what he got at Andersonville it was a king's feast. Mrs. Linden doled out careful portions to Jacob and to Holland Granger, the other boarder, who had recently been hired as principal for the new high school.

'There was talk of converting the old Bradford mansion,' Holland said, cutting into his fish with the side of his fork, 'but instead we're building a new building closer to town.'

'The Bradfords have left?' Jacob remembered the beautiful bay horses they kept, always a matching pair.

'Both their sons died, so they've moved to Burlington to be near their daughter.'

'You were living in Cincinnati before the war, if I'm not mistaken?' Mrs. Linden asked Jacob. 'Your father was so proud of your successes.'

Jacob doubted that. He probably just enjoyed having something to brag about, for once.

'A self-made man, he told everyone. Liked to take the credit. Well, but I was sorry to hear about your sister, though.' After his mother died, Jacob's father sent Gracie to Illinois to live with their Aunt Nell; Gracie later married a soldier from the same town, and that was where she died. It had been over ten years since Gracie had lived in Lark's Eye, but everyone knew everyone else's business here, present or absent.

Mrs. Linden passed him the platter of fish. 'Grace was about the same age as my Lizzie, if I remember correct. Lizzie got married last year but she's a widow already. Gets a pension from the government.' She eyed Jacob appraisingly. 'You have a wife back in Cincinnati?'

Jacob helped himself to a second piece of haddock, browned to the color of the sandy ocean road and almost as dry.

'No, no wife. Nothing like that.'

'Have another buttermilk biscuit. I'm sorry the rise is so poor. My Lizzie is an excellent baker, not like me.'

'Everything is delicious, Mrs. Linden,' Holland said. When Mrs. Linden wasn't looking, he caught Jacob's eye and winked. Delicious wasn't exactly the word to describe her cooking. It wasn't burned, at least.

'What were you up to in Cincinnati?' Holland asked Jacob.

'He was in shipbuilding,' Mrs. Linden said. 'Started his own business, even.' She seemed to know a lot.

'A small business, but yes, it was my own.'

Jacob was secretly proud of his successes. He had picked up the mechanics of steam power as though pulling the knowledge out of his pocket, a coin that had been there all along. At fourteen he started as a riveter's assistant, and he worked his way up until he knew enough at twenty to start his own shop.

But that life seemed like somebody else's now. When he enlisted, he left it behind. 'We have to go forward,' Caleb used to say in prison camp, 'since there's no going back.'

After dinner, the two men went to the porch to smoke. Holland walked with a slight limp, and Jacob noticed one of his shoes had a thicker heel than the other. Probably this was the reason he sat out the war.

'Why don't you come out to Swaby's and have a drink with me,' Holland proposed. 'We can get some decent dessert while we're at it. If you stay here you'll find a half a dozen girls on this very porch within the hour wanting to meet you.'

They heard the side door close and saw Mrs. Linden tying her bonnet as she hurried away.

'See there,' Holland said with a laugh, 'I knew it. A nickel says she's going to fetch that freshly widowed daughter of hers.'

Jacob tapped out his cigar and slipped the stub back into its paper. People were friendlier here than he remembered.

'Then we better be quick,' he said.

At the tavern a man barely taller than a child but sporting a beard was behind the bar lining up thick stein glasses, all of them cloudy with age.

'Evening, Mr. Swaby,' Holland said. 'This is Jacob Culhane, visiting from Cincinnati. You remember his father?'

Mr. Swaby looked him over sternly. 'I do. And I believe he still owed some on his tab when he died.'

Jacob said, 'Oh, I . . .' and was feeling in his pockets when Mr. Swaby cocked his head and pursed his lips into a thin-lipped smile.

'I'm having you on. Mr. Gideon settled six of your father's spoons on me. D'ya want them back?'

Jacob laughed. 'Not even if you paid me.'

After they settled themselves in with a bottle at a corner table, Holland lifted his glass. 'To fathers.'

Jacob didn't much want to drink to his father, the drunken bastard, but he nodded and put the glass to his lips. Mrs. Swaby came to their table with two plates of pie – strawberry rhubarb tonight – and he cut into the crust neatly and delicately. No tremors tonight, he noticed. That was good.

'Somehow I find I'm hungrier after one of Mrs. Linden's suppers than I was before it,' Holland joked.

Although they were only a year apart in age, they hadn't met before – Holland had moved to Lark's Eye after Jacob left it. He was born in Nantucket and came to town as a schoolteacher, but after a couple of years he was hired by Dr. Tenney to act as a private tutor for his children.

'And now,' he said, 'I'm in love with the doctor's daughter.'

'Dr. Tenney has a daughter?'

'Hair like sunlight. Sparkling blue eyes. Smart, but not overly so.'

'This would be Fred Tenney's sister?'

'The very one. Well, the angelic sister, not the shrew.'

'What about his brother?'

'There's no brother, only Fred. Poor man, he died right before the peace was signed. The family is beside themselves with grief.'

Jacob was sorry to hear it. He remembered Fred as being lively and fun. 'I didn't know the family, only the doctor if someone was sick, and Fred. Fred was friends with my younger brother Benjy. Every now and again we'd all go shoot water rats together.' Once, after Benjy died, Fred came by the farm with another young boy to see if Jacob wanted to go rat shooting – vermin hunting, Fred called it. This must have been right before I left Lark's Eye, Jacob thought. He could remember his mother folding corn cakes into a handkerchief for him to take along with him, her belly hugely pregnant.

'So what are your plans? Going back to Cincinnati? Or will you work your father's farm?'

Jacob poured himself another finger of whiskey. 'What, take on the life of a farmer? No thank you. I'll sell it if anyone will buy it. I mean to try out Boston next. River travel is pretty well finished, what with the war and the railways. There's nothing for me in Cincinnati.'

'Why Boston?'

'I'd like to find some investors for a patent I've been working on, and I have a feeling it will be easier there. Also my cousin lives in New Bedford. Well, my cousin's widow.'

'Oh, a widow, is it? Mrs. Linden will be sorry to hear about her.'

'No, no, nothing like that. Just the last of my family.'

'What's the patent for?'

'Boring, really,' Jacob said. 'A kind of glue.' He was drunk enough that he didn't trust himself to talk about the patent, or Caleb, or Andersonville. He didn't know what he might say.

Holland didn't press him. 'Well, good luck with it.' Then he said, 'I don't suppose you'd like a wife to go along with you to Boston? Dr. Tenney's got another daughter, and he's looking to pay someone to take her off his hands. He wants a double wedding – easier on his wallet, I suppose.'

Jacob pulled his head back. 'Not you, too!'

'You'll be getting it from everyone, my friend,' Holland told him cheerfully. 'Now that the war's over, we're all matchmakers, don't you know.'

CHAPTER FOUR

'In its full sense the reproductive power means the power to bear a well-developed infant . . . Most of the flat-chested girls who survive their high-powered education are unable to do this.'
(*Principles of Biology*, Herbert Spencer, 1863)

The First Parish Church was a building Vita wished she never had to look at again, although she did have to look at it – she had to look at it every Sunday, and go inside, and sit on a pew.

It was full of painful memories. The church's front lawn was where Freddy first reported for duty along with sixteen other Lark's Eye men. On the day they were called, the church hosted a picnic for the new recruits and set out long tables loaded with turkeys, roast beef, ham, biscuits, pickles, jellies, pies – just about anything you could think of. The men ate plates of food and drank cider and visited with their family and neighbors while a brass band played inspiring, patriotic songs. At four o'clock, when the men marched off in formation toward the train station (a good three miles away), a line of little boys followed them to the end of the town waving small paper flags.

Behind the church was the old curate's cottage where, once the war was well underway, Vita and Amelia used to sit with the other girls from Lark's Eye and tear bed sheets or old garments into strips, stitch the long strips together, and roll them up to make bandages. They also knit socks and made lint packs, and they loaded everything into wooden crates to send by train to the Soldiers' Relief Commission in Boston.

Vita was all thumbs when it came to stitching or knitting, and she wasn't even all that good at tearing up sheets. But she would do it, and a hundred times more, for Freddy. Mostly she packed the crates, with a book or newspaper propped open against one of them.

But even worse than the long front lawn or the curate's house was the graveyard next to the church. This was where Freddy was buried.

Inside, the church smelled of varnished wood, musty cotton, and lavender wax. This Sunday, as usual, Vita squirmed while Reverend Chenowith droned on and on from the pulpit, his voice warbly with age but strangely resonant. The weather had finally committed to summer, and hot sunlight streamed in from the long windows. At least, Vita thought, we're sitting on the shady side.

But when the reverend began to talk about the beauty of sacrifice and duty to your country – staring down at the widows and the families who'd lost sons and grandsons and nephews – she couldn't take it any longer.

'I've a headache,' she whispered to Mitty, touching the bridge of her nose. Her mother nodded.

'Faker,' Amelia whispered, as Vita left the pew.

It was just as hot outside but at least there was a breeze, and the short spurts of birdsong were a welcome relief after the reverend's self-important tone. Vita went into the graveyard because it was cooler, and also to look at Freddy's headstone. So far each time she visited his grave, it was with the feeling – not quite a thought – that this concrete, tangible object, this carved piece of stone, would settle her grief, or at least hold it, so she could let go of the worst of it.

But as usual, standing before it, the headstone seemed as unreal to her as everything else.

Frederick Arthur Tenney. 1846–1865. *Beloved son, brother, patriot.*

She stared at the words. One day they would have to clean moss and dirt from the chiseled letters and scrub off white worms of bird droppings, but as yet the stone was too new. It was hard to think of his headstone aging, while Freddy did not. Even harder was grasping the fact that Freddy's death was ongoing – forever.

Jokester, prankster, outdoorsman. He tamed injured birds and adopted motherless squirrels. Always and every day missed.

That's what she would have carved. She took off her glove and touched the top of the stone. It was smoother and colder than it looked. She could see little sparkles running through it.

From the corner of her eye she sensed movement; a man was walking toward her. She didn't recognize him, which was strange in a small town with no obvious employment to attract newcomers. The man touched his hat.

'Morning.'

He was passing behind her when he stopped; he must have read the headstone.

'Fred Tenney. I was sorry to hear that he passed. Was he your brother?'

'You knew him?'

'Only a little. Holland Granger told me. We're staying at the same boarding house, Mrs. Linden's. I'm Jacob Culhane.' He took off his hat.

'Oh!' Vita looked at him closer. 'I know you! We went shooting once together.'

'We did?'

'With Freddy. I was wearing a pair of his trousers. You showed me how to hold the gun.'

It was Jacob's turn to scrutinize her. 'I remember that, but I thought you were a boy. Freddy's brother.'

Had she not been standing in a graveyard she might have felt delighted that their trick had worked – as it was, her spirits lifted slightly. She turned to walk out toward the church with him. 'I wore my hair pinned up in a cap but Freddy said I looked like a girl just the same.'

'So you two played a joke on me.'

She smiled. 'That night we couldn't decide if you knew and were playing along, or if we had truly fooled you.'

The congregation was descending the church steps in splashes of black and deep violet, the color of mourning. Amelia stopped to speak with a few young women from town, but her parents separated themselves from the others when they saw Vita.

'Dar, this is Mr. Jacob Culhane,' Vita said. 'He used to live in Lark's Eye, he's Mr. Culhane's son. You remember?'

'Jacob Culhane! I haven't seen you since you were a boy. How many years has it been?'

They moved to the shade of an elm tree, where her father turned his back to the graveyard. As they shook hands, Jacob thanked Dr. Tenney for writing him about his father. He'd just been visiting his grave.

'Not at all, not at all. Yes, sad news for you. And you a soldier at the time. I almost didn't want to add to your burden. But a father's a father. He often spoke of you. Cincinnati, wasn't it? And your own shipbuilding business? A self-made man. We need more of your kind around here.'

'I was on the steam engine side. But I've given that up now. I thought I'd make a fresh start in Boston.'

Jacob's hand, Vita noticed, was trembling a little, and he slipped it into his pocket. He had thick dark hair and was clean-shaven, though she could see a few hairs under his ear that he'd missed. He wore low-slung trousers and dusty boots, and he was standing close enough for her to see a small brown mole near his eyelid. For some reason she had the impulse to touch it.

'Boston, is it?' Her father glanced at Vita. 'Well you must come and see me before you go off. How's tomorrow for you? I'd be interested to hear about your plans.'

The next day was another hot one. Vita had been working all morning on her Latin, and she brought her pages down with her to the kitchen when it was time for tea. Sweetie was perched on her shoulder, and Amelia sat next to her sewing starched black ribbons onto her hatband.

'I always say a girl can go so far and no farther,' Mrs. Oakum said as she lifted the heavy kettle from the range and poured hot water into their large, brown, everyday teapot.

Ever since they were little and one of Dar's male patients had made a sudden half-dressed dash through the dining room to the outside privy, Vita and Amelia and Freddy had had their tea down in the kitchen. While she waited Vita continued to conjugate Latin verbs in ink – ink, because that's how sure of herself she was. But what she was really thinking about was Dar's office, and how she could get in there again to look through his books. He mentioned Quincy, and someone named Cheselsomething who wrote about bones. Bones were particularly interesting to her, how they knit together again after a fracture, creating their own new material – but how? She was resolved to pursue her plans to study medicine. Somehow she would get around her father's objections.

'Only so far and no farther,' repeated Mrs. Oakum – Mrs. O. to the family – setting the kettle back on the range. She had a name for her range, which was Susan. 'Susan's acting up today,' Mrs. O. liked to announce when she could not regulate the heat to her liking. She had thin chestnut hair scraped into a bun, a pinched mouth, and eyes set so far apart she had the look of a wolf. This was one of her favorite subjects: what a young woman might expect from life (not very much).

Vita dipped her pen in the inkpot, ignoring the bait. But Amelia, the good child, looked up from her work. 'And how far is that?'

'Marriage, of course. A good, firm marriage.'

She made it sound like a spanking. Vita caught Gemma's eye as Gemma carried the teacups to the table, and they both made faces.

'What if you don't want to get married?' Vita asked.

'No one wants to get married,' Mrs. Oakum told her. 'But I'm sure I'll find you looking for it anyway soon enough.'

There had once existed a Mr. Oakum but he was long gone – 'dead of a faint heart,' Mrs. O. liked to say, though Vita had no idea what that meant. She slept in a small bedroom off the kitchen that smelled of camphor and violet water, and acted more like an impoverished aunt helping the family than the family housekeeper. In fact, there was a slim thread of kinship between Mitty and Mrs. O., a shared great uncle or a second cousin, Vita could never remember what. She was constant and eternal, and had a habit of contradicting everything that was said to her. Vita and Freddy used to make a game of it:

'Mrs. O.,' Freddy might start, 'what's for supper?'

'Stewed tomatoes and rabbit, not that you'll be able to eat the tough old thing Perry sold me for meat.'

'Sounds dreadful,' Vita said.

'Not as dreadful as last night's rooster disguised as chicken.'

'Oh yes,' Freddy agreed, 'that was terrible. But I'm sure tonight's rabbit will be much better.'

'Much better! I don't know about much better,' said Mrs. Oakum. 'We'll see if I still have my place in the morning.'

'Oh, Mrs. O., surely Dar won't give you the sack on account of a little bad meat!' Vita said.

'He wouldn't dare. You all could never do without me.'

'You're right about that,' Freddy said.

'Am I now,' Mrs. Oakum said, but there she stopped, not quite prepared to go so far as to contradict that statement. Then Freddy would laugh: he'd won. He always won. He was the only one Mrs. Oakum ever favored with a smile, and she often slipped him a wedge of gingerbread or a piece of cake on the sly. The day they received the black-edged letter, Vita found Mrs. O. leaning against the frame of the kitchen doorway, sobbing into her large, red hands.

'No one will want to marry me anyway,' Vita said, putting her pen aside, and she waited for Mrs. Oakum's reflexive contradiction. But to her surprise Mrs. Oakum said, 'True enough.'

Mrs. O. in agreement? Vita and Gemma stared at each other. Mrs. Oakum lifted the sugar bowl lid to check its contents and said, 'But for all that, they'll ask you anyway, and you'll do your duty by them.'

The world was right-side up again.

'Them?' Vita tried for a joke. 'How many husbands do you imagine I'll have?'

'As many as what's needed to tame you.'

'That will be quite a large number, then,' Amelia said.

Vita scowled. She didn't see why Amelia cared if she, Vita, got married or not. She's so conventional, Vita thought derisively (and not for the first time); she only wants what every girl is *supposed* to want: a husband, a tidy house with fitted carpets, and a pair of pearl earrings. The pearl earrings in particular vexed Vita; this was what her sister was asking Dar for, as a wedding present. 'To match my engagement ring.' When Vita pointed out that unless she walked about with her hand cupping her ear no one would ever notice they matched, Amelia looked peeved.

'I'll notice,' she said.

'You might try to notice something *actually important* instead. Just for a change.'

'Oh, you mean like irregular endings in a dead language?'

Amelia, for her part, wished Vita wouldn't draw attention to herself all the time. 'Don't read when you're in town. It looks so odd. And speak quietly, why can't you? No one here is deaf.' As if she were the older sister, not Vita.

'Get that bird off of you, now,' Mrs. O. told Vita, 'before you take one of my muffins.'

Vita walked Sweetie over to the birdcage near the kitchen door; Sweetie fluttered from her shoulder to her finger and then hopped onto the little swing inside the cage. Freddy had whittled the swing himself out of a birch stick. He'd also removed the wire door to the cage; he said he wanted all of his animals, even his pet squirrels, to be able to come and go freely.

'Say good-bye,' Vita prompted, and Sweetie raised one twig-like claw in salute, a trick Freddy taught her. (She could also bow and make a noise like a door hinge.) After Freddy left for war, Sweetie, in her anxiety, pulled out most of the feathers in her left wing; Vita made soft rolls of paper for her to chew on instead, and gradually Sweetie accepted Vita and Mitty in lieu of Freddy. A relief, but it also caused Vita a pang.

'Vita is only interested in dry, dull, book facts,' Amelia said, banking her needle. 'She has no interest in people. No wonder she doesn't want to marry.'

'That's not why,' Vita said, stung.

'Anyway, Dar's decided.'

Mrs. Oakum set a jug of milk on the table. Her hands were chapped and slightly clawed from all the scrubbing she'd done in her life. 'Decided what?'

'She's to marry the first man he can find for her,' Amelia said.

'What? How do you know that?' Vita asked.

'I heard him tell Mitty.'

She looked so neat and satisfied, her hands folded on the table, her blonde hair tucked neatly into its knitted black snood, that Vita felt a prick of pure hatred. Gemma made a small grimace, in solidarity, at Vita.

'That doesn't mean anything. He can't force me down the aisle.'

'So what will you do instead? Stay here and grow old alone?'

'I'll go to college.'

'College!' Amelia sniffed, her nostrils flaring like Dar's. 'Not that old idea.'

'Why not? I just need to find the money for tuition.'

'Well, there you are,' Amelia said as if proving her point, and she raised her left hand to admire her pearl engagement ring. Vita looked down at her own fingers, which were stained with purple ink. She wished that she hadn't said anything about college. When I'm a doctor, she used to tell herself as a young girl, I'll prescribe Amelia the most horrid-tasting medicines. Too bad bleeding by leeches was no longer in style.

'Vita. Amelia,' Mitty said, coming into the room. Sweetie flew out of her cage and landed on Mitty's shoulder, greeting her with a peck on her ear. 'Do you remember that Mr. Culhane was coming today? Well, he's here now, and Dar wants you to take your tea upstairs with him.'

'Drink tea with this man? This unmarried man?' Amelia raised her eyebrows at Vita: *You see?*

'Oh hush,' Vita told her.

Jacob didn't much care for social visits. He was a farmer's son; social visits unnerved him. He wasn't sure why he'd come today except that he'd been invited, and he was bored. Also, he had to admit, he was a little curious to see Fred Tenney's sister again.

This morning he met with Mr. Gideon at the Savings and Loan, and now he was just waiting to hear what the bank would offer for his father's land. He wondered if he should go back with his barrel glue plans; perhaps the bank would set him up with a loan as well. That and the sale of the farm would make a good start for his new business, if he could find a cheap workshop to rent. 'Locke and Culhane.' He liked to picture the wooden shingle over the door.

'We'll join the others in a moment,' Dr. Tenney said as they sat in his office. 'How are you, son?' He looked Jacob up and down, as though he were a horse. 'It must feel good to be back home. Or do you consider Cincinnati your home?'

The room was musty-smelling, with horrifying instruments on little tables around the room and framed insects on the wall. The floor was piled with old newspapers, and although Dr. Tenney knew Jacob was coming – he'd invited him here – he still had to clear a chair for him when his wife showed Jacob in.

Jacob smoothed his trouser leg with the palm of his hand. 'I haven't been back to Cincinnati since the war started.' He frowned. 'Yes, it's good to see Lark's Eye again.'

'Remind me what unit were you in?'

'The 130th Ohio.'

'A terrible thing, that war,' Dr. Tenney said. 'But inevitable.'

That's what everyone said now, and that's what everyone said before the war, too. It's inevitable. Maybe it was. The furious arguments over slavery, states' rights, and the value of compromise (was it weakness? was it wisdom?) had polarized the country. Statesmen – and commoners – in the South bitterly opposed those in the North, and vice versa; their mutual hostility was fanned by public orators and partisan newspapers. Everyone on either side claimed to be a true patriot. The ones on the other side were foolish at best, evil at worst.

When he joined up, Jacob thought he was a true patriot, too. He was fitted out with boots and a uniform and told he would receive three dollars a week. At the training camp he drilled with the other recruits and had a crash course in military formations, but (true to the North's inept beginnings) he was not given even one day's training in loading and firing a rifle – in his case an old Prussian musket, which Jacob had never before seen let alone shot.

He almost wished he had brought his squirrel gun from home. On their first skirmish, half the boys in his unit gave up trying to load their muskets and instead just found cover. The other half could load them but not shoot with any accuracy. Most of them were farmers, a few tradesmen, and one was the son of a county judge. Jacob got four shots off his musket before the mechanism jammed, and then he spent the next hour kneeling behind a thick oak tree trying to fix it, hoping he wouldn't get shot dead on his first day out.

He told himself he was doing his duty. Denouncing slavery and preserving the Union, however poorly the two sides fit. The South was the rural aristocracy; it was slaves working fields of tobacco, and house parties, and European manners. The North was factory smoke and railroads and crowded cities – modern life.

Jacob didn't say this to Dr. Tenney, but after his friend Matthew Ames was killed – not to mention all the others, many of them savagely – he stopped believing in the rhetoric of war. What honor was there in killing a man, in slashing or ripping or breaking his body? War was simply a neat rationalization for those who wanted something and could not get it by their intellect. Worse, they had other men do it for them: misguided men, foolish men, brave men, cowardly men, men who had a real desire to fight and hurt and kill, and men who told themselves that by fighting and killing they would somehow advance a greater good.

'Even now,' Dr. Tenney was saying, 'I understand there are some rebel soldiers who won't admit defeat. Skirmishes in Texas, and so on. Well, someday they'll see the value of our side. They'll be forced to.'

Forced to? Jacob looked at the framed beetles on the wall behind Dr. Tenney. Force just piled up bodies until there were not enough men left to fight. Slavery was against the law all across the country, and thank God for that. But as for the rest – the bitterness and distrust, even hatred, of the other side – well, the war hadn't settled that. Not at all. Men kept on searching out ways to be enemies. He'd seen that clearly at Andersonville among the prisoners, where they were all, supposedly, on the same side.

'Are they – are your daughters and your wife – are they waiting for us, do you suppose?' Jacob asked, trying to change the subject.

'Yes yes,' Dr. Tenney said. 'We shouldn't keep them waiting. First, though, I wanted to tell you a little about my daughter Vita. We're looking to settle her future. My wife and I. In case you're, ah, you know, thinking about your future, too.'

So Holland was right about that. Jacob felt himself flush. 'Oh. Well, that is – I'm not sure I want to make any changes at the moment.'

'Yes, of course. I understand. You're a young man just back from battle. Take your time and look about you, of course, of course. But, I thought I would – delicately you know – just mention our plans. In case they should fall in line with your own. Vita is not bad-looking, if I may say. She's, ah, quite healthy. And a good age for marriage. There will be a substantial dowry going with her as well.' He named it.

Jacob didn't know what to say. He thought of Vita standing by the grave of her brother, small but somehow sturdy, planted firmly on the pebbled path as the wind blew back the hem of her dress.

'No need to answer right away. Just something to consider as you begin your next venture in Boston. The money, and, ah, and so forth. Someone to run your house.'

'I see. Well, yes.' Jacob felt himself squirming, literally squirming, on the thin chair cushion. 'But of course, I hardly know your daughter.'

'Oh, these modern notions,' Dr. Tenney said with a strained laugh. 'You don't need to know much about a woman. Better not to, in fact.'

Mrs. Tenney and her daughters were sitting on a long, gray sofa when Jacob followed the doctor into the back parlor. Vita was reading a book the size of an apron pocket, while Mrs. Tenney and the other daughter – Holland's fiancée, he guessed – held embroidery hoops, although only Mrs. Tenney was actually stitching. He was surprised to see a little cream and yellow bird perched on her shoulder.

'My son's pet,' she explained when she saw Jacob looking at the bird. 'Her name is Sweetie.'

The shiny black fabric of Mrs. Tenney's mourning dress reminded him of the framed beetles in the doctor's office, and the bird on her shoulder added to this theme of nature caught and tamed. He smiled uncertainly.

'Let's show Mr. Culhane how Sweetie can balance like a seal,' Amelia suggested. 'Where's her ball?'

She was blonde and tall; Vita was smaller, with slanted blue eyes and dark eyebrows. She gave him a twisted smile, her lips compressed. 'The doctor is taking Fred's death hard,' Holland had told him at Swaby's tavern. 'I think he simply wants to be alone, no reminders. And Vita looks an awful lot like her brother.' Jacob had noticed that himself.

Dr. Tenney shooed the bird to the far end of the room. 'Now none of that nonsense.' He turned back to Jacob. 'Amelia is very good at the needle. She's embroidered every pillow in the room. And you've met Vita. My oldest daughter. She's good at . . .' He paused.

'Sugar in your tea?' Mrs. Tenney asked.

Vita, with an expression Jacob couldn't quite decipher (disappointment? hope?), said, 'I'm good at Latin and Greek, Dar. And science, too.'

Both disappointment and hope, Jacob decided – she wants her father's approval. A craving he remembered too well. Mrs. Tenney handed him a cup with a small almond cookie balanced on the saucer.

'Latin? Well, that is impressive. I only got up to the fourth grade, myself,' Jacob said. He took a sip of the weak tea – the import trade was still affected by the war – and set it down beside him. He looked at his hands, which so far were still, but nevertheless he flattened his palms on his thighs to hide any tremors that might start. Reminders of the war could trigger a reaction, the army doctor in Covington had told him, as well as uneasy situations.

No doubt this qualified as an uneasy situation.

He struggled to find something to say. 'Holland Granger, he was your tutor, I think?'

'That's right, but now that he's engaged, he's quit us.' Vita cocked her head like a boy toward her sister.

'So I hear.' He turned to Amelia. 'Congratulations.'

Amelia thanked him. Another pause. Ten more minutes, then he would make his excuses.

'So I suppose that means no more lessons for either of you.'

'No. Well, not from him,' Vita said. She glanced at her father. 'But I intend to go to college,' she went on, her voice getting louder.

Dr. Tenney put down his teacup. 'Now, now. There are no plans for that. If other proposals emerge . . .' He made a swooping motion with his hand toward Jacob, underscoring his hint.

Jacob nodded, but he was still watching Vita. 'What would you like to study in college?'

She hesitated. 'Science. I – I haven't quite decided which branch. I also like mathematics.'

'Mathematics?' That surprised him. 'Isn't that hard on a gentle brain?'

'A gentle brain?' She laughed at him, actually *laughed*, and he felt his face flush with heat. This was why he hated social calls. He was always making gaffes like this. Was gentle not a compliment, then?

'You think *I* have a gentle brain?'

'What I meant was –'

Her face had gone purple, and her voice rose louder. 'Tell me if you can, Mr. Culhane, what is the square root of two?'

'The square root?'

'I'll give you a hint: it's an irrational number.'

'Vita!' her father said sharply.

She rose from her chair so abruptly she knocked over the side table, and her cup managed to fall on the other side of the rug where it shattered into pieces. She glared at Jacob Culhane who was scrambling to stand up too, his mouth opening and closing like a fish.

Amelia knelt down to start picking up the wet shards of china while Mitty rang the bell for Mrs. Oakum.

'Vita, sit down! Amelia, stand up,' Dar said.

Amelia complied; Vita did not. A rhythmic pounding was sounding in her ears, like a teacher rapping on a fist of knuckles. To make matters worse, she felt tears spring to her eyes. Why was everyone always against her?

'Vita!' Dar said again.

'I won't!'

Jacob Culhane is an oaf, she decided. Yesterday he was all right, but today he's showing his true colors – prejudiced against women, like everyone else. As she rushed out of the room she caught a glimpse of her sister's compliant face, looking up at Dar for approval. The daughter who does everything right! Whereas I'm too loud, too opinionated, too interested in books. She felt as though she were being pushed on all sides by a mysterious force, a kind of sideways gravity, which squeezed her body and tried to keep her just exactly where she was: a worn-out whaling village thirty miles from Boston.

'Oh, now,' Mrs. Oakum said, meeting Vita in the hallway and seeing her expression. 'What can be as bad as all that?'

'Dar wants to marry me off and get rid of me. He doesn't ask *me* what *I* want.' She could hear the hysteria in her voice.

But Mrs. Oakum – who had fed Vita cups of beef broth by hand and slept in a chair by her bed for three days when Vita was ill with the measles – was clearly unmoved.

'No one asked me if I wanted to be a housekeeper,' she said, handing Vita a clean handkerchief, 'and yet here I stand.'

She was a snob. Was that her undoing? To be fair she also had the idea that she could help Arthur in his work. She could apply some of her intelligence; she could assist him with his research. Years later she read about another Marie, Marie Pasteur, who helped her husband test his famous vaccines. But as it turned out, once they were married Arthur didn't want Marie's help. He didn't even want, it seemed, her interest. 'This is for us men to sort out,' he began to say. 'You have enough to do with the children.'

Her job was to keep them safe. To prepare them for adult life. She sipped the bitter tea, willing it to work its magic. She hadn't failed, exactly, but it felt like she had.

The first year they were married, when she was pregnant with Freddy, Marie used to sneak into Arthur's office to read his magazines and journals when he was out of the house. *The Lancet*, *The American Medical Monthly*, *The Boston Medical Newsletter*. Once, he'd left his patient notebook on his desk, and she sat down to read it cover to cover. The notebook was a great surprise – not his childish handwriting (she'd had letters from him when they were engaged), but rather the conclusions he came to. For his male patients he wrote little enough, and for the women he often just wrote: *hysterical complaint*.

But her heart always lifted when she saw Arthur with his poorer patients – the mill workers, before the mill closed, or one of the farmers. He displayed real sympathy and spoke to them easily, without condescension. Quick to share a joke as he measured out medicine. This was where he shone.

Marie shifted on her cushion. She didn't want to think about Arthur. Her head was beginning to feel lighter; it was no longer the heavy iron ball it had been an hour ago. It was time. She set her empty teacup on the tray and pulled out

Freddy's *carte d'album*, which she'd hidden in the narrow cranny between her chaise lounge and the wall.

There on the first page was her Freddy, standing in uniform and smiling his wide, crooked smile. His ears flapped out slightly beneath his cap. Apparently a man – a civilian – equipped with a camera and tripod had approached the soldiers after they made camp; Freddy had explained it all in the accompanying letter, how the man offered to take staged photographs for a dime apiece for anyone who wanted them.

A day in the life of a soldier.

There was a photograph of men eating breakfast under a roped-up tent (Freddy on the right); men sitting around an open campfire in daylight (Freddy on the left, holding a tin coffee pot); and men digging a ditch (a partial view of Freddy's back). The last photograph was a formal portrait of the unit with Freddy in the back row holding up the company's pet dog so that her head was visible to the camera.

What was the name of that dog? She couldn't remember. In the photographs the men all looked hale and eager. Early days. If she saw them today they would probably have the same hollowed-out expressions she noticed in the soldiers now returning home. Even Freddy, she supposed.

Tucked into the back of the album were his letters. Marie slid one out and began to read from it randomly; this was the best way, she'd found, to make his voice come alive.

. . . I helped Dr. Boutwell as he went down the line of injured men. Since my father was a doctor, he said, I probably knew more and could help more than anyone else. One poor boy was in agony, his intestine was punctured. I couldn't even help him get comfortable as he died, and I'm most sorry for that. Mitty, I'm not sure if I'm meant to be a doctor, but Dr. Boutwell says it's always hard at first.

Freddy often mentioned Dr. Boutwell. Dr. Boutwell had been his closest friend in the unit. Besides helping him in the medicine tent, Freddy went bird-watching with him and they regularly hunted for mushrooms after an evening rain. When the doctor was mustered out, Freddy missed him sorely. It was another doctor, the replacement surgeon – an assistant, the commander wrote – who neglected, fatally, to take off Freddy's arm. Marie didn't know that man's name, and she didn't want to.

She turned to another letter.

. . . We have a company dog, a stray who followed our unit when we broke camp last week. I could tell right away she was suffering from worms, she was so skinny but with a pot belly, and constantly scooting herself along the dirt. I treated her with apple cider vinegar and chopped carrots, like Dar did with Riddle. Now she's beginning to gain weight. I've named her Pinecone, for her color, and we call her Pie.

Pie; that's right. Marie looked down at Riddle, whose paws quivered as he slept. Chasing a squirrel, perhaps, in a dream. How pleasant it would be to believe that Freddy was only away from home for a while, that he would return with Pie, who would make Riddle jealous, and tend to his animals again. Marie closed her eyes. Could she take enough of Mrs. Winslow's syrup to believe that?

'Mitty!'

She opened her eyes to see Vita standing in the doorway, her dark hair wild and loose. 'Didn't you hear me knock?'

'I didn't. I'm sorry.' Marie slid the album back into its hiding place. Vita came in and sat down on the bed across from her.

'Dar can't really think he can marry me off?' she said plaintively, without preamble.

Marie's face felt soft and still – not stiff, but without the means to move, like pond water on a windless day.

'Mitty, are you listening?'

'I'm a little tired. No, don't go,' she said as Vita began to stand up.

Vita sat down again and ran her hand over one of Amelia's embroidered pillows. She found a loose thread and began to pull at it. 'Does he truly want to marry me off, do you think?'

'I don't know. Possibly.'

'But it's so old-fashioned!'

'It is, I agree.'

'Can't you talk to him?'

Arthur didn't talk to anyone nowadays, unless it was about mistakes made in the war.

'Come and sit here, why don't you. And fetch my brush.'

Marie moved her legs aside so that Vita could sit on the seat cushion beside her. She began to brush Vita's long hair slowly, careful not to pull too hard. It was full of snarls. It usually was.

'I should go to college, you know I should. Why can't he understand that?'

They'd discussed college before, when they were alone. Women's colleges were cropping up everywhere. But secretly Marie always had her doubts about whether Arthur would agree.

'You said it yourself, he's old-fashioned.'

'Why did you let me share Freddy's lessons? I should have gone to the school in town.'

'A tutor is better.'

'If I'd gone to school in town, I wouldn't *want* to go to college. I'd be just like everyone else.'

'Would you?'

'I hope so.'

'I don't think you do.'

'I do, though. In a way I do. Anyway, there's no one left to marry. If that's really what he wants.'

'Well, you don't *have* to get married, you know. You can always stay here with me.'

Vita didn't say anything to that. And really, Marie didn't blame her for wanting to leave. It's a small town, she thought, and shrinking every day. The mill and the sail loft had closed before the war, and more and more men were setting off to find work in city factories. When she closed her eyes Marie could see the town literally shrinking: the empty fields spreading dust over houses, the ocean in a sparkle of blue lapping at Mr. Neeley's shop door. The laudanum inspired her imagination, gave it color and depth.

As she began to work out a knotty whorl of Vita's hair between her fingers, she thought of how she used to use a wet comb to try to coax a curl from Freddy's hair when he was a baby. His hair was black, too, but finer; a finely spun dark web. Vita's hair was soft and thick, like the mane of an exotic, wild animal. Marie always noticed how Arthur frowned whenever Vita quoted some passage from memory, but if Freddy quoted a passage, Arthur clapped him on the back.

'I often wished I'd had more schooling when I was a girl. I thought that if you were properly educated, you and Amelia, you'd be happier than I was. More prepared. But maybe it was a mistake.'

'It *was* a mistake,' Vita said angrily.

She was so full of energy and purpose. Arthur was like that once, when they were first married. Amelia was the most docile of the family, though she had spirit, too – it came out when she mimicked the townspeople or her aunt; she caught their inflections and absurdities perfectly. But

Marie noticed that Amelia never did this when her father was in the room. To him, she presented the picture of the daughter he wanted. Marie almost admired that; Amelia, out of all of them, knew how to get her own way.

Marie had to beg Arthur to let Vita share Freddy's lessons when Vita was small. 'She has a fine mind,' she'd said. This was obvious from the time Vita could talk. Arthur said it didn't matter, that brains were wasted on a girl. 'But it will save us money in the long run,' Marie argued. They were paying the tutor anyway, and the children could share books. 'Plus Vita could help Freddy.' 'You mean Freddy could help Vita,' he countered. Marie had paused, trying to be diplomatic. 'They'll help each other. They'll spur each other on.'

Arthur thought about that. 'I suppose a little competition can be good for a boy,' he finally decided.

Riddle, who'd lifted his head when Vita came in, was asleep again, and snoring. Marie put down her brush, divided Vita's thick hair into three long strands, and began to braid it. Maybe *was* her fault that Vita wanted to go to college. Maybe all this had simply been a chance for her to live the life, through her daughter, that hadn't been offered to her. Vita loved the process of following a logical thread to its end, and as a girl Marie had been the same way.

'I'll talk to your father,' she said, although she suspected she wouldn't get very far. If only she had her own money! But by Massachusetts law all her money became her husband's when they married. And even if Vita did find tuition money on her own, Arthur could always go to the college and drag her back home. That was his right as the father of an unmarried woman. Six months ago Marie didn't think Arthur would ever do something like that, but now she wasn't so sure.

'What are you reading at the moment?' she asked to change the subject.

'Pliny. Also William Harvey.'

'Ah. The circulation of the blood.'

'Yes, he's interesting. Pliny, though. Everyone speaks his name with such awe, but he thought women having their monthlies could wither plants and dim mirrors just by looking at them.'

Marie let out a tiny wisp of air – more of an acknowledgment that she should laugh, rather than a real laugh. 'Do you have a ribbon?' She was holding Vita's braid in one hand.

'No.'

She hesitated, and then with her free hand she pulled out Freddy's photo album from against the wall.

Vita turned her head – gingerly, as Marie was still holding her hair. 'Are those Freddy's photographs? I wondered where they were. Were you looking at them just now?'

Marie fished out the coral ribbon she used to mark her place in the album and wound it around the end of Vita's braid. The laudanum made her feel sleepy and open-hearted. Reflective. Almost soft. She was tired of the armor she wore every day, pretending she could simply carry on with daily life.

'I suppose I wanted him to be alive for a little while longer,' Marie said.

Vita pulled her braid around and felt the neat plait. She rubbed her fingertips against the end as though it were a paintbrush she was testing for dryness. Together she and her mother looked down at Freddy's smiling face, his dark hair, the way the uniform emphasized his shoulders. Marie couldn't help but think that the other men seemed less distinct. Milkier, somehow. Like Vita, Freddy had been full of enthusiasm, only not about books.

When Vita looked up, her eyes were wet.

'Me too,' she said.

The second suitor was just as bad as the first, and not nearly as handsome: Stephen Phelps. He wore tight crimson gloves, said 'Chooseday' instead of 'Tuesday,' and his mouth drooped on one side like an old man's – he had suffered a series of fits as a newborn. Phelps lived nearby in the town of Closbury; his father was one of Dr. Tenney's patients.

During the war Phelps served as secretary to someone he made sound very important, but whom no one had ever heard of.

'Captain Netherfield. I argued to do my part until my father found me the job. I write in a very fine hand. The army wouldn't take me otherwise, you see.'

This last he said to Holland Granger, nodding at him as if their infirmities made a bond between them. But that was unfair, Vita thought. Phelps had rheumy eyes and a persistent dry cough, and his eyebrows had been partially singed off the previous day. 'I lit a cigar carelessly,' he explained, 'but they will likely grow back.'

As usual they were sitting in the stuffy back parlor, only her mother was upstairs with a headache, lucky thing, and Holland had come by to see Amelia – and now he's trapped, Vita thought, like the rest of us. Even her father didn't seem particularly taken with Phelps, although he was the one who invited him.

'Your father tells me you have plans to go out west?' he said somewhat stiffly, and then folded his hands in his lap like a schoolmarm listening to a lesson.

'His property will go to my brother John, and the factories will go to James, but my father's given me the means to buy twenty-six acres in Oregon.' He coughed his quick, raspy cough. 'The money for the land, that is, but not enough to build on it. That's up to me to raise.'

Here he looked pointedly at Dar, and then at Vita. Vita tried to maintain a bland expression. She was determined today to keep her temper. Her new plan, as discussed with Gemma, was to play the role of the meek daughter, to bide her time, to promise and delay, until Amelia got married. A new plan had occurred to her: why not use her aunt's promise of house-buying money for tuition? Must it be used for buying a house?

'I can't give you a check before your sister, Vita, that wouldn't be right,' Aunt Norbert had told her when Vita went to see her last Thursday to ask about it. 'But I will give it to you on her wedding day, the same day I give Amelia hers. And if you are unmarried then, why, I suppose you can use the gift as you wish.'

If Dar won't help me, Vita thought, I'll do it myself.

'Oregon,' Phelps was saying, 'is a vast, ripe wilderness. Full of potential. But empty. You won't find any women there to cook or take in laundry. I must set out with the proper provisions.' Here he looked at Vita again.

Was she a provision?

'Don't tell me that the men there wash their own clothes!' she couldn't help saying.

'Vita!' Amelia laughed. 'You've never so much as polished a shoe!'

Phelps frowned. 'Is that right? You cannot clean leather?'

Vita remembered her game. 'I'm sure I could learn. After all, I've learned Latin and Greek.'

'Oh yes, ladies' samplers with their little inscriptions. So popular these days.'

'I mean proper Latin. I've been studying it since I was twelve.'

Phelps tilted his head, imitating someone who listened. 'As you're a man of science,' he said to Dr. Tenney, 'you might like to know about a few exciting new discoveries in the area of farming. Modern techniques on how to aerate the soil.' He turned back to Vita. 'To aerate means to add air,' he explained.

'I know that.'

He nodded. 'To add air, yes. Now in Oregon I intend to plant persimmon trees. The persimmon tree produces fruit from the seed in only four years, and the pounded bark can be used to reduce a fever. I happen to have some notes with me, if you are interested?'

Here he looked at Amelia, who said politely, 'Oh certainly.'

He stood to withdraw a sheath of papers from his pocket and sat down again, fussily, careful to keep his coat from wrinkling.

'The persimmon has many untapped uses,' he began, reading from his notes. 'When the fruit is well mashed and strained through a coarse wire sieve, it can make uncommonly good bread . . .'

Sunlight beat against the freshly washed windows, and the wainscoting beneath the windowpane seemed to melt before her eyes. Vita looked out to the yard, where she could see her mother's dahlias; at the moment they were only green stalks with large, tight buttons that waved in the wind like planted corn, but in a few days the buttons would begin to open into double buds with lilac and white petals, and fiery red single buds, and her mother's border dahlias, small white and peach piccolos.

Every spring for as long as Vita could remember, Mitty began her dahlias in pots in the greenhouse with a carefully calculated mixture of chicken manure, potash, and bone – testing for the correct balance of nitrogen and potassium – and then she replanted them in the ground after they sprouted. Mitty was always precise in her proportions, and she wrote down every new finding in a series of notebooks, much like Vita's own. Gardening, Vita realized, was the perfect cover for a woman interested in science.

When Freddy and Vita were little, Mitty sometimes wrapped their legs in bandages and pretended to make them a dose of quicksilver in a game they, not very creatively, called 'Ulcers in the Leg.' Since her father was a doctor and a professor of medicine at Yale – Dar had been one of his students – Mitty knew quite a lot. But she hid her knowledge; she even hid her curiosity. She gardened, and she read the monthly science journals that came to the house, but always on the sly.

'. . . the tender leaves can be made into tea and its bark used for dye,' Phelps was saying.

How could her mother stand it? Vita often wondered. How could she suppress her intellectual curiosity this way? It made Vita angry – angrier – at her father, but she was also (she had to admit) disappointed in her mother as well. I won't be like her, Vita promised herself. I won't.

'Pulverized, the bark can also be used to reduce a fever.'

Holland, his head resting against the high back of the sofa, was asleep. Amelia pinched his arm, but although he closed his mouth he didn't open his eyes. Phelps didn't notice. He came to the end of his page and lifted his wet, red-rimmed, eyebrowless eyes to look at Vita.

'Those are just a few thoughts of interest,' he said, as he began to fold the pages back along their folds. Vita could see her father pull back a yawn, and even Amelia seemed caught in a sleepy stupor. Vita didn't even try to appear interested. He was an oaf, like Jacob Culhane, but worse because of his silly pretenses. He imagined she didn't know what aerate meant! A life with him would be a life of being told facts she already knew.

'My plan is to leave on the first of October,' Phelps said. He looked pointedly at Vita. 'And I hope to be married by then.'

'Surely he hasn't made an offer already?' Vita said the next day, in her father's office, when he summoned her. He was sitting behind his desk and she stood before him like a penitent student. She felt a real moment of panic, but her father hesitated.

'Not in so many words. But matters move much more quickly these days. And you heard him, he's primed to leave in a couple of weeks.'

'But to leave so soon! Think of everything he has to do – all those persimmon seeds to gather.'

Her father didn't smile. 'Well, that *is* what he expects.'

She was half relieved and half incensed – how could Dar want to stick her with that bore for the rest of her life? He was her father; shouldn't he want more for her? His obvious disappointment in her was always in his voice, so unfairly. Hadn't she learned German and Latin and a fair amount of Greek? Couldn't she solve a calculus problem faster than Holland Granger could? But it did no good for Vita to think about all the ways she was clever. In fact it set her back, since it brought on a familiar knife-swipe of frustration.

'Dar,' she said, trying to appeal to his reason. 'Let me study medicine. I'll find a way to do it. It's my dream.'

'Your dream is to be laughed at and ridiculed?'

'No, to be a doctor. A lady doctor. I wouldn't be the first – there are hundreds of them now.' Over two hundred, according to the *Boston Medical Journal*.

But her father was not impressed. They were like old sparring enemies who came face to face every few months, neither one ever able to claim a lasting victory. He picked up the polished monkey skull on his desk that he used as a paperweight. His eyes glittered.

'A *lady doctor.*' Now he was mocking her. He bounced the skull from hand to hand. 'Do you know what that means in a city like Boston?'

'It doesn't mean a woman practicing medicine?'

'No, it doesn't mean a woman practicing medicine. It's the name of a woman who ends unwanted pregnancies for other women. It has nothing at all to do with being a doctor. Most *lady doctors* haven't read so much as a paragraph about the bodily systems. Never heard of chloroform.'

'First used as an anesthetic in 1847 by Sir James Young Simpson,' Vita said, falling back to trying to impress him with her knowledge of facts. 'Just tell me what to read, Dar, and I'll read it. You know I can do it!' She could hear her voice rising dangerously, emotionally.

'I know no such thing. You like to read, yes, and your memory is sufficient.'

With effort, Vita stopped herself from objecting. Her memory was excellent!

'But being a doctor is more than simply reading books. It requires patience, which you lack. Attention to detail, which you lack. And you must be absolutely thorough with every case, at every step of the way.'

'Dar, I can do all that. I mean, I can learn to do it. Please let me try!'

'As a doctor you have to concern yourself with other people, something I have never seen you do. A parakeet doesn't count.'

'Give me a chance to prove myself.'

'It's unnecessary.' This was the phrase he used whenever he wanted to shut down a discussion. 'I told your mother the same when she brought it up last night.'

'But it *is* necessary. It's very necessary!'

'Vita. Stop shouting. You're only proving my point. You don't have the temperament for higher learning. No woman does.'

His head seemed unusually small, wobbling on his neck, and his eyes would not meet hers. Why wouldn't he acknowledge her accomplishments? Growing up she'd learned to wind her emotions up like a skein of wool, make a tight ball of them, and then hold the ball in place for as long as she could. She turned to leave, afraid that she might pick up one of his antique bleeding bowls and throw it at his head.

'I expect I'll receive a letter from Mr. Phelps soon,' her father told her. 'And then you must abide by my decision.'

It was his parting shot, and she felt it.

However, the letter, when it came two days later, was not what they expected. 'As of yesterday evening,' Phelps wrote, 'I'm engaged to marry Phoebe Barnes, and could not be happier.'

CHAPTER SIX

'Be to her faults a little blind;
Be to her virtues a little kind;
Let all her ways be unconfin'd
And place your padlock on her mind.'
(Advice to married men, *Godey's Lady's Book*, 1834)

Phoebe Barnes was a thick-limbed farmer's daughter, a muscled little pony, who would be an excellent asset for a man going off to the wilderness; whereas I would be useless, Vita thought happily. Phoebe Barnes, what a goose. But thank God for her, really. Let's just hope she likes persimmons.

It was as near perfect a summer morning as one could wish for: sky like sheeny blue fabric, warm sunlight, a soft breeze with the slightest tang of salt to it. Vita went outside with her notebook in hand. There was a spot against the back of the house between two crooked rhododendron trees where she liked to read or do problems; the trees flanked the kitchen windows, with a cleared space between them. A small, dry refuge. The air smelled like the wild mint that grew in dark patches around the yard.

Vita spread her black crocheted shawl on the ground, settled herself against the house shingles, and opened her notebook.

Prove the sum of the first n integers = n x (n+1) / 2

The smell of bean broth wafted out through the half-open kitchen window, and Vita could hear her mother in the kitchen talking to Mrs. O.

'And maybe a nice Sunderland pudding for dessert,' she was saying.

Vita wrote:

1 2 3 4 5 6 7 8 9 10
10 9 8 7 6 5 4 3 2 1
11 11 11 11 11 11 11 11 11 11 sum

The sum of the first ten integers was 55; she wrote:

11 x 10 / 2 = 55

and then thought about Gauss, the mathematician who solved this proof when he was a boy walking to school, or so the story went. A boy genius, Gauss was. Vita wasn't a genius, she knew that. Often it took her weeks to work out a proof, and lately there were some proofs she'd had to abandon. She sensed she had gone about as far as she could go in mathematics – science was more her strength – but she still enjoyed trying to puzzle out answers.

She rubbed out a smudge on the paper with her rubber eraser and brushed the crumbs away. As a girl, before the war, she often hid in this spot; in late spring, when the rhododendrons were in bloom, the tree branches with their bright magenta flowers arched over her like an umbrella canopy, and she was almost completely concealed. Freddy might come out with a pet squirrel on his shoulder and never see her, or Mrs. O. to beat the kitchen rug. Vita watched them covertly from her spy hole, although they never did anything she didn't expect. She found it exciting to be invisible, but also a little lonely.

'I would think two pints, at least,' her mother said from inside the kitchen.

'I'd best check how much flour we have left,' Mrs. O. said.

Once Freddy enlisted, Vita felt even more isolated and alone. Who could she talk to about her interests, besides Gemma, who was busy with her own work? Amelia made new friends with the girls in town as they rolled bandages for the soldiers or packed lint in the old curate's cottage, but Vita was irritated by their bland chitchat. When she went along to help she always brought along a book or a newspaper, which she propped open on a barrel to read while she rolled up long strips of cotton cloth, ignoring the others. This was when her father began his obsession with getting the news from all over the country, as many newspapers as he could get delivered. In the Washington paper, Vita read an article about Dorothea Dix, who was in charge of hiring war nurses. Excited, Vita thought she might do something useful – more useful than rolling bandages – and maybe she could also learn from the army surgeons (she would have to be stealthy about that). But when she wrote to Miss Dix via the newspaper, Miss Dix replied in large loopy handwriting that all volunteer nurses must be 'homely' women over thirty years old who wore no jewelry or ribbons. Although Vita rarely wore jewelry and hated ribbons of any kind, she was barely sixteen.

She also read about Clara Barton, who took it upon herself to distribute food and water to wounded soldiers in the field – sometimes even when the battle was still raging. Clara Barton wasn't a nurse, although once she did extract a bullet from a young man's arm when no help was nearby.

Even better. Vita wrote to her, too. But, like Dorothea Dix, Miss Barton (though in tiny purple script) wrote back to say that Vita was 'too young to witness the barbarianism of the battlefield. But I commend your spirit, my dear.'

She kept that letter in her pocket for weeks until the paper became as soft as cloth and began to tear when she unfolded it.

Still, the two women gave her encouragement, if only just the fact of them. Maybe her own plans weren't crazy. Unexpected, yes, but not unimaginable. Over a decade ago, Elizabeth Blackwell graduated from a New York college with a medical degree – the first one awarded to an American woman – and a few years later her sister Emily received her medical degree as well.

Women could become doctors, this was a fact. Vita simply had to keep Dar from finding her an available suitor, and then let Aunt Norbert's money do the rest. She looked up at the spiky rhododendron branches above her and chewed the end of her pencil, making little mouse marks on the wood. She had to stick with her plan.

'We've not nearly enough.' Mrs. O.'s voice came drifting out again through the open window. 'We'll need another half cup for sure. And Gemma's already gone off to Fenegan's to pick up the doctor's boots.'

'What about Vita, can she go? Where is she?'

Vita held her breath. She didn't want to be sent on an errand, she wanted today to herself, but she heard Mrs. O. say, 'Oh she's right there at the window doing whatever she does out there. Vita!' she called out. 'Stop your eavesdropping now, we need you to go pick up some flour.'

Or maybe, Vita thought, shaking rhododendron filaments from her skirt, I'm not as invisible as I'd like to be.

❁

It was such a warm day that she didn't take her shawl with her. Walking over the stone bridge and along past Carver's farm Vita let her arms swing freely, like a man. She adjusted Freddy's old satchel, which she'd started carrying when he left for war. She didn't like going to town with a basket, it made her feel too much like the other women in town. Ordinary. Like Amelia.

At the top of the road she paused to look down at Lark's Eye Bay, sparkling in the sun; her aunt lived just opposite the pier in a large butter-colored house with black shutters. It was the largest house in Lark's Eye, with two cottages in the back for the gardener and cook. The Norbert family made their fortune in shipbuilding and, later, in canning factories along the coast. But as a widow – 'conveniently childless,' as she liked to put it – Aunt Norbert had made even more money, wisely investing in railroads and oil right before the war.

Aunt Norbert had firm ideas about money. She had firm ideas about diet, penmanship, and the proper size of engagement ring stones (small; or at least smaller than hers). She considered lemon juice a woman's first line of defense against freckling, and disapproved of men who wore pointed shoes or who said 'set' instead of 'sit.'

'I serve as a model for the town,' she liked to say. 'People watch me for how to act.'

'Or when to run,' Freddy used to whisper. His nickname for her was Lady Norbert.

Before she married Ezra Norbert, Clara Toombs had attended, for one year, the Mount Holyoke Female Seminary, which later became a college. 'My love of history began there,' she often said, 'under the tutelage of Mrs. Elvira Peterson, who also taught embroidery and health and had a tremendous head of hair for a woman of sixty.'

She was proud of her education, cut short when she visited her sister Marie in Lark's Eye and was proposed to by the much older Ezra Norbert – sixty, gouty, windy, but still with all his money the prize of the town. Vita felt certain that her aunt wouldn't protest if she used her gift of 'house-buying money' for college tuition. Hadn't she said that if Vita was unmarried on Amelia's wedding day, she could use the money as she wanted? Vita liked to think that Aunt Norbert would *want* her to further her own education. She couldn't understand why the men in her life – well, Dar – were so against it. Freddy would have been on her side. She imagined him arguing for her; she was sure he would have been her champion. And maybe Dar would have listened to him. Maybe, or maybe not.

In Neeley's Shop, as she waited for Mrs. Neeley to measure the flour, Vita looked out the window at the field they called Oak Field because it had once been a grove of trees. But every single one of the trees had been harvested long before Vita was born to make hulls and ship masts and spars. These days sand blew over the loose dirt, and nothing grew there but weeds. When it rained it became a gloppy shallow pond of mud. It was amazing to Vita that Amelia – that anyone – wanted to stay in this town.

'Give my best to your mother,' Mrs. Neeley said, handing her the sack of flour tied with twine. 'And tell your sister I have some nice buttons just come in from Boston if she wants to take a look. So much for her to do now, I'm sure! Well, I hope to hear of your being married next thing.'

Vita tucked the flour sack into Freddy's satchel. 'No, I don't think you will, Mrs. Neeley.'

Away from her father she had every confidence in herself. She was resourceful and smart. All her work, all her studies, had been preparation for leaving. Her ambition felt like an unused power; a mountain lion waiting to spring.

Poor Phoebe Barnes, she thought again; but standing outside the shop in the warm sunlight Vita found she couldn't muster up much pity for Phoebe, she was feeling too pleased with her own freedom. Really, she wanted to laugh. Aunt Norbert liked to say she didn't realize her own potential to be useful (and to command others, Vita silently added) until she moved to Lark's Eye. But I'll be more useful, Vita thought, by moving away.

Only not to Oregon with Stephen Phelps, thank God.

❁

As Jacob crossed the town green, he saw Vita Tenney walking toward him with a smile on her face. Why would she be smiling at him? Then he realized that he was smiling, too.

'Mr. Culhane,' she said, stopping to give him her hand.

He was in a good mood. It was a sunny day with a hint of sea breeze, and being back in Lark's Eye wasn't as painful as he had feared. In fact, he was beginning to warm to it. Being an adult, and not a trapped child, helped. It was also gratifying to be viewed as a war hero (he wasn't) and sought after as a bachelor (he was). Just last evening he sat drinking lemonade on Mrs. Linden's porch with three lovely young women who seemed to compete with their dimples. And here now was Fred Tenney's sister with her husky voice and sunburned nose, smiling up at him. She was really quite little, he noticed again, although she spoke in a way that commanded attention.

'I wasn't sure you would say hello to me,' he said, 'after our last meeting.'

'You caught me on a good day. Tomorrow I might not.'

He raised one eyebrow. 'I've been warned. Shall we develop a signal?'

She laughed. 'And why are *you* in a good mood?'

'Does it show?' He was carrying a roll of oversized paper, and lifted it slightly. 'I've just been to the bank. I've an idea for a patent, and Mr. Gideon has expressed some interest in it. I'm hoping to get a loan.'

'A patent for what?'

He hesitated.

'Don't worry, I won't give your secrets away.'

'It's a bit complicated,' he said.

Vita felt a black stab go straight into her heart. 'Oh, well then, if it's complicated,' she said, kicking herself for stopping to speak to him. As quick as that, her good mood vanished.

But he didn't notice her change; he was looking down at his paper as he began to unroll it. 'I'm not sure I understand it. No, that's not true. I *know* I don't understand it. It's a formula that my friend, a friend from the war, worked out. He's gone now, didn't make it.'

He spoke quickly as though to get through that last part as fast as he could. Vita realized he wasn't calling her abilities into question, but his own. They were standing next to the bandstand in a slice of shade. Jacob held out one end of the thick, curled paper to her and Vita took it, stepping up next to him to look at it.

'See here,' he pointed to sketches of labeled barrel parts; the staves, the hoops, the hoop rivets and hoop joints. Also bilge, chime, cant, head – parts Vita had no idea there were names for. 'We're trying to make a barrel that doesn't leak oil. They're fine for dry goods and even fish, a little water leaking out of a fish barrel is fine, but you lose money if your oil barrel leaks oil. Only a little lost oil in every barrel adds up quickly over time.'

Vita studied the equation underneath the drawings. A warm breeze played over the back of her neck. 'Is this the formula your friend worked out?'

'Yes, but it's not perfect. Caleb was still working on it when – when he died. And I'm not . . . well, I didn't have much in the way of schooling. I guess I told you that. I've a good mind for business, though, and once there's a model I can push it ahead, but I need a partner to help get the formula right. That's where the loan comes in, to pay for another salary. And for the workshop too, of course.'

'It probably needs a glue that's strong but quick-drying.'

'That's it, exactly! At first we were thinking of changing the shape of the barrel staves, but then we decided no, it's the glue.'

'Starch-based, or rubber?' she asked. She'd once read an essay on modern adhesives in one of her father's science journals.

'We thought casein glue, made from milk.'

'Of course; that's more water-resistant.'

'You've heard of casein?'

'I've read about it. Would you heat the barrels to set the glue?'

'Vita! Miss Vita!'

From the other end of the green Vita saw Gemma coming toward them; not running, exactly, but walking fast. Her thin face was flushed with excitement.

Jacob began rolling up the thick paper. 'Well, thank you for indulging me.' He touched his hat.

'It wasn't an indulgence.'

'Then thank you for turning your gentle mind in the direction of my problem.'

Gentle mind? Was that a joke? He was grinning as he turned to cross the road. So he *was* teasing her. Had he been teasing the first time he called her mind gentle?

She thought not. She smiled to herself.

'Vita, you'll never guess,' Gemma said, reaching her. There was an exuberance in her expression, like a woman who has just witnessed a great event – a flaming comet, or a tornado touching down.

'Ruffy's home,' she said. 'And I've seen him.'

Ruffy – Randall Barstow, Gemma's sweetheart – was back from battle.

No one had heard from him in six weeks, not even his mother. He was young, only seventeen, and had signed up in the last months of the war. It was hard to imagine Ruffy as a soldier. He had a slight frame and fine blond hair and was the gentlest boy Vita knew, though his skin was permanently sooty from working at his father's smithy. It was hard to imagine Ruffy as a blacksmith either, but that Vita had seen for herself.

'He wrote letters to his ma and to me from the hospital camp,' Gemma said. 'But they must have strayed. The nurse in charge of the mail had her hands full, he said, what with all the injured men.'

Ruffy included. One of his hands had been shot off, the left one. He aimed to raise horses now, he told Gemma. Working the anvil with only one hand was impossible, though in truth Ruffy barely had the muscle even with two. His father, who had been a thick, muscular ox as a young man, was bent and crippled after thirty years of heavy work. He was happy to teach his youngest son Rayburn the trade, who at fourteen already had a neck like a bulldog mastiff and the strength to match.

'Ruffy thinks he can use his army pay to buy a couple of horses. At the beginning he might have to gentle foals on the side, he told me, to raise money. He didn't have a ring but he asked me anyhow would I marry him, right there outside the post office, and he kissed me where anyone might see! He doesn't want to wait. I think Mrs. Barstow will give us his grandmother's ring. Unless his brother got to it first.'

'Rayburn is only fourteen!'

'Fifteen last week. He's got his eye on Phoebe Barnes.'

Too late there, Vita thought. She and Gemma were still standing under the shade of the bandstand. She squeezed Gemma's arm.

'Oh Gemma! I'm so happy for you.'

Ruffy was not muscular like his brother, but he was scrappy. He and Gemma would rise in the world; Vita had no doubt. And I'll rise, too, she promised herself – the words were a talisman. She could see the tops of the marsh roses that grew near the water, and Mr. Neeley, wearing his greengrocer's apron, stepped outside with a bucket and began to wash his buggy. An ordinary day in an ordinary town. She thought of Jacob Culhane, with his low-slung trousers and dark eyes. *Thank you for turning your gentle mind in the direction of my problem.*

A jokester, she decided. Like Freddy.

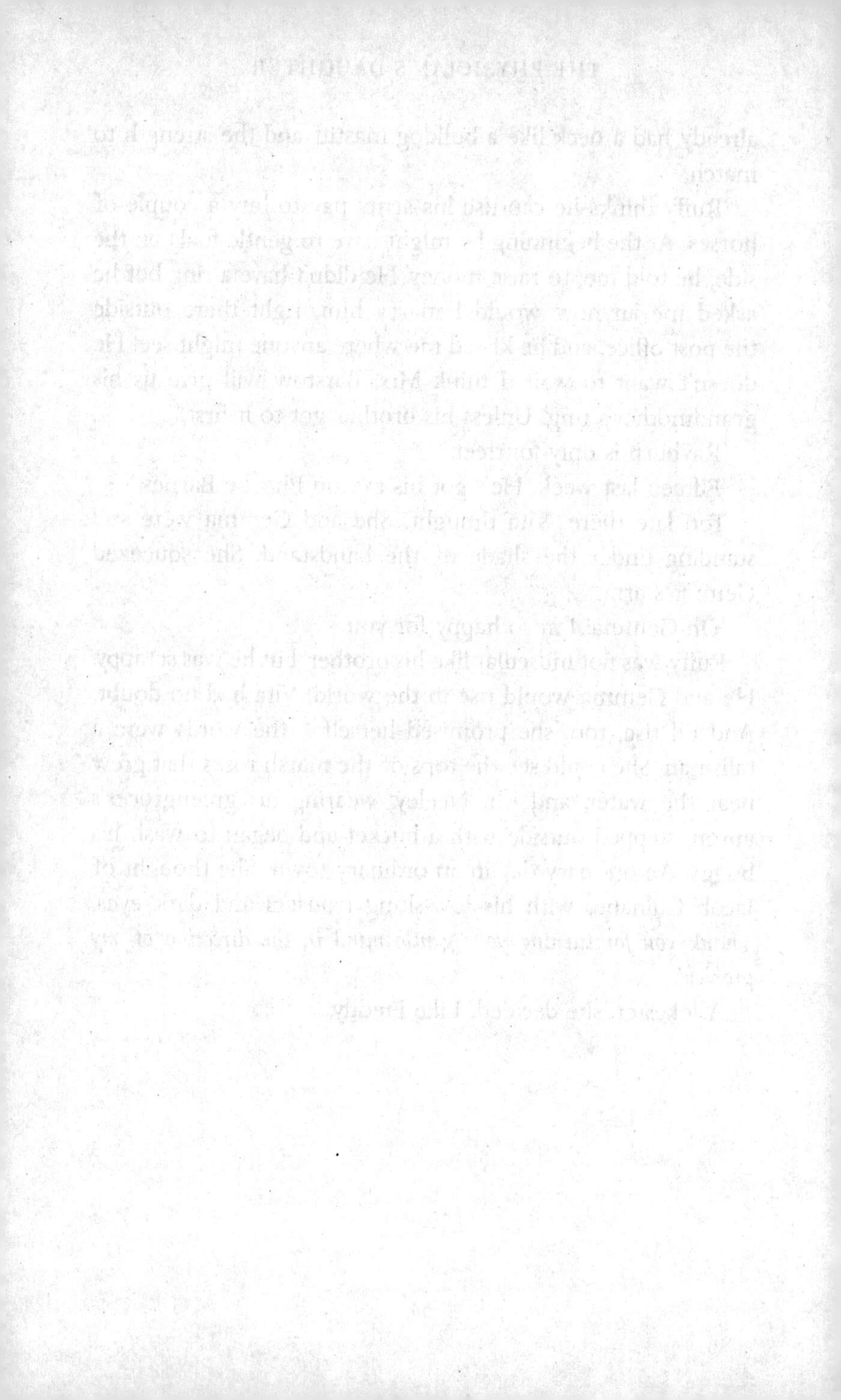

CHAPTER SEVEN

'Once the bride has donned her gown and turned off all the lights, she should lie quietly upon the bed and await her groom. When he comes groping into the room she should make no sound to guide him in her direction. There is always the hope that he will stumble and incur some slight injury, which she can use as an excuse to deny him sexual access.'

(*Instruction and Advice for the Young Bride*, Mrs. Ruth Smythers, 1894)

'I've made arrangements to dine out this evening,' Vita's father announced at breakfast a week later, 'and you two girls will accompany me.'

'To dine *out?*' Vita asked. They never dined out.

'Where, Dar?' Amelia asked.

'You don't know him. He wants to meet Vita.'

So, another candidate. I'll have to move fast, Vita thought. She was still building her case: she had Aunt Norbert's offer of money, which would answer for tuition, and she'd written to her second cousin, Maria Maag, asking if she might live with her in Philadelphia while she looked for a preceptor there.

After her apprenticeship she could stay in Philadelphia and attend the Female Medical College of Pennsylvania. Surely when her father realized she wasn't asking him for anything, he would agree.

Now she was just waiting for an answer from Maria Maag, whom she met only once at her grandfather's funeral in New Haven. That was over ten years ago.

'I would be happy to help with your children,' Vita had written, 'as part of my room and board.' Later she thought: Or does she even have children? She couldn't actually remember, since she barely listened to family news.

When the time came to leave the sky was filled with bloated, leaden clouds, and Dar agreed to give Gemma a lift home. Gemma lived with her aunt and two cousins on a road where the mill workers had lived until the mill closed down; many of the cottages stood abandoned with empty window frames and half-exposed roofs. Gemma's uncle had worked at the mill until he died, and her aunt made ends meet by making baskets in the winter and working in the Closbury dairy in summer, when they needed extra help.

'Thank you, Dr. Tenney!' Gemma said, stepping down from the carriage. 'For sure I would not have made it home in time.' She didn't actually make it home in time now; seconds after she started down the lane, the threatened rain blew in with a swift violence. Vita could see her half-running, half-jumping down the dirt road, which was quickly transforming itself into treacly mud.

'Poor girl will get soaked,' Dar said, watching her.

In town he was known for his sympathy. He wasn't from a wealthy family, not like Mitty; his father had been a postmaster in Connecticut. He'd worked his way through medical college at an apothecary shop, and was consequently one of her grandfather's favorite students – he'd had to do the same (and then, also like Dar, he'd married a woman with money). Grandfather Toombs himself had bought Arthur Tenney the medical practice in Lark's Eye, when Lark's Eye was still a prosperous town.

What had happened? Vita wondered. Was it grief over Freddy, or something more? She looked at her father's face, wishing she could understand him or anticipate his moods. When she was with him, and they weren't in the midst of an argument, she almost felt sorry for him. But as soon as he spoke to her, it was as if someone threaded a needle with pure silken anger, which rose twisting from her heart.

They headed inland, ribboning around the swollen marshes. The wind sounded like an urgent message in a language no one could understand. But after only a few minutes the sound of raindrops hitting the bellows top softened, and then subsided altogether.

Just a quick summer downpour.

The carriage pitched uncomfortably along the rough road. Vita peered through the smeary glass windows but the bay was no longer visible. When Mr. Healey turned the horses at the crossroads, Amelia leaned forward to look out, too. A moment later she said, 'Why, I believe we're going to Riverside,' and she stared at Vita with a mixture of surprise and disbelief.

The only person they knew who lived in Riverside was old Robinson Jameson. All at once Vita had a sinking feeling.

'We're not going to Mr. Robinson Jameson's house, are we?'

Her father was leaning back in the corner of his seat with his eyes closed. 'Oh, do you know him?' he asked without opening them.

Amelia and Vita gaped at each other, this time in horror.

'Dar,' Amelia said. 'He goes to church with us.'

'That's right, he's a Methodist. I forgot.'

Vita waited for him to say more.

'Does he have a nephew visiting?' she asked, not very hopefully.

'The man is worth a fortune,' he said.

Uncharacteristically, Amelia took Vita's hand. Vita could tell she was picturing, as she was, the long gray hairs in Robinson Jameson's ears, and how his eyes followed young girls as they left the pews.

'Stop,' Vita said loudly. 'Stop the horses.'

The horses continued at the same pace. She raised her voice. 'Mr. Healey! Please stop!'

Her father opened his eyes. 'No need to stop, Healey, let's keep going.'

'Dar,' Amelia said. 'You can't think to marry Vita off to Mr. Jameson. He's awful. He really is.'

'You have a better idea? She didn't like Culhane, and Phelps didn't like her.'

'But Mr. Jameson is so old.' Amelia was red in the face, struggling to speak. Vita couldn't help but feel grateful to her for trying to help; her sister usually went to ground at the first sign of trouble. But Robinson Jameson was too much even for her. 'He – there's something wrong with him. How he looks at us.'

'Oh, enough!' Dar snapped. He glared at Vita as though she had been the one to speak out, not Amelia. 'He looks at you how any man would look at you, with admiration.'

'Dar, I can't get married,' Vita said. 'I want to go to college, to become a doctor, like you. Aunt Norbert said she'd pay my tuition –' somewhat true – 'so there will be no burden on you. And I've already fulfilled all the academic requirements, algebra and Latin and so on. And I can stay with Mitty's cousins, the Maags.' Fingers crossed.

'In Philadelphia?'

'I'll look for a mentor there. A preceptor. Perhaps you know someone, a colleague? You wouldn't have to recommend me, you could just give me his name.'

'I wouldn't do that to him or to you.'

'Why not?'

'Or to myself either.'

'But why?'

'It's a disgrace, that's why. No daughter of mine will dishonor the family that way, not while I still have breath.'

Vita became aware of a faint but persistent rattle: one of the glass windows was loose in its frame and jiggled as they rode over the rutted road. They were approaching Riverside; up ahead she could see the first squat, brick buildings that led into the square. Amelia was still holding her hand. She began to speak faster.

'It's no disgrace! There are more and more women doctors every day. Why else would there be an entire college dedicated to their education? More than one college?'

'To keep them from distracting the men who are doing the real work.'

'Dar, I've dreamed about this since I was a girl.'

'Wanting something badly is not in itself a recommendation. No. Stop,' he said as she tried to speak again. 'I will not allow it. I won't.'

His voice was rising, too, and his nostrils flared angrily. The horses turned up a long, narrow drive flanked by silvery birch trees and stopped in front of a sand-colored stone house. Mr. Healey hooked the reins and came around to help Amelia out, but Vita's father opened the opposite door and Vita followed him.

For a moment they were alone; the carriage, streaked with mud and wet leaves, blocked their view of Amelia and Mr. Healey. Vita put her hand on her father's arm. She could hear, at a distance below them, the river that gave the town its name.

'I'm not asking you for anything. You needn't worry about a preceptor, I expect I can find one on my own. And with Aunt Norbert's money –'

He pulled his arm away and stared at Vita with such a raw, wild look that for a moment she was scared. His skin whitened, and his teeth, when he opened his mouth to bare them like a dog, were stained gray. His face seemed to suddenly shrink, and then grow.

'Am I not speaking?' he hissed. 'Can you not hear me? Are my words only an irritating noise, a fly against the windowpane, bump bump bump? Bump bump bump?'

His feathery tone had dipped into madness. Vita was so stunned she could say nothing, but nor could she look away. Her father's eyes solidified into glass and he narrowed them, observing her coldly.

'*You* are the pebble in my shoe,' he told her.

And then, just as quickly, he lost his mad expression as surely as if he had reached up to take off a papier-mâché mask. She watched his features gather and smooth themselves out like dirty fabric ironed into respectability, not quite fresh and clean, but close enough.

But now she'd seen a glimpse of it; the secret self he kept hidden away. No wonder he locked himself in his office all day. It must be a terrible strain. An expression of confusion came over his features, and he looked like the boy he must have once been, whose job it was to take in the world, to try to understand it, rather than to judge.

Shocked as she was, Vita nevertheless wanted to say something to console him, or even, if possible, to negate what she'd seen. She watched him pull out his handkerchief and touch it to his lips, resuming the bearing of that respectable man, Dr. Arthur Tenney. Not knowing what else to do, she followed him around the carriage toward the house.

'What just happened?' Amelia asked, seeing her face.

Vita's shock didn't wear off until they were nearly finished with the dinner Robinson Jameson had laid out for them: a joint of dry beef, overcooked peas, gummy rolls, and watery mashed potatoes followed by custard with raspberry cream. The long black table was crammed with dishes and candles, and pastoral paintings hung on every inch of the dining room walls, their dusty frames only a thumb's width apart.

A cramped and uncomfortable meal. Jameson exuded a strong smell of sherry when he greeted them at the door, and then proceeded to drink two bottles of wine more or less by himself at the table.

Vita picked up a tarnished dessert spoon and took a bite of the custard, only to find the cream had slightly but perceptibly soured. She was beginning to understand just how dismal her prospects truly were. Her father wasn't thinking rationally, so no rational plan would sway him. At the moment he was making mundane conversation – 'I hear the codling moth has spread to orchards in Iowa' – but his mask could slip again at any time.

Robinson Jameson put a huge spoonful of the spoiled custard into his mouth with no apparent distaste. Greasy food stains (not all of them recent) were spattered down his necktie; Vita felt queasy simply looking at them.

After dessert, not very convincingly, her father made an excuse to leave Vita alone in the dining room with their host, taking Amelia with him. Amelia shot Vita a parting look – *sorry!* – as she left.

To his credit, Jameson came right to the point. He didn't want Vita for her father's money, he told her. He had plenty of money. He wanted the companionship.

'It's getting harder and harder for me to button my trousers,' he said with a leer.

'Surely a valet can help you with that.'

'Ha ha!' He spit when he laughed. 'I like your energy.' He lit a cigar and looked her over.

'I just don't see myself marrying.'

'Maybe I can convince you.'

He put his hand on her upper arm, his thumb brushing against the side of her breast.

Vita pulled away. 'I have other plans.'

'Oh? And what are these plans?'

'I'm going to college.' The likelihood of that was smaller than she cared to calculate, but she could think of nothing else to say.

'College? For women? A female institution? I've always been curious about such places.' His tongue snaked out to touch his upper lip. 'Absolutely. By all means.'

Vita stared at him. 'You wouldn't object?'

'Of course not. Take a month, even two. Meanwhile I can do some business in Canada that's been pressing. We can marry at Christmas.'

Take a month or two. Only this morning this would have enraged her, but now there was a frozen stone in the middle of her chest.

She stood up and left the room. As she passed the closed parlor door she could hear her sister's voice but she didn't go to her; instead Vita went straight to the front door, hoping to get outside before Jameson saw her leaving. Luckily he was an old man and moved slowly.

There was still some light in the night sky, and the birch trees along the drive were like silvery columns creaking in the wind. Walking down to the road she felt numb and light, almost weightless. For so many years she'd set her sights on a certain future – leaving Lark's Eye, going to college, practicing medicine – and without it she didn't know who she was. She felt like nothing.

As she approached the stone footbridge she heard a tavern door open, and the faint leak of voices before it closed again. Robinson Jameson lived closer to the town square than she'd expected. For a while she listened to the babble of the stream below, the high and low notes of water pursuing its course over and around every obstacle as it rushed toward the sea. The smell of Jameson's cigar was still in her nose and she leaned over the footbridge. The edge was mossy and damp; the current swirled darkly beneath her. It was not a terribly long way down.

Quick footsteps sounded behind her and before she could turn a heavy hand landed on her arm.

'Careful there!'

A man was pulling her back from the edge. The smell of cigar was stronger – it hadn't been Jameson's cigar she imagined she smelled, but this man's. She twisted around to look at his face.

'Mr. Culhane,' she said, surprised.

Jacob had stayed on in Lark's Eye a week longer than he expected, and a week longer after that. To his surprise and (to be honest) mortification, the bank had after all turned him down for a loan: 'We think oil is a losing proposition, in the long run,' Mr. Gideon told him, 'and so we don't believe the barrels need modifying.' Added to that, they offered only a few pennies per acre for his father's farm. 'We're being conservative about land just at present.'

Suddenly he was no longer the war hero, no longer the local boy who did well and who should be rewarded. At least, that's how it felt. But instead of indulging his disappointment, he decided to forget about loans and begin tapping investors. Since he was here, he would start with Robinson Jameson, who owned a string of factories in the southern part of the state and two mills in New Hampshire. He put Jacob off twice, finally meeting with him only this afternoon. But he listened to Jacob's story for less than five minutes before shaking his head. He had a dinner to see to, he told Jacob, and in any case he'd already settled all his investments for the year.

Why in hell hadn't the man said so to begin with? Jacob had made it clear from the onset that he wanted to set forth a business proposition.

After their meeting Jacob went straight to the tavern down the road from Jameson's house where he consoled himself with food: stewed pork and glazed carrots and a rich plum tart for dessert. He was able to eat a little bit more at one sitting now, although this meal was the heaviest so far. The tavern keeper brewed a unique cider made with honey and skimmed milk, not as bad as it sounded, and more potent than he let on. Before going back to Mrs. Linden's, Jacob decided to walk up to the footbridge to clear his head.

That's when he saw a woman leaning over the edge.

His body drained of sensation. He was back in Andersonville, looking up to see Caleb lean out too far from the muddy stockade wall while doing the repairs he was ordered to, and about to get shot by a guard in the back of the head.

He rushed over and grabbed her by the arm. When she turned he saw it was Vita Tenney. Her chalky face seemed to float above her dark mourning dress, like a ghost.

'Mr. Culhane,' she said, surprise in her voice. She pulled away from his grip. 'What are you doing?'

'I thought – I'm sorry. Excuse me.' His right hand was shaking violently. He threw his cigar to the ground and stepped on it, hoping his movement would hide the tremors.

'Did you imagine I was going to do myself harm?'

'No, no. I thought . . .'

He trailed off, not wanting to explain himself, but she kept looking at him, waiting for him to finish.

'Sometimes – because of the war, I suppose – I overreact.'

'You overreact?'

He didn't want to go on, he knew it wouldn't make any sense. In that moment he really did see Caleb. He was back in the prison camp, trying to shout out a warning before it was too late.

'I'm sorry,' he said again.

She took a long breath. 'Well. You startled me.'

For a few seconds they looked at each other, not knowing what to say next.

'You're a long way from home,' he said finally. His heartbeat was beginning to return to normal.

'Yes, we were just visiting Mr. Robinson Jameson. My father and sister are still there. I'll go back in a moment.'

'That's a coincidence. I was there myself earlier today, hoping he'd invest in my patent idea.'

'The barrels?'

'That's right. But he turned me down.'

Vita looked out to the water. They were standing side by side in the middle of the bridge. 'I was there to hear a marriage proposal, but *I* turned *him* down.'

'You don't mean to say that your father is trying him now?' As soon as Jacob said this he regretted it. Vita snapped her head toward him.

'What do you mean, *trying* him?'

'Well . . .'

'My father talked to you about my dowry?'

He nodded, not wanting to meet her eye.

'I'm curious, Mr. Culhane. How much is my father offering for me?'

Jacob hesitated.

'It's all right, tell me.'

'Six thousand dollars.'

'Six *thousand*?'

'And a gold pocket watch that belonged to your grandfather.'

The sun had gone down but it was still light out, a long summer evening. The humid air felt like a pond you could swim in. Vita knew that watch – her father had never liked it. The money, however, astonished her. Six thousand dollars! More than she thought. Much more.

She turned to leave. 'You needn't accompany me,' she said as Jacob began to walk off the bridge with her. 'I'll be fine.'

'It's my pleasure,' he said, though he didn't sound particularly pleased.

The night air smelled gummy with pinesap and they kept to the middle of the road where it was driest. Neither one spoke. Vita felt as though she were in someone else's skin; or as if, after seeing her father's mad face, she had shrouded herself with a bed sheet. If only she could.

Six thousand dollars. She could do a lot with six thousand dollars.

When they came to Jameson's drive she looked up at the tiny lights in the windows above them and thought about Jameson's leering, scarecrow figure. *It's getting harder for me to button my trousers.* She had twenty-four dollars saved in a tea tin, enough to get her to Philadelphia and to live for a couple of months, but nowhere near enough to see her all the way through college.

Would Aunt Norbert still give her tuition money if it was expressly against her father's wishes?

Probably not.

She glanced at Jacob. 'I take it the bank declined to give you a loan? That's why you were meeting with Mr. Jameson?'

He nodded. 'That's right.'

The wind rustled the tree branches and she glanced up the driveway again. At any moment someone might come down, Jameson or her father, to look for her.

She took a long breath. 'I have a proposal for you,' she said. 'Perhaps we could split the dowry. Marry each other, and split the dowry. You would have money for your workshop, and I could go to college.'

For a moment, silence. Then he said, 'That's quite an idea.'

She could tell nothing from his voice.

'I want to go to medical college. But even before I apply I have to train with a doctor. A preceptor, he's called. That will cost money, and I'll also need money for living expenses and of course later for tuition.' One by one she put each card on the table. 'My father won't help me.'

'I expect not,' Jacob said. 'I mean to say, a lady doctor. Not anything I've ever heard of, frankly.'

'A female doctor. A *lady doctor* means something else,' she corrected him, as though everyone should know that. 'And yes, there are some. And there's no reason why I shouldn't be one of them. I have an excellent memory and excellent study skills. I'm certain I can carry it off.'

She wished she could see his expression.

'However, I should be clear,' she went on. 'Given my plans, I can't be a wife to you. A real wife, with babies and so forth, taking care of your home, planning the meals. I can only offer you the money you'd get from my father if you marry me. Half the money.'

'You don't think you can do both? Be a wife and be a doctor?'

'And see to the house and the cooking and nurse babies? While I'm also seeing patients? No.'

He took off his hat and wiped the top of his forehead with the crook of his arm. The movement brought with it his scent – hair tonic and tobacco and something else, something of his own. She remembered his hand on her arm when they stood on the bridge, the sudden nearness of him, startling and thrilling.

'Two households might be expensive, but remember, you'll have money to pursue your interests while I pursue mine.' She was a little amazed at herself; the plan sounded well thought-out even though it had been born not five minutes ago. 'Three thousand each. That's what I'm proposing. A marriage in name only.'

She waited. He looked down at the road, studying it.

'I don't want to insult you,' he began.

Her heart plunged but she said, 'Mr. Culhane, I am so flattened by recent events that I haven't the energy to be insulted.'

'I could spend the whole six thousand dollars for my enterprise,' he told her, 'and more.'

'How much do you need?'

'I was planning to ask five thousand from Mr. Jameson.'

She was silent a moment. 'Do you think you could find a sponsor for me? To act as my preceptor? He must be a respectable doctor. In Boston, is that right? That's where you intend to go next?'

'I think I could.'

'There's a medical college in Boston that accepts women. I could live there if you could find a preceptor for me.'

'Two households will be expensive. What do you say to one household with separate rooms – three or four hundred dollars should cover that.'

She thought it over. 'All right, I can agree to one house. Why don't we put five hundred dollars aside for the household, you can have thirty-five hundred, and I'll take two thousand. Anything left over from the living expenses can be yours at the end.'

Jacob laughed, which surprised her. She heard Robinson Jameson's front door slam shut and then a man's voice near the house.

'All right,' Jacob said.

'Yes? You agree?'

He held out his hand. 'You'd make a good man,' he told her. She could hear rather than see his smile, and his hand felt pleasantly warm, a giant's heavy paw clasping her own much smaller one.

A frisson of pleasure shot up her spine.

'I know that,' she said.

PART 2

CHAPTER EIGHT

'It is observed by the Ancients that the human
voice is either shrill and puerile,
or grave and masculine.'
(Dr. Boerhaave's Academical Lectures, 1757)

September 1865, Lark's Eye, Massachusetts

The mahogany table in the Tenneys' back parlor was crowded with wedding gifts: painted picture frames, narrow-neck vases, porcelain candy dishes, a perfume burner, two pastel drawings of lilies in gilded frames, a silver cruet set, fish knives displayed in a walnut case, and an ewer in the shape of a Roman helmet.

Amelia's thank-you notes had all been written and posted, but so far Vita had hastily scrawled only one, to her grandmother in New Haven:

Dear Grandmother Toombs,

I am looking for a copy of Osteographia (sometimes called The Anatomy of the Bones) by Dr. William Cheselden, and

I wonder if there's a copy left among Grandfather's things? I would be most happy if you would send that to me, should you have it. I can pay for postage.

Most Lovingly,
Your Granddaughter,
Vita
P.S. Thank you for the nutmeg grinder. It will be very useful when I need to grind nutmeg.

Grandmother Toombs did not think it worth her while to take the journey for only a wedding, but she urged her granddaughters by letter 'always to remember your duty' and enclosed a ten-dollar bill and a prayer card for each of them.

Wedding preparations were more tedious than Vita could have imagined, notwithstanding the quiet day they were planning due to Freddy's death and the recent war: a short ceremony in church followed by breakfast at the hotel in town. Mitty, with Sweetie on her shoulder, supervised the unwrapping of gifts and the packing of trunks with an energy Vita forgot she'd ever had.

She knew nothing of Vita's plans. Neither did Amelia. 'Our nefarious agreement,' Jacob called it, when they were alone. It gave Vita a little thrill when he said that.

The wedding was now only five days away. Standing on a footstool in the parlor while Polly Gauntt, the dressmaker, tucked and pinned white dress material around her, Vita could hear Amelia bumping a trunk along the upstairs hall. Sunshine streamed into the room, making the porcelain gifts on the table gleam like liquid. Vita angled her book away from the glare.

The arytenoid cartilages are two in number and are provided with muscles, by which the rima of the glottis may be contracted or reduced.

Polly Gauntt grunted. 'Your sister never jiggles.'

She had to prepare as much as possible before she went to Boston in order to impress her potential preceptor, whoever he turned out to be. She was hugely disadvantaged, being a woman; she must work doubly, trebly hard. Her right arm, holding up the leather-bound book, began to ache.

'Turn,' Polly said.

In an hour Jacob would arrive to take her to Reverend MacNair's house, where they would be witnesses for Gemma and Ruffy's marriage. Upstairs Vita's second-best dress was waiting on her bed; Gemma had ironed it and laid it out herself before she left. She would have an even quieter wedding than Vita's: a few words in the reverend's parlor followed by a private supper prepared by Ruffy's mother. Gemma planned to wear her nicest burgundy tartan – which, as she herself said, was practically new, as she made it last winter – and as a wedding gift Mitty had given her a strip of Irish lace she'd had since she was a girl. At Vita's suggestion, Reverend MacNair had agreed not to use the word 'obey' in Gemma and Ruffy's ceremony. When Jacob heard about that, he laughed.

'Why get yourself in a bother about a word you hear once in your life and never again?' he asked.

'You might hear it again,' Vita told him. 'My father says it.'

'Oh, well, your father's the old guard. Ruffy and me now, we're modern men. We don't believe all that nonsense.'

He and Ruffy, it turned out, had fought under the same commander, though a year apart. By the time Ruffy enlisted Jacob was already in Andersonville. However, to Vita's surprise, they usually spoke about horses, never the war.

She looked up at his face to make sure he was teasing.

'If you don't believe it,' she asked, teasing in return, 'then why object to changing the word?'

They were walking in her mother's greenhouse, where they could be alone. Vita felt the same wash of light-heartedness that she had – she now realized – relied on from Freddy. No one else in her family joked any more.

Jacob picked up a loose geranium flower that had fallen to the tiled floor and pulled off its leaf. He crushed the leaf and held it to his nose.

'Esteem, obey; doesn't it come to the same thing?' He twirled the magenta-colored bud on its stem before holding it out to her.

'I don't think it does,' she said, smiling.

'It's only a word.'

She took the flower. 'Then you won't mind changing it in our ceremony, too.'

He laughed. 'Well played,' he said, and leaned in to kiss her.

❁

They hadn't kissed when they got engaged that night near the footbridge; that had been a business transaction. And notwithstanding his white teeth and dark hair, the mole near his eyelid that she found so attractive, and the way his trousers hung loosely at his hips, Vita didn't know at first if she wanted to kiss him. Was kissing part of their agreement?

She was, she had to admit to herself, curious. Maybe even, as the first week went by and he did nothing more than touch her hand, a bit disappointed. At last, a full nine days after their night on the footbridge, in the blue darkness of a summer evening, Jacob said, 'You're my pledged bride, and yet I haven't kissed you. Do you think that's strange?'

Her chest immediately tightened. They were standing on the gravel drive in front of her house; they'd just eaten supper and Vita was walking him out. Jacob was half turned toward the iron post where his horse was tethered. He looked at her sideways.

'Not strange. Not exactly,' she said carefully.

'Perhaps that's not included in our nefarious agreement?'

She tried to match his levity. 'I'm not sure that it is.' Still, her chest continued to feel tight and, almost without meaning to, she took a step closer.

He stepped closer too, took her by the arm, and kissed her. His aim was slightly off target; he kissed her a second time, harder. It started more awkwardly than she had imagined kisses to start, and there was a kind of shyness to Jacob's first movement that she felt he was trying to cover up by that second, firmer kiss. As always, she could feel her brain thinking, observing, analyzing, pulling the action apart to study its pieces, while her body felt nothing like a scientist whatsoever: her middle seemed to soften and tingle at the same time.

'All right then,' he said, stepping back. He loosened the reins from the tethering post. 'Now *that's* done.'

For a moment she could only stare at him, her breath coming out in short, irregular blows. *There. That's done. Just a necessary formality.* Had he wanted to kiss her, or not? Fireflies – *photinus ignitis* – sparked in the twilight as he swung himself up onto his horse. She half turned away, willing her body to toughen up. Despite her declarations – a marriage in name only – she'd wanted to kiss him.

'However, I hope we can take up this same conversation tomorrow,' he said smiling down at her.

So. He'd wanted it, too.

After that there followed weeks of furtive kisses, and sometimes more: his hands on her hips, her face; her fingers finding his trouser pockets and pulling him toward her so they could kiss again. Something hungry in her had started, which she didn't understand. It was exciting and alarming. She wanted to make notes of these new sensations but she was afraid someone else might read them.

'The arytenoid cartilages are two in number,' she recited as Polly Gauntt pulled at the stiff white wedding dress fabric. Her arm, holding up the book, was getting tired. 'The rima of the glottis may be contracted or reduced.'

'What's that, Greek?' Polly asked, eyeing Vita's dress sleeve with suspicion. She slid a pin out from between her lips just as Amelia poked her head into the room.

'Jacob's coming up the drive.'

Vita's pulse immediately quickened. She wished, and not for the first time, that she could be cool and distant, not pulled into his – or anyone's – sphere. Polly Gauntt helped her out of her wedding dress, and as she left the room Vita stashed her book on the gifts table. She ran up the steps two at a time, wiping her sweaty hands on her thin cotton chemise. She felt as though something important was happening, but she wasn't sure if it had to do with doctoring – she was acting on her dreams at last – or Jacob. No doubt about it, their alliance was confusing and exciting. Was it practical, or sensual? Could it be both?

That was the question she couldn't answer.

❁

Amelia offered her opinion, though Vita never directly posed the question to her – 'Thank goodness you've come to your senses and are acting like a proper woman at last.'

In spite of the fact she would now share her wedding day with her sister, Amelia was pleased Vita was marrying

Jacob. Marrying anyone, really. A betrothal, to Amelia, was neither practical nor sensual, it was simply what you did. Vita didn't bother to argue with her. What was the point?

'Let me help you with your buttons,' Amelia said, following Vita into her bedroom.

'What about Jacob?'

'Polly will let him in. What about a black ribbon under your collar? Or a brooch?'

She had given Gemma six beautifully embroidered handkerchiefs as a wedding present. Vita had given Gemma a book.

After pinning her own brooch to Vita's dress, Amelia stepped back to view the effect. Ever since Vita announced her engagement, Amelia had slowly but surely assumed the role of older sister – Vita was in her realm, now.

'You need about a hundred more hairpins,' she said.

On the morning of Gemma and Ruffy's wedding, Jacob found himself thinking about a day he'd gone to the old quarry outside of Lark's Eye – not swimming, exactly, but walking in the stony-cold water, although he knew how to swim. This was when his mother was still alive, and also his brother Benjy. Benjy was with him that day. Benjy was a funny child, surprising and imaginative, always wishing for impossible, spectacular things. 'What would you like for your birthday, Benjy?' 'The moon on a string!' he'd say.

The day was fantastically hot, which was why they'd gone to the quarry. How old had he been, eleven? Twelve? And Benjy must have been around seven or eight. For more than an hour they played in the water around the quarry edges, but after a while Benjy climbed out to sit partly in the sun and partly in the shade, both drying off and staying cool. Jacob, not ready yet to leave the water, walked into the deeper parts. In town they said that a horse had fallen in here years ago, and drowned. Not understanding about decomposition, Jacob both feared and thrilled to the idea that he might step on the body.

Another step. Then another. Benjy was watching, or at least Jacob imagined he was, when the stone floor suddenly gave out and Jacob plunged into the wet darkness, which was more surprising than stepping on a horse, although (he thought later) much more likely. The murky water closed over his head and his arms floated up like wings. He didn't feel panicky, though; after the initial shock he opened his eyes to look around at the mud-green expanse. A sparkle of sunshine glittered to his right, where he could see, surprisingly, tiny snippets of fish. He had left one world and entered another. This world was cold and gripped him around his chest; it was only dimly visible, undulating, craggy, with a slightly metallic taste, but it wasn't hostile. He could leave it at any time.

Benjy was standing at the edge of the quarry looking for him when Jacob paddled up to the surface. But Benjy didn't appear worried. More like curious.

'What did you see? What was down there?' he asked.

Jacob's first impulse was to say something fanciful: a castle, a fairy garden. But Benjy was not a good swimmer, and Jacob didn't want him swimming out to see for himself.

'Nothing,' he said. 'Just water.'

Benjy's face crumpled. 'Are you sure nothing else?'

'Nope. Just muddy, cold water. Is that my shirt you're wearing?'

Benjy's expression – always so mobile – instantly transformed to a grin. He stepped back, clearly hoping Jacob would chase him. 'What shirt?' he asked.

Now, once again, Jacob felt as though he had taken leave of one world and dropped into another. The old world was cannon fire and imprisonment; it was tics and nightmares and tremors. But for the past five weeks he'd had nothing – not one nightmare, no tics, not even a slight shake in his trigger finger.

Every morning he woke up with a feeling of lightness. He'd come out on the opposite side, at last. And what was war's opposite after all, he thought, if not family suppers and kissing in greenhouses? He'd left a brutal, complicated world behind him for something much softer.

He didn't think of it as falling in love, though he didn't have much experience there. As a young man in Cincinnati, he had twice found himself infatuated with beautiful, unreachable young women – one was a state senator's daughter – whom he'd met at the charitable teas that were popular then. He wore his new, tight clothes and tried to match the tone of other young men, but he still felt like a farmer's son.

Araminta; that had been the name of the senator's daughter. He couldn't remember the name of the other one. Both now seemed as insubstantial as paper dolls compared to Vita.

Vita was energy made flesh with her quick mind and almost constant motion. She was always getting the side of her dress caught on a splinter of wood in a doorframe, or knocking into a side table. She wore the smallest hoop imaginable – maybe because of this need to keep moving – and once or twice he had sworn she wasn't wearing a corset under her dress.

He found himself thinking about that. What was under her dress.

At first he hesitated even to take her hand, not sure of the parameters of their agreement. But as the days went by he began to wonder if her hair was as soft as it looked. He noticed how he contrived to touch her, and how he liked to breathe in her scent – vanilla soap and lead pencil and, faintly, something of the leather-bound books she always carried. He liked the tones of her husky voice when she spoke to him, and the way she looked so intently at him when he spoke to her. And when they finally kissed for the first time, Jacob felt a sensation float like a rose petal from the base of his spine to the back of his head. He had an urge to lean in, to pull Vita closer, but instead he stepped back and tried to cover up his desire with a joke.

'Now *that's* done,' he'd said. Could she hear his forced jocularity? He mounted his horse quickly, not sure if he'd botched it or not. He wanted badly to kiss her again.

And they did kiss again. She seemed almost as eager as he was. And for all her intensity, he felt easier in her presence. She liked his jokes and teases; maybe that was part of it. His hands were steady as he encircled her tiny wrists and drew her closer. Before they kissed Vita always looked up at him with an expression somehow secret and personal, something meant only for him.

Castles and fairy gardens.

A world underwater.

'Did you decide to hire a buggy?' Holland asked him at breakfast. 'Or will you borrow the doctor's?'

Jacob had discussed with him how he would need a buggy to take Vita and himself to Gemma and Ruffy's wedding.

Holland, who was planning on buying his own carriage after his wedding, had been reading up on the latest models.

'I was able to get over to Tillings's yesterday after all, and his price seems fair.'

'A rather cumbersome contraption, as I recall,' Holland said.

'I'd rather not bother the doctor.'

He'd hired a horse from Mr. Tillings after he and Vita announced their engagement and he decided to stay on in Lark's Eye. The horse, Molly O'Grady, was a sweet-tempered bay although as slow as the summer sun, as his mother used to say. He rode her down to Tillings's soon after the church bells rang noon and, as arranged, he handed over a newly minted half-dollar for the use of their two-seated buggy for the day. The boy who worked for Mr. Tillings helped Jacob adjust the harness and buckle the crupper beneath the mare's tail. His name was Frank Pride, and his quick half-smile reminded Jacob a little of his brother Benjy. He had light brown skin and green eyes.

'Are you related to the Frank Pride who worked for Mr. Norbert some years back?' Jacob put a hand on Molly O'Grady's flank to keep her calm while Frank finished tightening the crupper.

'Yessir, that was my dad. Did you know him?'

'I used to run errands for him sometimes when I was a boy. I was sorry to hear he'd passed on.'

The boy bowed his head, acknowledging this, while still intent on his task. Frank Pride, Sr., had been the coach driver for Ezra Norbert – Vita's wealthy uncle. If Jacob was in town, Mr. Pride would pay him a penny to go into a shop and fetch whatever Mr. Norbert wanted fetching that day. He always asked after Jacob's mother and father. 'You make sure to help your mother today, son,' he would say.

Had Mr. Pride once been a slave? Jacob, as a boy, never wondered, but he wondered now as he and Frank rolled the buggy up behind the horse and pushed the shafts in place. During the war, there'd been two runaway slaves who lived with his company when they were stationed near Frankfort, Kentucky. Mag and Nathan, their names were; they'd come from a horse farm in the southern part of the state. They were thin and jittery, and stayed with the company for over a month before crossing the river to Ohio. Their dream, Nathan told Jacob, was to find their way to Canada. To leave Kentucky and this whole cursed country far behind them. Mag had a long, suspiciously straight scar from her shoulder to her wrist, as though someone had started to skin her. Nathan's back was crossed with whip marks.

'Is your mother from Lark's Eye, too?' Jacob asked Frank.

'No, she's Irish, she came from Dublin,' the boy said. 'She works in Mrs. Norbert's kitchen.'

'Well, try to help her out at home whenever you can,' Jacob said. He grinned. 'That's what your father always said to me.'

They adjusted the slanted buggy top and locked it in place. Jacob climbed up to the seat and touched his hat to Frank, who stepped back to look over the outfit with a professional eye. He nodded and smiled – *it looks fine* – and then he lifted his hand in farewell.

It was a hot day for September, the last breath of summer. Jacob drove slowly along the road and over the old stone bridge to the Tenneys' drive, halting the mare under the shade of two cuddling birch trees at the side of the house. He could smell the jasmine planted nearby and he stopped to take a long breath, his hands in his pockets. The sun felt warm on his back.

Before he could knock on the door the seamstress, wearing a hat that resembled a netted pincushion, came out. She was carrying her cumbersome sewing bag in two arms like a baby, and she told Jacob that Miss Vita would be down to the parlor directly. He thanked her as she nudged past him.

'And a happy day to you, sir,' she said.

Inside, the house was still and quiet and cool. He wondered if Dr. Tenney was locked in his office as usual. There was no sign of Mrs. Tenney or either of her daughters.

For a while he amused himself in the parlor by looking at the gifts table. He spotted a small leather book half hidden between two painted vases and picked it up; the author was a fellow named Boerhaave. Never heard of him. He flipped through the pages, impressed by the serious language.

'It is observed by the Ancients,' he read aloud to Vita when she came in, *'that the human voice is either shrill and puerile, or grave and masculine.'*

He grinned, holding his place in the book with his thumb. 'Has anyone ever told you that your voice is grave and masculine?'

'Fairly everyone.' She took the book from him and put it back behind the vases.

'Grave and masculine, despite your little size,' he continued as they went outside. "Though to be honest, I'm not sure I would prefer shrill. A shrill voice is harder to ignore.'

'You would like to ignore me?'

He put his hand on her elbow to help her up into the buggy. 'I could never ignore you,' he said.

'Because of my voice?'

'Mmm . . . and other things.'

She raised her eyebrows. 'What other things?'

'Oh no, I don't want your head to swell. Anymore than it is,' he amended. He settled himself on the seat beside her and took up the reins.

'My head isn't swollen! I know where I excel, that's all.'

'I don't suppose there is anything you think you're not good at?'

'Certainly there is. I'm no good at hat trimming, for one.'

He turned and looked at her small, dark hat, exaggerating his study. 'Yes, I can see that,' he said.

She laughed. It felt good to be outside, hot though it was, with a breeze blowing in the salty scent of the ocean.

'And what about me?' Jacob asked as they turned toward the old stone bridge. 'Does my voice please you? Or anything else?'

She pretended to think. 'Well, let's see.' One of the wheels bumped over a rock in the road and she put a hand on the side of the buggy to steady herself. 'You wear your trousers well.'

To her surprise, his cheeks reddened. 'Do I?'

'Oh yes. They cover your abdominal region adequately but not excessively, protecting your vital organs, and they are not too tight, which would infringe upon your digestion.'

By the time she got to vital organs Jacob's blush had faded and he began to smile good-humoredly.

'Well that is good news. I would hate to infringe upon my digestion.'

'It's one of your better qualities.'

'Perhaps my best.' He looked sideways at her. 'Why don't you take off your gloves, Vee. I want to feel your tiny hand in my rough and uncouth paw.'

'Can a paw be uncouth?' But she took off her glove. His hand was warm and comfortable. 'Amelia told me that Holland is only allowed to hold her hand if she has gloves on. And he can kiss her once a day, in the evening, on the cheek.'

'Poor fellow. It must be hard knowing that I got the better choice of Tenney daughters.'

Vita felt a prick of pleasurable surprise. No one ever preferred her over her sister. Had she secretly wanted this, too?

'And now,' Jacob said as the reverend's house came in sight over the hill, 'we should begin to practice our parts.'

'And what parts are those?'

'Two young people in love.'

She laughed again. Her heart rose in her chest.

'They'll never believe that,' she said.

Reverend MacNair was a kind, abstracted man who paid little attention to bodily comfort; his jackets and trousers were made from the roughest homespun, and his lean brick house, as small as a hat shop, was furnished with unpainted furniture and braided rag rugs. The rugs, made by Mrs. MacNair, were maroon and brown and matched the leather covers of the books in the bookcases. Despite her black lace mourning collar and cuffs, Vita felt overly vibrant in her royal blue dress; whereas Gemma, wearing a modest burgundy tartan, appeared perfectly in keeping with the parlor's decor.

Her face was glowing.

'Jenny dressed my hair,' she told Vita in a low voice. 'What do you think?'

Only this morning she'd been wearing her usual neat gray dress while she cleaned Dar's boot soles with a wire brush. Somehow she looked younger now: a little girl trying on her mother's clothes and practicing hairstyles that were much too grownup for her.

To Vita's surprise, she felt tears in her eyes. 'You look beautiful.'

Ruffy looked uncomfortable in his Sunday clothes and stiff new shoes. In contrast to Gemma, his face, weathered by the outside life of a soldier, seemed older than his seventeen years, although his eyes were the eyes of a boy in church, not quite sure how to look sufficiently solemn. The left cuff of his suit sleeve had been folded up and neatly sewn in compensation for his missing hand.

'Thank you for standing up for us,' Ruffy said formally to Jacob, who laughed and clapped him on his shoulder, saying, 'It's nothing, you old soldier.'

After a few minutes Mrs. MacNair showed them their places in the front of the room. It was a short ceremony. Gemma and Ruffy stood with their elbows touching as the reverend read from his Bible, spoke a few words about duty and love, and then asked them to repeat their vows. When he used the word 'esteem' instead of 'obey,' Jacob caught Vita's eye and smiled.

Afterward Mrs. MacNair served small glasses of elderberry wine that matched Gemma's dress and the rugs.

'May joy and peace surround you,' she toasted the couple.

Gemma blushed her own, peculiar blush that affected only the tip of her nose and her cheekbones. She was happy. A mundane observance, perhaps, but the truth of it felt like a thumb pressing on Vita's heart. Gemma was following the natural order of love, whereas Vita had constructed something artificial and planned.

She looked at Jacob as she raised her glass. Their secret was a bond between them, but it also made her feel lonely.

Afterwards they all went outside to see Gemma and Ruffy off. Ruffy had borrowed a little pony cart from the MacNairs, and someone – Mrs. MacNair, probably – had woven blue and white ribbons into the pony's mane. Ruffy, holding the reins with his good hand, gave a festive shake to start her going.

Yellow dust circled up behind the wheels. Gemma clamped a hand down on her hat and twisted around. 'Good-bye! Good-bye!'

They would eat a celebratory dinner and afterwards go to their new rooms above the Barstows' stables. Gemma would still work for the Tenneys but she'd been given leave to arrive later than usual tomorrow: half-past ten.

The MacNairs shook hands with Vita and Jacob and went back inside their house. Gemma is married, Vita thought. It felt strange, and not quite real. When she glanced up at Jacob she saw, to her surprise, that his face was solemn, too.

'What is it?' she asked.

From here they could look out across the road to the wide bare fields and marshes that used to be stands of hardwood trees. A few roofs were visible in the town beyond, and ribbons of spindly fir trees, newly planted, encircled some of the farmyards. The ocean was below all that, a hidden power, like memory.

'It's nothing,' Jacob said. 'Just – the toast Mrs. MacNair gave, that was something my friend Caleb used to say.'

'The Caleb who drew your barrel plans?' She tried to think back to the toast.

'*May joy and peace surround us before long.* He said it at Christmas, back at Andersonville. It was only the five of us – the Five Knights, we called ourselves. We shared a tent, a very sad kind of shelter –' he tried to smile, 'that Caleb and the others built a couple of weeks before I got there, but it was better than a lot of men had. We'd managed to get a little flour from somewhere and cooked up some pancakes. That was our Christmas treat.' They used tree sap as syrup – which also helped irritable stomachs – mixed with a bit of sugar that

Caleb snuck out in a twist of paper from the cookhouse, where he worked.

'Near the cookhouse was the storehouse, and just before Christmas the Sanitary Commission had sent two or three dozen hams for Union prisoners, but of course the rebels saved them all for themselves instead. Caleb got hold of a little chunk of one of them, about the size of your hand maybe, and we had that for our Christmas dinner, too. We didn't have any knives for cutting so we just took turns taking bites.'

Vita hesitated. 'Caleb was a good friend to you,' she said.

Jacob could feel the sun on the back of his neck, even hotter now than it was at noon when he rode out to Tillings's stables. Already it was hard to remember how hungry they'd been all the time, and how sick. Flux. Dysentery. Fevers. They used to dream about tunneling from the cookhouse to the storehouse – Caleb had even managed to pull up a kitchen floorboard – but it never came to anything.

'He saved my life,' Jacob said.

On his very first morning at Andersonville, waking up on the cold ground among the worms and flies and excrement, he found Caleb's piercing blue eyes watching him. He had a fuzz of blond hair and high cheekbones, and Jacob could still hear his voice, raspy and low, as if coming through a fine sieve: *Would you like a better sleeping spot?* Caleb was cheerful and smart, and he never gave up hope that they would be released. *There will be an exchange of prisoners before long*, he used to say; *the trick is to stay alive until that time comes.*

But it was more than a trick. It was the conjurer's last, most spectacular miracle. By the time they were liberated, more than half the prisoners were so weak they had to be pushed out in wheelbarrows, and of the Five Knights – Caleb, Ethan, Lewis, Tom, and Jacob – only Jacob survived. He might not have been tempted by Dr. Tenney's proposed dowry had it not been one way to keep Caleb's dream – the modified oil barrels – alive. And he wasn't taking advantage of Vita, he told himself, since she herself had proposed the deal.

He could feel her watching him now. Slowly he became aware of layers of sound: the wind, cicadas, a bird clacking, and something scratching in the hedge. He looked down the empty road where a loose swarm of insects hovered drunkenly above the dirt. Vita was standing very still beside him. After a moment she reached out to squeeze his arm, briefly, in sympathy.

He nodded. Then he took off his hat and, with his fingers spread flat, he brushed off one side and then the other. When he replaced his hat on his head he felt marginally better, as if by altering the hat's condition he had altered his own mood. He held his arm out for Vita to take, and they began to walk back to the buggy.

'Well, anyway, they've done it,' he said.

'Who? Gemma and Ruffy?'

He helped her up to the seat, which was covered by a thin washed-out blanket – once pink, he guessed, or maybe blue? – and as she sorted her skirts he climbed up beside her.

'You know what the Irish say.'

'What's that?' Vita asked.

'There's no cure for love except to marry.'

As he unhooked the reins he could feel her looking at him curiously – that intense, penetrating look of hers – as though trying to make out whether he was joking or not.

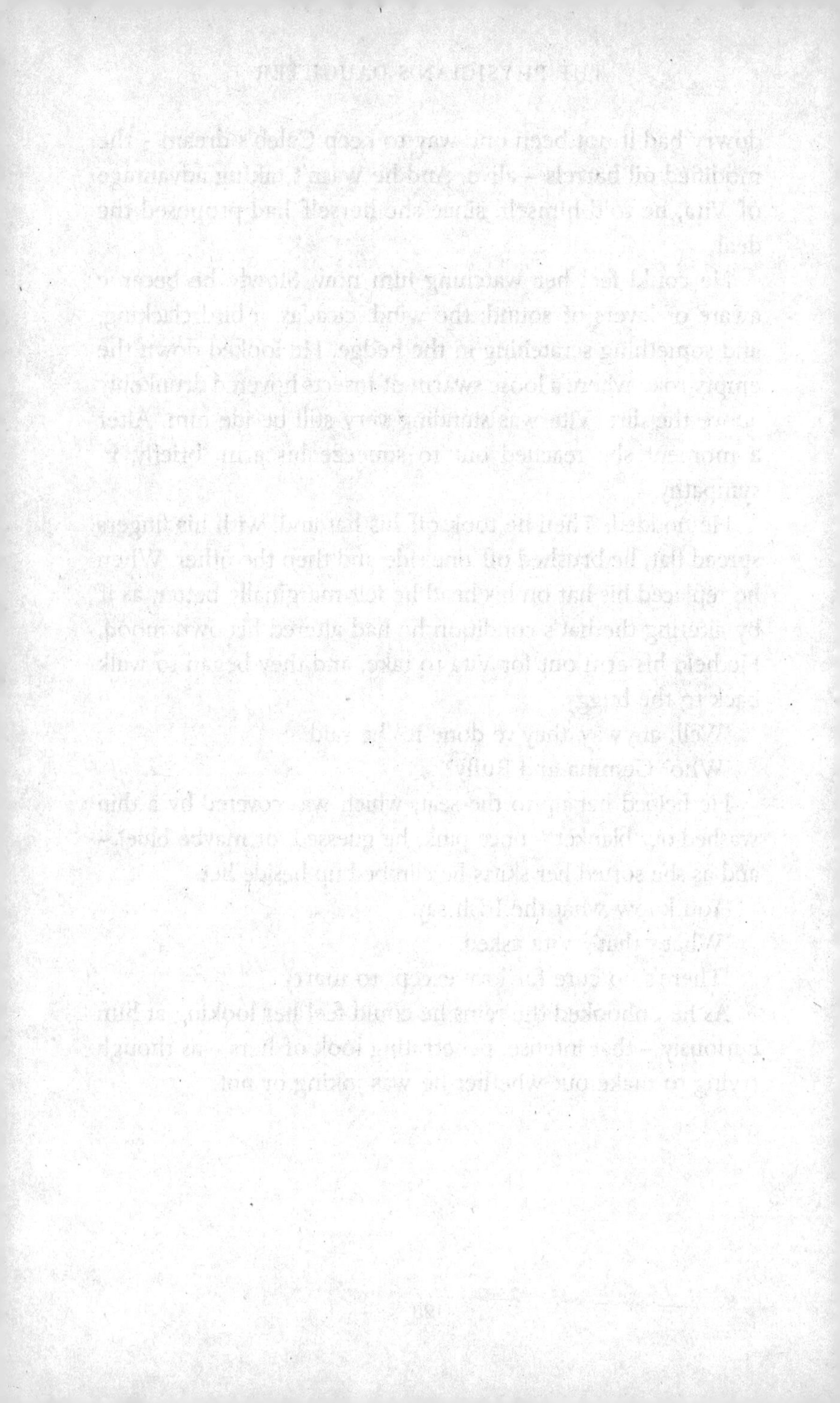

CHAPTER NINE

'A virgin's desire to marry is known by several signs:
her spirit is brisk and inflamed, her body is heated,
and she craves sharp and salty food.'
(*Aristotle's Masterpiece*, Anonymous, 1717)

The next morning Vita stood at the window with Sweetie on her shoulder a good half an hour before Gemma was due at the house. When Gemma did arrive, she didn't look any different. She was wearing the same gray dress she always wore, and in the kitchen she put on one of the three nearly identical aprons that she kept at the house; today it was the one with a little round hole near the hem where an oven spark had burned through it.

Mrs. Ruffy Barstow! It was hard to attach that name to Gemma with her bony shoulders and long thin hands.

'Well?' Vita prompted when at last Mrs. Oakum went upstairs to sweep the parlor carpets, and they were alone. Gemma began to make the codfish balls they were having for dinner. 'What was it like?'

Gemma's nose flushed pink as she chopped fish into flinty particles. 'I don't know. It was – well. At first I didn't know where to look, I was that embarrassed. And you know, I'd never seen his missing hand not covered up before. But it wasn't bad, just a knob, mostly smooth and regular.'

'Were you nervous?'

'Of course! And Ruffy, too, his breath was coming all quick.' Her knife stilled a moment. 'It was a bit squirmy, you might say, all arms and legs. I don't think I ever pictured it right. I was surprised at how close you have to be to make it happen.'

Vita pulled the bowl of butter from its shelf and looked for a spoon. She nodded to Gemma – *Go on.*

'Closer than close, every part of you. All your skin touching. I never read about that. You can't imagine how warm and lovely. Ruffy knew even less than me, I think. I had to sort of push his *hoochydink* around to where it needed to be.'

They both laughed. The tip of Gemma's nose was bright pink as she scraped the chopped fish into a basin of water with the blunt edge of her knife. Vita added a spoonful of butter the size of an acorn to the mixture, and Gemma cracked an egg into it.

'What did Ruffy do next?' she asked. 'Did he say anything?'

'He was breathing so fast he couldn't talk. At least not the first time.'

'The first time?'

'You don't have to do it only once in a night. He told me that. Also –'

'Also what?'

'Ruffy doesn't want a baby,' Gemma told her, not looking up. 'Or, not right away. He wants us to save up our money so he can start his own stable and breed horses. For a year, he said. And what do you think? He knows how not to make one.'

'How *not* to make one?'

Gemma added cold mashed potatoes to the basin and began stirring everything together.

'He got up a jar of water with vinegar and baking soda. Then he turned around while I washed myself.'

'Before, or after?'

'After. And then wouldn't you know it a minute later we were back under the covers and him telling me we don't have to do it just the once. It was dark out by then, or almost.'

'Tell me more about the vinegar and baking soda.'

Gemma wiped her hands on a striped dishtowel. 'It cleans you out down there, he says, and that keeps babies from starting.'

'Does it work?'

Gemma's nose flushed pink again. 'We'll see.'

Vita grabbed a handful of the sticky mixture and began rolling it between her hands to make a ball. Like most girls in Lark's Eye, Vita and Amelia were taught to help with household tasks – beating rugs outside in the spring, or making cider in autumn. They were New Englanders after all; they were not like the rich families their ancestors had fled from in Europe. They were made from, or had become, sturdier stock.

But Vita wasn't thinking about codfish even as she reached out to get another handful from the bowl. She was thinking about Gemma's cousin who had once gone to a woman – a *lady doctor*, as her father would say – hoping to get rid of a baby, although it didn't take. Ellie, who was unmarried, now worked in a herring factory on the coast while her mother raised the child. It was hard enough to stop a baby once it started, but Vita had never even heard of how you could keep a baby from starting in the first place. Except, of course, by not lying with a man.

She thought of Jacob's brown eyes, the dark mole near his eyelid, the way he listened to her and called her Vee. She could understand how Ellie might let that misfortune happen to her. And it *was* a misfortune for Ellie, a great misfortune, since everyone knew all about it and she had been lucky to get a job ladling glops of herring into tins in a factory line. Vita spotted Ellie a few weeks ago in town wearing cracked boots and a low hat pulled over her forehead. She walked like an old woman already, as if every step was an apology for the space she took up, although she wasn't much older than Vita.

'Do you think you could ask Ruffy what he put into the vinegar water?' Vita asked, wiping her hands. 'I mean precisely, the exact solution?'

There was a croak and a groan on the kitchen stairs. 'Stop your gossiping, girls,' Mrs. O. called out. 'I'm coming down.'

Vita reached out to squeeze Gemma's arm. 'You're a real married woman now.'

Gemma laughed happily. 'Hardly,' she said.

The morning after Gemma and Ruffy's wedding Jacob almost missed breakfast – unusual for him. He was filling out; his trousers fit him more snugly, and his cheeks had lost their slightly sunken look. He was able to eat more at one sitting, and his hunger had a different feel. Less desperate. Maybe it was simply knowing that there was food for him now any time he wanted.

But that morning he woke late and then lay on his back in bed feeling uneasy in a way he could not at first identify. Something brushed his face – a speck of plaster from the ceiling? He touched the soft pouch beneath his eye with his forefinger. *Pop.*

It wasn't dust. The tic beneath his eye had returned.

It felt like the heartbeat of a hummingbird, or a flea that had been caught under his skin and was pushing to get out. He waited, hoping it was temporary. *Pop, pop.*

His heart sank. He thought all that was over, just like his life as a soldier and prisoner was over. How long could the fingers of war keep their grip on a man?

It must have been Ruffy and Gemma's wedding that did it, he thought. It brought back memories, and not only about Caleb. Once at Andersonville there was a prisoner who'd found a white dress among the clothes sent every month by the Sanitary Commission, and he wore it all day long, pretending to be a bride. The man – a former sharpshooter from Pittsburgh – put a floppy collar on his head like a veil and he got a good laugh, and later a whipping when it became clear he hadn't worn the dress just for fun.

But who did anything in Andersonville just for fun? Even Jacob's own mates, the Five Knights, told jokes only because they knew they had to in order to stay sane, trying to maintain a distance from the horrors of prison life.

What's the difference between your greatcoat and a baby? One you wear and the other you was.

How are two lovers like two armies? They generally get along until they're engaged.

One guard had stuffed the sharpshooter's makeshift veil into the poor man's mouth while they whipped him. Jacob tried not to look, but the sight of a man being whipped in a dress was seared into his brain.

The smell of fried ham and coffee wafted up to his room, and he could hear Mrs. Linden's commanding voice followed by the sliding bang of the dining room door. He got out of bed and made his way gingerly to the washstand, keeping a careful balance as if he'd had too much to drink the night before.

He looked into the mirror. The tic wasn't noticeable unless he stared hard. He washed his face, and then slipped his hands into his two oval palm brushes, which had leather straps instead of handles. He dipped the bristles into the tepid basin water and, using both brushes simultaneously, smoothed back his black hair, one brush to a side. A gentle caress. This sometimes helped.

But the tic pulsed, and pulsed again. *Pop. Pop, pop.*

The brushes were a gift from his late cousin's widow, Samantha, a woman Jacob had once asked to marry him. This was right before war was officially declared and everyone was nervous, taking chances or acting out of character, feeling a sea change coming. Even at the time Jacob sensed he didn't mean it – it was an impulse born from fear rather than love.

Fortunately Samantha told him plainly that she planned never to marry again. She was independent for the first time in her life, and she liked it. Although she wasn't rich she could live within her means, perhaps taking in a boarder once in a while if she felt a pinch.

'But aren't you lonely?' Jacob had asked.

She smiled. 'Not at all.'

He put down the hairbrushes and peered at the side of his face again. Was the tic losing its punch? Maybe no one would notice it. But Vita was keenly observant.

I don't want her pity, he thought.

He could hear Holland Granger humming in the hallway, then changing the tune as he went down the stairs. They'd taken to eating breakfast together, after which Holland went to inspect the work being done on the new high school and Jacob wrote letters, finalizing plans for moving to Boston. He'd found a house and had engaged a woman to cook and clean. This afternoon he planned to stop by the bank to pick up the sale of purchase for his father's farm, and then he and Holland would ride over to the Tenneys' together for supper. In less than a week Jacob would be a married man living in Boston. But for a moment, he couldn't picture it. It felt like a story he'd heard, not a life he would live.

Maybe he didn't want to live it?

Was he anxious about marrying? Was that why the tic had returned? He thought again about how glad he'd been when Samantha refused him. How he realized that he didn't want to get married, not really. Maybe he still didn't.

Marriage is a cage, his father liked to say. Usually when his mother was standing nearby.

Jacob's cousin, Walter Friel – Samantha's late husband – had been a stockbroker, and he also inherited his father's furniture business. He was older than Jacob by a good ten years, but he was always kind to him when they met, treating him like a younger brother, listening seriously to his plans. The Friels lived in New Bedford, where Jacob's mother was from. This was her side of the family. Walter had been an only child and died childless. Before the war, he went to Cincinnati every six months or so for business and he used to take Jacob out for a meal when he was there. The last time they met they talked about the falling grain prices, the shuttered mills and factories, and all the men out of work. The newspapers were calling it the Panic of 1857. Jacob's own business held on, but barely; this was when he began to suspect that riverboats were a thing of the past; the future was in rail. Only a few weeks later Walter suffered a fatal stroke, and the next time Jacob saw Samantha – in New Bedford, at the funeral – she embodied what was now, after the war, a familiar sight: a young, beautiful, lively woman dressed head to toe in black.

As Jacob buttoned up a clean shirt he asked himself why he hadn't thought to invite Samantha to their wedding. She was his only living relative, even if it wasn't by blood. She still lived in New Bedford and could easily get to Lark's Eye by train. If he wrote quickly and posted it himself, the letter might get to her tomorrow.

He put a finger on his tic, trying to calm it as you would calm a worked-up dog. He didn't want to admit weakness, but at the same time he wanted support. Someone from his old world. Like Walter, Samantha always made him feel wanted, even important. Less alone.

He scribbled a note at his desk and slid it into an envelope as he went down the stairs, hoping he wasn't too late for coffee at least. As the tic pulsed under his eye he thought of the old quarry again; how the cold, stone floor disappeared so suddenly from under his feet. One minute he was above water, the next minute he wasn't. He could still remember the green murky world when he opened his eyes. The feeling of the slow float down.

Out here, he thought as he walked into the dining room, it's all shifting sand to begin with.

Vita wondered if there were any books or articles in her father's office about how to *not* start a baby. She'd been meaning to do another sweep of his shelves anyway, since Grandmother Toombs never did send her any medical books. This wasn't all that surprising since she was the least sentimental person Vita had ever met. She'd probably gotten rid of all of her late husband's tomes and journals within six months of his death. When, as a child, Vita went to New Haven for her grandfather's funeral, she had watched in amazement as her great-uncle Robert covered his face with a handkerchief, crying and blowing his nose. Vita had never seen a man cry before. Meanwhile her grandmother stood dry-eyed and as stiff as a lampshade in her panoply of black silk, composed enough to scold a maid when she dropped a wet umbrella on the floor.

And so, late in the afternoon, while her father was napping, Vita stole into his office. She had to be quick; Holland and

Jacob would be arriving soon for supper, and her father might wake up at any time.

She opened a window, trying to dispel the smell of sweat and spent coals. But as she turned back toward the bookshelves, her attention was caught by an open letter on her father's desk. The name 'Fred' leaped out from the page. *Fred . . . Fred*, and again, at the bottom, *Fred*.

She turned the letter over and looked at the signature. Dr. David Boutwell. She turned back and started to read from the beginning.

Cleveland, Ohio
August 4, 1865

Dear Dr. Tenney,

I have thought of my friend, your son Frederick, many times, and I was immensely sorry to hear of his death. The news of it came to me only this morning, and I wish to offer my most sincere condolences. Your son was a good soldier and a generous friend, and I am sorry that I could not be with him at his last, having left the unit six weeks earlier. Although he was liked by everyone, I believe we shared a special bond. We often went mushroom hunting together, and we were also both interested in identifying local birds and their calls. In fact we had a little competition going on in that area, which I believe he ultimately won.

I thought I might share with you a few of my treasured memories of Fred, times we spent together before I left the unit. In the hospital tent, where he kindly assisted me . . .

Dr. Boutwell described how Freddy bandaged wounded soldiers and held cups of water up to their lips. He assisted

Dr. Boutwell with minor surgeries and read to the men as they convalesced, or didn't. Once, miraculously, Freddy found some brandy 'from the Lord knows where' to put in a bowl of milk gruel for a man who was dying – who didn't last the night – and fed him by hand.

It may give you comfort to know what a fine young man you raised, Dr. Boutwell wrote. *He was unselfish and giving to the last.*

Vita wiped her cheek quickly, roughly, with the heel of her hand. She became aware of horses clopping up the gravel drive, and moments later voices floated through the open window. Holland and Jacob.

She turned the letter over and put it back on her father's desk. The Freddy in these stories was the adult Freddy, not her prankster brother. It was the man she didn't get the chance to know, although she could picture him frowning in concentration, giving an injured man the kind of thoughtful care he gave injured birds when he found them. At home she never saw him pay the same strict attention to any person that he'd paid to his birds and animals. People, to Freddy, were easy; they fended for themselves. They didn't need his care. Until, apparently, they did.

'Why not?' she heard Holland ask from outside the window.

'Most of the barrels were first used for other things, like beer or molasses, even turpentine. And they leak like the dickens. That's what I'm aiming to fix.'

Jacob was telling him about his patent idea, the modified barrels for petroleum.

'Is it a matter of binding the hoops more securely?' Holland asked. 'Or modifying the staves?'

By now they were standing so near the window that they would see her if she crossed the room. She straightened the letter on the desk with her fingertips. She wasn't ready yet to banter or be teased.

'More like the glue for the staves. I hear that Rockefeller only uses white oak for his barrels, and he cures the staves right where they're cut, to make them lighter. Cheaper freight costs that way, too. But they still need a better glue.'

'You know, it occurs to me that Vita likes that sort of thing.'

She froze. Jacob said something she couldn't make out.

'Oh, experiments,' Holland said. 'Recording results. Retesting, changing the variables. All that. She's quite disciplined. Too bad she's a woman.'

'Well, I can't agree with you there.' Vita could hear a smile in Jacob's voice.

'There was talk once of her going to college,' Holland said. 'Her mother mentioned it. Not a worthwhile expense, in my opinion. I mean, she's smart enough certainly, but what would be the use? For a woman, that is. Anyway, then the war came.'

'I don't see the use of it for anyone,' Jacob said. 'I can read and write and do sums. What more do you need? Anyway, Vita and I have an agreement.'

'Oh, yes? What's your agreement?'

Vita held her breath.

'She can read as many books as she wants, but only the books that I give her.'

Holland laughed. 'Well, then, you had better find a good number of books about oak barrels.'

He doesn't see the use for college? Is this what he really thinks? A tight knot of anger swirled in Vita's chest and lasted all through supper.

'You were the one who didn't want anyone to know,' Jacob said when she confronted him later.

'Because of my father! He's –' she didn't want to say *mad*. 'I don't know what he might do. Anything. Call off the wedding.'

'Lock you up in a tower?'

'Don't joke,' she said.

His cheek twitched, and he quickly turned his head. She was walking him out after supper. It was dusk, and the last of the fireflies were signaling each other. She thought of the first time Jacob kissed her, here on this very spot. She shoved the memory away.

'Is our agreement still on?' she demanded.

'Of course it's still on.'

'Has my father given you the check?'

'Why, are you worried?'

Knowing her father, he would pay up but not until after the wedding ceremony, when she was properly tied. 'I'm sure he'll be true to his word. He likes you. You're a self-made man. That's how he thinks of himself, too.'

Jacob reached out to touch her arm but the movement seemed forced. Was he hiding something? How did he really feel? It occurred to her that he never talked about her studies except as a joke. Like yesterday, when he found her Boerhaave book. Last week when she asked him if he'd found a preceptor for her, he told her not to worry. 'When we get to Boston I'll find one,' he'd said.

'Do you really think college is no place for a woman?' she asked him now.

'I didn't say that. What I said was I didn't see its use – for anyone. But I didn't actually mean it. I was throwing him off the scent.'

'I don't see why you had to.'

'You don't? All right.' He looked at his horse. 'But just so you know, I don't think that really.'

She wanted to believe him. She fingered the small book in her pocket, *Elements of Surgery*, which she grabbed at random from her father's shelf before she left his office. She indulged in an old fantasy: her father would see her performing some complicated procedure, and praise her skill. Her anger shifted, and then stepped back an inch.

'Well,' she said. 'I like that you lied for me.'

'I did lie for you. I never thought much about college one way or another until I came back to Lark's Eye.'

'But you'd like your doctors to be well trained, certainly.'

'I'd like you to be well trained.' He took her in his arms, and she didn't resist.

But she couldn't help reflecting that in truth she knew very little about him; he left Lark's Eye when she was still a child. He built a business, fought in the war, was captured, survived. He almost never talked about the war, not even to Ruffy who'd fought in it, too. His attention to her sparked a warmth in her that she hadn't known she wanted. Maybe they would execute their plan – splitting the dowry, using the money to pay for a preceptor for her and a workshop for him – and then stay together at the end of it. She was beginning to want that. She inhaled his clean smell of starch and soap, and the musky hint of hair tonic.

'By the way,' Jacob said as he pulled the stirrups down from the saddle. 'I've invited my cousin Samantha to the wedding.'

'Who?' She'd never heard of a cousin.

'Samantha Friel. My cousin Walter's widow. You'll like her, I promise.'

Vita looked up at him. 'Why should I like her?'

'She's very personable. And well read.'

Something bright and energetic colored his expression. He's proud of this cousin, Vita thought. This Samantha.

'Not as well read as you, of course,' he said. 'And her voice is considerably quieter.'

So they were back to bantering. But she felt crossed with uncomfortable feelings; one of which might, she feared, be jealousy. Why had he never mentioned this cousin before?

'Is she pretty?' she couldn't help asking.

'Of course!' He smiled at her. 'I make it my business only to associate with pretty women.'

Not really the answer she wanted.

CHAPTER TEN

'In the case of overexcitement before marriage,
a cure can be effected by sleeping on a straw
mattress and washing the genitalia with
poppy-heads, lettuce, and henbane.'
(*Aristotle's Masterpiece*, Anonymous, 1717)

In town Marie noticed a miniature paper flag in the whip-socket of an unfamiliar wagon. It was stopped in front of the hotel, and she guessed that another batch of soldiers was traveling through Lark's Eye on their way home. Some old whaling man was probably standing them a drink right this minute in the hotel bar, talking up battles and bravery. She decided to put off her errand inside.

'I thought you wanted to check on the food for the wedding?' Arthur said as she turned away. He walked as if balancing on uneven sticks; she'd persuaded him to come 'out in the sunshine' with her, with the added lure of going to the tavern to see if his favorite whiskey had been delivered. He liked to keep a few bottles at home.

He needed to get out in the world more, Marie thought. That morning, while he was eating breakfast, she took the opportunity to open the smoke-stained curtains in his office. She'd looked around in dismay at the stacks of newspapers on the floor, the piles of unopened letters, the browning curls of apple peels in the ashtrays. Dust mites floated to the carpet like coal detritus, heavy and spent. He'd made a small pocket of industry at his desk: one cleared space where he could set a newspaper to read. She was tempted to throw open the curtained French doors that led to the side yard for air, but she'd have to move two towers of old medical journals simply to get to them.

She spotted Arthur's red leather appointment diary on top of one of the towers. The last time he wrote in it was over a month ago.

Monday. Collect shoes. Inspect Wilkinson's horse. Call on Mrs. Everly, complaint of jaw pain.
Tuesday. Wilkinson's horse. Call on Mrs. Everly if time.
Wednesday. Horse. Call on Mrs. Everly.
Thursday. Call on Mrs. Everly, or ask Quane to see her. Jaw complaint.
Friday. Collect shoes.

Had he ever called on poor Mrs. Everly, who lived alone above her son's glove shop? Certainly he hadn't fetched his mended shoes – Mrs. O. had asked Gemma, finally, to collect them – and he never got around to seeing Wilkinson's horse, either. Wilkinson sold it to a dairy farmer named Dobbs, and Marie knew this only because Arthur complained bitterly about the sale at dinner. But the next morning, when she asked him if he planned to look at another horse, he'd already forgotten about it.

'Why would I need another horse?' he'd asked.

'I mean because Wilkinson sold his.'

'Did he? Well, it was an old sway-backed thing anyway.'

Marie became momentarily confused. 'So you *did* see the horse?'

His face clouded. 'Certainly. Of course.' He turned as he spoke, obviously lying.

Now as they shuffled along – Marie slowed her pace to match her husband's – she said, 'It's so nice out. I think I'll just sit on a bench and wait for you while you collect your whiskey. I can ask Mr. Cummings about the food later.' She didn't want Arthur to see any soldiers, it upset him.

But he said, 'Then I'll sit, too, and catch my breath.'

They crossed over to the green. Marie chose a bench that faced away from the hotel. Horses were tethered along the road, some attached to buggies, a few with feed sacks hanging from their necks.

She felt an ache in the back of her neck as though she'd been carrying a weight on her head, an ancient woman balancing a water jug on her skull. When they returned home she would go up to her bedroom, close the door, and drink her tea laced with Mrs. Winslow's Soothing Syrup so she could think about Freddy without quite so much anguish. And it was important to think about him, to keep him alive. Once when she was walking in town – this was years ago, before the war certainly – she saw a thin baby bird splayed on the sidewalk, its neck at an odd angle, dead. It was small and featherless, with veins like indigo thread. It must have fallen out of its nest. Its mother hovered and swooped, pecking at passersby, guarding the body. Marie stopped a few paces away to watch, amazed. But a half a minute later the mother bird flew off and didn't come back. Had she given up? Forgotten? Marie didn't know what was worse: to see your offspring die; or, after they died, to forget them.

And so she had her laced tea twice a week, and looked at Freddy's letters and photographs. His jug ears and his army tent. But what did Arthur have? All of his newspapers were nothing but painful reminders, yet she was afraid that without them he'd become untethered completely.

'I've ordered eggs, a decorated ham, birds in season, and fried oysters,' Marie said, trying to interest him in the wedding meal. 'And two cakes, of course, a bride's cake and a groom's cake. Vita is petitioning for chocolate cream, but Amelia is afraid for their white dresses.'

'Vita has always been stubborn,' Arthur said. 'Like you.'

Marie laughed. 'And you!'

'I'm not stubborn. I'm right.'

She looked at him, thinking this was a joke. But his face was pinched inward. It's still only been five months, she reminded herself. She wondered how long she would be counting time forward from April.

'Do you remember when Freddy and Vita used to go with you to see patients?' She should try to bring up pleasant memories – for her own sake as well as for his. 'It was such a treat for them.'

A sly grin crept across Arthur's face. 'Once I asked Vita to give Josiah Whetmore his medicine. I'd measured it myself, of course, first. When we were outside the house I coached her on what to say: 'Here's your dose, Mr. Whetmore. You must take it with a glass of water.' How we howled when she said that!'

'Why did you howl?'

'Because she looked so ridiculous; eight years old and about as tall as a minute, telling a grown man what to do.'

Marie still didn't understand. 'But you told her to do that.'

'When we started laughing she couldn't believe it. Her face! What's that color – that mixture of purple and red?'

He'd played her for a joke. Marie's heart burned. She could picture so well Vita as a girl wanting to perform well, expecting praise.

'Mauve?' he said.

The wind swirled up, blowing the tree leaves into an eddy of green. Marie told herself she was being foolish for feeling provoked. By now Vita had probably forgotten all about the incident (and poor Josiah Whetmore, she thought, remembering how he hung himself after his own family died). Still, Marie wished she could hug the eight-year-old Vita as she stood inside that farmhouse feeling humiliated and tricked. She wished she could tell her that she had done very well. But it only counted, somehow, if it came from her father.

'Vita just wanted your approval. She's always wanted that.'

Arthur paused and seemed to consider this idea. He stared at a colony of spiky goldenrods blooming by the bandstand. Then: 'What were we speaking about?' he asked.

His expression was like a little boy's again. Lost. Marie's irritation fell away, and in its place she felt impotent and lonely. She could smell a faint hint of dry leaves in the air. Soon it would be autumn and her girls would be gone. And then there would be just the two of them left in the house, plus Mrs. Oakum. Gemma might go off with Ruffy someday, but Mrs. Oakum would stay in Lark's Eye to the end. And Marie's sister Clara, of course. Marie thought about something her father used to say to Clara as a young girl: You are built for use, not for show. He said this because she was large and had a long bony nose. Marie was considered the pretty daughter, but what good had that done her? Later Clara had eclipsed her anyway by marrying into wealth.

Marie took Arthur's hand. It felt cold and knuckly. An old man's hand. 'We were talking about the wedding breakfast,' she told him. 'What flavor of ices would you like to order?'

Vita felt guilty about hiding her plans from her mother, who always encouraged her studies. But she couldn't risk it. What if Mitty, like Dar, thought that Vita would bring disgrace to the family? Or what if she told Dar, or let something slip?

A woman with a career. How disgraceful was that, really? Certainly there were other women who had careers.

'You're not other women,' Vita could imagine Amelia saying.

Up in her bedroom she checked her books – Tripler's *Handbook on Surgery*; Walshe on the *Diseases of the Heart and Lungs*; Leidy's *Elementary Treatise on Anatomy* – and then packed them carefully into her mother's old maroon carpetbag, which she planned to take with her on the train to Boston. Everything else was secondary – her dresses and monogrammed towels, the bars of vanilla soap Aunt Norbert gave her nieces each Christmas. New stockings, new dresses. Vita would wear the same dress every day for all it mattered to her. Only her books were precious.

The carpetbag had a thick strip of mustard-colored hide sewn onto the bottom to keep out the wet. Packed, it was heavier than it looked. As she pushed the bag under her bed with her foot, she thought about Jacob's cousin Samantha. Well read, he'd said. She imagined a haughty older woman who would instantly notice Vita's chewed fingernails. Or was Samantha young and amusing? Personable, he had said. What did that mean?

'Aunt Norbert is here,' Amelia announced, knocking two quick knocks on the door and then coming in without waiting for an answer. She looked Vita over. 'Better wash your face.'

Aunt Norbert had decided to deliver her wedding checks personally. The envelopes were sealed with her husband's crest, which was copied from the Norbaer family crest in Germany – no relation. She stood in front of the gifts table in the parlor and presented the envelopes with some ceremony and a little speech about economy that Vita didn't bother to listen to.

When Vita fingered open the envelope flap she gave herself a thin, sharp paper cut in her haste. She put her finger in her mouth. The first thing she looked at was the amount, five hundred dollars. Then she noticed the name: Mr. Jacob Culhane.

'You've written the check out to Jacob?'

'Of course.'

Vita looked down again at her aunt's spidery writing. 'But how do I make a withdrawal? Must I see the bank manager every time?'

'Oh my goodness, the bank won't give you cash money!'

'You'll receive an allowance from your husband,' Mitty explained. 'For housekeeping.'

'Like Dar gives Mitty,' Amelia said.

Aunt Norbert frowned. 'Do I get a thank you from you, Vita?'

She rose to kiss her aunt. The check was printed on pale yellow paper with a pinkish tint, like a bloodstain. Her father's check would be made out to Jacob too, of course; she had known this without really thinking about it. In fact, until this moment she had never stopped to consider the practicality of their arrangement.

'Why can't I go to the bank myself?' she asked.

'Oh Vita!' her aunt said. 'Any money or property that a woman brings to a marriage becomes her husband's. You must know that. It's all kept in his account.'

Had she known that? It dawned on her for the first time that she would be entirely dependent on Jacob's honor to keep his side of their bargain.

'Women are born for sacrifice,' Amelia said. This was one of Aunt Norbert's favorite sayings, although she generally said it about other women, not herself.

Aunt Norbert glanced at Amelia sharply; then, satisfied that Amelia did not mean it as a joke (Vita knew that she did), she nodded. 'Quite right.'

Vita slid the check back in its envelope. The men in this world had thought of everything. Should she worry about Jacob's intentions? Would he split the money with her as he promised? She would have no lawful recourse if he didn't. She thought again about this cousin, Samantha. A cousin she hadn't once heard him mention until yesterday. His words to Holland floated back to her: *I see no use for college.*

But he'd explained that.

But what if he'd been lying?

Outside the sky darkened dramatically and there was a crack of thunder. Moments later the rain began falling so hard they could hear nothing else, and they went up to the window to watch it. The clouds were long and mottled, like warped marble columns thrown up into the sky. There was another crack of thunder, and then all four women reeled back as something crashed against the window and fell.

Vita stepped up again to look. 'A robin. It's dead.' It was lying on the ground with its tiny beak turned toward her like a beckoning finger. Only seconds ago it had been on the wing, battling the rain, drawing breath. Then: a sudden blow and the heart stops. Vita looked back at Sweetie, safe on her perch in the corner of the parlor.

You're in charge of my animals while I'm away, Freddy had said. Who would take care of them after she went to Boston? She must talk to Mitty about that.

'Poor thing,' Amelia said, about the robin.

'Poor thing?' Aunt Norbert fluttered her hand toward the window. The rain was coming down heavily, at a slant. 'I don't know what it thought it was doing, flying about in all that.'

CHAPTER ELEVEN

'The chaste man enjoys greater brain power.'
(*Private Lessons in the Cultivation of Sex Force*,
Anonymous, 1913)

Ezra Norbert had been a tall man with a sizeable head, and his portrait, which was as long as a door, did not attempt to disguise this. Although also tall, Aunt Norbert's head was much smaller, a fact she emphasized by wearing her hair scraped back and oiled.

'My husband took the pledge and I along with him,' she announced when they were gathered in her front parlor. 'But as he is gone, I do, on special occasions, allow myself a drop.'

It was the night before the wedding. Aunt Norbert was hosting a 'family evening' that included supper and, Vita imagined, some tedious but well-meaning speeches. Her manservant Hunt poured wine from a crystal decanter into enormous cut-glass goblets while Uncle Norbert looked down from his portrait, hard-eyed and judging.

Aunt Norbert handed the first glass to Jacob's cousin, Mrs. Samantha Friel, who had arrived by train that afternoon. Samantha was younger than Vita expected, tall and good-looking, with a sharp chin and a heart-shaped face. Her top lip curled amiably when she smiled, which was often, and she had dressed her hair in thin ringlets that somehow drew attention to her well-spaced gray eyes. Vita, who allowed Gemma to make braided loops out of her own hair, felt like an unraveling ball of yarn.

'Please call me Samantha,' Samantha had said when Jacob introduced her. 'After all, we'll be cousins starting tomorrow.' She claimed she'd been born and raised in Boston, but her voice had a flatness that Vita associated with Maine.

In the dining room, Aunt Norbert's table was set with her best gold-rimmed china, and all the candles were lit although it was barely eight o'clock. Jacob pulled out a chair for his cousin, who had a large field of skirts to organize. On her index finger she wore a ring with a flat white stone. It seemed to Vita that Jacob held her hand, his thumb covering the ring, longer than was strictly necessary.

Vita sat on the opposite side, facing the two of them. As the soup was ladled out her father turned to Samantha.

'And what business was your late husband in, Mrs. Friel?'

He had had two glasses of wine already and was almost like his old self, attentive and outgoing, although Vita noticed her mother watching him carefully.

'Walter was a stockbroker,' Samantha said. 'Mexican and European bonds, mostly.'

'I can't say I know much about bonds.'

She smiled. 'Nor me.'

She bent her head to say a few private words to Jacob. The sleeves of her shimmering blue dress did not quite reach her elbows, and her bare arms and neck added to her raw, powerful presence.

She raised her glass.

'To the brides,' she said.

After that they spoke generally about rain – would the present good weather hold? – and train travel – Samantha's cloak had been covered in soot just walking through the Boston station – and Aunt Norbert's dishes of creamed herring – fresh that day from the nearby fisheries. Over the beef, Samantha began to describe an organization she'd recently joined, the American Social Science Association.

'I've heard of them,' Vita said, although she hadn't.

'Then as you know they believe that science should be applied to solving our social problems. We should study them methodically.'

'What problems specifically?' Holland asked.

'Poverty. Overcrowded housing.'

'I always think that these issues could be very well addressed by money,' Vita said. She was forming her opinions on the spot.

Samantha smiled. 'In a perfect world, yes.'

She commanded attention from all the men at once, even Holland. Vita could sense their interest like a musky odor circling the room. In comparison she felt inconsequential; a dry, dead beetle on a windowsill.

'Sounds a good cause,' Dar said. 'The occupation of any woman should be that of service to others.'

'Quite right,' Aunt Norbert agreed, whose own service to others usually took the form of unwanted advice.

Samantha was still looking at Vita. 'My cousin tells me you're a scholar,' she said. 'I went to Berwick Academy for a couple of terms, but I'm afraid it did me no good.'

'Don't let her fool you,' Jacob said. 'My cousin is quite smart.' He sounded like a defending lover.

'What reading can you recommend?' Samantha asked. 'My husband had a subscription to *Punch* for many years, but I'm afraid I let it lapse during the war.'

'At the moment I'm reading a book on heart and lung diseases,' Vita said, her voice loud and strong although she felt exactly the opposite. 'But that probably wouldn't interest you.'

Both Mitty and Dar looked over at her sharply. 'Do you mean you're reading Walshe?' her father asked.

'You should try *The Atlantic Monthly*,' Holland suggested. 'A very good magazine for the modern reader.'

'You don't read that,' Amelia said.

His face colored. 'Yes, I do. Sometimes I do.'

A tedious meal, and a long one. When Hunt came in with dessert plates, Aunt Norbert rapped on her water glass with the bowl of her spoon.

'My sister and I have a present we'd like to give on this very grand occasion. From our late father.' She directed Amelia to fetch a gray silk bag lying on the table under the window. Inside were two gold coins, like tiny burnished buttons.

'The last of his collection,' Mitty said.

Samantha craned her long, white neck. 'How lovely. May I see?'

Vita noticed how eagerly Samantha watched as one of the coins was passed down the table to her. She examined it closely, turning it over in her fingers while at the same time keeping it in clear view like a customer at a jewelry shop, anxious that no one suspect her of thievery.

'It's so small.'

'But worth a good deal for all that,' Aunt Norbert told her.

'How much do you reckon?'

Vita waited for her aunt to frown and say something dismissive about money discussions. But instead she said proudly, 'I've been told they could fetch over one hundred dollars each.'

'My gracious!' Samantha smiled at Jacob. 'A nice little nest egg.'

'It's an heirloom,' he said. 'It's not meant to be sold.'

'You, refusing money!' Samantha laughed. Her face was flushed and her manner seemed almost reckless – the effect of the wine, probably. When Jacob saw Vita watching him, he smiled. Slyly? Contritely? Samantha passed the coin back up the table.

'I'll see that they're put in the hotel safe,' Aunt Norbert announced, drawing the bag closed with her large, knuckly fingers. The two couples planned to spend the night at the Lark's Eye Hotel after the wedding and then take the early train to Boston the next day. 'Best not to keep them lying about – the maids, you know. There's one coin for each of you.'

Vita started to say thank you but saw her aunt was addressing her remarks to Holland and Jacob.

'Mrs. Norbert,' Holland said, 'you've been very generous.'

'You must call me aunt now,' she said, nodding once to Holland and once to Jacob. As if counting them, Vita thought.

❁

Despite her uneasiness about Jacob and Samantha – or maybe because of it – Vita drank more wine than she was accustomed to; later, up in her bedroom, her fingers felt sweaty and clumsy as she fumbled with her dress buttons.

She had to get out of this corset. She had to get out of these shoes. She was on her stomach looking under the bed for her shoe buttonhook when her mother walked in. Vita had pushed the carpetbag out from its hiding place and now it stood in the middle of the floor gaping open with all the medical books she'd taken from her father in plain sight. Her mother stared down at them.

'So you're reading Walter Walshe,' Mitty said as she began to unbutton Vita's dress for her. Vita could feel the happy tug and release down her back as one by one the buttons came undone – sixteen tiny orbs of annoying blue silk. 'And also Paget? What's this sudden interest in medicine?'

Vita hesitated. The wedding was tomorrow. What did it matter if she told her mother now? She stepped out of her dress and Mitty began loosening her corset.

'I want to be a doctor.'

Mitty stopped working on the corset. 'You want – you want to *work* as a doctor?'

'Yes. Like Dar. I want to be trained, go to classes, all of it. And then practice.'

She could smell the last of the whale oil burning in the glass lamp on the mantelpiece. She pulled off her corset and turned around to check her mother's expression. Surprise, concern. No dismay; but no delight, either. Mitty bent to pick up the brass oilcan that Vita kept next to her fireplace, refilled the lamp, and turned up the flame.

She sat down on the corner of Vita's bed. Then, in a gesture that Freddy used to call 'Mitty Being Patient,' she folded her hands in her lap and tilted her chin up.

'Why the sudden interest?' she asked.

'It's not sudden. We used to talk about college, remember?'

'But you never mentioned medicine. When did you decide this?'

'I've wanted to for years. Before the war even. Ever since I was little.'

'And what about Jacob?'

'Jacob knows all about it. He said he would help me.'

'Help you with what?'

Vita blew out air, frustrated. 'Go to college! Use Dar's money, the dowry, to pay for medical college, and also to pay for a preceptor before that. And living expenses and so on.'

'In Boston,' Mitty said. It was a question.

'Yes. In Boston. The only thing is, I realized – I'm beginning to realize – that if Jacob changes his mind, I'll be left with nothing. I'll have no recourse if he decides to use the dowry for – for something else.' She thought of how Samantha looked at the little gold coin, assessing it. '*You* refusing money?' she'd said to Jacob.

'So this is not a real marriage.'

Vita thought about their kisses and embraces and she flushed, as though she were betraying Jacob, or both of them – but why? Her mother was right, it wasn't a real marriage. *Our nefarious agreement.*

'Mitty, what did you expect? Dar told me I had to get married.'

'He couldn't force you, you know.'

'He wasn't – he isn't going to pay for any more schooling, or any more anything, he made that clear. What should I do, just stay here, in this house, in this room, growing old and stupid?' She was angry now.

'Is that what you think I am? Old and stupid?'

'Of course not! But Mitty –' It was impossible to make her mother understand. She was still sitting on Vita's bed with her hands in her lap, but there was movement, her thumbs rubbing against each other, revealing her agitation.

'Vita,' she said, 'listen to me. A woman always has choices. I've had choices. I keep my mind busy with my dahlias, my soil experiments. I've learned to look for ways to engage my intellect. I read the science journals your father subscribes to after he is through with them. It's difficult here in Lark's Eye;

it's not impossible, but it's difficult. That's why I wanted more for you. Boston will have so much more to offer. Even if you don't become a doctor or anything else.'

Vita was standing in her chemise, half-facing her mother, her hand on the opposite bedpost. She traced a nick in the wood with her fingertip. What about your tea, she wanted to say. You want to feel numb; you need that. Twice a week that's what you need, and you'd probably do it more often if you thought your health wouldn't suffer. But she couldn't say that. It wasn't Mitty's fault that she was stuck here, bored. Was it?

She felt cold, and she wanted her mother to comfort her. Or better yet, help her to get what she wanted. She plucked her shawl from the foot of the bed and wrapped it around herself, and then sat down on the window seat. 'Why *shouldn't* I become a doctor?' A challenge.

Her mother's eyes met hers in the mirror over the mantel.

'It's as you say, Jacob might change his mind. And you can't do anything without a husband's permission.'

'A husband's permission!'

'Or his help.'

'But it's *my money*. It doesn't seem right that from tomorrow on Jacob can spend *my money* however he likes.'

'Your father's money,' Mitty corrected.

'But it was your money first. Wasn't it? Money that Grandfather Toombs gave you?'

'Well, yes and no. He gave it to your father, same as your father is giving money to Jacob.'

'And it was your mother's money before that.'

A slight pause. Vita waited. Mitty inclined her head.

'Don't you see how unfair that is? It's like we're being sold.'

'Would you rather have nothing?'

'I would rather be able to have some say in how my money is spent.'

'It's the law. I know it doesn't seem right. But it's the law.'

'It's wrong,' Vita said.

Mitty let out a long breath. 'All right. It is wrong. But be realistic. Jacob is a man, and men like to have their creature comforts, no matter what they say beforehand. That's simply a fact. I thought your father was – would be – different. But after we married – well. Men get more conservative after they marry.'

Vita felt waves of self-pity coming at her again and again almost jauntily, belying their aggressive nature: *You can't, You can't, You can't.*

'Just think, Vita, you'll be living in a city after tomorrow. A large city, where there'll be many opportunities for you. Public talks and lectures, museums. No matter what, you'll be able to engage your mind, you can live an interesting life. You don't need a profession to do that.'

Her mother's face, in the dim lamplight, was as still as stone. As a headstone, Vita thought. I can't help it; I want more. But she didn't know if she could trust Jacob – that was the hard truth. She thought of their last kisses outside Aunt Norbert's house, when they were saying good-bye. They were facing the water and she could see a twinkle of lights from houses across the small bay. His hand was warm on her arm, and she felt a stirring beneath her skin as though she could trace, inch by inch, the web of blood within her.

'Tomorrow's the day,' he'd said. Had he sounded cool? Calculating?

'You won't be safe as a woman alone,' Mitty told her. 'A woman in that profession. But if you really *must* take up something, maybe train as a nurse? That way you could still uphold your wifely responsibilities.'

'I don't want to be a nurse. I want to be a doctor.'

'But being a doctor is very demanding. You've seen it yourself – patients at all hours. It's not suitable for women.'

Vita leaned back against the wooden side panel of her window seat and stretched her legs out lengthwise, sliding her toes under the pillow at the other end to warm them. Why was it so hard to convince everyone? Jacob, in retrospect, was the easiest to persuade. She didn't really think he had a secret plan with Samantha. That seemed too underhand, too sly.

She closed her eyes. Her father always praised Jacob for being an honest, self-made man. But Jacob's father had been a drunk. That's what people said. A mean drunk. You couldn't trust him, they said. They said this even as he lay in his little farmhouse, dying.

Maybe she couldn't read the signs.

'You don't understand people,' Amelia liked to tell her. 'You spend too much time with your books.'

She could picture her sister's expression, hard and knowing. But what can I do, Vita thought. It's too late to run away, and anyway that seems melodramatic and childish. Mitty said something she couldn't quite hear. A moment later the sun was shining brightly in her face and Amelia was leaning over her, shaking her awake. Vita was still stretched out on her window seat. Her bed quilt was draped over her, and Mitty was gone.

'What are you doing here?' Amelia said. 'It's time to get dressed.'

In the morning, dressed in his tight wedding clothes, his head pounding, Jacob found parts of the previous night difficult to remember. He had taken a room at the Lark's Eye Tavern, which was closer to the church. Mrs. Swaby had tapped on the door to wake him up. Before he left, he stood at the bar and downed a mouthful of brandy. The liquid sparked his throat, burning a path as it traveled. After that his head felt marginally better as long as he didn't turn it too quickly.

His hired gig and driver – young Frank Pride, Jr., dressed in a dove-gray suit and cap – waited outside for him.

'Be careful of your coat, sir,' Frank said. 'Pull it down behind you before you sit back, that way you don't wrinkle it.'

'You're a good man, Frank Pride,' Jacob said, and Frank smiled from ear to ear.

They drove around the town green with the gig's top down. Thankfully it was an overcast day, otherwise the light would have been painful. This morning Jacob almost wished that he hadn't invited Samantha to the wedding. Her carefree façade irked him in company. Also her need for everyone to admire her. Of course, he'd known that about her before. She understood so well how to charm. Her smiles contrasted sharply to Vita's irritated scowls during the meaningless dinner talk. Samantha, he could tell, had despised that scowl. Small talk was her forte.

As they turned up the church drive the sun found a crack in the cloud cover, and Jacob felt it like a spear in his eye. It was important to hold his body naturally, to climb down from the gig steadily, and to stand with a half-smile on his face as he looked up at the church (looming, enormous) while Frank tipped his cap and said, 'A very happy day for you, sir. Will you need me to wait?'

He couldn't remember the plan for leaving.

But here was Mrs. Norbert – Aunt Norbert, as he was to call her now – wearing a dress like a tiered purple cake with white icing. She walked toward him faster than a heavy woman in a large tight dress should be able to move.

'Right on time!' she told him.

He took her proffered arm, plump and commanding.

'Thank you, Frank. That's all, I guess. Best of luck to you.'

They went into the dim church vestibule. His neck felt stiff and he tried not to look around or think too much about what was happening. Best just to fall in line, like a soldier. At least his tic was gone. No tremors, either. When it came time to go up to the altar, Jacob matched his pace to Holland's; even with his special shoes, Holland still limped if he walked too fast. Jacob didn't see – or look for – Samantha in the pews.

But when the congregation stood and the music for the brides began ('Here we go, old man,' Holland said under his breath) and Jacob saw Vita emerge in white silk and lace, her tiny shoulders carrying the weight of her massive dress, her expression a mystery behind the dotted, cream-colored veil, Jacob felt a warm but strangely light feeling bloom in his chest like a question. He tapped his fingertips against his thighs as he watched her walk toward him, slowly.

Here we are, he thought. Here we go.

CHAPTER TWELVE

'The majority of women (happily for them) are
not much troubled by sexual feeling of any kind.'
(*The Functions and Disorders of the Reproductive Organs,*
Dr. William Acton, 1883)

The wedding breakfast menu was, pompously, irritatingly, written in French – Aunt Norbert's doing, no doubt. *Galantine en Bellevue, Pâte Mélange á la Parisienne, Terrapins á la Maryland.* Vita had a startled moment when she saw their names at the top of the sheet: Madame Vita et Monsieur Jacob Culhane; Madame Amelia et Monsieur Holland Granger.

Vita Culhane. That was her name now. It sounded like the name of someone she had recently met and would presumably get to know, though at the moment she was a stranger. Was this how gamblers felt when the dice left their fingers but before the rolling came to a stop? Time wasn't suspended so much as empty, a thin slice of space between action and consequence.

She was married.

Jacob leaned in, pressing his forearm against hers. They were sitting at a round table – crystal goblets and maroon-rimmed plates with the hotel initials, set on a white linen cloth – that seemed much too large for only two couples. The blank unreality Vita had experienced in the church was slowly receding, and in its place she felt all the discomforts of her stiff, unyielding dress. She was a puffy caterpillar, *Lepidoptera larva*, looking up as the hotel waiter set down yet another fresh plate in front of her. Pickled eggs served with a sprig of parsley.

'I don't believe your aunt has any feet under that dress,' Jacob said.

Vita looked over at Aunt Norbert, who was circulating among the tables. Her dress, dyed a vibrant lilac that made her lips and eyelids appear blue, was wider than anyone else's in the room, even Amelia's, and completely hid her shoes.

'Might there be wheels instead?'

She played along. 'And tiny mice to pull them.'

'Muscular little fellows.'

They both laughed.

'I deposited your coins in the hotel safe, marked with your names,' Aunt Norbert announced to the two couples, braking to a stop at their table. 'Be sure to collect them before you leave tomorrow morning.'

All four glanced at the dining room door as though they might see right through it to the hotel desk and the safe. Beyond the desk was the wide staircase that led to the guest rooms and beds. The marriage bed. Vita felt a hot pull at the thought of it. After the wedding ceremony, in the church vestibule, Gemma had leaned in to whisper, 'You must write me straight away. Tell me everything.'

When the grandfather clock in the corner chimed the half hour, the groom's cake was cut, and then the bride's cake. After that the two couples stood by the double doors to say good-bye to their guests. The sun glinted through the sparkling clean windows, making Vita sweat. At least she didn't have to speak with Samantha again; she'd gone back to New Bedford on the noon train, and missed the breakfast.

Her parents were the last to leave.

'I know you'll be happy in Boston,' her mother said.

And then Dar: 'Be good, and try to speak softly.'

Try to speak softly? This was his advice for marriage? His hair, which Mitty had trimmed that morning, was looking very gray. Would he ever forgive her for 'disgracing' him by becoming a doctor? Her old dream fluttered up: Maybe, as time went on, he would learn to be proud of her.

'I will,' she lied.

❁

It took two maids and twenty minutes to get her out of her dress, and ten more minutes to get into the next one. In between Vita sponged herself with water from the basin to cool off. When a soft knock sounded on her door, she assumed it was her sister. But she opened the door to Jacob.

'Oh! Amelia was just going to check up on you and Holland,' Vita said. 'She wants to take a stroll before dinner.'

'We could do that.' Jacob looked at her. His face was half in shadow. 'Or we could stay here.'

Her heart rose and began to beat faster as she stepped back to let him in.

He closed the door behind him. Then, without preamble, he bent to kiss her. It was an awkward kiss, as if he recognized this was an important moment and that made him nervous. She was nervous, too. She stretched up trying to reach him, and they both felt the strain at the same time and laughed. After that, it was better.

They kissed again. She could smell wine on his skin. He slid his hands up the sides of her dress and she felt a slow thrill begin at the base of her spine, like a snake uncurling. He stroked the pearl buttons going up her back, each the size of a ripe summer pea.

'That's one,' he said, unbuttoning it. 'Two. Three.' At twelve he said, 'You must have an army of monkeys helping you dress and undress every day.'

She laughed. 'Why monkeys?'

'With their tiny little fingers.'

He kissed her neck and skimmed the dress off her shoulders. They were standing next to the canopied bed, ignoring the candied walnuts and dried fruit arranged on a white platter on the table, left for them by the hotel management along with a bottle of wine.

They worked on her layers first: her dress and camisole and petticoat; her corset; her garters and stockings. As layer after layer fell onto the floor, Vita began to feel as though she were preparing to do something extraordinary, like fly. Jacob kissed her bare forearm and then her neck again. She bent to unbutton his pants. By this time they were both sweating and hot.

'This is hard work,' she said, 'this getting to bed.'

He laughed, and she wondered: have I ever made anyone laugh before? Her bridal nightgown had been folded neatly by the hotel maid and placed at the foot of the bed. When she reached for it, Jacob said, 'No.'

He drew her to him, embracing her tightly. They were both unclothed but she didn't feel embarrassed. She felt, instead, as though this was right and the other – the heaps of clothes on the floor – was alien and unnatural.

They pushed the pillows off the bed and lay down on top of the coverlet, facing each other. Jacob traced his forefinger down the side of her right breast and over her ribs. He drew an invisible circle on her belly, and another circle lower down. Drawing his desire.

'I'm going to go slowly,' he told her. 'So we can get to know each other.'

'A little at a time.'

He touched her nipple. 'A very little at a time.'

The hot September sunlight, creeping in through the gaps in the curtains, gave the room a watery, undersea haze. After a while they started working out the details more seriously, the positions of legs and arms and mouths. As they settled into a spot in the middle of the mattress Vita found herself thinking: here it is. It felt as though doors upon doors were opening inside her, and she understood so much that she never understood just by reading. She didn't know if she liked it yet, there were moments of raw pain followed by careful adjustments. Still, she felt supernaturally awake and alive. It was as if all at once, and without even thinking, she could speak the language she'd been studying all these years.

But then Jacob pulled himself away and turned onto his side.

'What is it?' she asked.

There was a box near the bed, something he'd brought in earlier with his shaving kit. When he lifted the lid she rose up on one elbow to see.

'A French letter,' he said. 'So you don't get pregnant.'

He explained how it worked while he unrolled it, and when he turned around she saw the sheath, thick as a butcher's apron, on his penis. A new element entered, raw and cold, but she didn't want a baby, it was true. He pulled her close again.

Afterward he lay on his back, his arm beneath her neck. He caressed her shoulder lightly. She was staring at the ceiling, warm from this new experience, which she wanted to talk about.

But instead she fell into a light sleep. When she opened her eyes again it was darker. The afternoon had passed into twilight. She could hear people talking in the hallway. Through the open window, the unmistakable scent of pipe smoke wafted into the room as someone, whoever was smoking, sat on a rocking chair on the hotel porch beneath them. For a while she listened to the *creekah creekah* of the rocker. Jacob was lying on his side, watching her.

'Well,' he asked. 'What did you think?' His teasing tone. She considered her answer.

'I think I'd like to try it again,' she said, and he laughed.

They heard the dinner gong but they did not even pause. As Jacob moved inside her she felt closer to something, she didn't know what. It wasn't so painful, at least. An early owl hooted, and hooted again. Jacob made a noise in his throat and afterward lay very still for a minute before rolling over and peeling off the second French letter. After that they both slept for a long time.

The third time it was so dark Vita could no longer see anything beyond the bed. They had missed dinner but contented themselves with the walnuts and fruit and the tepid bottle of wine left in their room. After they ate every morsel, they peeled down the coverlet and slipped into the cool sheets.

The wine made both of them tipsy, almost giggly. Once again Jacob began slowly and Vita was reminded of music, the quiet beat of a repeated tempo. It was then she felt the thing like a wave coming, followed by a pulsing burst that stayed within her. A kind of light settled on the top of her head and the hotel went absolutely silent. No owls, no other guests roaming the halls. All the night creatures had retired and the morning birds had not yet awakened. She herself hardly breathed. After a few moments she pulled away and then pressed herself against Jacob's side, hot and sweaty and in awe of what just happened.

She forgot about the third French letter until he moved his hands down, jerking it off. Coming back into the bed – he scrounged to get under the tousled sheets – he kissed her shoulder. She was trying to think what to say to him when she heard his breath deepen in sleep.

For a while she lay awake beside him. Her body felt heavy, both old and young – how could that be? She touched her bare elbow, embracing herself. Every part of her was tired, and although she hung in this state for several minutes she did not fall asleep. Her neck was uncomfortable, and she swung her arm down to the floor to feel for a pillow.

'Lift your head,' she told Jacob. He obeyed, rising just enough for her to slide the pillow beneath his head. Then she found one for herself. When she settled back down on the mattress, he felt for her hand. After a while she thought maybe he had fallen asleep again.

But then he said, his voice groggy, 'Thank you, Samantha.'

Every molecule in her body seemed to freeze in place. 'What?'

He turned his head and half opened his eyes.

'You called me Samantha,' she told him.

'Did I? I must have been dreaming.'

'*Were* you dreaming?'

'I don't know. I don't remember.' He pulled her closer and put his nose against her neck. 'You always smell like vanilla,' he said. 'Why is that?'

'Is there something between you and Samantha?'

'No. No. I was asleep, that's all. Well, I did ask her to marry me once, but that was years ago.'

She knew there was something. She pulled out of his embrace and stood up from the bed.

'Obviously she said no. Where are you going? Come back.'

'So you were in love with her?'

Her voice was tight, as though she were holding some of her breath back for another purpose. Jacob realized the mistake he'd just made. 'No. I wasn't. Not at all. I was lonely. It was right before the war. An impulse. I was relieved when she said no.'

His eyes were adjusting to the dark but still he could only see shapes: the two long rectangular windows, a block of an armchair in between them. Vita was a slender tree with no branches.

'Come back,' he said again.

'No.'

Ivory moonlight trickled in through the curtain. He watched Vita shrug on her chemise and go to the armchair by the window. She sat down, pulled a pillow out from behind her, and held it to her stomach.

'Have you found a preceptor for me in Boston?' she asked.

'Can't we talk about this in the morning?'

'*Have* you?'

He sighed. 'Not yet. And actually,' since the conversation felt inevitable, he struggled to sit up, 'I wanted to propose something to you.'

There was a decanter of water on the bedside table; he poured a splash into one of the glasses and swallowed it. He felt a little more awake.

'I was thinking. I wonder if instead of working with a doctor, you might want to work with me on my patent idea? I mean the modified barrels. The formula for the glue compound. Holland gave me the idea. You're good at science, at experiments;

he told me that. Together we might figure it out. A shared project. A partnership.' It was an idea he'd been thinking about for a couple of days.

A pause. 'You're proposing I work on barrel glue,' Vita said, 'instead of studying medicine?'

He couldn't make out her expression. 'Just for six months or so, maybe a year. Or even, if we both like it, for longer. A partnership,' he said again. She was silent. 'Vee, I know you were thinking of becoming a doctor. But is that really feasible? What I'm suggesting is, here's another way you could put your mind to use. And with me, your husband, as the front man, well you see how much easier that would be for you. As a woman. You wouldn't have to do it alone.'

'In other words, my gender wouldn't get in the way.'

'Exactly!'

Another pause. 'What if I don't want to work on the problem of barrel glue?'

'I think you'll find it interesting, actually. But it's late, let's talk about it tomorrow. I can explain it all better when I'm not so tired.'

He was struggling again to keep his eyes open. He felt like he was half dreaming already. His words, like the furniture in the room, appeared in his mind like differently shaped blocks, visible and material. A partnership, had he said that? That part was important. But he couldn't help himself, he was falling asleep.

'All right?' he asked. But he couldn't stay awake long enough to hear her answer.

Vita felt as though the pillow she was holding on her lap had become a repository for her emotions; if she didn't move, if she didn't shift the pillow, she could take in what Jacob was saying without really feeling it. But that only lasted so long. A syrupy sensation began circling in her body, like a terrible sadness. At the same time her arms and neck felt wooden, and her voice, when she spoke, sounded to her like the strings of an instrument growing slack and taut intermittently. But at last Jacob stopped talking, which was better. Every sentence he said made her feel worse. After a while she could hear his breathing change.

'Jacob?'

He didn't answer; he was asleep.

She looked out the window.

So; it was true. They'd made a pledge but he didn't take the pledge seriously. He didn't take her seriously. He didn't want her to study medicine; he didn't think she could do it. Just like everyone else. And now, legally speaking, she was his. She had no money of her own; every penny was her husband's by law and he could do what he wanted with it. If he didn't want to pay college fees, if he didn't want to pay for a preceptor, no one could make him. She couldn't make him.

It was not easy to think, and she had to think. Her feet were beginning to feel cold and she got up to look for a blanket. On impulse, she picked up Jacob's trousers and felt the outside pockets until she found his little black coin purse. In it was the folded check from her father – 'Payable to Mr. Jacob Culhane,' useless to her – and also two one-dollar coins. She took the coins and left the check.

Her heart was beating hard in the way it did when she knew she was going to argue with someone, usually her father. She looked in Jacob's jacket pockets but found nothing, and then she remembered the little box by the bed with the French letters. She carried it to the window and, by the light of the moon, sifted through it. Four more dollars and his signet ring. Also, and this was a surprise, the little sealed envelope from Aunt Norbert containing the gold coin. When had he retrieved it from the hotel safe?

Outside the sky was shifting from jet black to coal black. Vita dressed quickly, her heart still pounding like a hammer against her ribs. A signal she was doing something foolish, or brave? Her worn carpetbag was at the foot of the bed with her books, and she wedged in all the clothes she could fit. Should she write him a note? What could she say?

Downstairs, a slender young man with thinning hair and a walrus mustache sat on a stool behind the hotel desk. For all that it was early, he looked alert and rested.

'I left something in your care last night,' Vita said. 'A small envelope in the safe.'

'Your name?'

'Mrs. Holland Granger.'

The cast-iron safe sat on the counter behind him, a gray box the size of a lion cub with curlicues outlining the door and the scripted word 'SAFE' above the lock in case anyone had their doubts. Shuffling through a few items, the clerk found an envelope with the name 'Granger' in Aunt Norbert's handwriting. The coin was a lump at the bottom, scarcely bigger than her dress buttons. Worth one hundred dollars, her aunt had said, and now she had two of them. Enough to make a start.

When she asked when the next train to Boston left, the clerk took out his pocket watch. 'Mail train in twenty-six minutes. First passenger train's an hour after that.'

The mail train, then.

'Would you like me to fetch the conveyance,' he asked, 'for you and Mr. Granger?'

'We're traveling separately. Yes, the conveyance would be helpful.'

'Shall I get your trunks? Are they in the back?'

Amelia would forgive her (maybe) for the coin, but never for taking her dresses.

'That's all right. My husband will see to our luggage.'

When the clerk went to find the driver Vita stepped into the small coatroom by the hotel door. On the women's side she found a heavy wool cloak with maroon trim, and put it on. A pair of calfskin gloves had been folded together and left in one of the pockets. Vita measured them against her hand. Too long in the fingers, but they'd do.

She went outside. By now the sky was the color of chimney smoke, and a light but steady breeze was blowing in from the ocean. Lark's Eye appeared wasted in this light, as though every bush and tree had been dusted with ash. The rockers on the hotel porch looked like a line of tombstones. For so many years, all she wanted was to leave this town and find her true place in the world. She thought about Jacob asleep in the room above her. If he went to the window now, would he see her? She could picture him in bed with his arm slung over his eyes, one foot exposed. For a moment the urge to leave her bag and purloined cloak on the porch steps and go back upstairs, slide under the starched cotton sheet, and feel his warm, long body against hers was stronger than any urge she'd ever felt. If the hotel carriage hadn't come around just at that moment, she might have.

PART 3

CHAPTER THIRTEEN

'No man should yield to temptation without a struggle.'
(*Private Lessons in the Cultivation of Sex Force*, Anonymous, 1913)

January 1866, New Bedford, Massachusetts

Jacob could remember having the feeling of desire, but desire itself seemed to have left him. The butter biscuits that Samantha was loading onto the small, gold-rimmed plate might just as well be cardboard discs for all they appealed to him. She added a couple of sugared ginger slices and a caramel, and then handed him the plate.

'I know you'll like these little ginger bites,' she said with a smile. 'But tell me what you think of the caramel. I had a box sent from New York.'

The thick coating of sparkling sugar on the ginger slices made his stomach tighten. He put the plate on the little wicker table beside him, next to his untouched cup of tea.

'Is your rug new?' he asked.

'Do you like it? The old one had been stretched so many times that I couldn't even tack it down any longer.'

She'd redecorated since he was last here. Everything was gold and pink, or else white. Even the two slender maple trees outside the window, their branches muscled with snow, matched her color scheme. But had the room always been so crowded? All these hanging lamps and table lamps, pearly pink vases with dried flowers or pussy willows, a dozen framed watercolors on the wall, and miniature busts of German or Russian composers facing out on the bookshelves? He was hemmed in by the bric-a-brac, a feeling he never remembered experiencing here before.

'Your parlor feels very . . .'

His body jerked at a noise – the coal fire had shifted, and a couple of sparks ticked loudly up the chimney like gunshots. He glanced at Samantha but fortunately she hadn't noticed his jumpy reaction. She was looking around the room with a pleased expression.

'Cozy,' she said.

Cozy. All right. He felt the tremor in his thigh start up and he flattened his palm on his leg to hide it. His teeth felt like tombstones in his dry mouth but he didn't dare try to take a sip of his tea because his hand had begun to shake, too.

'Now Jackie; you must tell me everything!' Samantha said. Alone, she always called him Jackie, just as his cousin Walter had. It was the name Jacob's mother had called him.

'I kept expecting you to write! And where's your little bride, why hasn't she come with you? I sent her a lovely note congratulating the both of you, but she never replied.'

He hesitated only a moment. 'She's gone.'

A look of horror. 'What!'

'No,' he said quickly, realizing how that sounded. 'I don't mean, she isn't . . . She just left. She left me.'

'She left you?' Samantha stared at him. 'When? Why?'

He did not gloss over the timing. 'Immediately. The next day. In Lark's Eye.'

'You don't mean the very day after your wedding?'

He nodded.

'But that was months and months ago! Oh, Jackie.' Samantha set her plate down on the table, leaned forward, and took Jacob's hand.

'It doesn't matter,' he said, though he didn't pull his hand away. 'Marriage is a cage. I'm better off out of it.'

He'd been telling himself this for months; he'd even said the same, more or less, to Mrs. Tenney when she came up to Boston to see him. By then his tumult of feelings had settled into a dull, smoldering anger. Marriage was a cage. Just like his father always said. And Jacob had had enough of cages to last a lifetime.

Mrs. Tenney had looked at him sadly. 'You're hurt and angry. But don't worry, we'll find her. I've been writing people I know. Discreetly.'

She was right; he *was* hurt and angry. But the fact was, his hurt and anger had taken him in another direction – he didn't want to find her. He didn't want to look.

The coals shifted again, and Samantha squeezed his fingers. 'Well, I thought there was something. Look at you. You're not yourself. Wearing those old trousers, and who is seeing to your shoes? Have you any idea where she went?'

He let out a long breath. Tried to steady his nerves. 'She wanted to study medicine, that's all I know.'

'Of course! We talked about books at that awful dinner party, oh I'll never forget those dishes of herring!' Her mouth twisted itself back into a frown; she almost laughed. Jacob was surprised. Perhaps he didn't look as bad as he felt, in spite of his scuffed shoes?

'I haven't, I'm not myself,' he began, but Samantha interrupted.

'Of course not. Jackie, you must look for her! You must find her. She's your wife.' Her hand was still on top of his.

'You're wrong. I don't have to find her,' Jacob said. 'I'm not going to look.'

'But you're ill over it! I can see that you are ill.'

'It's not that . . . it's not her, I mean.' He realized that each of them was being careful not to call Vita by her name. 'It's not Vita,' he said firmly. 'It's. . . it's the other thing.'

'What other thing?'

'The war.'

'What war? Oh, you mean the old war?'

The *old* war! This was going about as badly as it could go. Samantha took her hand from his and sat back. A sharp expression came into her eyes.

'It's come back to me – I can't let go of it. It's making me ill. I can't get away from it.' His voice had risen pathetically. Well, that's why he was here, wasn't it? He had to speak of it, no matter how he sounded.

'You mean memories of battle and so forth?'

'Mostly the prison. Camp Sumter. In Andersonville.'

'O-oh.' She pursed her lips, studying him. 'Well, yes,' she said slowly, nodding her head, 'that was very bad. Everyone is talking about Andersonville. That, and everything else related to the war. Almost a year later and it's still all people can talk about. It's all so . . . Oh, Jackie. I can see how it might be difficult for you.' She leaned forward and took his hand again, clasping it with both of her own, but he sensed that she had just stopped herself from saying, *It's all so tiresome.*

'You must simply stop getting the newspapers for a while,' she told him. He could smell her warm breath, stale from the biscuits. 'A complete break.' She leaned back again, as if it had all been sorted.

'I haven't. I mean, I don't read them, not for weeks. It doesn't help.'

'Well then, you must simply make yourself think of other things!'

'I thought that maybe, if I stayed with you a while, I might be able to shake it. You sometimes take in boarders, don't you? I could board here.'

Samantha drew back her chin. He noticed how sharply her chiseled cheekbones contrasted with the soft plush velvet of the armchair.

'I haven't taken in boarders since Walter's last block of railroad stocks came to term.'

'I have money . . .' He was thinking of Vita's dowry. 'I could take you to plays, we could go into Boston at night. Go to restaurants. I could help you live well.'

'I already live well.'

'Well then, live better.'

'No,' Samantha said. The word was like a rock. 'That won't do, Jacob, I'm afraid. You can't come here.'

'Why?' He hated himself for sounding so pitiful – he could see her face harden as they spoke. He would have done better had he not mentioned prison camp. The conversation had gotten away from him, and now he couldn't remember what else he'd planned to say.

'People will talk,' she said.

'About a boarder? But you've had boarders before.'

She shrugged. *It still happens.*

'Then we'll go away. Find someplace new.'

'In truth, I like where I live. I like it very much.'

'*In truth*,' Jacob said, mocking her, 'you don't want to help me.'

'Jacob, it's not that. Don't think that. I *can't* help you. That's all.'

That's all. His hand began to shake again but he did nothing to hide it, and he watched her look down, take note of the tremor, and look away.

'Well?' he asked. It had been a fool's dream to come here.

She paused. 'I don't know what else to suggest. Perhaps a doctor?'

The irony didn't escape him. 'Doctors are selfish fools,' he said.

He walked back through the slushy streets to the station, ignoring the passing cabs. The train was already at the platform when he arrived and he chose a seat in one of the forward coaches, where he could smoke. A group of soldiers jumped up into the car just as they were beginning to push off; they swayed with the car's jerky movements and fell on each other as they sat down, laughing. One of them brought out a square whiskey bottle and, without the inconvenience of glasses, the bottle was passed from mouth to mouth.

The last soldier in line offered the bottle to Jacob. It was wet at the neck and smelled of strong home brewing but Jacob took a pull anyway, feeling the peppery liquid coat his mouth. The soldiers were loud and rowdy, one or two starting songs that the others either took up or booed down. An older man wearing a glossy black hat like brushed cat fur took the opportunity to change cars at the next stop.

Jacob didn't mind them. Their noise was a distraction. He stared out the window at the passing fields, crusty with old snow, and wondered why he ever imagined Samantha would take him in. It was a battle doomed from the start. Moreover he had delayed his retreat too long, and now he felt too tired and defeated to do anything except brood on topics best avoided – Vita, or the war. His stomach rumbled; he wished now he'd eaten one of those biscuits.

When he'd been captured in the war, it was also because he'd been hungry. This was in Tennessee, near Dandridge, and his regiment was both fending off Confederate gunfire and retreating, although the other side was also retreating. Another blunder by Union commanders – who couldn't believe an enemy was ceding ground if any bullets were flying – and another successful deception by the Johnny Rebs, as the Union soldiers called them.

The war, which was supposed to last only a few months, just kept going on and on. Two years. Three years. Rumor had it that the rebels had begun using poisoned bullets, and at the time Jacob could well believe it; he'd seen one man's hand, merely scraped by a musket ball, swell to twice its size and turn black and blue overnight.

It began to rain during their skirmish near Dandridge, and it continued to rain for three days while they retreated. Everyone was hungry and cold. On the third night Jacob and a few mates decided to get off the road and sleep in an abandoned schoolhouse, where it was drier. When they woke up it was no longer raining, but they discovered that the other command had left them behind. Still, there were other Federal units around, so they decided to eat some breakfast before looking for their own men again. A half an hour later when they left the schoolhouse they found a group of six Confederate soldiers outside with their pistols raised, commanding them to halt.

As soon as he saw the men in their ill-fitting gray uniforms, Jacob was filled with the irrational desire to turn back time and make different choices, a physical urge he felt as truly as a poisoned bullet. Within minutes everything of value was taken from him: gun, haversack, overcoat, blanket, boots. He and the other prisoners spent the night in a tobacco warehouse, where he was able to buy back his blanket with the fake greenback money he'd hidden in the lining of his army cap. It was a regular, government-issue wool blanket, brown with a darker brown stripe, very worn, stinking of gunpowder and fetid mud, but it saved his life.

After another day's march he and the other prisoners were loaded onto train cars, and Jacob huddled under his blanket, trying to pass unnoticed, waiting for the chance to slip out. But the boxcar doors were fastened on the outside and there were no windows, only slits in the siding. Guards sat in each corner of the car near the water barrels, which were only half full. Six days later they were unloaded at midnight and marched by torchlight to the prison camp – an enormous palisade of huge, squared logs standing upright in the ground, maybe thirty feet high.

At first, when the gates opened and they were pushed inside, Jacob could only make out piles of rags scattered on the ground. There was no moon and it was hard to see even with the low torches the guards carried, which smelled strongly of pinesap. But when he heard a groan Jacob realized these were men, not rags. There were no tents in sight, and the ground was strewn with excrement. Later, in the daylight, the excrement and dirt would glitter with scurrying lice. A smell of rotting meat came at him as he stood there – the smell of death. Men were buried once a day in shallow pits of mud just outside the palisade, and corpses were stacked against the walls until the time came to bury them.

If only I hadn't suggested a hot breakfast, Jacob thought. If only I hadn't gone into that schoolhouse. If only I hadn't enlisted. But if wishes were horses, as his mother used to say, then beggars would ride.

'Welcome to hell,' a prison guard said, shoving him hard.

Jacob had felt the same urgent desire to turn back time the morning after his wedding day, although at first, waking up alone in the hotel bed, he hadn't been worried. Vita probably went downstairs to ask the clerk about trains, he thought, or she was conferring with her sister, or seeing about breakfast. It wasn't until the hotel maid came in with a basin of hot water and a stack of small, clean towels and left again, closing the door softly behind her, that Jacob saw the note:

I've changed my mind. I've left. You can have the money. V.

The note was held in place under a clear bottle of violet water on the washstand; he had already begun to lather his cheeks for a shave when he spotted it. He wiped the soap from his face with one of the clean towels and read it again.

I've changed my mind. I've left.

He could hear the maid rap on a door down the hall, 'Hot water, sir,' and also a pounding from outside as if men were working on the hotel's foundation, breaking a piece off or adding something new.

I've changed my mind? What did that mean? He was standing in his nightshirt and a dressing gown hastily put on for the maid, though he hadn't tied the belt properly and it was now hanging open. Something tugged at the base of his neck as though that was the spot where rational thought began; later he would feel nauseous, and then angry, and then incredulous, and then angry again. At the moment he was simply dumbfounded. He stood in his open dressing gown holding the heavy, cream-colored paper with her new initials – VTC – in his damp hand while outside the window a bird sang out: *glee, glee, glee.* Not a warning, but an aside.

While he dressed he kept picking up the note to read it again but it was no use, he could not understand it. He needed to talk to someone. He fastened his tiepin with some difficulty – his right hand had already begun to tremble – and went downstairs. From the boy at the front desk he learned that Amelia and Holland had left already on the early train.

'Will you and your wife be breakfasting with us? Would you like a table by the window?' the boy asked.

Jacob looked into the dining room, the room where only yesterday they had eaten their wedding meal, now set for breakfast. An older man sat with his wife at a table near the door, both of them wearing traveling clothes. A silver-plated rack of toast stood on the table between them. Neither one looked at the other, or spoke.

'Sir?' The desk clerk was so young that his voice cracked, and his earnest expression reminded Jacob a little of his brother Benjy. He resisted the impulse to take Vita's note from his pocket to read yet again; or to show it to the boy and ask his advice. He looked down at his hands as though to pin them in place and saw with a shock that the left one was black and blue, grotesquely large, as though he had been struck by one of the poisoned bullets – a myth, the papers were saying now. He lifted his hand quickly but as it came into the light it shrank and his fingers resumed their natural color.

The clerk was still waiting for an answer. Jacob felt something loosen and crack open. Where was she? What should he do? He had the strangest sensation that the air inside him was slowly spilling out. He must somehow turn back time. But turn it back to when?

'My wife had to take the early train,' he told the boy, 'so it will just be myself for breakfast.' He paused, wanting to say more. 'A window will be fine.'

❁

He left for Boston that afternoon without telling anyone about Vita, and he spent the last week of September and all of October waiting for her to write or appear. He joined a reading club, then a philosophy club, and then a botany club, but after the first meeting of each one he never went to another. The newspaper boy on the corner, the man who ran the cigar shop, and the woman who came to cook and clean, Mrs. Humphrey – these were the only people he spoke to. Although he did his exercises faithfully his tremors grew worse, and at night his dreams became furious battles with death. He was hung, he was chased, he was shot. Every night.

'Shall I change the sheets today, sir?' Mrs. Humphrey regularly asked. They quickly turned sour from waking up so often in a cold sweat. Also he was losing weight; his belt had become a necessity. 'My sister can cut out some new clothes for you, if you've no mind to go to a tailor,' Mrs. Humphrey told him. 'She lives right near.' That suited him, though it meant one more person to talk to.

Pride kept him from writing Mrs. Tenney until November. But it turned out she already knew; Vita had sent her a note soon after she left. Jacob and Mrs. Tenney arranged to meet to discuss it; she told her husband she wanted to go into Boston to shop. Apparently Dr. Tenney wasn't in on the secret.

'My husband can't know,' she'd said. They were sitting at a black iron-wrought table at the station restaurant, and she leaned forward to put her gloved hand on top of Jacob's. 'He's just starting to – to get control of his emotions. This would set him back. And even if it didn't, he would probably make all sorts of trouble. I think we should try to quietly look for her on our own.'

'Why would she do such a thing?' Jacob asked heatedly, drawing his hand away. He was thinking: *to me*.

'I honestly don't know. She's always been . . .' The black wrought-iron chair tilted on its uneven legs as she sat back to consider. Jacob waited. Rash, he thought. Strong-willed. Selfish.

'Fearful,' Mrs. Tenney said.

'*Fearful?*' He almost laughed.

'Not of a new challenge, but fearful of being, oh I don't know. Like everyone else. You two had an agreement, isn't that right? She was to study medicine? And you approved?'

'That's right.'

'Then I don't understand it.'

Had Vita planned to bolt all along? He was angry, but he also couldn't shake the worry that it was somehow his fault. But it wasn't his fault. He couldn't very well find a preceptor in Boston when he was living in Lark's Eye; he didn't know why she kept pressing him on that. Or was it the barrel glue? Was he wrong to suggest working together? If so, she was selfish and cruel.

He wanted to think the worst of her. Or at least part of him wanted to. The angry part.

Only last spring he thought that all he wanted in the world was enough money to make Caleb's final plans a reality – Caleb, to whom he owed his life! Then Vita came along with her penetrating stares, her soft mouth, her humor, her intensity. A lingering scent of vanilla and lead pencils. Always with a book in her pocket. She was interested in his opinions but had opinions of her own, too. Maybe that's why he thought of a partnership.

Anyway now Jacob no longer believed he could gin up a model. He'd tried, in October, to work in the little shack of a workshop that he'd rented outside the city, only a couple of train stops past Boston. But he couldn't do it. He couldn't be alone. On his very first visit his throat closed up and he started to panic. It felt like a prison.

So instead he just went once a week to check that the locks still functioned, that no vermin had gotten inside, and that the roof wasn't leaking. Then he re-locked the door and caught a train home. He had leased it (foolishly, as it turned out now) for a full six months.

He couldn't be by himself all day, and he couldn't work with a stranger. What was left for him? Going to see Samantha had been his last, desperate resort. But he was off the mark on that one, too.

By the time the train pulled into the Boston station it was so dark that Jacob could see only his own reflection in the window. The soldiers, who'd been singing 'Danny Boy' as the train clamored to a stop, were still struggling into their overcoats when Jacob stepped down onto the platform.

All he wanted now was to get home quickly and eat the dinner Mrs. Humphrey had left for him. But as he walked among the throng of people toward the exit, he suddenly smelled the strong scent of vanilla.

Vita's scent.

He stopped abruptly and looked at the women walking by. For a moment he thought, *She's here!* His heart felt warm and soft; his anger vanished. On their wedding night he'd wrapped himself in this scent, burying his nose in the nook between her shoulder and neck. She'd flattened her palms against his back, and they'd found their way together so naturally, so perfectly. Sometimes when he woke in the morning even now, just for a moment, he let himself imagine that she was lying next to him.

The smell of vanilla vanished. Maybe it was only a trick of the senses.

He noticed an old, disheveled soldier – still wearing his regulation cap and coat – sitting on a station bench watching him. He was as different as could be from the soldiers on the train. His skinny neck seemed to be on its own plane, pushing his head out unnaturally, and his cracked, unlaced boots yawned open. As Jacob approached, the man uncurled his fingers to reveal lines of oily grime on the palm of his hand. Close up, he wasn't as old as Jacob first thought. Misery drifted from him like a swamp fog.

You won't survive alone, Jacob wanted to tell him as he fished in his pocket for a coin. Even out here, in peacetime, you won't survive it.

CHAPTER FOURTEEN

'When I see a girl under twelve with a book in
her hand, I always feel an inclination to
throw it at her head.'
(Sir Benjamin Brodie, as quoted in
Gaillard's Medical Journal, 1886)

January 1866, Cleveland, Ohio

Vita pressed her fingertips against the stuffed rectangle of cushion on the chair arms to keep her concentration while Mrs. McDove cut into the cake. *The heart functions to circulate the blood*, she recited inwardly; *the right side of the heart with venous blood, and the left side with arterial blood.*

She'd wanted to stay up in her bedroom and study, but Mrs. McDove fairly commanded her to the parlor, it being a holiday – Old Christmas Day, which some called Twelfth Night. Up and down the street families were lighting bonfires in the slushy two-week-old snow and burning evergreens to ensure prosperity in the coming year. Even Mrs. McDove had built a small fire at the end of her yard, though by this time it was thoroughly doused. She wore a sprig of mistletoe pinned to her collar for luck.

'And here you are, Mrs. Culhane,' she said to Vita, handing her a piece of the apple cake. She picked up a small white pitcher. 'Cream over it?'

Mr. Nowicki, a thin cabinetmaker from Warsaw, also came down to celebrate the holiday. He was a kind, slightly reticent man who wore rimless glasses and played whist every Monday evening at the Polish Club downtown. He'd come to Cleveland last year after the Polish Uprising, and he once showed Vita the long scar on his forearm where a Russian soldier had sliced through his shirt with a saber.

He smiled his thanks as he took a plate of cake.

'And shall we indulge in a glass as well?' Mrs. McDove asked them.

But just as she put her hand on the sherry decanter they heard the front door open, followed by the loud scraping of shoes and a dramatic cough. Reverend Simpers was announcing himself home.

Mrs. McDove took her hand off the sherry. The three listened without speaking, all of them no doubt hoping they might escape the reverend's attention. But Mrs. McDove's scruples got the better of her.

'Oh, well, I suppose I should . . .' and she went out to the hall to invite him in.

Mrs. McDove was short and plump with a very round head, and usually wore pale gray dresses, as befitting her name. She ran the house with Gracelin, her maid and cook, with an efficiency Vita admired. Mrs. McDove offered fair weekly rates that included breakfast; suppers and laundry were extras. She had a softness for sweets and dessert wine, which she was happy to share in exchange for some company.

Reverend Simpers, on the other hand, possessed only an artificial veneer of kindness. Tall, with thick blond hair that curled away from his forehead like the marbled tresses on a Greek statue, his looks alone commanded attention. He had broad shoulders, a thick chest, and muscular arms; it was his heart that kept him from the war. 'It's not all that it should be,' he explained.

An understatement, Vita thought.

The two other lodgers – a pair of gentle and not quite impoverished sisters, the Misses Pickens – were out visiting an old school teacher. Their father had owned a toll road in Connecticut and they lived off his savings, supplementing their income by crocheting baby socks and making infant shoes out of broadcloth. They favored three-cornered shawls and liked to dress in matching outfits, and they carried peppermint drops in their purses for any child they encountered. They lived in a suite of rooms on the second floor, down the hall from Mrs. McDove and her son, while Mr. Nowicki and the reverend each had smaller rooms on the third floor. Vita lived in the attic.

'Well, well,' Reverend Simpers said as he stepped into the parlor behind Mrs. McDove. His gaze stopped at once on the three upturned sherry glasses. 'Not drinking, surely, at this time of day?'

He had a way of making everyone feel miserable about themselves except for the elder Miss Pickens, who could not see past his beauty. Walking through the room with an air of ownership (like a buck in his forest, Vita thought, who had been looking forward to the sherry), he wove around the motley collection of chairs before selecting Mrs. McDove's armchair to sit in, which was too small for him.

'Please, reverend, you'll be more comfortable here.' Mrs. McDove tried to usher him into a larger chair, but he liked to discomfit others when he could.

Vita and Mr. Nowicki began eating their cake a little faster. Mrs. McDove turned the sherry glasses over, and then, as if that action meant nothing more than that she was tidying the room, she straightened the needlework portrait of her late husband, which hung on the wall.

'Twelfth Night, is it?' Reverend Simpers said as he stabbed at his cake with his fork tines. His manners were not as refined as his features. 'A pagan holiday. Harmless, I suppose, but we should not make too much of it.'

He did not need to glance at the sherry decanter to make his meaning clear, although he did.

'To be sure,' Mrs. McDove said, her face reddening. 'You're quite right.'

'I've been told that in Wales they believe seals take on human form on this day.'

'Seals! My goodness.'

'Have you ever seen a seal, Mrs. McDove?'

'Well, now, let me see. You mean in the lake?'

'Lake Erie? A seal in Lake Erie? Ha ha ha! I should think not.' He watched Mrs. McDove's cheeks flush a deeper pink before he turned to Vita. 'Our kindly landlady wonders if she might have seen a *seal* in *Lake Erie.*' His laughs, like all his laughs, pretended to be good-natured but was not. There was nothing Reverend Simpers liked better than catching people out.

Vita, who did not want to share in a joke at Mrs. McDove's expense, resolved not to accept another piece of cake. Only five minutes ago the room had been a cozy respite with its glowing coal fire, its worn and comfortable chairs, and, in the back corner, Mrs. McDove's collection of mirrors hanging from chains, jingling slightly when the air stirred. Through the long windows on either side of the fireplace Vita could see the city air full of smoke, which turned crimson in the late afternoon on account of the factory furnaces. The odors wafted through the thin walls of her attic bedroom, which overlooked the street, and sometimes woke her in the morning after the furnaces were relit for the day.

It was in the morning that she was most homesick for Lark's Eye, for the smell of long, wet grass and salty wind. She missed her bedroom window seat, and Mrs. O.'s warm kitchen, and Sweetie nudging her ear. Of course, here she could skip supper entirely and study in her room past midnight. She could do whatever she wanted. Last night she placed a thin sheet of onion paper over a textbook illustration charting the course of the brachial artery, and when she finished tracing it she tacked the copy above her desk next to her other drawings: the blood vessels of the lungs, the contours of digestive organs, and the course of the femoral artery down the thigh. The human body was so complex, so neatly compact, bone and vein and muscle tissue interlayered but also distinct. She liked to stand in front of her desk in the mornings and admire the drawings. The beauty of the machinery.

But there was no Gemma to talk to, and no Mitty, and no Sweetie. Instead of sand dunes there were trees, and instead of hills there were long brick factory chimneys. Even the water tasted different here.

She tried not to think about Jacob.

'And what has our little doctor been doing today?' Reverend Simpers asked, landing on Vita as his next victim.

He had white, pointed teeth, like a cat's. If she used vocabulary he didn't know, he smiled at her as though she were a precocious yet misguided child.

'I've been studying arterial blood flow.'

When Vita first moved into the house, she tried to make her case as a war widow in need of employment. 'My father is a country doctor,' she explained, 'so it feels quite natural.' But the reverend made no secret of his disapproval.

'In my opinion,' he liked to say, 'women can enter any profession they wish just as soon as they learn the right way to get off a streetcar.' He always attacked with a smile on his face.

But before the reverend could form his assault on her there was a banging from the hallway and Mrs. McDove's son Stewart – Soot – came into the room, knocking his shoes on the bottom of the door. He was eight years old but carried himself like the man of the house.

'Hello, my young sir,' Mr. Nowicki said, smiling gently. 'Out looking at the bonfires?'

'Oh, Soot, my precious, mind your feet,' Mrs. McDove scolded.

Soot paid his mother no attention but made his way straight to Vita. 'Did you bring your book down with you?'

'You don't have to do your learning today,' Mrs. McDove told him. 'It's a holiday.'

Vita was giving Soot lessons as part of her rent. When he did well she let him look at her anatomy book as a reward; Soot loved its gruesomely vivid illustrations.

Reverend Simpers cleared his throat. 'Stewart, why don't you tell us what Christian deeds you've been up to today?'

Soot ignored him. He lifted his foot and knocked his heel a few times.

'Won't you go get your slippers on?' Mrs. McDove asked. 'My floor will thank you for it.'

'No it won't! Floors don't have feelings. Or a mouth.'

Vita and Mr. Nowicki looked at each other and smiled. Soot was a favorite with all the lodgers except Reverend Simpers, who resented any distraction away from himself. He caught their smile and forced a laugh.

'Well! I see you do have a brain in that pumpkin shell, don't you?'

'He's a smart boy,' Mr. Nowicki said in his soft, melancholy voice.

The reverend must have taken this as a criticism of his comment, for he said more forcefully, 'Pumpkin shell. That's what we call a head like that.'

Mrs. McDove held out a hand to her son. 'Well, come along then and give your mother a kiss.'

But instead Soot went to the window to look out at the neighbors' bonfires. 'Why do we have feelings, anyway?' he asked after a moment.

'Why, to tell us right from wrong, of course!' Reverend Simpers boomed importantly.

Soot didn't reply. Somehow it was obvious from his back that he didn't care for that answer.

'If we didn't feel pain from a fire,' Vita said, 'we wouldn't draw our hand back from it.'

'You saying pain keeps us alive?' Soot asked.

She hadn't thought of it that way. She glanced at Mr. Nowicki, who had been beaten nearly to death by the same Russian soldier who sliced up his arm.

'It's good we have a brain to remind us what can hurt,' Mr. Nowicki told Soot, 'so we don't make the same mistake again. To remember the feeling of pain, that is what helps us.'

'What about heart feelings?'

'Heart feelings!' The reverend laughed. 'My little man, you don't have to worry about that, not for years.'

As if children don't have strong feelings, Vita thought. Soot was facing her now, his young soft face working hard to look serious. It was a serious question. *The heart functions to circulate the blood*, she thought. She felt sorry for the elder Miss Pickens, who was in love with Reverend Simpers; he knew she was in love with him and he played with her as though she had a chance. Mr. Nowicki had been in love with a young woman lost in the insurrection – that was how he put it to Vita – and Mrs. McDove's husband had died in a mill accident when Soot was a baby. Even the younger Miss Pickens had lost someone, a fiancé who'd been killed in the first year of the war.

What *about* heart feelings? Vita wondered. Jacob's warm breath came back to her, his dark eyes, the mole near his eyelid, the way he watched her closely when she spoke. It had been nearly four months since she'd left him in Lark's Eye. She didn't want to think about him, but she did.

She set her fork down on her empty plate. 'That's something else,' she said.

Her plan was to finish reading Quincy's *Dispensatory* while it was still light out, but as she was going up to her room she heard a knock on the front door.

'Why, Dr. Boutwell,' Mrs. McDove said. 'Come in, come in – there, let's get you out of the wind. I'll fetch Mrs. Culhane.'

Dr. Boutwell, Vita's preceptor, sometimes came to fetch her if he was on his way to visit a patient at home. Part of your training, he explained.

'A young girl with a toothache,' he told Vita as she fetched her cloak. 'Might be infected. Her mother sent me a note.'

He looked the part of a doctor in his long, fitted gray coat and matching brushed hat. He was a trim, compact man in his late forties with closely cropped black hair, a thin mustache like an upside-down U, high cheekbones and slanted almond-colored eyes. He carried his doctor's bag in his left hand and a brass-topped cane – he had a weak ankle – in his right. Vita could see a couple of cigars wrapped in letter paper leaning out from his coat pocket; he handed these out to male patients after a difficult treatment. In the other pocket he kept a waxed bag of sugared almonds for children.

'Never noticed the name of your rooming house before.' He glanced at her. 'Is that why you chose it?'

The name of it was The Frederick.

'Yes,' Vita said.

Dr. Boutwell had been Freddy's closest friend in the army and the reason why Vita chose Cleveland – that and the fact the Cleveland Medical College admitted women as students as well as men. Vita remembered the letter he had written to her father about Freddy. Surely, she'd thought on the train leaving Lark's Eye, he wouldn't refuse to help his friend's sister?

Outside, streams of lint-colored smoke curled up from the house chimneys, and passing horses wore blankets over their necks. Vita tried not to look down at the gutter, which was strewn with wet paper, potato peelings, and the glistening blue edges of spoiled meat. Garbage collection in the city was at best inconsistent; only that morning she had read in the newspaper a new ordinance against throwing dead cats in the street.

At the corner Vita noticed a group of soldiers lined up near the steps of the Methodist church, waiting for soup. All of them were ragged and hungry-looking. A few had sewn their coat sleeves closed to protect the stub of arm they had left, while others simply let their empty sleeves flap listlessly in the wind. A flag of the defeated, regardless of which side they fought for. Just as Vita and Dr. Boutwell were passing, the minister came out of the church doors; he smiled down at the two of them as though they shared something with him merely by their proximity, or maybe because they were still whole, whereas the soldiers lined up for soup were not.

She wondered where Jacob was now – in the little house he'd found for them in Boston? She still felt her breath catching in her throat when she went to the hall table after breakfast to look at the mail. Of course there was never a letter from him. How could there be? She knew that she was to blame, if there was blame. She'd panicked, that was the truth. But he didn't believe in her, either – he didn't think she could do it. And now she had a carefully arranged life, a proverbial house of cards. She couldn't risk anything – anyone – dismantling that.

'It's just up ahead,' Dr. Boutwell said.

Maybe he was living with Samantha. She tried not to imagine that.

They turned down a narrow street with identical wooden houses standing shoulder to shoulder. Two lines of bare, winter trees stretched their spindly branches over the road as if hoping and failing to grasp each other in the middle. For all that it was Twelfth Night, no one was lighting bonfires on this block, as there were no yards to speak of. Just houses and mud.

A young woman with smallpox scars on her cheeks opened the door. As she took their wraps she looked at Vita curiously but only said, 'You can follow me up, if you please.'

In the small bedroom at the top of the stairs a girl was sitting up in bed, her eyes red-rimmed and swollen. She looked to be about eight or nine, Vita guessed. Her mother sat on a wooden kitchen chair beside her, holding a vinegary-smelling piece of bread against her daughter's jaw.

'Home remedy,' Dr. Boutwell told Vita later. 'Other times I've come in to find a patient with a mouth full of salt.'

Besides the bed, the room had a washstand and a long trunk covered by a fringed biscuit-colored shawl. The walls were painted white and there was a plain wooden cross hanging over the washstand in lieu of a mirror. There were no books or pictures, and only one window that looked out at the chipped roof shingles of the house next door, an arm's length away.

The mother, standing up to give Dr. Boutwell her chair, thanked them for coming.

'Of course. Toothache, is it?' he said in his gentle voice as he sat down. 'Oh my, that's painful.' He folded his hands together to show the girl that he was not going to touch her yet. 'What's your name?' he asked her.

'Elsie Ann Archer,' she told him, trying not to move her mouth too much. She wore several knitted shawls over her nightdress.

'Elsie Ann, what a pretty name. I've seen your neighbor, Mrs. Crocker, and she recommended me to your mother.' He smiled at her. 'So that means we're not complete strangers. Now then, Elsie Ann – or do they call you just Elsie?'

'Just Elsie,' Elsie answered.

'All right, Elsie. My assistant will look at your tooth first, and after that I'll take a peek.'

Mrs. Archer looked around for the assistant. By now Vita was used to that. She pulled the washstand stool over to the other side of the bed and asked Elsie to open her mouth. A sour odor like a rotten egg exuded from her mouth when she did.

'A little wider, please,' Vita said. After Dr. Boutwell's soft voice, her own seemed to crash through the room. Elsie's mouth was small, with neat rows of white teeth resting on her pink gums like tiny wet pearls. Vita looked curiously at the line of necks and crowns, the sharp canines used to tear meat, the molars for crushing it. The mechanics of breaking down food starts here. She was most interested in the enamel, which was, she'd recently learned, even harder than bones.

She could see one tooth that was darker than the others. The gum tissue beneath it was swollen and inflamed.

'Lower jaw,' she said. 'Left mandibular.'

Still with her mouth gaping open, Elsie's eyes followed Dr. Boutwell as he leaned over to peer in himself.

'Right, the second molar. Very good.' Dr. Boutwell sat back. 'You can close your mouth now, Elsie. Thank you.'

He told her they were going to have to take the tooth out, and that after that her pain would be over. 'It's a back tooth,' he said, 'so no one will see that it's gone, even when you smile, and it's a baby tooth, which means that another one will grow in its place. What do you think? Is that all right? Can we take it out for you?'

Elsie's eyes filled with tears but she nodded. He was a gentle, thorough, considerate physician, and even new patients seemed to trust him.

'It won't hurt much. It will hurt a little, but not much. And we'll be quick about it.'

Vita washed up while Dr. Boutwell instructed Mrs. Archer to make up a poultice for her daughter, writing out exactly what it should include. He asked her to boil some water as well and bring that up, too.

'Now then,' he said, turning to Vita after Mrs. Archer had gone downstairs. 'Think you can do this?'

The poultice-making had been a ruse to get the mother away. Elsie looked over at Vita with such scared eyes that Vita felt she had to say, 'Of course!' right away, trying to convey utter confidence. But her heartbeat quickened. She'd watched Dr. Boutwell pull teeth a half a dozen times over the last few months, but she had never pulled one herself.

After she helped him organize the instruments, Vita sat down next to Elsie. Elsie stretched open her mouth again and closed her eyes as Dr. Boutwell handed Vita the small metal pincers. Vita clamped them on Elsie's carious tooth.

She tried to imitate Dr. Boutwell's gentle smile, but it felt like a grimace.

'All right?' she asked. Elsie's scanty eyebrows went up and she closed her eyes. Inhaling, Vita gave the tooth a tug. Nothing. She tugged again, but the tooth didn't budge. Elsie, her eyes still shut, whimpered softly.

'Nice and strong,' Dr. Boutwell instructed.

Vita tightened her grip on the pincers and yanked hard. A loud crunching noise came from the girl's mouth.

'Mm-aah,' Elsie cried.

Vita pulled the pincers out. A white, bloodstained tooth with a long root was dangling from the instrument's blunt blades along with, to her horror, a piece of gleaming white bone. I've broken off part of her jaw, she thought in a panic, and her stomach tilted and then constricted. Meanwhile Elsie's mouth was running with blood. Dr. Boutwell handed Vita squares of white gauze and she began stuffing them into Elsie's mouth.

'Gently,' Dr. Boutwell reminded her.

She told herself to slow down. She packed the gauze against Elsie's gum, and when the gauze was soaked through she lifted it out with a pair of smaller pincers and packed in another pad. She lasted three rounds of this before she turned away and made for the washbasin, where she was sick.

'That's fine, I can finish up now,' Dr. Boutwell said behind her in a calm voice. 'Elsie, you were a brave girl and now it's all done. You're going to feel very much better after this. Tell me, do you rinse your mouth out every night before going to bed? Just nod or shake your head.' He then proceeded to give her instructions for the care of her teeth.

Vita, wiping her sick away with her handkerchief, felt as if every bone in her body was made of tissue paper. Would Elsie's jaw get infected? Would she die of gangrene? She was afraid to look at Dr. Boutwell.

'You broke off the tooth socket, that's all,' he told her when they were back on the street. By this time it was fully dark out, and the trees on either side of the road looked like a line of skinny dark soldiers standing guard.

'You mean that wasn't a piece of her jawbone?'

'Is that what you thought?' Dr. Boutwell laughed, but not unkindly. 'No, no, nothing like that. Only a bit of the socket. Don't worry. You did fine.'

But she could not break free from the image of the tooth socket, the raw hole in Elsie's mouth, the odor of rotted eggs. The first time she went on a patient visit with Dr. Boutwell it was to see a young boy with a broken arm, and as Dr. Boutwell was setting it Vita had to turn away to be sick. That had been in a tiny, hot bedroom that was more like a closet, and she told herself the closed space was the reason. But she was sick again when she watched Dr. Boutwell pull a ball bearing out of a man's shoulder with a pair of needle-nosed pliers, and when he cleaned a grocer's festering chest wound, and when together they examined a woman's head lesion to find it crawling with tiny red insects.

'You'll get used to the sight of that,' Dr. Boutwell told her each time.

Now he said, 'Pulling a tooth takes a bit of practice,' and then, when Vita said nothing, he patted her arm. 'Next one will be easier.'

Mrs. McDove was in the hallway when Vita walked in. 'Oh Mrs. Culhane, you're home. Supper's in ten minutes if you're taking it.'

She had no money to pay for the meal but she heard herself say, 'Thank you, yes.' She was hungry and tired, and Mrs. McDove wouldn't give her the bill until next week. She tugged off her cold gloves and scrunched her fingers to warm them.

'Is that our little doctor back from her house call?' Reverend Simpers called from the parlor. Before she could escape he came out, newspaper in hand. 'So what was the terrible emergency you had to rush off to?'

He was so much larger than she was, and he liked to hover. Vita stepped back, trying to regain her own space. 'I pulled a tooth.'

'A tooth! Did you really? You pulled a tooth? My, my.' He smiled at Mrs. McDove and then at Vita, enjoying himself. 'All your months of training, and finally you can perform that delicate operation! You've learned at last to pull out instead of push in? Ha, ha!'

His laughter was over in two breaths, like the back and forth of a razor.

'My old granny used to pull our teeth. Afterwards she gave us lumps of sugar to stop us howling. Perhaps you should take your lessons from her. I'm sure she would charge you much less than the doctor!'

Vita felt a familiar swirl of anger in her chest. 'And I'm sure she didn't know the first thing about teeth or anything else,' she snapped.

This was just what he was hoping for.

'Oh now, don't be angry, Mrs. Culhane. I was merely making a joke! My, you do have a temper, don't you?' He shook his head. 'I'm not sure you have the patience to be a doctor. Or the self-control, or the discipline. All traits that a woman naturally lacks. Am I right, Mrs. McDove? Can you imagine a woman commanding a ship?'

The ventricles, after expelling blood into the arteries, immediately begin to dilate, Vita recited to herself, trying to keep from saying anything more. His leap from doctors to ship captains had so many logical discrepancies that she didn't know where to begin, but battling him would only result in further insults – she had been on this roundabout before. She couldn't let his prejudices stop her, just as she couldn't let her father's prejudices stop her. After she finished Quincy's *Dispensatory*, she wanted to organize her reading for next week. Tomorrow she'd have to sell Aunt Norbert's second gold coin. Soon, before she was out of funds completely, she needed to write the Cleveland Medical College requesting an interview, and then she would probably need to find another job – more tutoring? – to support her while she attended classes.

'Off to study up on how to pull a splinter from a fingertip?' Reverend Simpers asked as she turned to go upstairs. She didn't have to look at him, she could practically hear his smug smile. She forced herself to take the stairs slowly, to ignore his taunts. But when she was in her own room at last with the door shut behind her, she pressed her pillow against her face and began to cry.

No, the thing that would stop her was the impossibility of it all.

CHAPTER FIFTEEN

'And when the ladies get degrees
Depend on it there's naught will please
Till they have got our chairs and fees
And there's an end of you and me.'
(Boston Medical and Surgical Journal,
Anonymous, 1873)

When she first came to Cleveland, Vita cried every day. She cried because she was anxious, or exhausted, or discouraged, or simply overwhelmed by all the new experiences piling up one on top of each other without pause. She was never overwhelmed back in Lark's Eye. In Lark's Eye, she was the one who knew everything, or thought she did.

'It will be a waste of your time and money,' Dr. Boutwell had said when she first approached him about being her preceptor. They were standing in his office, two small rooms above a Levantine store that sold patterned carpets. Vita had found his address in the city directory.

'They won't accept you into the medical program here,' he told her. 'I'm sorry, but they won't.' He meant because she was a woman.

'But Emily Blackwell graduated from the Cleveland Medical College.'

'You mean Elizabeth. She graduated from a college in New York, and originally she was accepted only as a joke.'

'No, not Elizabeth; her sister, Emily,' Vita had said. 'Emily received a degree from the medical college here.'

She'd been in Cleveland for only three days but had already found her way to the medical college, an imposing stone building on St. Clair Avenue. Vita, staring up at the windows, could imagine the classrooms inside: rows of desks facing a podium, diagrams sketched in chalk on a blackboard. Her heart lifted at the thought of sitting on a stool, taking notes among students who, like herself, were excited to learn about arteries and endemic fevers.

'Well, they might have accepted her a few years ago,' Dr. Boutwell said, 'before the war, but . . .'

Vita stopped listening and began instead to recite to herself the bones of the hand – *scaphoid, lunate, triquetrum, pisiform* – because she'd learned from long experience that the first answer always was no. She was also trying to suppress her worries over what she'd done; to appear mature and confident. The office window was open a crack to let in the breeze – it was just as humid here, even in September, as it had been in Lark's Eye – and she watched glittering crumbs of dust float down toward the floorboards.

Dr. Boutwell's office building was the runt of the block, but it was downtown, just off Public Square, right in the heart of the city. That was exciting. Riding the horsecar, which here they called a streetcar, was exciting, too, and also watching the enormous barges slough their way across Lake Erie, a body of water so vast it might easily be called a sea.

Iron and oil had changed Cleveland overnight from a village to a full-blown city. Almost twice as many people lived here now, Mrs. McDove told her, than lived here before the war began. Cheap wooden houses with taverns on every corner could be found in The Haymarket, south of Public Square; yet not too distant from that was Euclid Avenue, which they called Millionaires' Row for its lavish mansions and the stately elm trees lining the road. There was a new city fire department with a telegraph system to sound the alarms, and the downtown streets were lit with gas lamps from sunset to midnight. Mills, foundries, wholesale houses, shipyards – almost any imaginable industry could be found on the waterfront along the Cuyahoga River, known as The Flats. It seemed to Vita that every Clevelander was busy at all times either making money or spending it.

Lark's Eye, which had felt isolated and dull before, now seemed so slow in comparison that it might be dead. In spite of her fears, or maybe because of them, Vita vowed to herself that she would stay in Cleveland until someone dragged her away or buried her standing up, facing her enemies, like an ancient Irish warrior. She wouldn't back down.

'Still, for Freddy's sake,' she'd said when at last Dr. Boutwell finished listing all the problems with her plan, 'won't you take me on?'

For a moment she thought she had him. But then he shook his head and began telling her no all over again.

It took her three tries to convince him. On the last visit, when he opened his door to find her standing in the hallway yet again, Dr. Boutwell had sighed theatrically and raised his shoulders, giving up.

'But only because you might be able to find work as a midwife, or work with a doctor later as his assistant. You can at least earn a living that way.'

'I'll be a doctor,' she insisted, 'not an assistant.'

She kept in her pocket a list of women doctors:

Elizabeth and Emily Blackwell, now practicing in New York
Linda Folger Fowler, now teaching in Rochester
Harriot Hunt, practicing medicine since 1835
Trotula of Salerno, an 11th-century Italian doctor and professor
Aspasia, a specialist in obstetrics in Greece, 450 B.C.

There was also:

Jane Hawkins, denounced as a witch in 1641 and expelled from Boston
Margaret Jones, denounced as a witch in 1648 and executed in Boston

'But medical colleges, all of them, are notoriously difficult –'

'I'll prepare like nothing else,' Vita interrupted. 'The one thing I know how to do is study.'

He paused. 'As a doctor you must learn how to listen, too.'

'That won't be a problem,' she promised.

He had opened his office door holding a small kettle in his hand; now, motioning her in, he turned to put it on the coal stove. 'Well you'll have to get your own teacup,' he said, 'because I only have one.'

❁

The morning after she pulled Elsie Archer's tooth, Vita walked to work as usual to save money. The temperature had dropped overnight and slushy piles of old snow lining the street had frozen into pitted drifts.

She saw patients with Dr. Boutwell in his office from Monday through Thursday, and on Fridays they both volunteered at the Old Soldiers' Home near the train station. On very cold or rainy days Vita took the streetcar to his office, but in truth she preferred to walk. She liked the bustle of the crowded sidewalks and the sense of urgency as men hawked their wares – knife-sharpeners, rag collectors, muffin sellers, and every other kind of tradesmen she could imagine.

'Outta my way there!' a man rolling a barrel down the sidewalk shouted at an errand boy trotting toward him.

'Oy! Git gone yourself.'

Men in well-cut coats and brushed hats greeted each other from opposite corners, raising their voices to be heard over the grumbling delivery carts: 'Are you going to Nisbet's next week?' 'Wouldn't miss it!'

Such an exchange would never happen in Lark's Eye, where a lifted hand might begin the conversation and another hand lifted back would end it. In Lark's Eye, merchants waited in shops for customers to find *them*, but in Cleveland everything was a public hustle. Maybe it was like this in every growing city.

She'd written to her mother from the train station in Boston while she waited for the connection to Cleveland. After she left Jacob that morning, trying to come up with a plan, Vita remembered Dr. Boutwell's letter to Freddy. Cleveland, then. She didn't want Mitty to worry, but she also didn't tell her where she was.

I've gone to train to be a doctor. As we discussed. This has been my dream forever and I know I can do it. Please don't worry. And please don't tell Dar. Jacob isn't with me, but I'm perfectly safe. P.S. Take care of Sweetie for me.

Two days later, she wrote to Gemma:

I'm in Cleveland and I'll send you a fixed address as soon as I'm settled. Please write to me with news. No one else knows where I am, and I don't want them to know. It's strange to live in a city.

Let me know if you hear anything about Jacob.

But Gemma, as she told Vita in her return letter, had heard nothing about Jacob.

Clouds ruffled overhead and coupled with blowing smoke from the factories. Vita pushed thoughts of Jacob away yet again. She needed to concentrate on her studies, only her studies. She'd made her choice. As she neared Public Square the lake wind grew fiercer, slapping her cheeks with an icy hand. She wished she'd stolen a warmer cloak from the hotel in Lark's Eye.

'Tea?' Dr. Boutwell asked when Vita got to the office. 'The water's just boiled.'

He came in early each morning to light the stove, which meant the little office was always warm by the time she arrived. Vita nodded, unwinding her half-frozen scarf and taking off the mittens she was wearing over her gloves. She pulled off her boots and placed them in the wooden crate near the door, and then she stepped into the pair of soft-soled shoes she kept in the office. The black smock she wore every day over her dress had two large front pockets, which held a pencil attached to a long notebook, a silver-plated tongue depressor, plasters and small splints, and thumb-sized capsules of quinine, iron citrate, tincture of cardamom, and other doses of what they regularly administered. Dr. Boutwell kept his larger instruments rolled up in a long leather strip, which he unrolled on the windowsill (for the light) when he needed to choose one. The entire office was comprised of two small rooms, plus a tiny office in the back – a closet really – where they kept tonics and pills and unmixed powders for medicine.

Vita mixed up a basin of chlorinated water and began washing her hands. Dr. Boutwell had drilled into her the importance of this.

'A Hungarian doctor, a man named Ignaz Semmelweis, discovered that doctors with unclean hands could carry diseases to their patients,' he'd explained on her very first day. 'That was almost twenty years ago now, and the evidence keeps mounting, although there was a great outcry, I can tell you, when the man first published his findings.'

Dr. Boutwell had all the current medical journals delivered to his office and he loaned them, along with his textbooks, to Vita with a generous spirit. He'd been only fourteen when he got a job as an apothecary boy in Cleveland, delivering powders to doctors. Later he studied at the University of Toronto, where his first practical study was the human wrist.

'I'll never forget my surprise over the beauty of the tendons,' he said. 'I had expected many things, but not beauty.'

Vita dried her hands and checked the water level in the corner barrel. Her goal today was to make no mistakes. That was her goal every day.

'Shall I turn the shingle?' Dr. Boutwell asked.

He went to the window and flipped the wooden sign so it faced the street: *Dr. D.A. Boutwell, Physician and Surgeon.*

The day had begun.

❁

Their first patient was a lean man with a bad stomach; Dr. Boutwell asked Vita to mix a dose of Columbia powder with magnesium for him to take home with him. After that they saw a tall, bony woman with sores in her mouth (rosewater, ammonia, and honey mouthwash), an old man who needed gout pills (gum guaiacum and camphor with ginger syrup), and a young boy who slunk in behind his mother.

'He's dizzy and sick at his stomach all the day and he's got headaches at night,' the mother explained. She was a short woman with long, full lips that drooped into a permanent frown. 'Yesterday before supper he fainted right there in my kitchen, almost caught the corner end of my stove.'

Dr. Boutwell touched the boy's forehead. He looked at Vita. 'Do you have any questions for the lad?'

She could tell he knew already what the trouble was, but she was at a loss.

'Maybe his eyes?' Dr. Boutwell prompted.

'Have you had any trouble with your eyes?' Vita asked.

'Spots sometimes,' the boy whispered. He was only eleven or so, all elbows and knees like a fast-growing colt. 'White spots.'

'Did you see them before you fainted?'

'I did, ma'am.'

She had to bend close to hear him. His lips were swollen, she noticed. She touched his belly, which felt swollen, too. She asked the boy more questions, eliminating dropsy, bilious fever, and cholera, but she was still no closer until Dr. Boutwell asked the boy how his appetite was.

'Eating my cupboards bare,' the mother said for him.

Ah. 'Ringworm?' Vita looked at Dr. Boutwell.

'Tapeworm, more likely.'

Tapeworm! She should have thought of that immediately, but the fainting put her off track. The commonest cause is the commonest culprit, Dr. Boutwell liked to say. He was still looking at her expectantly.

'For that we give,' Vita said, hoping her voice would prompt her memory, 'for that we prepare . . .'

'Kousso,' Dr. Boutwell reminded her.

The kousso plant. Of course. She found the powdered mixture in the little closet in the far room where they kept their supplies, and although she could not hear Dr. Boutwell from there, she felt sure he was giving the boy a sugared almond while asking the mother to return with him next week so they could check the efficacy of the cure. He kept a lined accountant's notebook in which he recorded every patient's ailment and the medicine he prescribed. The indigo ink he favored faded to purple as the months went by, and Vita knew this because he often asked her to look up a case; he remembered dates with an accuracy she envied.

Just as they were about to close for lunch, a young man came into the office wearing a striped scarf and matching cap in two shades of blue. He introduced himself as John Gaines, and told them he was suffering from headaches and what he called 'heart ticks.' He had a lean face, and this along with his ginger hair and darting eyes put Vita in mind of a fox who'd wandered into a city. Out of his element, perhaps, but more curious than afraid.

'Heart *ticks*?' Dr. Boutwell asked. 'What do you mean by ticks?'

'Up and down. Sudden spurts.'

Dr. Boutwell looked at Vita. 'Heart palpitations,' she suggested, and Dr. Boutwell nodded in agreement. He asked the young man to sit.

'My ma tried the clamshell and sugar cure on me, and also the cold water cure of standing in cold water up to my ankles. A doctor over on Pearl Street said not to eat limes, pickles, or currants, but that didn't help neither.'

'Would you kindly hold out your hand? My assistant will take your pulse.'

Like Elsie Archer's mother, John Gaines looked around for his assistant. When Vita stepped closer he drew his head back and narrowed his eyes at her.

She turned his wrist over and found the artery. 'Heartbeat is normal,' she said after a minute, and then gave him back his hand. John Gaines touched the place where her fingers had been.

'You been helping the doctor long?' he asked her. His breath smelled like rank pork and molasses.

'I'm studying to be one,' she said.

He narrowed his eyes again, considering that. His chin was small and sharp, and his long nose seemed to point to it.

'What do you do for a living, Mr. Gaines?' Dr. Boutwell asked.

It turned out he did nothing. When he came back from the war, his mother didn't want him to stray too far so she could keep an eye on him.

'My ma takes in boarders and I look after things like fetching the coal and keeping up the fires,' he said. 'But then a shaking moved into my heart and I couldn't carry coal no more for fear that something might burst in me. I'm thinking I should take to my bed. Am I dying?' he asked stoutly, almost as if he hoped he was. 'You can tell me straight out.'

The sudden lift in his voice made Vita think he wanted some excitement. Dr. Boutwell must have thought so too, since after examining his eyes and throat, touching his lymph nodes, and then touching his back to check the size of his liver, he told John Gaines he was nowhere near dying.

'You need more employment; that's all. You're a strong young man. And the war is over.'

'Not fer my ma it ain't.'

'She'll learn to live without you during the day. After all, she lived without you when you were off fighting.'

'What about my, what d'you call 'em, my palprations?'

'Palpitations. I can give you some iron pills,' Dr. Boutwell told him. He turned to Vita. 'Will you fetch the young man a cup of water? I'll return directly,' he said as he went into the back room.

John Gaines's eyes followed Vita as she made her way to the barrel in the corner. Sinking the dipper into the water a strange feeling came over her, as though a thin string of spider web had brushed up against her skin. When she turned around John Gaines was standing right behind her, close enough to touch. How had he crept up so silently?

He leered at her. 'So you aim to be a doctor, do you?'

For some men, a barrier went down once you touched them; after that, according to a logic Vita couldn't fathom (but by this time recognized), you were fair game for being touched yourself. She had learned to step back quickly, but John Gaines was quicker and he grabbed her by the forearm.

'Let me thank you for checking my pains.' His lips were open and wet.

'That's enough,' she told him, wrenching her arm away.

He grabbed her again. 'Oh, now, don't take offense.'

She tried to pull away again but this time his grip was firmer.

'Unless you're the type that don't care for a man's thanks?'

'Let go of me.'

He was still grinning. With his free hand he tried to grab the space between her legs but all he got was a fistful of black smock. Spreading his long fingers he went for her breast but Vita dodged sideways, her back twisting painfully. He made a sound – *tchunh!* – his tongue popping from the roof of his mouth. He tugged her arm hard, trying to force her into a better position for his grabs.

'Let go!'

'Only if you promise to meet me later.'

With her free hand Vita made a fist and cuffed him on the ear just as Dr. Boutwell came back into the room, a paper twist of pills in his hand.

'Ow! Hey there!' John Gaines shouted, letting go of her to clutch his ear.

'What's happening here?' Dr. Boutwell asked, although he could tell at a glance what was happening and quickly stepped between them.

'Here are your pills, Mr. Gaines, and now you can pay me fourteen cents and be off. Go back to your doctor on Pearl Street next time, or go see Dr. Neville up the street. But don't come back here.'

John Gaines still had his hand clapped to his head. 'I should get the pills for free on account of my burst ear.'

'It's not burst. My fourteen cents, if you please.'

Vita, her heart still racing, disciplined herself not to rub her bruised arm. She didn't want to let John Gaines know how much his grip had hurt – to give him that satisfaction. After he left, Dr. Boutwell closed the door and locked it. It was almost noon anyway, when they usually closed for lunch. Vita sat down on the wooden stool in front of the stove, opened the little door and, as if to change the subject, began pushing around the ashy coals with a poker. She was trying hard not to cry.

'Oh, Vita,' Dr. Boutwell said, putting a hand on her shoulder.

He was like an older brother to her; he was like Freddy. It was his sympathy more than anything else that brought on her tears. Dr. Boutwell pulled a handkerchief from his pocket.

'He's a troubled young man. He doesn't have enough to occupy him, but that's no excuse.'

'It's not only him,' she said, wiping tears from her chin. 'It's everything. All of it. It's all so . . . so physical.'

Touching patients' wrists, their damp foreheads, the insides of their mouths; and having some of them, like John Gaines, try to touch her back – she hadn't anticipated how hard that would be. She was someone who read books and memorized lists. The parts of the outer ear. The bones of the hand. That's what she thought doctoring was about. But in common practice she was failing, hardly able to diagnose a condition even if she'd read and memorized the symptoms, like tapeworm.

How could I be so bad at all this? she wondered. Back in Lark's Eye it never occurred to her that her usual diligence and concentration wouldn't be enough. She loved reading about the intricacies of the nervous system, or the infection rate of smallpox, or the earmarks of malaria, but when faced with an actual patient she always seemed to falter. Even with John Gaines, she had faltered. She might have thought of iron pills.

Would she ever be able to diagnose an ailment on the spot? And if she did, would the patients believe her? Would the men? There were more John Gaineses in the world than she had imagined.

'You're tough,' Dr. Boutwell said. 'But it takes time, and it also takes practice.'

She'd been at it for over three months. Maybe she couldn't do it.

'Wanting to do something is a long way from doing it well,' she said.

'Well, that's true. And it will be harder for you than for the others, for the young men. But I don't have to tell you that.'

Jacob had warned her that her gender would get in the way. He was right.

'I thought doctoring would be hard,' she said, 'but hard like solving an algebra problem is hard. If you've memorized how parts of the body function and break, and the mechanisms to fix what breaks – medicines and so on, surgery, whatever is needed – well then, it would simply be a matter of memory and application. I'm good at that. But there's more guesswork than I thought. And the patients, they move around and talk.'

He smiled at that, as she meant him to, but she was thinking: And grab at you, and make lewd suggestions.

'Some of them talk quite a bit,' he said. 'And they don't always tell you the truth.'

'I'm not good with people. I never have been. I didn't think it would matter.'

He frowned in sympathy. 'All we can do is listen and look. And ask questions. Think of your patients as textbooks, if that helps. The clues are there to be read.'

It sounded easy, the way he put it. But it wasn't.

'It should be Freddy sitting here, not me. He's the one who should be here.'

She hadn't known she was going to say that. She hadn't even known she thought that. Looking up, she saw an expression flick over Dr. Boutwell's face, like a butterfly touching down on a flower only briefly before changing its mind.

'But you know,' he said, 'Freddy wouldn't want to be here. He wanted to work with animals, be a horse doctor perhaps, a veterinarian, only he was afraid of what your father would say.'

'Is that true?' Vita was surprised. It sounded like Freddy, but Freddy had never breathed a word about this to her.

'You look so much like him. But he didn't have your ambition.'

'My father hates my ambition.'

'I'm sure he would be proud if he saw how hard you're working.'

Would he? She always hoped Dar would be proud of her; she couldn't remember a time when she didn't. The idea of his respect was like a child's pretend friend, useful but imaginary. She usually avoided talk of her parents, letting Dr. Boutwell assume that they knew what she was doing. She was even more secretive about Jacob. A war widow, she called herself. Sometimes, in her weaker moments – like now – she wondered if Jacob would take her back. Maybe she should abandon this experiment.

She looked down at Dr. Boutwell's handkerchief and rubbed the initials, *DB*, embroidered in tiny yellow cross-stitch in the corner. David Boutwell. She knew so little about him, really. He lived with his wife and twin sons on the Near East Side, and on Sundays they went to the Congregational church on Erie Street. His father had been a failed inventor; he told her that, once.

'Was it hard for you when you started?' Vita asked, handing him back the handkerchief.

Dr. Boutwell cocked his head. His mustache, so neatly trimmed and waxed, tilted into a fishhook. 'I was miserable,' he said.

CHAPTER SIXTEEN

'It is enough for women to love,
to pray to God, and to spin.'
(Molière)

February 1866, Lark's Eye, Massachusetts

Arthur's eyes were closed, but he opened them immediately. Marie, walking into Freddy's old bedroom, felt a sudden shock – like she'd come upon a corpse.

'What are you doing here?' she asked.

He was lying on Freddy's bed.

'Just resting a moment.' He made no move to sit up, though he didn't close his eyes again. 'Actually, I was thinking of moving my things in here. To give you more room.'

'Moving in here to sleep?'

'Yes, to sleep!' he snapped, and she immediately felt chastened. But she persisted.

'Every night?'

Now he closed his eyes. 'Mm.'

Sweetie, perched on Marie's shoulder, rubbed her beak against Marie's jawline and pecked at her cheek three times in quick succession. Herding me, Marie thought. She crossed the room to open a window, which was the reason she'd come in here – to air the room out. She did this once a week.

Freddy's room still had the simple curtains and white-washed walls from babyhood, since one of her son's quirks was that he never wanted anything altered. Even when Amelia and Vita had their rooms wallpapered and fitted with new carpets, he refused to do the same. The only thing that changed was an increasing number of shelves and cupboards, which he built himself, to hold his own collections: a set of miniature wooden globes; variously sized mineral nuggets; a real but non-functioning telegraph key that Uncle Norbert had brought back from a trip to New York many years ago; and old nursery toys, including a small wooden wolf with a fleece covering that came on and off.

After she drew back the curtains, Marie heaved up the middle window and propped it open with a stack of three books; adventure novels with bright orange covers. When Freddy first left for war, Amelia rearranged the objects on his shelves so that 'the displays matched,' as she put it, and she placed the toy wolf on a shelf with his games – cribbage and an old Faro set – and his adventure novels next to his schoolbooks. But the next day, Amelia reported, someone had moved them all back. Arthur? Vita? Mrs. O.? Marie wondered if they all came in here occasionally, as she did, to sit on Freddy's bed and look at his things.

Would Arthur pack away these boyhood collections? Make the room his own? That would be a good thing, probably. Forward movement. But she didn't think he would. What he wanted, she suspected, was to lie among the relics.

'If you'd like to move in here, of course you should. I'll ask Mrs. O. to come help.'

'Thank you, my dear,' Arthur said in a gentler voice. He wasn't heartless, she reminded herself. He was ill. Sunlight pushed through the windows intensely for a moment, and the sudden glare evoked in her the old feeling of waiting. But the waiting was over. Freddy would never come back.

There was a time when Marie believed that nothing would ever top the shock of hearing about President Lincoln's murder, the complete stupor she felt all the day after. Like Arthur, she read the newspapers word for word, page after page, following the story from every angle. Even a week later her mind felt incapable of taking in anything else. But that was a pinhead's worth of water compared to the drenching she felt when the telegram about Freddy arrived. The awful truth was, once she learned about Freddy, she no longer cared so much about President Lincoln, although of course she would never say that to anyone. A terrible act, shooting a man in the back while he watched a light comedy with his wife, but it was remote, whereas Freddy's death was close and tangible. She could still remember the feel of his fine, two-year-old hair as she combed it with a wet comb and wound a dark strand around her finger to curl it. The newspapers – all their words, all their arguments – could never erase what happened. They could not even explain it, although they held out that promise every day.

Sweetie pushed her little head against Marie's cheek again, and she heard the *shrush* of feathers against her ear. All right. She hadn't meant to get maudlin. She was almost at the door when Arthur said, 'What have you heard from Vita?' Still with his eyes shut.

Marie hesitated.

'She and Jacob are moving to a larger house,' she told him.

'Are they? Well.'

'Apparently they had to lay all new carpets in the downstairs rooms.'

'Mm.'

'And they've had two of the back windows enlarged.'

'Such industry! He's an energetic young man. Exactly what she needs.' Marie waited for the punch. 'To tame her.'

She was standing at the foot of the bed and could smell the sour smell of his stockinged feet. His hair was shiny with grease, and a dirty tendril was plastered in place over his left temple. When was the last time he bathed?

'I'll leave you to your rest, then,' Marie said, shutting the door behind her.

Her lies to him were getting increasingly elaborate. It soothed her to imagine Vita's home. A brick house, a front door painted forest green. She didn't know who she was trying to protect with these stories, Arthur or Vita. Or maybe herself?

She had written to her connections in Boston, wording her letters carefully, striving for a light tone. 'My daughter owes me a long letter; please scold her for me if you see her!' They both wrote back that they hadn't yet seen her, but would certainly scold her roundly if they did. And how is your dear husband? And your sister Clara?

They were Mrs. Caroline Abbot and Mrs. Deborah DeLong, two old school friends from New Haven who currently lived a few blocks from each other in Boston. Who else did she know there? She didn't want to ask Arthur. Maybe she should try her cousin Maria Maag in Philadelphia? Of course, she could only use the excuse of wanting a letter from Vita once; after that, Marie just had to hope they would mention it if they'd seen her.

She would have to keep up the correspondence, then. Renew past friendships. Write more regularly.

Perhaps that wasn't a bad thing.

She went to her room and took out her little portable writing desk and, like Arthur, went to her bed although it was only three o'clock in the afternoon – the little clock on her bookshelf chimed the hour in muffled coughs. Vita was capable and confident, but also unworldly. And she was still her child. It was Marie's duty to keep her safe. The trouble was, Vita didn't want to be kept safe.

Sitting up against the pillows, Marie arranged the desk over her lap. Then she flipped open the top of the ink well. Dipped her pen nib. Took a moment to think.

Dear Maria, she began.

CHAPTER SEVENTEEN

'There are many arguments against the female doctor. In the first place, in the majority of cases, she is an unnatural being.'
(*St. Louis Medical Mirror*, Editorial, 1892)

February 1866, Boston, Massachusetts

Jacob thought he might as well start his search here in Boston, although he didn't really believe Vita would run away to the place where they planned to set up house together. Of course, her choices were limited.

She would be studying with a preceptor and preparing for college, so naturally it made sense to visit colleges where she might eventually apply. The New England Female Medical College was located near Boston's Back Bay, and Jacob's idea was that she might look for a preceptor among the professors.

But she could be anywhere, really.

If he had found a preceptor for her before they were married, like she'd asked, then he would know where she was. But it did no good to think this way. It wasn't his fault. Anyway, his immediate job was to find her and take her home. She was his wife. He needed her, he now realized. One thing he'd learned from Andersonville was that your best hope of survival was to, in Caleb's words, form a shield wall. Lone prey were targeted and picked off. Not only by the guards, but by the starving inmates too.

Their shield wall was made up of five men, the Five Knights as they called themselves, and they worked together to stay alive. Caleb had been the leader, and the one Jacob felt the closest to. He grew up on his father's farm near Kirtland, Ohio, and his mother had been one of the first women to graduate from Oberlin College – which was also, Caleb told Jacob, a 'hotbed' of antislavery fervor. His parents were ardent abolitionists, and Caleb joined up as soon as the war began. He'd been captured while tearing up a railroad six miles south of Petersburg, Virginia, and sent to Belle Isle prison camp before being transferred to Andersonville. He was among the first prisoners to arrive, and he told Jacob that slave women were still setting logs for the stockade wall when he got there.

Caleb had a quiet voice, slightly husky, and except in death the corners of his mouth were always slightly stretched, giving the impression he was about to break into a smile – which he often did. He was cheerful but serious, intent on keeping them all alive with a methodical regimen: exercise, cleanliness, and adequate shelter.

'There's no police, no magistrate, and the guards don't care about ten thousand Union men brawling or starving to death,' he explained. Later the numbers would swell to twenty thousand, then thirty thousand. Jacob didn't know it then, but he was lucky in a way (the luck of the unlucky) to have got in early, since the later captives had to dig holes like wild animals to try to stay warm, and most of their belongings were stolen during their first night at camp when they didn't know enough to protect themselves better. Fresh fish, they were called.

Caleb led Jacob back to his tent on that first morning, where three other men – all bones for arms and bones for legs – sat around a small, smoky fire. They were introduced as Ethan, Lewis, and Tom. Tom was boiling water in an impossibly small tin pot. The prison was spread over sixteen acres with a creek running through it, providing the men with drinking water. The problem was, they also washed themselves in it.

'That's why we boil every drop we drink,' Tom told him. Tom was a Michigan man. Lewis grew up near Chicago, and Ethan, like Jacob, was from Massachusetts. Ethan had made a deal with one of the guards to buy his used tobacco chew, which he dried out to make into snuff and then sold.

'We're always on the lookout to find ways to barter for extra food,' Caleb said.

Maybe it was the gentle whisper of his voice, or maybe it was the sight of the lone man ten feet away from them who was lying in a shallow rut running brown with diarrhea, too weak to move, staring at Jacob as though peering out from his grave. Jacob understood in that moment that he couldn't survive by himself.

Caleb outlined their rules for him:

1. *Drink no water until it's been boiled*
2. *Clean your body every morning*
3. *Exercise every afternoon*
4. *Talk, joke, and make light of things – don't allow yourself to get despondent.*

It was almost impossible to keep clean without soap, something Jacob never saw in all the months he was there. But they could at least scrape the lice off their bodies each day – most of the lice – and rub their skin with a frayed wet rag. Caleb and the others called the lice graybacks, and they called the rebel soldiers who guarded them graybacks, too. Although the guards were there to keep anyone from escaping, they didn't mind if the Yankees fought among themselves; in fact they liked to collect around the fighting prisoners and bet on the outcome. Strange at first to Jacob: many of the guards wore blue Yankee uniforms.

'The Sanitation Commission regularly sends clothes to us,' Caleb explained. 'But the graybacks go through the barrels first.'

If any man spoke sharply to a guard he was taken outside the stockade where he was bucked and gagged: made to sit on the ground with his arms tied around his raised knees, with a horse bit shoved into his mouth. And if he stepped over the deadline – the flimsy rail fence that ran around the prison about fifteen feet in from the stockade walls – he was shot. Many of the prisoners were barefoot or had muddy rags tied around their feet, and all were skeleton-thin. Every stage of hunger could be witnessed within fifteen minutes of walking around the camp.

'The Southerners are not a business people,' Lewis told him. 'They can't manage their treasury, they can't repair their railroads, and though they say they are going to erect tent shelters for us, they can't coordinate the supplies. Best not to expect any better than what you have now. And don't for God's sake ask for anything, it'll just get you in trouble. Don't even talk to the guards if you can help it. Like the Southern Confederacy itself, you should only want to be let alone.'

Prison camp was almost worse than battle, because prolonged, although after his friend Matthew Ames died Jacob had stopped believing in the rhetoric of war in any case. At Andersonville they were all crowded together, all these heroic soldiers of the North, most of them suffering from dysentery and near-starvation, with lice crawling over their soft bruised flesh as if devouring them alive. The prisoners took each other's beggarly possessions by stealth if they could and by force if not. Their weapons were knives stolen from the cookhouse, and sticks that they sharpened as best they could, and rocks aimed at another man's head with precision.

They were all Union soldiers. They were all, in theory, on the same side.

'Keep your spirits up,' Caleb liked to say. 'It's a matter of will.'

A matter of will and, Jacob thought later, a good dose of make-believe. He arrived in late March and was liberated the following year in May. Confederate Camp Sumter, Andersonville Post Office, Anderson Station, on the Sumter–Macon county line. In those fourteen months he never received any packages or letters, and only after his release did he learn that his sister had died while he was imprisoned. Even the Five Knights died off one by one, except for him. Lewis and Tom died of dysentery, Ethan caught pneumonia, and Caleb was shot by a guard in a sentry box while he was repairing the embankment after a heavy rain – a job he'd been ordered to do. Caleb had leaned an inch too far out over the edge, trying to do the job properly, and the guard shot him in the back of the head.

The *Boston Post* claimed that work was still going on filling in the Back Bay with dirt hauled in from Needham, twenty-five miles away – the idea was to build more housing once it was filled – but one-horse tipcarts continued to dump refuse collected from wealthier neighborhoods into the marsh, and the neighborhood exuded an odor of dung, rotting onions, and coal ash. Jacob kept to the lanes and alleys where the mill hands lived – rows of low brick houses with pig pens and chicken coops in the yards, wet sheets hanging from windows (one or two dried to a frozen stiffness), and broken whiskey jugs on the street leading like a trail of breadcrumbs away from the taverns.

A half mile past the cheap brick housing some larger dwellings remained; among them was the college Jacob was looking for. It was a square mansion with dormer windows and a long stone staircase leading up to a set of imposingly wide front doors. Clearly a former residence. It was a bitterly cold day – the air felt sucked dry of any moisture and an icy wind found the knife-edge of skin between his glove and coat sleeve – but inside the college it wasn't much warmer. The large front hall was empty. There was a row of wooden pegs to his right, with various cloaks and coats laying claim to them, and next to that a door that looked to be painted shut. To his left was the office – or so he assumed; its door was propped open.

'You must get the wind every time someone comes in,' he said to the woman sitting behind a large table that doubled as a desk. She had strong, square shoulders and massive auburn hair piled up on her head like a basket, and wore a pince-nez on her nose. She took the pince-nez off and let it dangle from its chain.

'I should close my door but the idea is to be welcoming.'

Jacob asked her if she knew a Vita Culhane in the college. But the secretary, or whatever she was – Mrs. O'Reilly, she introduced herself – said there was no one by that name enrolled as a student (he hadn't held out much chance of that anyway). When he asked about professors taking on students as apprentices, she shook her head again.

'I keep the professors' schedules. I would recognize the name.'

'No Vita at all? How about Vita Tenney?'

'No. I would know.'

She looked, indeed, like she knew everything; more than perhaps you wanted her to know. She was watching him shrewdly.

He offered, 'I've just come back home from the war. I was in prison camp, and then I was ill. I'm her brother.'

'And you're certain she's in Boston?'

'No. I only know she wanted to study medicine. It was her dream.'

Mrs. O'Reilly suggested he go to Baltimore. A couple of women physicians lived there, she told him, and one had recently given a lecture at their college.

'They might act as preceptors for young women,' she said.

'So there *are* female doctors?' he asked. 'Practicing, I mean?'

She gave him a tired look. 'More than you might think.'

❦

A week later Jacob took the morning train to Baltimore and checked into a small hotel near Calvert Station. Baltimore, although only three degrees south of Boston, felt much closer to spring: a cold but not icy breeze played along the streets, and he saw a handful of budding green leaves on the trees. He passed women dressed in vibrant, spring colors – chartreuse, emerald green, cobalt blue – and near the packing houses there was a powerful scent of fresh oysters.

Somewhere a band was playing 'The Star-Spangled Banner', or maybe it was only a handful of men on a corner with an empty hat in front of them. He couldn't listen to that song anymore without seeing the slow advance of army supply wagons – their company bandleader, a man called Chicken because of his skinny legs and the loose flesh of his neck, – began playing it as soon as the lead wagon was spotted. But the supplies, when they finally came, were never enough. Not enough meat, not enough flour, not enough medicines. He hoped never to drink chicory coffee again.

Dr. Rebecca Coleson lived in a corner house near a busy intersection where jostling merchants rang their bells trying to rustle up jobs: 'Glass put in! Glass put in!' 'I'll grind your horseradish!' 'Rags, any rags?' Jacob felt suddenly engulfed as he shouldered his way among them. He stopped in the middle of the sidewalk and felt his right arm and then his left, pretending to adjust his coat, until his panic subsided. Crowds could do this to him now. He made himself picture the openness of Lark's Eye, where ducks waddling across the town green usually outnumbered the townspeople sitting on the benches. Eventually his breathing returned to normal.

To Jacob's surprise, Dr. Coleson answered her own door.

'I don't take in many students,' she said when Jacob explained his purpose. She was tall with a long beaked nose, and she hardly bothered to open the front door all the way to speak to him. 'Men would rather study with men, and a girl has never approached me.'

Her practice must not be very lucrative, he thought as he crossed the street again, given the state of her house, which was weedy in front and needed a new coat of paint.

Dr. Deerview, on the other side of town, did not know Vita either, although her round dimpled face looked friendlier and she offered him coffee, which he declined. The mustard and white shingle hanging over her door announced her practice but not her sex: *Dr. J.S. Deerview, Physician.*

'Have you tried the female medical colleges?' she asked. 'A student, a potential student, might go there first to look for a preceptor. That's what I would do if I hadn't had an uncle who could help me.'

'I did, yes, the one in Boston.'

'There's one in Philadelphia, too. And I believe the Cleveland Medical College admits women as well as men, although I'm not certain about that.'

✻

Jacob had a third address in his pocket: Marshall Windsor, a fellow he'd known at Andersonville. Marshall had lived in the 'tent' next to his – another makeshift affair made of sticks and rags and, in Marshall's case, ripped shirts sent to the camp to be used as bandages. Marshall worked in the hospital tent; he was the one who helped Jacob carry Caleb to the Dead House after Caleb was shot. Although they had exchanged addresses the day they were released, they'd never written to each other until Jacob sent a note last week saying he was coming to Baltimore. Would he care to meet?

The address Marshall sent in reply was for a downtown dining club – he lived with his married sister, and it was more convenient to dine out. At first Jacob didn't recognize him sitting at a corner table with two glasses of ale before him. When he saw Jacob he stood up and waved him over.

'You've gotten very fit!' Jacob said, greeting him. Stout was the word he was thinking.

Marshall laughed. 'You can see what a body will do for itself on three meals a day.'

At Andersonville the rations were doled out once a day, at four o'clock, and a quarter-pound spice can was used to measure out each man's scanty portion of cornmeal, along with two ounces of bacon and, every third day, a half-teaspoon of salt. After Jacob's second month there, the bacon disappeared.

'To your health.' Marshall raised his glass and nodded to the second glass for Jacob.

Jacob took it up. 'And yours.'

A waiter brought them slabs of roast beef and separate plates of mashed peas, small discs of carrots, and brown bread with molasses. They drank slowly and ate quickly, like men who'd been starved for months on end. Jacob wondered if he always ate this way now, or if it was the effect of being with a fellow prisoner again.

The room glowed from the hurricane lamps on every table; some men dined alone reading a newspaper, while others raised their voices, trying to be heard in a group. The walls had dark wood paneling and framed pictures of hunting scenes. Every once in a while a dessert trolley wheeled slowly by on the thick carpet, as though advancing on sand. They spoke about the price of cattle and oysters, and Marshall told him about a new cracker manufactory in town, which his brother-in-law was managing.

'To go with the oysters here, you see.'

Marshall worked as a clerk for the railroads, and Jacob found himself wondering if he could get him a job. If he wasn't going to pursue the barrel glue idea, he needed to start looking for something else. He didn't want to use up Vita's money. He still thought of it that way: Vita's money.

Marshall's face had filled out and his hair was thick and shiny. The day they were liberated, he and Jacob and everyone else looked more dead than alive with their bony shoulders, their necks like flaccid rope. Jacob himself was so thin that a man collecting dead bodies had come toward him with a shovel. Jacob opened his eyes when he felt someone move his arm, and scared the poor man half to death.

'We made it,' Marshall had said to him outside the tall palisade gates. Their pace was as slow as a crawl. 'We're free. We can walk off in any direction at any time.'

He'd walked off in the direction of Baltimore and seemingly never looked back. Did he ever have tremors? Did he suffer from nightmares? All the questions Jacob had wanted to ask felt swallowed up by the room's warm lighting, the plush chairs, the brandy he was sipping. Now that he was here, he didn't want to risk losing this comfort.

Instead he asked, 'What's it like living in Baltimore?'

Marshall liked it. 'Lots of boat clubs and hunting clubs, lots of socials. The young ladies here have a style to their humor, I can't rightly explain it, and they're also very pretty. Sometimes I take a Saturday off and a buddy and I take a couple of girls out to Gwynns Falls. I like my job, too. The pay's good. The B & O has the best equipment in the country right now, what with all the locomotives it bought from the government. Making money hand over fist. Everyone wants to travel!'

Jacob nodded. To get away after months – years – of not being able to go anywhere in safety. He understood that.

'We could use men like you,' Marshall said, as if reading Jacob's thoughts. 'I can look around for open positions, if you like.'

But as soon as he offered it, Jacob knew with a heavy certainty that he didn't want it. He couldn't say why.

'Good of you, thanks. Might be just the thing. I'll let you know.'

'You could let me know now! I'll start poking around in the morning.'

Jacob hesitated. 'To be honest, I'm not sure I want to move house.'

'I know what it is. You have a girl back in Boston. Am I right?'

Marshall was smiling, pleased with himself. Jacob thought about how Vita was open like that – her thoughts written plainly on her face for anyone to read. He remembered the afternoon of Gemma and Ruffy's wedding, how Vita looked at Gemma. And how her expression softened with sympathy while she listened to his story about Caleb and their Christmas dinner. Even now, without warning, he sometimes pictured her walking in the greenhouse with her brother's bird on her shoulder. 'She loves chopped-up carrots, when I can sneak any away.'

He wished he knew where she was. He was pulled to her without wanting to be. The last time he saw Marshall he'd been thinking he would sell his father's farm and start a new life in Boston; he'd planned to work up a business and leave the war behind him, just as he'd left his father behind when he ran away to Cincinnati. Why was it so much harder now? He felt the tic start pulsing under his eye, blast it.

But Marshall didn't seem to notice. They didn't mention Andersonville until the end, and even then not directly. Saying good-night on the street, Marshall struggled to button the middle button of his overcoat and then laughed when he saw Jacob watching.

'We survived. We owe it to ourselves to live well.'

'We do deserve it.' Jacob shook Marshall's hand. 'We surely do.'

He watched Marshall slowly cross the loosely cobbled street with his head thrust forward and down. When he was out of sight, Jacob turned and walked in the other direction to the harbor. The gas streetlights cast an oily light on the water, and he thought he could make out, down the pier, men loading crates onto a frigate. Dark brick houses rose up behind them – closer to the water than he would have expected – on the narrow street.

This spot, the place he was standing, was the furthest south he'd been since the war. Without looking away from the water, he pulled out from his coat pocket a small wooden rectangle on a string: the identification tag Matthew Ames had made for him after they'd been fighting for a year. The scrap of oak was so thin it had been hard to puncture a hole in it; Matthew used his penknife and broke two before he got the hole into this one. Jacob could still picture him at night carving the tiny, crooked letters: *J. Culhane.* Behind him the hillside was dotted with campfires like theirs, and tents, and men.

Jacob swung back his arm and lobbed the tag into the water, where it landed noiselessly and – he assumed, since he could no longer see it – sank. He'd wanted to talk to Marshall about the war and prison camp; he thought he might even show him his tag. But Marshall's new interests – jobs, girls, the future of railroads – were no doubt healthier, and better suited to dinner talk. A dog barked near the frigate, and Jacob felt the tic pulse beneath his eye again. He didn't want to hold onto the past, but he also didn't know how to release it. The dog was still barking, high and menacing, as he turned and began walking along the darkened street toward his hotel, wishing he could believe in the power of gestures.

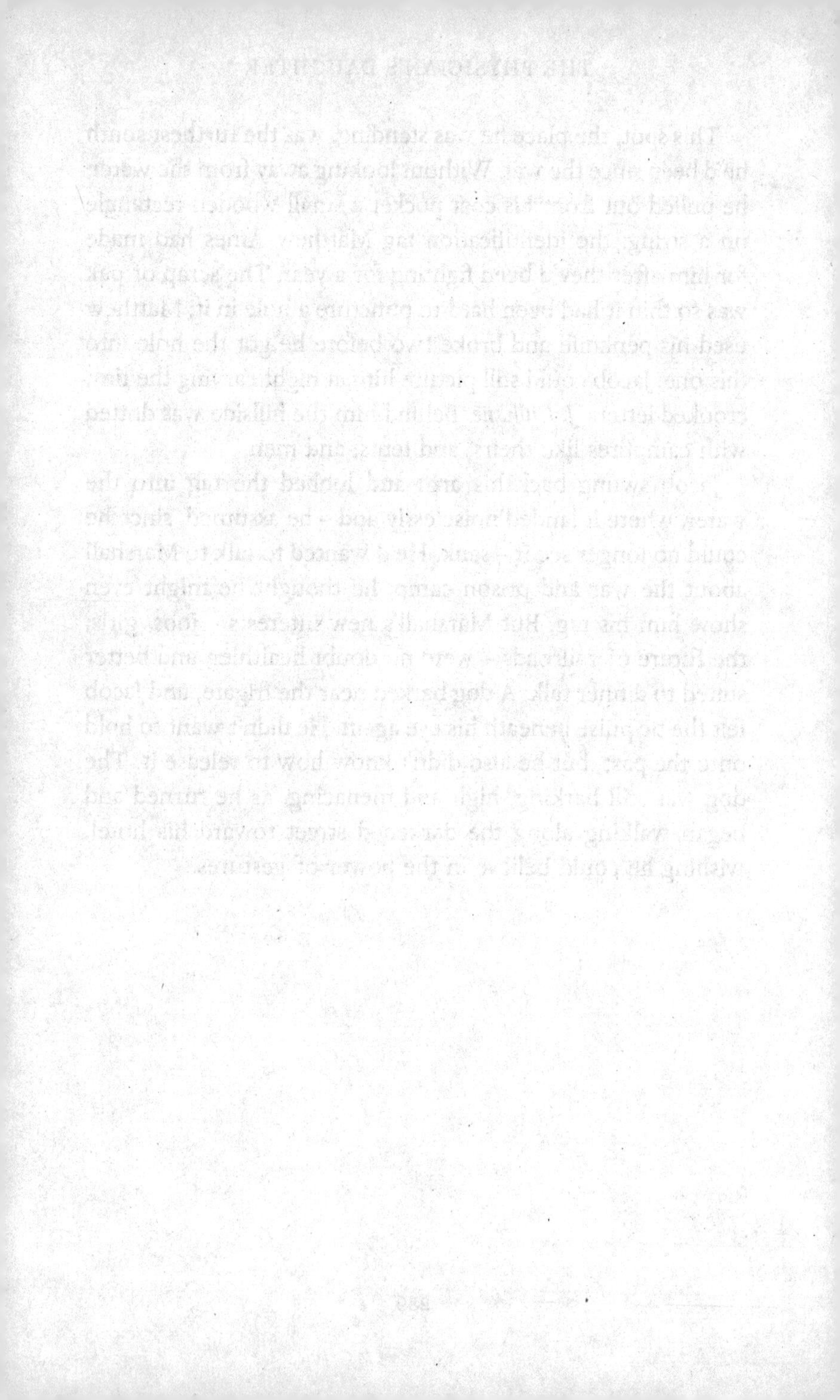

CHAPTER EIGHTEEN

'Little women are more apt to conceive than great; slender, rather than gross; fair, rather than ruddy. To have great swelled breasts is good.'
(*Dublin Quarterly Journal*, Dr. John Denham, 1862)

March 12, 1866
Lark's Eye, Massachusetts

Dear Miss Vita,

I wish I could see the tall buildings you describe. Aren't you fearful being so high up, lest you fall out? There is not much in the way of news here. Your sister ordered material from New York with a Dutch windmill design and she wants me to make them into curtains for her kitchen. She complains that she's bored and sometimes goes to the high school to help with I dont know what. It opens in less than a month. Only boys will be allowed to go, but last night Mr. Granger says he might let a girl in whose interested, and Miss Amelia says oh like Vita, and he says yes like you.

About once a week your sister asks me if I know anything and I always say no but I think she suspects me. Sometimes I bring your letters with me to reread them when I have a moment to myself, but I should stop that as she's a terrible snoop. Your father is much the same though he's begun to see a few patients again. Your mother is writing letters to people in New Haven now as well as Boston. I see the addresses when I post them. I suppose she wonders if you are there.

Pocket, our new horse, is wonderfully handsome and healthy. Ruffy has started studding him out. We're going to build a house closer to town, we've almost got enough saved for the lot we picked out, and we can have it the bank says for just a deposit but Ruffy wants to buy it outright. I get awfully tired walking from our house to your house to Miss Amelia's. I'd like to work in just one place but Mrs. O. says to go where I'm needed, the pay's the same either way.

To answer your last, I still haven't seen anything more of Mr. Culhane. Amelia says he's in Boston, in the house he leased for the two of you. I'm sorry I dont know more.

Yours very truly,
Gemma

March 31, 1866
Cleveland, Ohio

Dear Gemma,

I wish you could tell my mother not to worry about me but of course you can't. Or maybe you could say, Oh Vita is very capable, I'm sure she's fine. Though in truth I don't feel very capable right at the moment. Doctoring is hard. Almost every day at four o'clock I wish I were sitting at the kitchen table with you and Mrs. O. and Amelia. I'm learning so much and I know the practical experience will be useful.

How is Sweetie? Would you give her rolled-up bits of paper to chew on? I don't want her to be anxious.

Now I'm off to study – I've read through nine medical volumes since I've been here! But I have about a hundred more to go.

All my love,
Vita

April 12, 1866
Lark's Eye, Massachusetts

Dear Miss Vita,

I saw your mother last week when I went to help stretch the rugs and I waited until your name was mentioned and I said, 'Oh Miss Vita will be a success in anything she tries.' So I hope that was all right. Maybe she felt better. She didn't say anything to it.

Sweetie is fine. She was sick on Easter week but your mother nursed her back with sugar water. I gave her extra paper rolls, like you asked. Riddle is getting very arthritic but he still climbs up the stairs every night. He sleeps in your mother's bedroom. Your father has moved into your brother's old room. He says he is writing a book about the war but I never see him writing, only reading.

Why don't you write Jacob a letter? Ruffy thinks the world of him. I've enclosed his address in Boston. You probably have it already.

If you go to the theatre in Cleveland tell me and tell me the whole play. I wish we had a playhouse here. A traveling company came last week and did Piramas and Thisby in the schoolhouse for three nights running. Ruffy and I saw it the last night and we laughed so hard. We got those French letters you told me about, Ruffy had to send away for them by mail. We'll have a baby after the horses start to pay, Ruffy says. I'm glad no one but you reads my letters.

I'm still working for your sister.

Yours very truly,
Gemma

Vita folded up Gemma's letter again – she'd read it four times now – and looked at the slip of paper with Jacob's address in Boston. *If* he was still there. She'd never seen the house; 'Anything's fine,' she told him when he showed her the lease before he signed it. That must have been, what, three weeks before their wedding? Four? He was wonderfully efficient about some things.

His face swam up at unexpected moments: once when she passed a flowerbox planted with crimson geraniums, and another time when she was looking at the Columbus Street bridge over the vast, tea-colored Cuyahoga River. The bridge was nothing like the little footbridge where they met in Riverside, but still, for a moment, she saw him so clearly. The mole near his eye. His dark hair. The fine wrinkles fanning out from his eyes when he smiled. She felt as though something small but vital had been torn from her skin, and even now, seven months later, the spot was still sore.

But what could she say in a letter? Nothing seemed right. *I'm alone in Cleveland; will you come see me?*

That sounded pathetic.

Might we talk?

That sounded as though she had something particular to say.

I'm having second thoughts. I might have made a mistake.

No. She would not say that.

She had forty-one dollars left, which she kept in an old rolled-up stocking in her dresser drawer. Her boot leather had gotten so thin that the damp came through but she couldn't afford new shoes, so instead she began lining the insides with newspaper, which worked as long as she changed the paper out every few days.

Today, since it was Friday and the day she and Dr. Boutwell volunteered at the Soldiers' Home, she had to spend a precious nickel to ride the streetcar – the Soldiers' Home was too far to walk to. It was housed in a narrow, two-story stone building near the train station, and during the war it served as a stopping place for soldiers to get medical care and rest before returning to battle. Now it was half clinic and half hotel. Mustered-out men were shuttled from one Soldiers' Home in one city to another, hopscotching their way across the country back to their farms, their towns, or to a new life elsewhere – many just kept going west.

She walked through the front room – a makeshift office where lines of soldiers waited to receive free clothes or to get help with pension forms – to the hospital ward, which always smelled of carbolic soap and burned coffee. The whitewashed walls had been festooned with flags and company regalia, and Vita felt the urge to salute the doctors, many of whom wore small Union buttons pinned to their lapels.

Although there were easily thirty beds, most of them occupied by soldiers, the ward had a womanly feel. Clusters of nurses in pinned hats and carefully ironed gray and white dresses removed breakfast trays and spoke to the men like commanders. ('One last bite, there you are, if you could just hand me the spoon now.') They'd been trained in the war, they were determined to do their duty even now at war's end, and they were legion.

It was like falling asleep, Vita wrote to Gemma, and finding yourself in a dream world of crisp, bright, sanitary order maintained by mothers and sisters and aunts. The cadre of women, as precise as an army in formation, kept the floors swept and the beds tidy and the men fed and washed. They distributed the meals – today, by the smell of it, porridge with bacon – and changed damp bandages and made fresh coffee and wrote letters for those who couldn't and distributed clean socks and a hundred other tasks besides. From the far window Vita could see two nurses beneath a canvas tent pushing wet laundry around in a tub; the wooden paddles they used were so long they slanted over their shoulders like rifles.

Dr. Boutwell stopped at each bed, checking wounds and asking soldiers about their symptoms, while Vita pulled from her pocket a long notebook with a pencil attached so she could take notes. Many of the abler veterans helped out by carrying heavy trays or basins of water for the nurses; she nearly stepped on one man who was scrubbing blood off the floor.

'Oh, pardon!' He tapped the air near his forehead, the brim of an invisible cap.

All of the men had been ticketed and registered; slips of paper tied to each bed marked their conditions, their names, and the names of their hometowns. One boy, according to his ticket, had been shot in the shoulder during the last battle in Texas, fought after the peace had been signed but before his general knew it. Dr. Boutwell asked Vita to check his wound while he took a look at the man a few beds away, whom they could hear breathing in a raspy struggle.

Vita helped the boy, whose name according to his slip was Alec Martin, to sit up. He wore a gown with a drawstring around the neck to make it easier to examine his wound.

'He relives a battle,' a passing nurse told her in a low voice. 'Whenever I bend over him he grabs me by the arm. I think he's trying to drag me away from a bursting shell.'

Sure enough, as Vita bent over to adjust the bandage he grabbed her wrist.

'It's coming! Get down!'

She waited a moment, feeling her pulse in her ears. Even after all these months it was still a struggle to adopt the tone of distant but professional concern that the nurses so easily maintained.

'It's all right now, Mr. Martin,' Vita told him, 'it's safe,' and he lowered his hand. 'I'm just going to take a quick look at your shoulder. Does it itch?' The bandage felt moist and she began to unwind it. 'Oh, it's healing very nicely,' she told him. She cleaned the wound and wiped the edges with a small piece of oiled lint, noting as she did so the color (slightly red), the level of oozing pus (none), and his skin temperature (normal). Doctoring, at this level, was a checklist, a satisfying process.

'It don't seem possible that such a little tear could kill me,' the boy said.

'This won't kill you, Mr. Martin.'

'Something will.'

After she tied the bandage ends together he asked for water, cupping his palm as if he wanted her to pour it into that slight indentation. There was a tin mug on the table beside his bed, but when Vita looked inside she saw a rim of film on the water's surface.

'I'll get you a fresh cup,' she told him. When she returned she found him still holding out his cupped palm.

She put the cup to his lips. After a moment, as if deciding, he opened his mouth. He didn't swallow until she pulled the cup away.

He wiped his chin. 'Thanks, Ma.'

That stopped her. She'd heard nurses say that sometimes soldiers like this – the hard cases, they called them – mistook them for their mothers or sisters, but this was the first time it had happened to Vita.

A strong sense of Mitty came over her: her square fingernails and tapered fingers; the way she cut a muffin in half by cupping it in one hand. Vita adjusted Alec Martin's shirt and pulled his striped, regulation wool blanket up over his chest. He followed all of her movements with his sad, round eyes. When she looked at him he nodded: *there, that's done.* He was a boy no older than Freddy had been when he left home. Vita's heart felt tight; every single aspect of doctoring challenged her in a different way. Would Alec Martin ever get better?

'Some of them do,' Dr. Boutwell told her, washing his hands later at the nurses' corner, which was what they called the curtained-off space – not even a room – at the back of the ward near the kitchen, with a small Franklin stove used for boiling water for tea, and bars of soap, and clean towels stacked up beside a white china washbasin.

He took a towel from the top of the stack and began to dry his hands. 'The body is very resilient,' he said.

She'd made a friend at the Soldiers' Home, a nurse called Lucy Frost. Lucy was tall with a long face, close-set eyes, and thick straw-like hair. She wore a blue pinstripe dress and a long white apron with an eyeglass and a syringe on two thin chains pinned to the waistband.

'In the war they only let married women nurse, but they let me train because I'm so ugly,' she said frankly.

Vita had thought her ugly too at first, but she didn't anymore. Lucy was cheerful without being cloying, remembered every instruction, and always seemed genuinely glad to see her.

What's more, she had nerves of steel. Vita had watched Lucy clean and re-bandage a man's empty eye socket without blanching, and sponge-bathe another man whose back was covered in weeping pustules. In secret, Lucy had married one of the wounded soldiers she'd met in the ward; they lived together with her mother across the river on the Near West Side. It was forbidden for a nurse to see a soldier outside the Home, and marrying one could get you dismissed. ('Can't encourage anyone else to break the rule, I suppose,' Lucy said.)

Her husband had one good leg and one prosthetic leg (donated by the army for his service), and he was good with numbers. Last week he interviewed for a job checking accounts for Mr. John D. Rockefeller at his downtown office. Today, with a beaming expression, Lucy told Vita that he started work there yesterday.

'Standard Works. They're making a fortune refining petroleum and shipping it east.'

They were remaking a bed together and Vita, pulling up the starched sheet, thought about Jacob. Again. 'Shipping it in barrels?'

'Probably.'

'Do the barrels leak?'

Lucy gave her a quick, probing glance. 'I don't know. Why?'

'Oh, someone I knew, a soldier, he was interested in that.' A wave of guilt swept over her. Someone she knew? Only her husband.

'All done, Mr. Paxton,' Lucy said to the soldier coming back to his freshly made bed. 'Now let's take a quick look at your sprain.'

Mr. Paxton sat down on the thin mattress, facing them. After they unwrapped his arm Lucy declared herself pleased with his progress. She showed Vita how to gently position Mr. Paxton's arm in a right angle to prevent hyperextension, and how to wind the clean white bandage firmly but not too tight. Alone at night, Vita studied gray line drawings of the human skeleton: the curved bones of the ribcage (*thoracic cavity*); and the knotted end of an arm bone (*humerus*) where it nestled against the shoulder socket. But real arms were heavy and cumbersome. Learning how to handle them took practice.

'Have you ever heard of Duke of Simpson strapping?' Lucy asked. 'That's for the knee.'

'Show me.'

After they settled Mr. Paxton, they went to a man they could practice on, Captain Marcus Jonathan. He wasn't ill but he had no family and nowhere to go, and since there wasn't a shortage of beds the nurses made up little ailments for him so he could stay longer. He didn't mind being used for training, even claimed to like it. Lucy crisscrossed his left kneecap with a bandage, used another one around his lower thigh, and then wove a third bandage around his knee and up his leg and back again to keep everything in place. Vita practiced on his other leg, handling the cloth awkwardly, trying to match Lucy's motions.

'Ouch!' the captain said suddenly, and Vita jumped back. What had she done wrong now? But he winked at her and laughed.

'Don't pay him any attention,' Lucy said, smiling and shaking her head at him. He had stripes of purple scars like claw marks going up one side of his face and had lost an ear in battle, but he joked as though it all meant nothing.

On Saturday Vita and Dr. Boutwell visited one of their pregnant patients, Mary Eileen Doherty, at her home in Irishtown

Bend – a flat, swampy neighborhood that the Cuyahoga River looped around and isolated from the rest of the city. Tall factory smokestacks loomed up from behind the houses, and a persistent oily fog blanketed the streets.

The price of food had shot up during the war, and fatherless children sold newspapers and matches on the corners, or swept the streets for pennies. More and more women landed in jail – theft, mostly. Mary Eileen Doherty was one of the lucky ones. At fourteen she found work in a factory sewing umbrellas for three dollars a week, minus the cost of needles and thread. She got married at fifteen, and now at sixteen was having her first baby.

Vita took the streetcar and met Dr. Boutwell on the corner. They walked past wooden houses with tin and tarpaper roofs that were built on stilts above the mud. Black embers from the factory smoke floated over the river.

'Tell me, if you can,' Dr. Boutwell said, 'the four types of labor according to Denham.' He liked to quiz her as they walked.

'Natural, Preternatural, Difficult, and Anomalous.'

'And the difference between Difficult and Anomalous?'

'A Difficult labor lasts more than twenty-four hours, and an Anomalous labor requires assistance.'

Two bareheaded boys scooped up horse manure in the street with their bare hands – 'They'll sell it for fuel,' Dr. Boutwell told her – while women wearing impossibly thin boots skidded along the icy sidewalks, their arms full of ale jugs or straw baskets or babies. Sometimes all three.

Mary Eileen lived in a shack that leaned heavily toward its neighbor, as if drowsy or drunk, with three freshly swept wooden steps leading to a horsehair rope doormat.

'You just missed it. She was having a fit,' Mary Eileen's mother, Mrs. Keene, said at the door as she took their wraps.

Mrs. Keene always looked at Vita with a slightly puzzled expression, as though trying to work out what, exactly, it was about Vita that she did not like. She wore a man's overcoat and an old-fashioned cap with frayed strings hanging down over her ears like two frizzy ringlets. The kitchen was small and cramped with gingham-blue curtains faded almost to white. Vita could hear the wind whistling through the walls where the tarpaper had peeled.

'I was only cold,' Mary Eileen protested. She was sitting by the stove with her feet raised on a stack of pinewood – they didn't have money for coal. Her normally pretty, heart-shaped face looked puffy and yellow. Her husband – a boy not much older than Mary Eileen – used to dig extensions for the canals until the railroads took over. These days he bet on horse races while he waited for spring and the carpentry jobs that came with it. His preferred place to wait was in the corner tavern.

'No, not with cold. And not the Ague neither.' Mrs. Keene suffered herself from bouts of the Ague – malaria, as it was called now. There were times every summer when she was struck with shaking for days on end. And that, Dr. Boutwell once told Vita in private, would never go away.

'A convulsion? Well then, we must begin your labor at once,' Dr. Boutwell said.

Mary Eileen blanched. 'What, today?'

'Begin it ourselves?' Vita had read nothing in her books about that.

'She's still near a month from her time,' Mrs. Keene protested.

'Mary Eileen has what is called eclampsia.' Dr. Boutwell smiled gently, trying to calm their anxiety. 'Mrs. Culhane can list some of the common symptoms, if you like.'

'Swelling, headaches, nausea, or vomiting,' Vita recited. 'Changes in vision, shortness of breath, or convulsions. Denham recommends bleeding up to forty ounces.'

Bloodletting, however, was going out of style, so she wasn't surprised when Dr. Boutwell said, 'Very good, though of course we won't do any bleeding today, that's proved ineffective. Let's give her an opiate to ease the convulsions, and then small doses of ergot to begin her contractions.' He turned to Mary Eileen's mother. 'You can forgo the dime, at least.'

Normally Dr. Boutwell charged three dollars for common labor and five for labor with instruments; for confinement visits, he charged twenty-five cents. In Irishtown Bend, however, he dropped his prices to a dime a visit and two dollars for labor, no matter what kind, and he would also take payment in food. He was liked here, even welcomed, because he charged so little and was 'soft-hearted,' as Vita heard one granny say, although some still preferred the local midwife when they could fetch her sober enough from the tavern.

Dr. Boutwell pulled a stool over to Mary Eileen. She'd gone as stiff as a schoolgirl who didn't know her lesson.

'Will I die?' she asked in a teacup-thin voice.

He took her hand. 'Oh my dear, I've delivered many a baby this way, don't you worry. You'll be sitting up asking for raspberries and cream tomorrow, with your little one snug in your arms.'

Mary Eileen laughed a tiny nervous laugh. 'Raspberries in April!'

❁

The kitchen was not much bigger than Vita's attic bedroom. That was good; it would be easier to keep warm. Two rickety wooden tables stood together at the end of the room piled with basins and mismatched plates; beneath one of them Vita found a rag basket, and she began stuffing rags along the windowpane to keep out the wind. Meanwhile Mrs. Keene dragged in a mattress and tucked a clean sheet over it.

Trying to start a woman's labor has been attempted since time immemorial, Dr. Boutwell told them as he boiled his instruments. The Egyptians drank a mixture of honey, wine, and fresh salt. Indian women made tea from powdered rattle-snake rattles and the bark of a pine tree.

'But we won't make you drink anything like that,' he promised, smiling down at Mary Eileen, who had gone white again. 'We have modern medicines at our disposal.'

After scrubbing his hands thoroughly, Dr. Boutwell proceeded to examine Mary Eileen.

'Os uteri admitted a finger. Now I'll break the membranes. That usually begins dilation.'

The accounts of eclampsia Vita had read about were vague, usually skipping over the actual birth, which was where she felt most in need of instruction. A typical case study might only be a few sentences long:

> *In another case of eclampsia there was profound uraemia, but no convulsions. Delivery was hastened by the use of forceps. The child died of marasmus on the third day.*

Marasmus was malnutrition. Not much to help her, there.

Later she would read up on ergot; a German botanist discovered that the black fungus that grew on rye stalks could, as he put it, 'awaken the pains of the womb.' European midwives – and after their success, doctors in England and America – began to grind the fungus into powder and use it to induce labor. But the powder, ergot, had recently been denounced by an American doctor, Dr. Hosack. If given in too large doses, ergot could cause intense contractions that the woman's body wasn't ready for, and the baby could suffocate or strangle. The medicine had to be measured very carefully, and the source of the ergot was also important. However, Dr. Hosack advised abandonment rather than caution, even though a mother with eclampsia might well die from her seizures. Because even in that dire case – the mother's death – the baby might still be extracted. And better for the mother to die than the child.

He renamed ergot 'Death Powder.' Hard to overcome a moniker like that, and most doctors stopped administering it. But Dr. Boutwell still made cautious use of it, 'because I don't care to lose my mothers,' he told Vita, 'if there's any help for it.'

They made Mary Eileen as comfortable as they could and kept the wood stove burning hot. Dr. Boutwell carefully measured out the ergot – three separate doses – and checked for fever. At first Vita read her textbook, occasionally sponging Mary Eileen's face and neck or giving her sips of beef broth, and then – as the labor progressed – she helped her to stand or sit or lie down as her pain dictated. Mary Eileen's mother went to the corner tavern and brought back ham sandwiches and fried potatoes, which they ate in shifts – all except Mary Eileen, who had vomited after the third dose of ergot. Vita was prepared to spend the night – she had done this before, at one of the fancy Euclid Avenue houses where the wealthiest Clevelanders lived – but shortly after sunset, groaning and crying, Mary Eileen delivered a slippery infant with a scrunched face like an elderly statesman.

Vita was euphoric. A baby boy. A healthy baby boy. He was greasy and covered in blood, and when he cried his first cry he urinated a thin trickle onto Mrs. Keene's sleeve. Vita watched his skin color deepen into red as the blood moved through his tiny, threadlike veins. Her head and chest felt light, and as she watched Mrs. Keene swaddle him, mentally noting her technique, she found she couldn't stop smiling.

But when she turned to Dr. Boutwell she saw that he was frowning. He gently pressed Mary Eileen's stomach with the flat of his hands. 'I do believe you are hiding another one from me.'

'What's that?' Mary Eileen asked.

'Twins,' Dr. Boutwell said. 'One crouched behind the other. Don't worry, your next baby will be faster.'

He put his hands on Mary Eileen's belly and gently felt for the head.

'Transverse lie,' he said, straightening up. 'We'll have to pull this little one around.'

He went to his leather medicine case, which was on one of Mrs. Keene's little tables. 'If we have trouble,' he said to Vita in a low voice, 'we'll have to use forceps. I'll boil them now.'

Her euphoria vanished. There existed – though not in Dr. Boutwell's bag – longer instruments she didn't want to think about: the blunt hook, the curette, the lever; she'd seen line drawings of them in her books. 'Tools to extract a dead child,' read the caption.

'What's tranver-lie?' Mary Eileen asked.

Dr. Boutwell looked at Vita.

'Transverse lie,' Vita said. 'That means your baby is lying across your belly instead of up and down, and so we must turn him round and pull him out. The best way is to pull by the feet. We call it the podalic version. Podalic means foot, you see, in the Greek.'

'Will it hurt?'

'Yes, I'm afraid it will.'

Mary Eileen turned to Dr. Boutwell. 'Can you do it?'

'Mrs. Culhane will perform the procedure with my assistance. Here now, breathe this.' He held a handkerchief under her nose. 'Just a drop or two of chloroform to ease the pain, but not too much because we need you awake.'

Anxiety clawed at Vita's stomach. She had seen Dr. Boutwell perform a podalic version once and she had read about the procedure, but she had never performed one herself.

'The heel, Mrs. Culhane, is what you feel for,' Dr. Boutwell reminded her, his hand resting on Mary Eileen's shoulder. 'Fingers can be mistaken for toes but the heel is unique to the foot.'

Slowly, Vita pushed one hand inside Mary Eileen and kept her other hand, her outside hand, on Mary Eileen's belly. Not only did she have to rotate the baby but she had to deliver the baby feet first, an arduous process. After Vita found one foot, she felt for the other one. Dr. Boutwell checked her position and nodded. 'You have both feet? All right now, carefully but firmly pull.' Mary Eileen, although dosed with chloroform, groaned.

Vita's first tug was too jerky and she nearly lost hold of a foot. 'Smoothly; nice and slow,' Dr. Boutwell said.

She took a breath and gripped the two slippery feet more firmly. Her heart was beating fast but it was important to stay calm, to keep herself from racing through the procedure. Slowly, inch by inch, she drew the baby down. But when at last the feet emerged, she saw that their color was a frightening grayish blue. The legs, the rubbery torso, even the nipples – all blue. Moments later she saw why: the baby's cord had wrapped itself not once but twice around her waxy neck. A baby girl, not breathing. Not alive.

Vita tried to speak but it came out as a moan. Dr. Boutwell took over, taking the tiny infant from Vita, wrapping her in a blanket, and then laying her little body on Mary Eileen's chest.

'I'm afraid this one didn't make it. I'm sorry, my dear. Her cord got around her neck, it probably happened sometime in the last week. Nothing to be done about it. But you still have a fine baby boy.'

Mary Eileen's eyes were wet with tears. 'A little girl?'

'Chances are that you'll have another, but you'll have to say good-bye to this one.'

The baby had fine, reddish-gold hair and fingers that gently curved inward. Puffy cheeks, broad lips, hardly a neck to be seen before her shoulders began. Her partially closed eyes suggested, though Vita couldn't say why, that her spirit was alive somewhere, just not in her body.

Babies die even as they're trying to be born. That's been true forever. But it still doesn't make sense, Vita thought, looking down at the tiny, still, perfect body. While Mrs. Keene showed Mary Eileen how to nurse the boy, Vita helped Dr. Boutwell deliver the placenta, which came out wet and glistening, embroidered with crisscrossing blue veins and a shimmer of gold. Even as she looked on it was flattening in his hands; an organ, when it was out of the womb, like a spent heart. Vita wiped the sweat from her eyelids with the crook of her arm and wrapped the placenta in cloth, to be carried out with the trash or buried beneath the mud on the riverbank. Her heart, so buoyant before, now felt like an anchor.

Another failure. This was worse, much worse, than being sick to her stomach, or misdiagnosing tapeworm. Dr. Boutwell said the cord had strangled the baby before labor had even begun, but how could he know?

'It's difficult and sad,' he said later, when they were outside and walking back to the streetcar stop. 'Very sad. But there was nothing you or I could do.'

The night air retained a scent of burning oil from the factories, though the smokestacks were no longer pushing out smoke. In spite of Dr. Boutwell's assurances, Vita couldn't help thinking that it must be her fault. Did I turn the baby the wrong way? she wondered. Is that possible? Or was it an earlier mistake, something else I did? Sick at heart: she understood that phrase now.

'We must count the successes,' Dr. Boutwell told her.

Count the successes. A depressing thought.

CHAPTER NINETEEN

'Study as she likes, and labour as she likes,
[the female doctor] will never equal the first-class
London surgeon, but she can nevertheless make
the village happier, teach hygienic laws which
prevent disease, or remove by a little skilled
advice the suffering [of a patient].'
(*The Spectator*, 1862)

April 1866, Boston, Massachusetts

After he returned from Baltimore, Jacob suffered from nightmares more vivid and frightening than ever. He tried sucking on horehound candy during the day and eating crackers with milk before going to bed – both cures Mrs. Humphrey, his charwoman, suggested – but his dreams only got worse, not better.

He didn't want to blame it on his old mate, Marshall. Maybe it was from the stress of travel? He'd become accustomed to his little house in Boston – in truth half a house, with an older married couple on the other side. He was used to its particular knocks and groans, the lean of afternoon shadows in his bedroom, the chipped third step going from the front door down to the sidewalk. Part of him wanted to just stay inside all day.

In almost every nightmare he was back in prison camp, usually trying to find food. But one night he dreamed that he was hiding, shivering with wet and cold in a muddy hole, petrified with the knowledge that if someone found him he'd be killed. After he climbed into the hole he'd pulled a man's putrid corpse over him as cover, and he could feel the weight of the man's back on his own back, dead flesh pressing down on his own. Though he tried to keep himself quiet and still, three men with red paint on their faces found him anyway. They pulled him out but somehow he managed to wrench himself away from their grip, and he began running down a dirt path alive with worms and maggots. The men caught up to him; one grabbed him by the back of his shirt. When they turned him around, Jacob realized that it wasn't paint on their faces at all, but blood. His blood. He looked down to see a gushing, bleeding wound in his abdomen and he made a gargling sound, more of a moan than a scream, as they dragged him back to the scaffold and the waiting noose.

He woke up shaking and sweating, his heart thundering in his chest. He had dreamed he was Junius Cray.

Junius Cray wasn't the worst thug at Andersonville, but he was fairly near the top. He was one of the Raiders, a gang of men who patrolled the camp in groups of five or six, scouting out victims. It was rumored that many of the Raiders, Union men all, came from the notorious Five Points in New York, but Jacob had come across more than one with a flat Midwestern accent.

Sometimes a lone Raider was captured and beaten or had half his head shaved, but usually it was the other way around – the Raiders, in a pack, pouncing on men who wouldn't give up their meager portion of cornmeal, pummeling them bloody. There were 'streets' and 'neighborhoods' in the prison camp, even a marketplace where you could buy an egg for a dollar, or a quart of sour milk for three. Junius Cray, like most of the Raiders, lived in what was known as Raiders Island in the middle of the camp's swampy middle; anyone foolish enough to wander into their territory was instantly robbed of whatever they carried or wore. There were no makeshift tents in Raiders Island, just holes in the ground where the men slept or ate.

Caleb used to say that the Raiders were too lazy to build proper shanties – they certainly had the means to steal whatever they needed from their work details or from other men. But Jacob believed they were cannier than that. They understood that these holes helped to enforce their reputation as savage dogs. They lured new arrivals to Raiders Island with promises of food or clothing, only to rob and beat them once they were there. In particular they targeted Tennessee men, since the guards had it out for them, too – southerners who were betrayers to the Southern cause. None of the guards looked twice if any Tennessee soldier 'accidentally' died.

Toward the end of the war, when the Raiders began stealing even from the camp's own stores, Junius Cray was sentenced to hanging. But somehow he escaped from the makeshift platform and hid himself in a hole beneath a corpse. Jacob had been one of the men who found him there. Junius struggled and kicked and tried to bite them as they hauled him back to be hanged.

When he awoke Jacob was terrified, and then confused, and then relieved as he recognized the green glass lamp on his bedside table. He switched it on, a hiss of ignition. The table was covered with a stiff white cotton drape yellowing with age and long immobility, like a doll's dress. When he turned his head he could make out the ironwork grill outside his window; it was closer to morning than night.

Gingerly, he felt his arms and then his face. No tics. A slight tremor in his left hand. Gradually his heartbeat slowed. The sight of the glass lamp and the yellowing table drape – ordinary objects in an ordinary bedroom – calmed him.

But he knew he wouldn't get back to sleep. He washed and shaved and dressed in the clothes he'd laid out for himself the night before. There was a medical college in Philadelphia that admitted women – exclusively women – and he'd planned to take the train there today, to look for Vita.

Out on the sidewalk he could smell the usual mixture of chimney smoke and something sea-rotted. Cabs pulled by weary-looking nags clopped slowly past him; he could wave one down, but he wanted to walk off the shakes if he could.

On the train, a grandmother-type carrying a cat in a bird-cage passed him a tin of biscuits, and two brothers – identical twins – offered him their extra newspaper. 'Delivered by mistake,' one said. For the first two stops, the four of them were the only ones in the car.

Jacob folded his coat to use as a pillow and closed his eyes, hoping to catch up on sleep, but instead he found himself thinking about the little business he and Caleb had got up in camp. They used to cook pancakes out of shared rations and some flour bought from one of the camp sutlers, which they sold in the prison marketplace – 'Broadway,' the prisoners called it – in the morning. With the extra money they could buy milk or medicine. One morning, it was sometime in the winter, a priest visited the marketplace distributing religious tracts in a drizzling cold rain.

'Repent your sins,' he told the prisoners, pushing the tracts into their hands. 'Read the Bible and repent.'

He spoke as if it was God who'd imprisoned them, and who was judging them (none too compassionately) even now. Two skeletal men began to lob clumps of mud at him: 'We want bread, not prayers!' Others followed suit. The priest, red-faced, puffed with anger, with a long smear of mud on his coat and – when he ducked the wrong way – the side of his face, called them animals. 'You reap what you sow,' he had snarled at them.

He thrust the tracts into the hands of a young boy and turned on his heel. Later Jacob saw the boy using the paper as kindling.

You reap what you sow.

Why had he dreamed he was Junius Cray? Did he feel guilty about something? About Vita? Now, all these months later, he could admit that maybe he hadn't taken her dream of becoming a doctor seriously enough. He joked when he was uncomfortable, and he saw how that might have been confusing. But she wasn't direct with him, either. She ran away without giving him a chance to explain himself. The morning she left, hot sunlight had streamed in through the thin hotel curtains, baking the room even after he struggled to open a window. He waited until the afternoon to leave for the train station, pacing that stifling room, hoping against hope she would return.

He missed her; that was the truth. He was still angry, though, too. But setting his brain to the task of sorting out his emotions was like trying to find water with a peach tree stick. The train car lurched and righted itself, and he could hear the old woman coo to her little cat. After a while the train's repeated shush and clank began to feel like a lullaby, and Jacob fell into a light, fragile sleep in which – thankfully – Junius Cray did not make an appearance.

Philadelphia was colder than Baltimore, and the women on the sidewalks seemed more subdued; certainly they wore drabber dresses. As he left the train station Jacob felt the wind brush the back of his neck, and when he looked up he could see masses of dense gray clouds inching across the sky as though being pulled by an invisible rope.

The Female Medical College was small enough to fit into a few rented rooms in the Women's Hospital, which was – he pulled the scrap of paper from his pocket to check the address – on North College Avenue. He shifted his carryall to his other hand and began to walk down the street. If he found a decent hotel along the way he would reserve a room; if not, he would just have to find one later.

He had only gone a couple of blocks before small, hard drops of rain started peppering his shoulders. He stopped to open his umbrella. He was standing outside a tavern with the 'Best Dutch gin in the city,' according to a card in the window, and he considered going inside to wait out the rain but instead he pressed on. The wind began blowing behind him, and by the time he turned onto North College Avenue his trousers clung wetly to the backs of his knees.

The hospital was a dark brick edifice in the middle of the block, with the aloof appearance he associated with banks. As if he had willed it, a young woman came out the front door and down the steps as he approached. She was hugging a load of heavy books in front of her chest and she wore a man's gray overcoat, which was oddly fetching. Her air of inner concentration reminded him of Vita.

'Excuse me,' he said. 'Are you a student here? At the college?'

She nodded, taking him in with cool, blue eyes. Her expression changed – it became just as shuttered as the brick building behind her.

Jacob paused, trying to decide which of Vita's names to use.

'Do you have a question? Or did you only come here to scoff?'

'Scoff?'

She made a face to illustrate, presumably, his opinion of her. '*The woman doctor*.'

'No, no. Nothing like that. I'm looking for someone, that's all. Vita Tenney. Or Vita Culhane.'

'Which one? Or are there two?'

Now she was mocking him. The rain came down harder. The girl had no umbrella and Jacob offered her his.

'No, thank you.'

He persisted, holding it over her head. 'I have another,' he lied.

She shifted her books and took it. Her fingers were stained with ink. Also like Vita.

'Vita Tenney Culhane,' Jacob said.

'Why do you want her?'

'I'm her brother.'

How was it that 'husband' seemed threatening? But it did.

'Well, I don't know her. And as there are only eight of us, I can say for a fact she's not going to the school.'

'Is there anyone she might be apprenticing with? I'm thinking of a professor, a doctor. She would be looking for a preceptor.'

The girl thrust the umbrella back, ready to be rid of him. 'I haven't heard anyone mention anyone called Vita.'

'Please, you keep it. Just one more thing. Do you know if the Cleveland Medical College admits women students?'

'They don't, the rogues. Not anymore. They used to.'

She was holding his umbrella with her left hand and she jiggled up her books with her right. 'All right?' She wanted to be off.

'Thank you,' he said. When she was a few feet past him he turned and called, 'Good luck with your studies!'

Nothing, not even an acknowledging shrug. Is this what Vita will be like? Jacob wondered. Hard and embittered? Defended against – what did the girl call it – *scoffs*? Before he'd stopped her, she'd had a different look altogether, absorbed and placid. He was the one who disturbed that. Raindrops collected on the brim of his hat.

He ducked into the bar with the good Dutch gin and had a drink, and then another one, and then he went to a hotel around the corner that the barkeep recommended. In all that time the rain never stopped, though it never got worse, either. It was still raining when he got on the train the next morning, and the wet weather lasted all the way to New Haven. Boston was overcast, but dry. When Jacob unlocked his front door and scooped up the mail from where it had pooled under the mail slot, he saw the letter from Amelia on top.

CHAPTER TWENTY

'Ladies are all very well in their place, and that is looking after the latest Paris fashions and making tea at home.'
(*The Medical Press and Circular*, 1870)

April 1866, Lark's Eye, Massachusetts

Marie was helping Mrs. O. clean the lamp chimneys when she heard the front door open and a slow, heavy tread as someone descended the kitchen stairs.

'Mitty!' Amelia said, coming into the kitchen. She kissed her and plunked herself down at the table. 'Oof, I didn't think I would make it.' She unfolded a napkin and mopped her forehead and cheeks. 'It's as hot as summer outside.'

Marie had her sleeves rolled up and a big apron tied around her neck. She pulled on a pair of old cleaning gloves, tied a piece of sponge around the end of a long pine twig that Mrs. O. had snapped off from one of the trees in the yard, and began rubbing the inside of a lamp chimney. As she worked on the smoke-coated glass, it began to look as though someone were etching out a secret code, like the Irish *Ogham* – scratches on a post. Meanwhile Mrs. O. was constructing new lamp wicks out of strips of canton flannel.

'Would you like to help us?' Marie asked Amelia.

'Let me catch my breath first.'

Amelia was six months pregnant and enjoyed the pretense of frailty. However, if anything she seemed healthier and better-looking than she was a year ago. Her lips were full and very red, her face had widened, and her cheekbones were more prominent. But she liked to heave herself about a little, and beg off chores. Gemma had begun working for her in town, and with Arthur's practice only recently stuttering back to life, Marie was glad to have Holland pay Gemma's wages for a while. She wasn't worried – not very worried – but she had to be careful.

'We were discussing your sister,' she said.

Amelia rolled her eyes. 'What else?' But Marie noticed a sly look coming over her. 'Any news?'

'No, nothing.'

Mrs. O. measured a long piece of flannel and folded it down to the width of a wick, overcasting the edge. 'She's just getting herself to some college talks. Isn't that what you said? No doubt she'll come back when she's spent all her money.'

'I do wish she'd send her address.'

'Maybe she's afraid Jacob will find her and drag her back.' Amelia's eyes glittered at the thought.

'She's all right,' Mrs. O. said, 'only stubborn. But I'll say it again: it was a wicked thing for a girl to do.'

Marie picked up another lamp chimney. 'She and Jacob must have quarreled. He didn't say so, but they must have.'

They kept their voices low although Arthur was, as usual, shut away in his office reading newspapers, or cutting out articles and pasting them into a new scrapbook he was making all about one battle, the first battle of Bull Run, and the mistakes that were made there.

'Maybe I should go to Boston myself to look for her.'

Mrs. O. blew out air. 'It's the husband's job to do that, not yours. Not anymore.'

Marie had had a letter this morning from her friend Deborah Delong, and another last week from her cousin Maria. She found she was enjoying her renewed correspondence with its family news, gossip, even recipes. But no one had seen Vita. Marie considered putting an advertisement in city papers ('Please write to this address if you have seen . . .'), but that made Vita seem like a criminal, or a dog. She swung back and forth between thinking she was doing too little or too much. These days, between her renewed correspondence – she'd begun writing letters to acquaintances in Pittsburgh and Baltimore, and even to an old neighbor who'd moved to the Dakota Territory, although she didn't think Vita would get that far – and her work with Mrs. O. now that Gemma wasn't there every day, she'd nearly stopped having her biweekly tea. There was too much to do.

'How's Sweetie?' Amelia asked.

Sweetie had not been as upset when Vita left as she had been when Freddy left – she pulled out a few of her feathers but was mostly content to chew on paper rolls – however she fell ill again last week and Marie had to feed her sugar water through a dropper every four hours, even at night.

'She's recovered. Dar likes to have her in his office now.'

'What?'

'He's moved her perch in there.'

'But he hates Sweetie!'

'I wouldn't say hate.'

'He thinks she's *unhygienic*.' Amelia mimicked her father's tone. No one smiled.

Marie was scraping the bottom of the filmy lamp glass in short, hard thrusts. 'Sweetie reminds him of Freddy, he says.'

Freddy had had the same black hair and dark blue eyes as Vita, and for a long while, before he shot up like a bean on a pole, they were the same height. People used to think they were twins. Vita was always better at their shared lessons even though she was younger, but she also didn't mind if Freddy teased her – perhaps that helped balance things out. Marie suspected Vita sometimes finished his schoolwork for him so they could go out and climb trees. Arthur liked to praise Freddy's work but Vita's was never neat enough, or the graph line she drew wasn't perfectly straight, or she didn't completely erase a previous answer. There was always something.

Marie pulled out the dirtied sponge and said, 'It's a comfort to him now, having Sweetie.'

'If only that war had never happened,' Mrs. O. said. 'That's what I blame this on. The war's what gave Vita ideas.'

'Vita's always had *ideas*,' Amelia said.

Once, when the war was going badly – and in the first three years the war was always going badly – Marie had gone in secret to a Copperhead meeting down at the little schoolhouse on the other side of the Lark's Eye Bay. She'd hitched up Miss Freckles, their old pony, to the pony cart, and drove herself with only the light of the moon as a guide. She was tired of only contributing tablecloths and sheets to the cause; she wanted to do something, anything, to end it. She rode past the stone farmsteads and, closer to town, two-story clapboard houses with double-deck porches. A lamp was burning in the school window as a signal, and there was an armed sentry at the door. Copperheads, who were opposed to the war, had to meet in secret.

It was after midnight when the meeting began. When Marie walked in she saw to her surprise that there were probably forty people cramming themselves on the squat benches meant for children, all Northerners who wanted to end the war. Many of them Marie didn't even recognize; where had they come from, up the coast? Like a Quaker meeting, the men (she was the only woman) rose from their bench when they wanted to address the room. At first the speeches felt sympathetic – we don't want the slaughter of our boys to continue – but it quickly turned ugly. An old man with long ragged hair and a boil on his neck declared that slavery wasn't the cause of the war, but abolition. Abolition, *that's* what needs to be abolished, he'd said. Marie had been sickened by the yells of agreement and stamping feet. The next man spoke of the importance of keeping free blacks from northern soil. 'We don't want 'em either,' he said. She couldn't even bring herself to nod to the sentry as she left. When she picked up the pony cart reins, she saw that her hands were shaking with anger.

Amelia was stroking her stomach gently with one outstretched finger. 'I wonder how it is that Gemma isn't pregnant yet. She got married before I did.'

Marie and Mrs. O. exchanged a glance.

'Amelia, you know there are ways to keep from getting pregnant,' Marie said.

'Why on earth would you want to? No, it's because I'm lucky. I'm always lucky.'

Marie felt a prick of irritation but she tried to get past it. 'Well yes, you and Holland have been very fortunate.'

'I'm always fortunate,' Amelia said.

'Don't tempt fate,' Mrs. O. warned. Using a fork, she spread apart the new wicks she'd made, which were soaking in strong-smelling vinegar in an old pie tin. Amelia wrinkled her nose.

'I mean it. Many girls won't have husbands now, because of the war, or their husbands will be defective – no, Mitty, it's true; however sad it is, we have to admit that it's true. And Holland is – well, you can't even tell that he limps anymore, not really, not with his new shoes. He has a good job, and he's handsome. And soon we'll have a beautiful little baby. Vita has missed out on everything. She could have had it but she threw it away. Really, Mitty, I have no sympathy for her.'

'Yes, I can tell.'

'Jacob is handsome, too. A little jittery from the war, but that's all. She was cruel to leave him. Don't you think? You agree with me, don't you Mrs. O.?'

Mrs. Oakum sniffed. 'Well. Not that I'd say it like that.'

'And don't you think that if we can help Jacob we should?'

Marie could feel the muscles at the back of her neck tighten. She put down the sponge. 'Amelia, what do you know?'

Amelia grinned in victory. 'Look at this.' She pulled a letter out of her dress pocket. 'From Vita to Gemma last week.'

'Amelia! You took someone's letter? Someone's private property?'

'Gemma left it at my house! And the house *is* my property. It was in a kitchen drawer, just stuffed in, maybe she forgot it.'

'You know that that's wrong.' Marie felt competing emotions unfurl within her: shock and disapproval and gratitude.

'I'll take it,' Mrs. O. said. She held out her hand. 'And so's you know, I agree with your mother. Never once in all my life in this house has anyone taken my letters.'

'You don't get any letters,' Amelia said, but she handed it over.

'Now I'm not going to read it, I'm only going to look at the return address.' Mrs. O. glanced at Marie. 'Cleveland,' she said.

'I know! I was shocked! I've already written to Jacob,' Amelia told them, not bothering to hide the triumph in her voice.

'You wrote to him? Without talking to me first?'

'I think he has a right to know,' Amelia said.

She looks very prim, Marie thought, but she can be as sneaky as Freddy. 'What did he say?'

'He hasn't answered yet. I only just wrote on Tuesday.'

Cleveland. Was there a medical college in Cleveland? Marie didn't know. She wanted to read the letter. But she shouldn't. She shouldn't even ask Amelia about it, but she couldn't help herself. 'And Vita, is she all right?'

'She's working with a doctor. Boutwell, his name is.'

Boutwell. The name rang a bell. One of her sister Clara's acquaintances? It would come to her. The lamps had all been wiped, and were lined up on a clean cloth on the kitchen table. Marie turned her back – glad that her face was hidden – and began loading them on a tray.

'I'll bring these upstairs,' she told Mrs. O.

Her heart was singing with relief.

CHAPTER TWENTY-ONE

'To live a chaste life, avoid food containing aphrodisiac stimulants, such as coffee, eggs, and oysters. Remember that it is chiefly the action of the mind that stimulates excessive secretion.'
(*Tokology, A Book for Every Woman*,
Dr. Alice B. Stockham, M.D., 1905)

May 1866, Cleveland, Ohio

There was a blacksmith up the block from Dr. Boutwell's office who worked with the long double doors of his workshop thrown open to the sidewalk; passersby learned to cross the street to avoid flying sparks. On her low days, the hammering thuds, sometimes crisp and sometimes muted, made Vita think of goblins knocking at her heart.

Not only had she left Jacob, but she had left him for nothing. She was no good at doctoring. She could memorize conditions and cures all she wanted, but when it came to actual patients she kept getting it wrong. One night she dreamed that she was back in the little tarpaper kitchen with Mary Eileen Doherty, but instead of attending to Mary Eileen she was staring at the kitchen curtains as they shifted about in a draft. When she looked down, she found the dead baby in her arms. Cold legs, little blue toes, toenails like grains of rice. She woke up thinking: it's my fault for not paying close enough attention.

She always thought she was different than Amelia and the other girls back in Lark's Eye, that she was smarter and more capable. But she wasn't. Don't give yourself airs, Amelia often told her. Don't read books in town, don't memorize Latin conjugations, don't want anything more than what's placed before you. Maybe she should have listened.

She dreaded going back to sleep and dropping into another dream, so Vita lit a candle and reread Denham's chapter on anomalous births until it was time for breakfast. In the dining room she found Soot already at the table holding *Frank Leslie's Illustrated Newspaper* unfolded in front of him.

'G'morning!' he said. 'Do you have the book?'

Last night he had successfully recited his multiplications tables up to and including the eights; as a reward, he was allowed to keep Vita's anatomy book for the whole day today.

'I left it outside your bedroom door. Your mother doesn't like you reading at the table, you know.' ('I don't think it's very nice to look at a man's private innards while you eat.')

Soot shook his newspaper irritably like a middle-aged banker, and Vita tried to hold back a smile. She could so easily picture him wearing a little mustache, a walking stick at the ready. Small for his age, Soot had to hold his elbows up to keep the newspaper off the table; at last he gave up, folded it in thirds, and laid it beside his plate.

Outside the window, Vita could see men walking down the sidewalk with handkerchiefs held against their mouths and noses. The morning was unusually dark, and a black, greasy smoke hung in the air. Another fire probably at one of the oil stills. It was cold, too, a shift back toward winter, although a few days ago, at the Soldiers' Home, it felt almost like spring. A couple of windows at one end of the ward were open, and Vita felt a fingertip of breeze on the back of her neck as she bent to clean a boil from a young soldier's shoulder. Her father used to call a boil a wen. She thought of Dar, who had a very gentle touch, as she mixed an ounce of origanum oil, an ounce of spirits of wine, and an ounce of spirits of turpentine in a shallow bowl. She spread the mixture on a rectangle of soft linen and tried to apply it as tenderly as she could to the boy's soft skin.

His name was Walter Cutter, and like Jacob his hands shook when he was anxious or if he heard a sudden noise – they had to relocate another soldier because he kept a loud pocket watch on the wicker table between their beds. While Vita cleaned his boil, he tried to hide his shaking hands under the bed sheet. But he saw that she noticed them anyway.

'Don't tie my hands, please don't,' he begged her; this was Dr. Hotchkiss's treatment for shakes.

Her heart had turned over. He had a round face, hooded eyes, and his voice was light and timid. Only the finest baby hairs grew over his top lip. He was not much older than Soot – he'd been a drummer during the last six months of the war.

'No, I won't do that, Mr. Cutter. How about some warm milk instead?' Lucy liked to recommend warm milk with a dash of vanilla to offset tremors. 'I can help you with the cup,' Vita assured him. But she saw he was afraid of her, that he mistrusted her. She didn't know how to inspire confidence the way Dr. Boutwell and Lucy could.

Add that to the list.

Before she served herself breakfast, Vita gave Soot a professional look-over. Last month he'd had a mild case of pneumonia and was slowly – *very* slowly – recovering. He had no great wish, Vita suspected, to go back to school.

'Let me feel your lymph nodes,' she said, and Soot allowed her to lay two fingers on his neck. She hated to think of him drumming into a battle like Walter Cutter. But if Soot had been born two years earlier, he might have done.

She took her hand away. 'Not swollen in the least. I think you're completely recovered.'

'Yes – just about.' He managed a cough.

While she helped herself to eggs Soot stirred several large teaspoons of sugar into his coffee cup, which, by the look of it, contained mostly cream.

'What'll you do today, d'you expect?' he asked. Since he'd been ill she'd been telling him patient stories; as a double benefit, this also worked to help her remember the cases and cures.

'It's Monday, so we'll see patients in the office.'

'Will you see that girl with the butter bean plant growing in her ear?'

'No, we removed that.'

'Can she hear again now? Could she hear this?' He whistled softly.

'I've no doubt she could.'

'If she had pushed the seed into her eye,' he asked, 'would it have grown itself there?'

'A seed likes a warm, moist spot. An eye isn't really warm enough. Also, don't you think it would have bothered her much sooner if it had lodged in her eyelid? The *palpebra*. That's the lower lid.'

A delighted expression washed over his face. 'If she didn't, it would creep up all over her eyeball. What's the science name for eyeball?'

'Scientific. The eyeball has a number of different parts. The *cornea*, the *choroid*, the *retina* . . . look it up in the book, why don't you. When I get home this afternoon I'll quiz you on that, and on your nines and tens.'

She stacked her empty coffee cup and saucer on her plate and stood up. She could hear Reverend Simpers coming down the stairs with his slow, important-sounding gait. Did she have time to slip something for lunch into her pocket? She shook out her handkerchief.

'Tens are easy! Will I get to keep the book longer this time?'

'I need it tonight, but you can have it again tomorrow. *If* you've got your nines and tens memorized.'

'Good morning Stewart,' Reverend Simpers said.

She hadn't been quick enough. The reverend stood in the doorway surveying the room with his usual air of ownership. Everything about him from his stiff collar to his waved hair – how long did it take him to wave it every morning? she wondered – was precise and unyielding and stern. He was like a false prince in a fairy tale: handsome but sly.

'And how's our little doctor? I wonder,' he said as Vita tried to make her way around him, 'if you don't mind, would you pour me a cup of coffee before you go? My hands are a bit shaky this morning.'

His hands were as still as tree stumps but he loved to find excuses for women to wait on him. She could smell the lemon he used in his hair to keep it yellow – this according to Soot, who overheard him asking Gracelin, their cook, for one. She poured him the cup of coffee, skimping on the cream. Then, before he could ask for anything else, she made her escape into the smoky street.

To Vita's surprise, Dr. Boutwell was already with a patient when she got to the office. A young man was sitting on the stool near the window, holding a bloodied grain sack against the side of his face.

'Found him waiting by the door. An accident with a hook in his meat truck.'

Blood was streaming down the young man's temple, though some of it might be the cow's, he explained. Dr. Boutwell flushed the wound with water, and then he threaded a small needle and selected a needle holder, which resembled a pair of scissors with flat blades and grooves at the end to grasp the needle.

'Some say that a scalp laceration can be closed by tying the hair on either side of it into a knot, but I've never seen how that can work. Blood makes everything slippery.' He handed the needle holder to Vita. 'You must avoid the hairs of his eyebrow, if you can.'

The slice was about an inch long. Vita applied pressure in the direction of the needle and she rested her forefinger on the flat surface of the needle holder to keep her hand steady. Curve and sweep upward, she thought. After four stitches she looped the long end of the thread around the needle holder, grasped the shorter end, and pulled the wound ends together. Then she looped the long end of the thread around the holder in the opposite way.

Dr. Boutwell nodded. 'Now once more, for a firm knot.'

If she pulled too tightly the skin would pucker; that had happened before. Slowly now, she thought, bending over her work.

'Well done,' Dr. Boutwell said when Vita snipped the thread end and stood back. The stitches were tiny and perfect, and she had created them. She wanted to just stand there and admire each one.

'Will I have a scar?' the man asked as Dr. Boutwell began wrapping a clean bandage over his wound.

'You're lucky you aren't a quarter inch taller,' Dr. Boutwell told him.

❁

That afternoon Vita saw her first case of syphilis. They were treating a man who had overturned a coffee pot in the back office of his shop and badly burned his hand. Dr. Boutwell immersed the man's hand and wrist in a solution of sodium carbonate, while Vita prepared a lotion of carbolic acid and olive oil. The shopkeeper, Mr. Mankrik, watched Vita with an annoyed expression, as though she were responsible for his accident. When the lotion was ready Vita applied it to the scaly areas of his skin with cotton batting.

Afterward, Mr. Mankrik tested his hand, curling it into a fist. 'By the by, can I have something for my throat?' He spoke with a low, hoarse voice. 'It's been acting up this last month. A gargle, if you have it?'

'Your throat has been sore for a month?'

'Maybe two.'

'A month or two!' Dr. Boutwell turned to wash his hands again. 'I'd better have a look.'

Mr. Mankrik took off his collar and tie. There were white patches on his throat and a speckled rash that started below his collarbone. Dr. Boutwell asked the man to unbutton his shirt.

A glance at Vita. 'What, and with her here?'

'She's my assistant. Remember who bandaged your hand for you?'

The sky was still hazy with factory smoke, and Vita brought over another kerosene lamp for more light. Dr. Boutwell found the primary lesion, which was already healing, but the rash had spread over the man's barrel chest.

'Why didn't you see me about this?' he asked. 'You have syphilis. You'll need to be treated. I'll give you medicine to rub on yourself, and you must use it every day. Come back and see me next week.'

Syphilis! Vita looked at his rash more closely. Coppery rash; hoarse voice; throat inflammation; yellow skin. It added up. The man had curly hair that was thinning on top, a thick neck, and close-set eyes behind spectacles. Not someone you would peg as a Lothario.

'Are you married?' Vita asked.

'Yes.'

'Tell your wife she must come in, too.'

'But her throat is fine!'

'She'll need the medicine, in any case.'

Mr. Mankrik looked at Dr. Boutwell for confirmation. 'She will?'

'You heard Mrs. Culhane,' Dr. Boutwell told him sternly. 'Bring your wife in tomorrow, Mr. Mankrik. And any other woman with whom you've had relations.'

'But I never!' Now he looked scared. 'I go to church every Sunday,' he protested.

Dr. Boutwell raised his eyebrows. 'Many men do.'

On Friday, at the Soldiers' Home, there was another case.

'A coincidence?' Vita asked. The man had heavy eyelids and a droopy lower lip. An inexplicable smell of moss hung about him.

Dr. Boutwell shook his head. 'This is what happens after a war. Soon enough women will start coming in with their children; the men infect them by sharing their bowls and spoons. Be sure to wash your hands with mercury compound after every examination.'

He asked Vita to mix up the ointment while he continued his rounds. After she put the ingredients together, she sat on the empty bed near the infected soldier and began to stir it with a short wooden spoon. There were more empty beds today than occupied. The Soldiers' Home was thinning out. Most of the soldiers passing through Cleveland now only received a check-up and a meal before they went on their way. Vita missed the one-armed veteran, Mr. Bollinger, who used to go around reading Dickens to soldiers confined to bed; he'd found a teaching job in Dayton. And Captain Marcus Jonathan, who let them practice bandaging on him, left to be a janitor in the Finnish Hall, where he was given a bed in the basement. Soon the Home would be shut down altogether, although the streets were still full of veterans looking for work or begging for coins near churches.

'Army sent me all the way to Texas,' the soldier told Vita while she stirred up his black ointment. 'Not much war going on in Texas.' He sounded aggrieved.

'You're lucky. You could have been killed.'

'Me? There's no bullet made could kill me.'

'No one is safe from a well-aimed bullet, Mr. Drummond.'

'I've got a buffalo hide. Bullets jump right off.'

Vita pushed the ointment into a squat jar. 'This is for you to take with you. You must spread it on yourself every day for a month.'

Drummond took the jar, slumping forward and cocking his head to look into it. He had a bad eye, she realized. Toward the end of the war they were taking almost anybody, thrusting a gun in their hand and hoping for the best.

'How about if you lather it on for me?' he asked slyly.

'Certainly. And I'll put a good dose in your mouth as well, which might stop you from talking nonsense. No man has buffalo skin. And your condition, syphilis, that's a serious condition.'

But he didn't seem the least bit ashamed or fearful. After writing him out instructions – 'Can you read, Mr. Drummond?' 'Most every letter,' he joked – Vita went to find Dr. Boutwell. He was standing with an orderly by the bed of a soldier who'd arrived just that morning, and had been trying to leave ever since. His name, according to the card attached to his belt loop, was Captain Tamby.

'Let me go, I'm hot, I'm drowning,' Captain Tamby kept saying.

'Sepsis, I'm afraid,' Dr. Boutwell said to Vita in a low voice. 'The arm will have to go. Take a look.'

She asked the captain if she might take a look at his arm and, turning it over, saw the telltale red line stretching up from his infected hand toward his elbow.

'I've sent for Dr. Hotchkiss. One of the nurses told me that he stepped out for a newspaper.'

'Why wait?' Vita asked.

'We need a surgeon.'

'But you're a surgeon.'

'We can wait for Dr. Hotchkiss. Ten minutes won't make a difference.'

'But –' Vita looked at the distressed soldier, who was breathing rapidly. She put a hand to his forehead. 'He's got a fever.'

'His lips aren't blue and his heart rate is fine.'

She put two fingers alongside Captain Tamby's throat. 'It feels a little elevated to me. Don't worry, I can assist you.'

Dr. Boutwell shook his head, not meeting her eye, and she thought: He doesn't trust me. I've failed too many times.

'I'll be all right,' she assured him.

'We'll wait.'

'I promise I can do this.'

Dr. Boutwell snapped. 'I won't take it off, I tell you!'

Both she and the orderly stared at him in surprise, and Captain Tamby took advantage of their inattention to wrench himself away and pull up his shirt. 'I need a bath, I need water. Water for my belly, can't you see.'

'What's all this?' Dr. Hotchkiss asked, coming up to them. Lucy, who'd gone to fetch him, stood behind him still wearing her heavy cape.

'Dr. Hotchkiss,' Dr. Boutwell said, clearly relieved. 'A case of sepsis, I'm afraid. The man's all right; a little delirious though.'

Vita listened as the two men consulted with each other. She had never seen Dr. Boutwell refuse to help anyone before. He was a generous man who considered his patients before anything else, and the most competent doctor she knew – certainly more knowledgeable than her father, even in his good days.

'Best to start straight away. You'll assist me?' Dr. Hotchkiss asked Dr. Boutwell.

Dr. Boutwell smiled stiffly. 'I'm afraid that isn't possible. But Mrs. Culhane, here . . .' Both men looked at her. 'She is quite able. She can assist in my place.'

Vita and Lucy hurried along after Dr. Hotchkiss to the little surgery behind the ward where they performed minor procedures. Vita felt for her notebook in her dress pocket while Lucy switched on the string of overhead lights and checked the stack of clean bandages. She gave Vita an encouraging smile. Vita smiled back, she hoped convincingly, and turned to help the orderly lift Captain Tamby onto the high, white bed. Then they all washed their hands.

The mattress had cloth straps sewn into its sides, and they had to tie the captain's wrists down so they could examine him. Dr. Hotchkiss asked Vita to take his pulse, and she felt the inside wrist with her fingertips.

'Very weak.'

She shook out a few drops of chloroform from its lemon-colored bottle onto a clean sponge and held it under the captain's nose while Lucy held his head still. His nostrils, flaring angrily, were very white, the rims like curved fingernail clippings. But after a minute the drug took effect and he closed his eyes, relaxing his shoulders. Lucy pulled down the bed sheet just enough to expose the captain's infected arm.

The orderly took a step toward the door when he saw Dr. Hotchkiss strapping a tourniquet onto the captain's arm. It had a leather strap and a steel buckle, and once he got the contraption positioned where he wanted it, he tightened the buckle's metal screw. Vita saw the orderly blanch and put his hand to his mouth, and although Lucy shook her head vigorously at him he slipped out anyway, closing the door behind him. The lights – gas lights, donated by the gas company at the beginning of the war – flickered for a moment.

Dr. Hotchkiss chose a large, single-edged knife from the instruments laid out on a clean towel on the trolley. He began making a circular incision below the elbow. Vita felt warm saliva pool on her tongue and she disciplined herself to inhale slowly, exhale, and inhale slowly again.

'Mrs. Culhane, please use forceps to clamp this vessel.'

Vita picked up a pair of tiny sterilized forceps from the trolley. The skin of the man's arm was pulled back to reveal a roadwork of vessels; each one looked like a little white pipe. She clamped the forceps on the one he indicated, and Dr. Hotchkiss said, 'Fine, keep going.'

She turned for more forceps, clamping them on the vessels, until at last Dr. Hotchkiss said that would do. He was ready to saw the round bone. It seemed impossible, but Captain Tamby was still breathing; Vita could see his chest moving while the doctor cut through the round bone. After the arm fell away, Lucy covered it with a sheet and took it from the room while Dr. Hotchkiss began sewing up the man's skin with large stitches.

Vita pulled out her notebook. There was still wet blood on her knuckles – she wiped her hands hastily with a rag – but she wanted to make a drawing of the doctor's stitch before she forgot it.

'Keeping notes, eh?' Dr. Hotchkiss asked, picking up a clean towel. He mopped perspiration off his beard, and then folded the towel to a point and dabbed at his mustache. 'They train all you ladies quite rigorously here. You'll make a good nurse one day.'

She supposed he could tell she wasn't one of the proper nurses because she was not wearing the long fever-proof dress they all wore, nor the tall round hat that served no purpose, as far as she could tell, except to mark them as professionals.

'I'm studying to be a doctor,' she told him. She was feeling reckless and proud. The last time she was in the little surgery with Dr. Hotchkiss, it had been to re-stitch a soldier's chest wound that had reopened. After he removed the old sutures and cleaned the area, Dr. Hotchkiss had taken Vita's hands without asking and positioned her fingers on the torn flesh to hold it closed while he sewed. She tried not to look at the man's yellow-and-plum-colored wound, shaped like an upside-down funnel, but when Dr. Hotchkiss finished and left the room she had vomited into the wastebasket.

Now she was elated with herself not only for her work but also for not getting sick. It had been weeks, she realized, since a procedure had made her sick. Maybe there was hope for her.

'Well you'll do very well,' Dr. Hotchkiss said. He had the deep, well-modulated voice of a man confident in his opinions. 'Very well indeed.'

For a moment, Vita glowed.

'Why don't you come see me at the Charity Hospital when the Soldiers' Home closes, and we'll find you a nursing job. After you've completed your training.'

She realized that he hadn't heard her. She raised her voice.

'Yes but you see, I'm studying to be a doctor, not a nurse.'

'Mm, that's fine,' he said, beginning to sort his instruments. Without looking up, he asked if she would bring him some tea.

A warm wave of embarrassment flooded through her. *Tea!* She strode out to the ward, her cheeks burning. Half of the blows came unexpectedly, like this one. At least with Reverend Simpers she knew to put up her defenses immediately. When she'd been clamping the tiny white vessels, she'd imagined her father standing there with Dr. Hotchkiss, watching with his hands behind his back. In her fantasy, he was nodding approvingly at her work. She knew it was childish, but she wanted recognition. *You'll be a fine doctor one day.*

Still, she found she couldn't ignore Dr. Hotchkiss, as he ignored her. He had just saved a man's life. Two older nurses – real nurses, with the silly round hats – were making up one of the beds at the end of the aisle. Vita made her way over to them and relayed the doctor's request for tea.

❁

Afterward she found Dr. Boutwell in the front room near where the veterans lined up to get pension forms. He was leaning against the wall smoking a cigar, his creased doctor's bag on the floor by his feet. As soon as he saw Vita he held out her cloak to her. He was already wearing his overcoat.

'I wasn't sick!' she told him. 'I didn't feel sick at all. I even helped clamp the blood vessels.'

Dr. Boutwell said, 'That's wonderful,' and watched her do up her cloak's large brass buttons.

'He told me I would make a very good nurse.' She tried to laugh it off. 'Even after I told him I was studying to be a doctor.'

Outside the wind rose to meet them, bringing with it the smell of burned oil. Dr. Boutwell seemed far away; was he even listening? They crossed the busy street to walk along the lake, where barges were chuffing to bring in their cargo. Further out over the water a mist had begun rolling toward the shore, like an army of men in concentrated pursuit of their prey. A few soft raindrops fell against her face.

'Why wouldn't you assist Dr. Hotchkiss yourself?' Vita asked. She was hoping he would say something complimentary – I knew you could it, or even, it's good training for you – but instead he said, 'It's better for me not to.'

That surprised her. 'Why?'

He was looking straight ahead. She thought he hadn't heard her over the wind.

'Why is it better?' she repeated.

'I performed too many of them.' His voice was strained and high.

'Too *many* of them?'

She glanced at his face. He still wouldn't look at her. As they approached the corner, horses clopped by in either direction, competing with the wind.

'I shouldn't go there. I thought I could help, but I shouldn't go.'

'You mean to the Soldiers' Home?'

'I shouldn't even be doctoring, but I have to make a living, don't I?'

'You shouldn't be doctoring?' That made no sense. 'You're the best doctor I know!'

He frowned. 'It's been a long day,' he said, 'and it's starting to rain. I'll pay for a cab.'

'But we're so close now.' The streetcar stop was half a block away.

He raised his cane anyway. A cab drove by them, the horse kicking up water from a gravelly puddle. Vita had never seen Dr. Boutwell downhearted before. She felt the urge to comfort him.

'You were a good friend to Freddy. I know he missed you when you left.'

'He was the only one who did.'

'I'm sure that's not true!'

'It is true. They wanted me gone. They told me so.'

'Who told you?'

'After I took off Maddock's arm in Chancellorsville. The lieutenant colonel. He said to me, "I needed my arm, and you took it from me."'

'Then he was a fool. You probably saved his life.'

'I did save his life, but it didn't matter. They thought I was using the army hospital as my own personal training ground. As if I would do anything but try to save those boys! You can't imagine the piles of arms and legs outside the hospital tent. The ears, the feet, even scalps. And the dead house, that was its own kind of hell.'

Vita didn't know what to say.

'After his arm was gone, the lieutenant ordered me to cut back all amputations by half. But how could I do that in good conscience?'

'What did you say to him?'

'What *could* I say? I left.'

'You left? But –' she thought about Freddy's letters. 'I thought – Freddy wrote – that you left because your mother was dying? The army reassigned you to Cleveland, so you could be near her.'

'*Honorable discharge*,' he said with bitterness.

A thought began circling like smoke, half-formed. 'So it was your idea to leave the unit?'

'They wanted me gone. I obliged them.'

She looked hard at the street traffic trying to distract herself, but the thought landed anyway: If he hadn't left, if he had stayed with the unit, he would have known to take off Freddy's arm, and Freddy would have lived.

'The surgeon who replaced you,' she said carefully, 'he didn't believe in amputations.'

'Another fool. The army was full of them.'

Despite the light rain, her face felt hot. Dr. Boutwell lifted his cane at another cab, and the approaching horse raised and lowered his head as if checking their respectability. Vita thought about the captain back in the Soldiers' Home. The stub of his arm would be bandaged by now. He'd be lying in the regulation cot on the ward, maybe waking up and taking some broth. Why does he get to live, and not Freddy? Why did Freddy have to die? It was not fair to have these thoughts, but it was impossible not to. The question never went away. It could never be answered.

The heart in its action produces two sounds; the first is a sound of propulsion, and the second is a sound of arrestment.

The cabbie shouted down a cheerless greeting at them as his horse came to a halt, twitching its tail.

Vita said, 'I think I'll take the streetcar anyway. I can see one coming.'

Dr. Boutwell didn't try to persuade her. His face was closed and unreadable, like the chloroformed captain on the operating table waiting for something to be cut from him. He climbed into the cab and rested his cane beside him on the seat. He barely nodded good-bye. Vita watched his cab drive off while the streetcar rang its approach in repeating jangles like a mockery. She found an empty seat next to a woman holding a chicken on a leash, and she stared at its little hemp collar trying to stave off the emotions gathering inside her, getting ready to bloom, already uncomfortable. Dr. Boutwell had done more for her than her own father would do. He was her ally. How do you forgive an ally? Raindrops spat in through the glassless windows and the wind seemed to turn as the street turned, so that Vita kept getting wetter and wetter. By the time she got home she felt damp right through, as though the rain had soaked into her veins where it circulated with her blood.

The rain, it raineth every day, Vita thought. What was that from, some poem? Shakespeare? Her mother would know. She wished she could conjure up Mitty beside her, feel Mitty's hands brushing her hair. Up in her room she got into bed and – since she should be studying –propped *Researches on Fever* against the pillow beside her as a kind of compromise.

It wasn't Dr. Boutwell's fault. Rationally, she knew this was true. If he had known what would happen to Freddy, he would have stayed. She felt sure this was true also, although it didn't make her feel better. She burrowed beneath her blankets and rubbed her feet together to warm them. She didn't want to leave her bed for a long, long time – maybe ever.

She must have fallen asleep. When she opened her eyes the dinner bell was ringing, but she didn't know if it was the first or the second.

To her surprise she felt marginally better. She took the time to look for dry stockings, only to realize after some silent minutes that she must have heard the second bell, not the first.

As she ran down the stairs she could hear the reverend's voice droning importantly from the dining room.

'The political dissidents with their violent natures were bent on aggression,' he was saying from his place at the foot of the table. 'Naturally they had to be stopped by whatever means possible. The Russians understand how to put down a crowd.'

Unbelievable; he was lecturing Mr. Nowicki on the Russian and Polish conflict, the one which had driven Mr. Nowicki from his home in Warsaw. Mr. Nowicki had suffered from the clash firsthand – Vita had seen the long scar down his arm – but that didn't stop the reverend from being the authority on the matter.

Vita, murmuring an apology, pulled out a chair across from Mr. Nowicki. She could see he was trying not to reply.

'What the rebels failed to understand,' Reverend Simpers went on, 'was that the Russian government was there to protect the Poles. But peasants are ignorant. Excuse me, *students*.'

But this was too much. 'Protect?' Mr. Nowicki said. 'They killed the students and strung up their bodies on Alexander Street and left them to rot in the summer heat.'

'Quite rightly. Punishment must act as a deterrent.' The reverend often mistook ugliness for righteousness.

Vita helped herself to the fried walleye. She wished she could come to Mr. Nowicki's aid but she knew nothing about the student demonstrations. He was looking down at his plate now, chewing furiously. Meals were fast affairs in Mrs. McDove's house. But Reverend Simpers kept pushing.

'Summer. I imagine the odor was fierce. Like sinners in hell.'

Mr. Nowicki glanced at the little clock on the sideboard.

'You seem in a hurry tonight, Mr. Nowicki,' the reverend said, catching the glance.

Mr. Nowicki swallowed and admitted that yes, he had an appointment later.

'An appointment? An evening appointment?'

'Yes, that is so.' He was wearing his Sunday vest, Vita noticed, and his collar looked stiff and new.

Reverend Simpers put down his fork and cast a shrewd eye over him. 'What's this, a *romantic* assignation?'

Mr. Nowicki's face flushed red, giving himself away. To her surprise, Vita saw a blush creep up on the younger Miss Pickens's neck as well. Fortunately, Reverend Simpers was so intent on Mr. Nowicki's discomfort that he didn't notice Miss Pickens.

'And you're all spruced up! Oh ho! A romantic appointment, well!'

He began to talk with his usual authority about love, a subject delightful to him since it managed to make everyone at the table uncomfortable at once. He didn't even pause when Gracelin banged open the door as she brought in the toasted cheese, marking the end of the meal.

'A man is at his most magnetic between the ages of twenty-five and forty-five,' the reverend was saying. 'For a woman, sixteen to twenty.'

'Only four years!' Vita protested. 'That hardly seems fair.'

'In some cases,' he said, pointing his guns at her, 'even less.'

She leaned forward to reach the toasted cheese, which the reverend liked to start passing around himself while saying a prayer. But tonight he was still warming to his topic, so Vita took the first one and passed the plate herself, forgoing the prayer.

'I was reading the other day about a new powder developed in France,' the reverend was saying. 'It's been used with great success for keeping at bay those illnesses stemming from love. You might want to take a dose of it, Mr. Nowicki, before venturing out.' He smiled his weaselly smile.

'Oh, reverend,' the elder Miss Pickens said, 'what kind of illness could come from love?'

Syphilis, Vita thought. Gonorrhea.

'High emotions affect the body. This powder prevents that.'

'What's the name of the powder?' Vita asked him.

'Badrolle . . . badoche . . . It will come to me. Something French, of course.' He patted his vest pocket, as though that particular memory might be stored in its cheap fabric.

'Baudruche?' Vita suggested.

'Yes, that's it. Baudruche.'

'It's not a powder,' she told him.

'Certainly it is. I read about it only the other day. The common name is French letter; I imagine it comes in an envelope.'

Mrs. McDove made a little noise and put down her triangle of toasted cheese. Vita remembered the French letters Jacob had used on their wedding night, each one like a sausage casing with a smell like the inside of a rarely used cupboard. There was a pale yellow ribbon at the end for easy removal.

She hesitated. Soot always ate an early supper in the kitchen with Gracelin, but she didn't want to further disturb Mrs. McDove, who clearly knew, as Vita did, just exactly what the reverend was describing. But the opportunity was too tempting.

'A French letter, yes. But it isn't a powder.'

'It is, I tell you. I read about it myself.'

'In an advertisement, or a news article?'

'An advertisement, but it was very detailed.'

'A French letter, or *baudruche*, prevents pregnancy,' she told him, 'and also diseases like syphilis. It does this by covering the man's – *manliness*.' She couldn't come up with anything else with the two Misses Pickens staring at her intently, looking not so much shocked – yet – as confused. 'It covers a man's *manliness* during marital relations. He pulls the French letter over himself like a glove.'

The reverend drew back his head. 'What's that? No.' His face was turning a brilliant crimson, right to the tips of his ears. 'It can't.'

'We give them out at the Soldiers' Home. Syphilis is a terrible problem in the army.'

For a moment no one spoke. Vita could hear Gracelin pumping water in the kitchen and a bang from upstairs, which could only be Soot. The reverend was having difficulty recovering himself. He patted his dry, blood-red lips two or three times with his napkin. For once he had no bullying words to say back.

A bubble of emotion rose in her throat. There was no denying her delight at besting him. She watched his face change colors, while at the same time she tried to keep her own face still. Don't laugh.

'Is this discussion quite . . .?' the elder Miss Pickens finally squeaked out, although what it quite was or wasn't she left dangling.

Mrs. McDove rose from her chair, releasing everyone at the table from their frozen spell. 'Why don't I ask Gracelin to bring out coffee to the parlor, just this once, for anyone who wants it. I can get up a fire in no time. The latest *Harper's* came this afternoon, and we might take turns reading it aloud.'

Buoyed by her victory, Vita ran up the stairs to her room two at a time. On her desk she found the card she'd written out with the name and address of the dean at the Cleveland Medical College. Quickly, before she could let herself think, she cleared a place on her desk and fished out a sheet of writing paper.

Dear Professor Cassels,

This letter will, I hope, serve as my application for a place in the summer term of the Cleveland Medical College. For the past nine months I have been studying with Dr. David Boutwell here in Cleveland, and he has supervised a course of reading for me that includes anatomy, physiology, and infectious diseases. I feel prepared to begin instruction at your institution with the goal of getting my certification as a physician. I am available for an interview prior to the term at any time convenient to you, to determine my eligibility.

Thank you for considering my request.

There she hesitated. After waffling for a few moments, she wrote:

Yours Very Truly,
V. Culhane

He would find out she was a woman eventually. But she would burn that bridge when she came to it, as Mrs. O. liked to say.

CHAPTER TWENTY-TWO

'No married woman can . . . ride about the
country attempting to address imaginary wrongs
without leaving her own household in a neglected
condition that must be an eloquent witness against her.
As for spinsters, we have often said that every woman
has a natural and inalienable right to a good
husband and a pretty baby.'
(*Sunday New York Times*, editorial, 1868)

She did not expect an answer the day after she mailed her letter, nor the next day (although of course she looked – there was only a butchery bill addressed to Mr. Stewart McDove, and a card advertising Hasheesh Candy). Leaving the house Monday morning, Vita decided not to say anything to Dr. Boutwell. Partly, she didn't want to jinx it. She was also unsure how she would feel seeing him again. But when she opened the office door he was leaning out the window trying to adjust the shutter, and he seemed so ordinary, so human, with his shirtsleeves rolled up and his mouth set in a line of concentration, that Vita couldn't feel angry with him. Freddy might have died anyway. She knew this professionally, and she knew this in her heart. Even with all the care and medical acumen in the world, he still might have died.

Dr. Boutwell straightened up and closed the window. 'That'll do for now.' His expression held no trace of the tight anxiety she'd seen on Friday, only his usual thoughtfulness. He didn't say anything about the Soldiers' Home, and neither did she.

They got to work sterilizing instruments (Vita) and checking the stores of medicines in the closet (Dr. Boutwell). And when patients began filing in, they were too busy to talk about anything else.

But at lunch, Dr. Boutwell invited her to his home that night for dinner. 'My wife has been at me to ask you. I should have done so before now.'

She understood this was by way of an apology. Before she could answer, he went on, 'I'll not be going back to the Soldiers' Home for personal reasons.' He unwrapped the wax paper from the sandwich he'd brought from home. 'But it is still good training for you. Mrs. Hauser is used to you now, it doesn't matter if I'm there.' Mrs. Hauser was the head nurse.

Vita felt like a baby owl, the last to fledge. 'I can go in by myself?'

He handed her half his sandwich and she poured him half the milk she'd brought with her in a glass jar. Their regular lunch. 'Of course.' He smoothed the used wax paper flat and then refolded it, saving it for another use. He took a sip of milk, which he drank from his teacup. 'Mm. You've heard of Asclepiades? The Greek doctor who founded the first medical school in Rome? All the early doctors in Rome, they were all Greek. Asclepiades thought that proper digestion would heal every illness.'

She had heard of Asclepiades, in fact. He believed that the Hippocratic Oath was a meditation on death. But she didn't mention that to Dr. Boutwell. Of course, he probably knew this already.

First, do no harm. This was a harder mandate, she understood now, than it seemed.

❁

After they closed up for the day, Vita washed her hands and face and tried to tame her hair with a wet comb and too-few hairpins. Outside the clouds were long and dark overhead, and a lamplighter was already lighting the gas streetlamps. There was a moving clatter as shopkeepers rolled up awnings and pushed their wheeled carts back inside the stores. Vita could smell the greasy refinery smoke lingering in the air, and also newly cut lumber. Now that it was spring half the buildings on the street were being extended or modified. She noticed the Italian organ grinder had come back to the little park in Public Square: a sure sign winter was over.

They passed the corner where they usually parted, and Dr. Boutwell, as was his custom when they walked together, began to quiz her:

'What is Quetelet's index?'

'A man's weight in kilograms divided by the square of his height in meters.'

'Also known as?'

'Body mass index.'

The sky deepened into turquoise with a line of copper at the horizon – or was that the lake? They were walking north, toward the water. Behind them was Euclid Avenue, Millionaires' Row, where wine glass elm trees lined both sides of the street and Italianate mansions were set back behind tall, wrought-iron fences. The mansions were built on a hill with views of the lake; they had broad green lawns, a militia of gardeners, and, in at least one of them, running hot water from a pump in the basement – or so rumor had it. In winter, the street was famous for its sleigh races. Vita had gone with Mr. Nowicki and the two Misses Pickens to see one on Christmas Eve, and the number of fur hats and fur coats and fur blankets on display could have depopulated a forest in Russia.

Dr. Boutwell – far from being a millionaire – lived in a small, pale brick house on Grove Street with a white door and white trim. The street was full of nearly identical houses, although some were built with deep maroon bricks instead of yellow.

'Until last year there used to be a log cabin on the corner,' he told Vita as he unlocked his front door. 'I was almost sad when they tore it down.'

'Looks like you just missed the weather,' Mrs. Boutwell said, greeting them inside.

She was a tiny woman with dark hair in a low bun, flat cheekbones, and warm brown eyes. Her two boys stood shyly behind her.

'Marcus and Nathan, say hello.'

Vita shook their hands and then brought out the two sugared almonds she'd taken from the office. Dr. Boutwell gave her a wry smile when he saw that. 'You've been in my medicine cupboard,' he said.

The two boys ran off, snorting laughs, with their hands over their mouths as if afraid their father might reach in to pluck the treats out.

When Vita stepped into the front room behind Mrs. Boutwell 'for a glass before we sit down,' she saw a small dog uncurl itself from the sofa.

'Pie, you know you're not allowed to sleep there!' Mrs. Boutwell scolded.

Vita felt momentarily confused. Pie? She knew that name.

'Our company dog,' Dr. Boutwell said.

Now she remembered. Freddy's dog. He'd written about Pie.

'Our mascot. He was really your brother's. But when I left, Fred smuggled him out to me. 'To bring you luck,' he said, 'and to keep Pie safe.' I carried him on the train in an old shawl I found somewhere, like a woman carrying an infant. All the way back here to Cleveland.'

He paused; Vita thought he was going to say more, but he didn't. She'd seen pictures of Pie in Freddy's photograph album. She smiled at the little dog as he sat facing her on the rug, brushing it with his wagging tail. He was smaller and cleaner than he looked in the photographs.

'He's a good dog,' Mrs. Boutwell said, pouring three glasses of sherry from a sepia-colored carafe. 'Only he likes that sofa too much.'

✿

Dinner was simple but delicious: lamb with mint sauce and small potatoes and something Dr. Boutwell called 'greens' though Vita had never heard of that.

'My mother was from Raleigh originally,' Mrs. Boutwell said. 'It's a southern dish.' It looked like cooked lettuce but tasted almost sweet.

'That's the onions,' Mrs. Boutwell told her. 'I cook them until they get sugary.'

The two boys ate with them, stiffly at first as they tried to remember their manners, and later communicating to each other from across the table in a series of eyebrow lifts and head nods (right, left, up and down) in their own muted language.

'Twins,' Dr. Boutwell explained, after they were excused from the table. 'Always some secret plan or game afoot.'

Mrs. Boutwell nodded. 'When they were very little I used to understand their codes, but now they've gotten too complicated.'

'They have their own language?'

'Unspoken, but yes.'

Vita felt a pang, thinking of Amelia. She would have so liked a twin, or at least someone who shared her same interests. Instead she was the odd duck in the family. She was surprised at the longing she felt, witnessing this family life. She'd always thought that if she could only be allowed to study medicine she would want nothing else.

After dinner she helped Mrs. Boutwell carry the dishes into the kitchen. 'I have a girl who helps me, but her mother is ill so I sent her home.'

'I don't mind,' Vita said.

'She'll come back to do the washing up just as soon as her mother is settled for the night. Anna Rose. She has a sister, but Cassie works for the Eells family up there on Euclid Avenue and sometimes has to stay quite late.' Mrs. Boutwell stacked the plates in the sink. 'The Eells have a balcony in their parlor, Cassie says. Inside the house! Can you imagine? Fortunately, they live down the street from us. I mean Anna Rose and Cassie, not the Eells.'

Dr. Boutwell poked his head in to say that he'd be in the parlor. A new *Boston Medical Journal* had come to the house that day.

'He still reads like he's a student,' Mrs. Boutwell said. 'There's always a new discovery, a new procedure. It's nice that he has someone to talk to about it all.'

'I feel the same way.'

Vita watched as Mrs. Boutwell put scraps on a plate for Pie.

'The army was not a good place for him. The officers never accepted him, they all came from money. David had to borrow a horse whenever they moved camp, or else walk with the infantry. Your brother used to carry the box of medical supplies for him. One box! They had so little, especially toward the end.'

She put the plate down on the floor for Pie. 'In his letters, he used to ask me to send handkerchiefs and needles. Handkerchiefs, he liked to say, were like angel visits: few and far between. He gave them out whenever I sent him a box, I'm not sure he kept any for himself. And he helped the boys mend their shirts and coats. When the war first started there was a saying among them, "A hole is more honorable than a patch." But after a few winters, didn't they begin to patch their clothes anyway. They used lint from the Sanitary Commission if they didn't have any other scraps – David gave them whatever he could spare. When the officers turned on him . . .' She looked down at Pie, who had finished his meal. She picked up the plate.

'He told me about the officer who was so angry when his arm was amputated,' Vita said. 'The reason he – he left the army.'

Why he ran off, she'd been about to say. Hadn't she run off, too? She pushed away the image of Jacob asleep in their hotel bed.

Mrs. Boutwell rinsed the sherry glasses and Vita set them upside down on a cloth. 'He felt betrayed, you see, from the boys in the unit. They began to question his abilities. His motives. That hurt the most.'

Someone you take care of, turning on you. That's betrayal. Or someone who is supposed to take care of you – Vita was thinking of her father. Does Jacob think of me that way? she suddenly wondered. But of course, he must.

'Not your brother, though,' Mrs. Boutwell said. 'He stuck by him.'

'The others, they didn't understand,' Vita told her. 'They didn't know how the body works. I'm sure he saved the life of that officer.'

Mrs. Boutwell sighed. She had gentle eyes that seemed to smile even when her mouth was sad. 'Thank you.'

Vita held her hand out to Pie and he came over for a sniff. Then he licked her fingers gently, with his tongue tip.

'David still talks about Fred,' Mrs. Boutwell said. 'He was a good friend. It must have been hard for you; first your husband, then your brother.'

It took Vita a moment to remember the story that she was a widow. She was becoming adept at telling lies and half truths in order to get what she wanted. This was how criminals lived, she supposed.

In the taxicab going home, which Dr. Boutwell insisted on hailing and paying for, she stared out the window. The low brick houses looked like they had been built on the same day with the same plan, traced and repeated. When the cab turned onto Euclid Avenue, however, the houses changed and enlarged: mansions with long front lawns, and lights twinkling in the upper windows like distant stars.

Leaning back on the worn carriage seat, Vita felt tears in her eyes. She had a pile of the latest medical journals on her lap, which Dr. Boutwell was loaning to her, and she liked Mrs. Boutwell, who seemed every bit as kind as her husband. But seeing this family life – this happy family life – that was too hard. You might want two things, she told herself, but you can only have one of them.

She resolved to make some excuse in the future if Dr. Boutwell invited her to his home again.

On Friday, after breakfast, Vita found a letter addressed to V. Culhane on the hall table: a stiff, cream-colored envelope with the address of the Cleveland Medical College embossed in the corner.

All the moisture left her mouth. She turned it over, strangely conscious of her fingers. Almost, she did not want to open it. She hooked her finger under the corner edge, as though the envelope slit was a gill on a fish and she was checking it for freshness.

Dear Mr. Culhane,

Thank you for your inquiry. I would be most happy to meet with you on Thursday, May 10th, at two o'clock, if you are available on that date.

Very truly yours,
Professor John L. Cassels
Cleveland Medical College

Her heart felt like it was opening multiple sets of wings, one unfolding after another. He would see her! She wanted to hug the letter to her breast like a newborn. She left for the Soldiers' Home with it in her pocket, taking it out on the streetcar to read its few lines again and again. Clouds tumbled overhead, thin and pretty like shining halos with the sun burning behind them. Soon, maybe in a month, she could write Mitty. And Jacob. She would write Jacob a long letter, explaining everything. Or would that be a mistake? There were regular accounts in the newspapers of wives who'd run away and were dragged back home by their angry husbands; the judges were not a bit lenient, at least not to the wives. Wives were the property of the men they had married, like a house or a horse. But Jacob wasn't like that. Was he? As always, she was back to the same question.

But she didn't want to spoil her mood by worrying about that now. Not today. At the Soldiers' Home, Vita spotted Lucy standing at the end of a row of beds holding a folded piece of flannel. On a square, rickety bamboo table beside her were two metal basins half filled with water, and a tin can of plaster of Paris.

'Can I help?' Vita was bursting to tell someone the news, although she worried Lucy might think she'd been hiding her plans. Which, of course, she had been.

'Fractured ulna,' Lucy said, indicating the soldier sitting up in the bed at a slight lean, like something shifted by the wind. 'The doctor's just set it. I'm preparing bandages for the splint.'

'How d'you do, I'm Mrs. Culhane.' Vita smiled at the soldier. 'You must tell me if you need anything.'

'Anthony Sergeant,' the soldier introduced himself, 'though I'm only a corporal.' He must have told this joke a hundred times, but clearly he still enjoyed it. He was thin with a rubbery look, as if his bones – even the broken one – were divining rods bending toward water. His bucked-out ears were made more noticeable by his closely shaved head.

'How did you break your arm, Mr. Sergeant?' Vita asked. He was holding it across his belly, and she could see it was swollen like a log of rising dough, with purple and yellow bruises along his wrist. She asked a passing nurse for razor and shaving soap. Meanwhile, Lucy continued cutting flannel into strips.

'It was on account of the train ride back from Mississippi. My unit was stationed there for a few months to ensure the peace, you see, and when we were finally discharged I thought it would be nothing to get home. Only the train stopped about every ten minutes to switch cars or switch lines because of the sabotage. Toward the end, I had to ride in a hay cart to an inland town where the railway line was undamaged.'

A line creased his forehead. He took a slow breath and exhaled – almost, but not quite, a whistle. 'I saw what seemed like a thousand acres of burned fields with skinny children picking them over looking for something to eat. They say the whole of the South is like that now. Makes you wonder, it really does.'

Vita began shaving his injured arm carefully so the plaster wouldn't stick to his arm hairs. 'Those poor children.' She knew what it was like now to go hungry, but for her it was only a day here and there. Nothing like ongoing starvation. And they were children! Their growth, she knew from her studies, would be adversely affected. They'd suffer from crooked, lightweight bones; heart problems; and for girls, difficulty conceiving when they were adults.

'Here in the city,' he said, 'everything feels like it's beginning – all the buildings going up, and the factories working, pushing out smoke. There it feels like it's all at an end. When we finally got to the train station I got to talking to a man who was waiting for a delivery of planked wood, and he said he'd feed me for the week if I would stay and help him rebuild his silo, which I did. Not many men around, you see. But on the last morning I tripped and fell on my arm. I don't even know what I tripped on! Heard it snap like a twig in the woods.'

'You traveled all the way here?' Lucy asked. 'With your arm broken?'

'It was only a day's journey, and I didn't like the looks of the town doctor. Well, his smell, really – rum and peppermint, and more rum than peppermint if you know what I mean. I figured the army had taken care of me so far. But I can tell you, I felt every bump and jolt along the way.'

A boy with mismatched shoes came walking down the narrow aisle between beds, selling peanuts for five cents a bag. 'Come back when I'm fitted up,' Anthony Sergeant told him, 'and I'll buy a bag for myself and each of these ladies.'

Lucy poured a measure of plaster into the basin of water, and stirred it to the consistency of thick cream. She added a couple of pinches of salt so the mixture wouldn't set too quickly. When she looked around for the doctor, Mrs. Hauser, the head nurse, noticed and came over carrying a second bamboo table.

'Dr. Hotchkiss asked me to begin applying the splint, he's tied up for the moment. But I see you two have it all in hand.' She set the little table down, covered it with a clean white cloth, and gave the plaster mixture a stir. Niblets of grit rose up to the surface. 'Good. Bandages all ready? All right then, let me know if you need help. I see I have to roust out that boy with the peanuts again.'

Vita felt a surge of excitement. She had never applied plaster of Paris herself. 'Why don't I dunk,' she told Lucy, 'and you flatten.'

'But I've never done this before, have you? Maybe we should get another nurse to do it.'

'It's not hard. We've seen it plenty of times. It's just like wrapping a Christmas package. Come on. You can dunk if you want, and I'll flatten.'

Lucy, after another moment's hesitation, began to immerse the flannel strips in the plaster mixture. After they were soaked through, she spread them on the bamboo table, where Vita smoothed them flat with the palm of her hand. Then together they gently applied the porridgey strips to Anthony Sergeant's arm, fitting one roller bandage snugly over another.

'Not bad!' Lucy said after a few go-arounds.

'How are you doing, Mr. Sergeant?' Vita asked.

'Tip-top.'

'How does your arm feel?'

'Very snug, thank you.'

While Vita tied the bandage ends, Lucy cut a few smaller strips for his wrist.

'Now,' Vita said, 'try to keep your arm still until the plaster has solidified. Won't take more than fifteen minutes or so. Meanwhile I'll see if I can't get a bag of peanuts for you before Nurse Hauser catches up to the boy.'

Her hands felt gritty and damp, and she rubbed them with a dry towel as she walked along the ward. Did she even have any money? She thrust her hand into her pocket where she found, happily, two nickels kissing in the corner. It was a day where nothing would go wrong.

She and Lucy had just finished stacking the basins to be washed when Dr. Hotchkiss came to check the drying plaster. Anthony Sergeant, still sitting up in the bed, had fallen asleep.

'Very well done,' Dr. Hotchkiss said, fingering it with his index finger and thumb. He nodded his approval at Lucy, who said, 'Mrs. Culhane deserves most of the credit.'

Vita nestled the bag of peanuts in the bent crook of Anthony Sergeant's good arm; he would see it when he woke up. 'If he doesn't crush it by mistake!' Lucy said, laughing. She was pleased by the doctor's words. They both were. Vita felt again the butterfly wings in her heart.

'I want to show you something,' she said to Lucy. They went to see if they could get tea at the nurses' corner. A pair of young nurses, waiting for the kettle to boil, stood with thick white mugs in their hands. Both were as small as teenagers; Vita, though not any taller, nevertheless felt decades older.

Lucy looked up from reading the card Vita had handed her with a confused expression. 'Who is V. Culhane? Your brother?'

'It's me. I'm applying to study medicine.'

'At the medical college here?' Lucy looked at the card again. 'But they don't accept women.'

Not this again. She tried to hide her impatience. 'Yes, they do. They accepted Emily Blackwell; that's Elizabeth Blackwell's sister. She graduated over ten years ago. And other women besides her.'

'But not after the war began,' Lucy said. 'They took a vote, the faculty did, and decided to stop admitting women. I wasn't interested myself, but I knew a girl who wanted to apply and she was told to go to the Female College in Pennsylvania.'

'What do you mean, took a vote?'

'You've heard of the American Medical Association?'

'Of course.' It was a new organization that wanted to regulate the practice of medicine – separating real physicians from the charlatans out peddling cures. There were too many untrained practitioners, they said, and too many branches of medical science vying for hegemony – homeopathic, botanical, eclectic. She could hear her father's voice: 'Something must be done to get rid of them.'

'Well, they came out against co-education in medicine. They published a report about it. And after that, the CMC faculty voted not to allow female students to attend their lectures anymore.'

'That can't be. I know for a fact . . .' Vita looked out at the beds in the ward, so many of them empty. What *do* I know? *Dr. Emily Blackwell, Dr. Nancy Talbot Clark, Dr. Myra Merrick.* All graduates from the Cleveland Medical College before the war. It never occurred to her that something gained could be revoked, a half-eaten slice of cake snatched away.

'They did let one woman in,' Lucy said, 'a couple of years ago, but that was because her husband was already a student there. She left without graduating, to have a baby.'

'But I've been studying all this time with Dr. Boutwell. He would have said if they didn't admit women.'

'You told him about your plans?'

'Oh yes, he knew.'

Lucy handed the card back to Vita. 'There are other colleges. One in Philadelphia, and one in Boston.'

'But I need a letter of recommendation, and they won't know Dr. Boutwell.'

'Maybe that doesn't matter.'

A soldier, struggling to open a top window with a long hooked pole, lost purchase and the window slammed shut with a bang. Vita waited for her emotions to gather into a storm cloud, to feel her old companion: fury. But although hot spears of thought struck her brain one after another – it isn't fair, it can't be true, they have no right – her usual full-blown anger didn't rise. Instead she felt unbearably tired. Also strangely vaporous, like a vessel filled only with air.

'Tea,' Lucy said, watching her,. 'that's what we need.'

One of the young nurses opened the cupboard where they kept the mugs. 'Oh bad luck, only one clean cup left,' she said, pulling it out.

Nothing for me, Vita thought with bitterness. But Lucy said, 'That's all right, we can share it.'

❀

'This came for me this morning.'

Vita held the letter out to Dr. Boutwell defiantly, an accusation. She found him in his office just starting his lunch. He put down his roll, wiped his fingers on his handkerchief, and took the envelope from her.

'From the Cleveland Medical College,' he said. '*We are requesting an interview . . .*' He looked up. 'Why, this is wonderful news!'

'But, you know, don't you, that they don't take women students.'

He studied the note again. 'V. Culhane. Is that how you signed your letter to him?'

'Why didn't you tell me? After everything, all you taught me, all I did . . .' She could almost hear Aunt Norbert saying, Speak in whole sentences, Vita. She took a long breath. 'You must have known that they don't allow women to attend their lectures anymore. Why didn't you tell me so?'

Dr. Boutwell looked surprised. 'Why, I did tell you!'

Vita shook her head. 'No, you didn't.'

'But I did. Many times. You wouldn't listen. I said – and I believe these were my exact words – "They won't accept women."'

'You – no, what you said was –'

Now she was confused. *Had* he told her? Her face grew warm as she considered that, actually, maybe he had. She'd stopped herself from listening to his arguments, one of her old tricks for getting what she wanted. She had trained herself from childhood not to listen to no.

'Then for heaven's sake,' she said angrily, 'why did you take me on?'

'You were so determined. I couldn't break your spirit. Nor did I want to. And there was always midwifery. If well trained, that's a proper profession.'

'I never wanted to be a midwife! You know that.'

'Or you might find work as a doctor's assistant.'

Vita let out a stream of air from between her teeth. Oh what does it matter, she thought, I'm failing the whole enterprise anyway. So she could apply a plaster cast; what did that signify? She couldn't save Mary Eileen Doherty's baby, and half the time she couldn't diagnose simple ailments. And even if she did, no one believed her because she was a woman.

She would never be a doctor. She couldn't do it, and they wouldn't let her: two sides of the same coin.

'Perhaps you could stay here,' Dr. Boutwell suggested, 'and assist me.'

'There isn't enough money coming in to support two of us. I've seen your books.'

He raised his eyebrows, acknowledging her point. 'Yes, but that could change. I could advertise, or . . . I don't know.' He stood to fill the kettle, keeping his back to her. 'The fact is, I've enjoyed having someone to consult with. Someone in the office with me. I was saying this only last night to Augusta after the boys went to bed. After the war, well, I thought I just wanted to be alone. Work alone. But in fact now I think it's better to work alongside someone else.'

'You don't want to work at the Soldiers' Home, though.' It was cruel, but she said it. She saw his shoulders tighten.

'That's something else.'

She knew he didn't like intimate disclosures; he was trying to be honest. Still, how could she help him? 'It's no use,' she said. 'I'm no good.'

'That's where you're wrong. You're still learning. And you're getting better.'

Was she?

'Even if I did stay,' Vita argued, 'I would never be a doctor. A real one, I mean.'

He hesitated. 'No,' he agreed. 'Not without a medical degree.'

'Well then, what's the point?'

'The point is that you help take care of people. You use your fine mind to diagnose and to cure wherever possible.'

'I never particularly wanted to help people. I liked the science.'

'Well, I could see that in the beginning. I did wonder why you kept at it.'

She didn't want to talk about her father, or even think about him. He would never see her perform some calculated procedure, and praise her. He wouldn't be proud of her. She'd been delusional about that, too.

'Anyway, I haven't changed,' she said.

'Haven't you?'

'I can't be one of those simpering women who want to do good in the world. They just get used up, as far as I can tell, and nobody appreciates them anyway, or even likes them. I don't want to become that.'

Dr. Boutwell's mouth twitched a little at one end. 'No, I don't see you that way. That's not what I meant. You're curious and hard-working, and you listen to your patients. Am I right?'

'They're a puzzle. I want to work it out.'

'Yes, but there's more. Tell me, who did you see this morning at the Soldiers' Home? Did you talk to any of the men?'

She thought of Anthony Sergeant as she last saw him, asleep with the bag of peanuts tucked under his arm. 'A corporal with a fractured ulna. Nurse Frost and I applied the splint.'

'Was he a textbook passage to you? Or a laboratory specimen?'

She flushed. 'No.'

'Well then,' he said, his point made.

But she wouldn't concede. 'Will that convince the college faculty?' she asked. 'Will they let me in if I mention Anthony Sergeant by name? If I know more about my patients than only their symptoms? If I care about them?'

She watched him draw breath, and then hesitate.

'No. I thought not,' she said.

CHAPTER TWENTY-THREE

'To give this position to Miss M. E. Zakrzewska is dangerous. She is a prepossessing young lady, and from coming in contact with so many gentlemen she must necessarily fall in love with one of them, and thus end her career.'
(Letter to Dr. Joseph Schmidt protesting Marie Zakrzewska's appointment as Director of the Hospital Charité, Berlin, 1851)

Jacob hadn't expected Cleveland to be so crowded and so noisy with delivery wagons and cabs and private carriages rumbling by in the streets, the streetcars ringing their bells, and hawkers trying to make themselves heard over it all. Brick office buildings and stone banks designed like Greek temples lined Superior Avenue without an inch of air between them, while people rushed along the sidewalk, hardly bothering to look up.

The last time he was here, when he was a boy, a little one-story house stood by itself on the corner of Public Square; it was white with lime-green trim, with a balcony on its roof and four or five slender young maple trees giving it shade. For years he had fantasized about growing rich and living in that house. It wasn't a mansion, but it was charming and graceful. Attainable, somehow, if he worked hard enough.

But the house was gone, and in its place they'd built an iron-gray office building that thrust upward four stories – high, impersonal, and commercial. Commanding, yes, but not a place you'd dream about.

He'd come with his father that time. They walked along Lake Erie's southern shore, gazing at the steamboats coming in and out of the port. His father had had a couple of good years and was seeing a Cleveland banker about buying more land. Why a Cleveland bank? Jacob didn't know. But within a few months there would be another silver crisis and another run on the banks, and Jacob's father would lose what little he'd saved. He'd been at the peak of his success that summer, and although he thought his fortune would continue, in fact it was already waning.

He let Jacob pick out a penny postcard from a corner kiosk to send home. Jacob still remembered the thrill of looping his l's and p's as he wrote to his mother in his best hand, and he felt another thrill as they went to the new city post office to mail it, a huge stone edifice half a block long. Inside there was enough empty space to stable every horse in Lark's Eye. It smells cold in here, Jacob said to his father, who laughed at him for that, and liked to bring up the remark later, in ridicule, after his fortunes had changed.

Only the wind is the same, Jacob thought, pushing his hat down again. Unceasing.

He went into the little park in the middle of Public Square and sat down on one of the iron benches facing the fountain. When he was last here, Superior and Ontario were called streets, not avenues, and both had been cut off to prevent traffic from going through the park. They still were cut off, but the city had since erected a white double-railed fence to underscore the point, which gave the park a captured feeling.

For a while he watched the spray of fountain water change direction and change again as the wind pushed it this way and that. A posted sign claimed the water was pumped in from Lake Erie; the dark droplets were like shakes from a pepper grinder. When he left the hotel this morning, he meant to go straight to the address that Amelia had sent him, but instead he circled the city, walking and walking, trying to come up with a plan.

My dear brother Jacob,

I hope this letter finds you well. I thought you might be interested in the current address of my sister Vita, if you don't already possess it . . .

It was a short letter. Amelia didn't say how she came upon the address; whether Vita had written her, or if she'd found it some other way. Nor did she say how Vita was faring. In fact, nothing about her at all. That made him nervous at first, and then fearful. But perhaps Amelia simply didn't know.

A couple strolled up to the fountain arm in arm and stood watching the spray. After they walked off, Jacob could see a lone woman standing on the other side. When their eyes met, she began to make her way toward him. Was she coming to solicit him? At this time of day? Her fringed shawl and high-buttoned collar gave her the look of a poetess rather than a prostitute, and there was something whimsical in the cut of her dress sleeves. Behind her, the dark pointed spire of the Old Stone Church rose up like a finger blaming God.

She smiled widely, revealing two gray teeth. 'Care to know your fortune?' she asked.

The wind lifted the rim of her flat hat at a slight angle, like a ghost taking a peek at him over her shoulder.

'My name is Miss Mary Light. I know what's already happened and what will happen yet.'

Jacob stood to offer her a seat on the bench, thinking that as she sat down he would take his leave. But she didn't sit.

'Even from far away I could see that you're lovesick. You're afraid that your girl isn't true. Am I right?'

He felt himself flush, surprised to be caught out. But he was a man sitting alone on a park bench in the middle of the day, dressed like a businessman and yet not at work. She didn't have to be a seer to know something was troubling him, and love was as good a guess as any.

She said, 'For a penny I can help you realize your love.'

He tried to joke. 'So much for only one penny?' He could see tiny repairs in her dress, and a rust-colored stain near the pocket. When she cocked her head uncertainly, he felt bad and fished out his coin purse.

She nodded, back on familiar ground. 'Now, then,' she said. She took hold of his two wrists, another surprise, but that was only to lower him down again to sit. Then she sat down next to him, turning to face him. She smiled her wide, child's smile. Those two gray teeth again.

'Here's what you must do. In between the hours of nine and twelve, on a night with a moon, go catch a gray dove and kill it. Mix its blood with wheaten flour to make a cake in the shape of a heart, and after it's baked prick the cake with the initials of your name. Then eat a slice before going to bed. Do this for two nights in a row. On the third night, write the name of your beloved on a clean piece of white paper and put it under your pillow.'

She spoke with the slight lilt he associated with children of Irish immigrants. She was watching him closely as if trying to determine whether or not he was memorizing her instructions.

'If on that night you dream of your beloved, then your beloved is true. If you do not dream of her, then she is false.'

She touched one of his wrists again, two gloved fingers pressing the bone. But Jacob was distracted by the word *beloved*. He thought of Vita's small hands, her intense glances, her husky voice. An eddy of emotion swirled in his chest.

'Now. You mustn't perform this during Passion Week,' Miss Mary Light told him. Passion Week was ten months away. 'Or on the eve of St. Jude's.' That was in October.

He gave her another penny, thanked her, and touched his hat. A dove's blood and wheaten flour – what would the chef at the American Hotel say to that? Of course; use my oven! But Jacob found he couldn't joke himself into amusement. He felt uneasy, as if Miss Mary Light had started to unearth something he didn't want unearthed. His hands, which had shook all day yesterday as he traveled, were completely still. He watched her circle the little park, as if seeking another customer, and then open the little iron gate and leave.

He left the park, too, but went off in the opposite direction. After a block he stopped and consulted the map that the hotel clerk had drawn for him that morning, and then he continued to the corner and turned right. He passed a line of men digging trenches for water pipes and, on the next block, more men grading the street.

He turned again, this time toward the lake, and for a while he strolled along a quiet street off of St. Clair. Boxy white boarding houses filled the block and a line of elm trees gave shade to the sidewalk. A kerosene wagon rumbled by him, then stopped at a house up ahead to deliver two small barrels. The faint smell of oil was everywhere, traveling on the lake wind. That morning Jacob had spoken to a man in his hotel lobby who was in Cleveland, he'd said, to see the horse races. He told Jacob that the fumes from all the city refineries – almost thirty of them now – turned butter rancid 'faster than fast,' especially in the homes near the river.

Vita's street had nothing to distinguish it from the other streets except for a squat stone church on the corner. He came to the address Amelia had sent him; a house made of the same blond brick as the other houses along the street, with white trim and a stone lintel over the door. A black and gold sign hung from the lintel: 'The Frederick'.

Jacob put his hand on the gate's cold iron finial and then hesitated. He could still leave if he wanted. Next door, a young boy had set up a show making animal figures with his hands: a wolf, a hawk, a swan. All that was missing was a white sheet and a candle. Two little girls crouched, not quite sitting, as his audience.

Jacob pushed open the gate, which yielded with a complaining squeak. To his surprise, the boy from next door got to his feet and called out. 'Hey! Mister! Stop a moment.'

He was a thin boy, eight or nine, dressed in a dark gray cap and short trousers. Jacob watched him squash through the knee-high hedge that separated the two houses. His sharp shoulder blades reminded him of bird wings.

It turned out that the boy lived at this house, The Frederick. 'And we don't need any penny photographs or ribbons or book subscriptions neither,' he said importantly.

'Do I look like I'm selling something?'

Jacob spread his empty hands as if opening an invisible hymnbook.

'I'm looking for Mrs. Vita Culhane.'

'The widder?' the boy asked.

So she was calling herself a widow.

'Not exactly. I'm her husband, you see. Mr. Jacob Culhane.' He began to pull out a card from his vest pocket before he realized the foolishness of presenting his credentials to a child. But the boy had seen Jacob's movement and held out his hand.

He read the card carefully, and then turned it over to look at the back.

'Why aren't you in school?' Jacob asked.

'I been out all month with my pneumonia. This is the first day my ma let me outside.'

'Pneumonia! That's serious business.'

The boy shrugged off Jacob's concern. 'Only one lobe. If it was both lobes it'd be double pneumonia but it was only the one. Mrs. Culhane explained it to me when she gave me my medicine.' He wedged Jacob's card into his front pocket, which was already bulging with whatever eight-year-old boys carry these days – in Jacob's time, acorn tops and string and a thin piece of metal he could bend into a fishhook.

'She told us that her husband was passed on.'

'Perhaps she meant missing.'

The boy cocked his head, suspicious. 'P'raps.'

'What's your name, son?'

'Stewart McDove.'

'Well, Stewart, I take it Mrs. Culhane lives here with you? Is she at home now?'

'She's out doctoring. You like to wait for her?'

The boy led him inside and down the hall to the back parlor; a room crowded with furniture and pictures – 'cozy,' as Samantha put it – and, along the far wall, four or five decorative mirrors hanging from chains. But this room really did feel cozy, with chairs that were worn and smooth, perhaps even ugly if examined one by one, but taken as a whole comfortable and unobtrusive. Compared to this, Samantha's efforts seemed obvious, even false. The boy offered him a chair near the unlit fire and then, to Jacob's surprise, he sat down to wait with him.

He offered Jacob some pages of a newspaper from the round table beside his chair, while he himself selected the page with news of that day's estate sales, which surely could hold no interest to him.

But he shook the page importantly. 'I could ask for tea, if you like?'

For the first time that day Jacob felt a true smile creep up, and he tried to bury it. The boy's toes dangled above the chair's oval footstool, almost touching its needlepoint cover.

'I wouldn't say no to a glass of water,' Jacob said.

The boy pushed himself out of his chair to fetch one. 'When I was sick in bed,' he said, 'I got to try whiskey.'

'Whiskey? Really? And how did you like it?'

He shrugged. 'I found that it's not to my taste.'

When she came home that afternoon, Vita was surprised to see Mr. Nowicki rise from the straight-backed chair in the hallway as though he'd been waiting for her. The lodgers usually sat in that chair only when pulling off boots or to open a piece of mail they didn't want to wait, for some reason, to read up in their room.

'There's a gentleman in the parlor,' Mr. Nowicki told her, 'and he has a card, and printed on it the name Mr. Jacob Culhane.'

She felt the blood leave her face.

'He has been in there for almost one hour with our Soot. I thought it best you should not be surprised.'

Had Mr. Nowicki been sitting in that uncomfortable chair all this time, waiting for her? Her heart warmed to him.

'Thank you, Mr. Nowicki.'

She looked into the hall mirror. She had imagined this moment; both dreading it and hoping it would come. And now it has, she thought, but she didn't know how she felt. Her shirtwaist was neat and her collar was clean. Her once-wild hair was smooth and neatly bound, even after removing her hat, because she'd begun to comb a little lotion into it at night, at Lucy's suggestion. Patients felt less fearful if their attendants were tidy. Vita pulled out a hairpin and angled it back into place. For some reason she couldn't seem to swallow.

Mr. Nowicki was watching her. 'Is Mr. Jacob Culhane your husband?' he asked.

Part of her was glad that the pretense was over. 'Yes.'

'Your husband is not dead?'

'No.'

'But you wished to hide from him.' He was looking at her anxiously.

'I'm sorry I lied to you, Mr. Nowicki.'

'You had a good reason,' he said firmly, not knowing the reason but knowing – or so he believed – her.

'I thought I did.'

'Of course you did. And you protected yourself.'

'But I didn't tell you the truth.'

He shrugged. 'Truth!' he said.

He might have said, 'Courage!' or 'Rubbish!' or 'Dog!' A rubbery word, *truth;* a word that could evoke anything or nothing. They smiled at each other, she had no idea why. He nodded encouragement.

'I'll wait right here. If you need me.'

When she opened the parlor door, the light in the hallway behind her seemed to shrink. Jacob was sitting near the fireplace and stood up when she came into the room.

There he was.

Vita felt prickles on her skin, like small mushrooms popping up in the dark.

'Mr. Jacob Culhane,' Soot said, hopping off his mother's chair.

She waited for something to come to her, what to say.

'Is he your husband?' Soot asked. 'Like he says?'

'Yes.' She felt her face flush again and she bent to fiddle with an oil lamp, turning the flame higher. 'Where's your mother?'

'She was out marketing until a minute ago. Now she's in the kitchen getting us tea.' He paused. 'So I guess he didn't die in the war, only went missing? But you didn't know?'

Like Mr. Nowicki, he was trying to protect her.

'I'm sorry, Soot. I knew he was alive. I shouldn't have lied.'

Soot looked at her as though she were a disappointing puzzle. 'Then why did you?'

Jacob was also watching her closely. The shape of his head, his squared shoulders – all so familiar, as if she'd seen him only minutes ago, not months. He still hadn't spoken.

'Well, as you know, I wanted to be a doctor. And he was going to stop me from doing that.'

Footsteps sounded in the hallway.

'You thought I wanted to stop you?' Jacob asked.

Mrs. McDove opened the door and came into the room carrying a tray. 'Now, then, why don't we . . .' Then she saw Vita. 'Oh, Mrs. Culhane, you're here, are you, and what a shock you must be having. Sit down, please, I'm going to light the coals for you.'

Vita allowed herself to be directed to the armchair and given tea with lots of milk and sugar. Mrs. McDove had been deceived but here she was, solicitous and kind, putting a pale pink teacup into her hand. Vita felt herself struggling to say something.

Soot got there first. 'She thought he was dead but he only went missing.' Lying for her.

'Of course, and what a happy surprise that he's here! Now, no more about it. It's a miracle, is what it is. Soot, you and I must leave them alone so they can talk. Let me just start the fire.'

Vita could not tell if Mrs. McDove believed the story or not. Soot hesitated, looking at Vita for confirmation. In the space of ten minutes he seemed to have grown into the little man he had for months pretended to be.

'I'll be in the dining room with Mr. Nowicki if you want anything,' Mrs. McDove said in her generous, light voice, but Vita saw her stare hard at Jacob's face for a few seconds, assessing him. 'Soot, come along.'

Jacob sat down again after they left, but pushed his footstool aside with one foot as if he wanted to be ready to spring up at any moment. They sat half-facing each other, each on one side of the fireplace. The smell of burning coal – which Vita usually found comforting – mixed with the scent of kerosene oil for the lamps and woody furniture polish. She didn't know what to say. That she was sorry? Was she?

'You've made friends here,' Jacob said. It sounded like an accusation.

'I have, I suppose.'

She heard the front door open, and the bird-like voices of the two Misses Pickens rang out in the hallway.

'Or we could wear our blue merinos.' A growly goose – the elder Miss Pickens. Then the sparrow: 'But do you think they will be warm enough? Why, hello Soot.'

Here the voices went lower, and Vita imagined Soot telling them not to go into the parlor and why. She felt like a bird herself; not a goose or a sparrow, but something more furtive – a starling on a stolen nest. Ready to defend it, but also, confusingly, ready to give up and make room for the intruder.

'Jacob –'

But he started to speak at the same time. 'Why didn't you talk to me; why did you just leave? Your note at the hotel – were you deliberately trying to be cryptic?'

'No. I don't know. I was in a hurry.'

'But why? Why leave?'

'You know why! You decided that I should work with you on your barrels instead of becoming a doctor.'

'I – that's not true. It was only a suggestion.' He said this aggressively.

'You never wanted me to go off to college. I heard you say to Holland that you never saw the use of it. Those very words.'

'But I didn't mean it, I told you that. Anyway you were the one who wanted to keep our deal a secret.'

'But was it a deal? A *firm* deal?'

'Of course it was.'

'So you were planning to keep your word? Even if I didn't help you with the barrel glue?' She wanted so much for that to be true.

'Of course! That is . . .' He pursed his mouth. 'Well. Maybe I did think it would all come to nothing, once we were married and settled. It seemed rather unlikely that any doctor would agree to mentor a woman. And then, I also had the feeling that you were growing fond of me. And so was I. Of you. And maybe we . . .' he searched for the right words. 'Maybe it could be a real marriage, I thought.'

She watched him lace his fingers together. It was true; she had grown fond of him. More than fond.

'The boy, Stewart, he tells me that you'll be going to medical college in the fall.'

'That's all fallen apart,' she said, getting up to tend to the fire. She might as well be honest with him. The loose ashes squeaked as she prodded them down through the grate. She took another minute to scrape the larger coals together into a pile, trying to work up a better glow. When she turned back she saw that Jacob had made a loose fist with his left hand and was tapping each knuckle with two fingers from his right hand. Four taps up, four taps back. Then he switched hands.

'A doctor taught me this. To stop my tremors. Soldiers' Complaint, he called it. Supposedly it will help with the nightmares, too.'

'I didn't know you had nightmares.'

'Of course you didn't. They started when you left.' His voice rose. 'When you left me, that's when it all started up again.'

'I've seen quite a lot of soldiers suffering from tremors. It's not uncommon.'

But that was the wrong thing to say.

'Have you? Have you now? You look after these soldiers, but you won't look after me?'

'I didn't know you needed looking after.'

'No, you didn't, did you? How would you?'

The fire crackled and shot up a red spark. For a moment they stared at each other.

'I want you to come back to Boston with me,' Jacob said.

'Why?'

'*Why?*' She was his wife; he didn't have to say it. He shook out his hands as if drying them in the air and looked at them. The right one still trembled slightly, as gentle as a hummingbird treading air. He began tapping his knuckles again.

'Do you have any other symptoms?' she asked. 'Shortness of breath? Hallucinations?'

'No. Nothing like that. Just tremors and nightmares.' He glared at her as if to say, *Aren't those enough?*

At the Soldiers' Home Vita had seen Dr. Hotchkiss swab a man's shaking hands with strychnine and tie his wrists together; 'binding the tremors will stop them,' he said, although it didn't. She thought about poor young Walter Cutter, hiding his hands under the bed sheet.

'Does the tapping work?'

'Not very well.'

'Stay a moment. I'll be right back.'

She went to the kitchen and returned carrying a cup of warm milk.

'With some extract of vanilla and a drop of whiskey. It's not a cure, exactly, but it might bring you some relief.'

Jacob took a cautious sip and then set the cup down on the table beside him. Close up, Vita could see dark rings under his eyes. In the silence she heard muffled voices coming from somewhere in the house. He was right, she had made friends here. She'd built a life without noticing. A gust of wind came down the chimney, causing Mrs. McDove's mirrors to rattle on their chains. The coals were dying again, down to their last ashy crumbs. In a minute she would stand up and scoop new coals from the coal box and coax the fire back to life. Or maybe she would just let it die.

'How would we support ourselves in Boston,' she asked, 'if you're ill?'

'I still have your father's money. Most all of it. If you could help me get better, to recover, I can look for a job.'

She nodded.

Then he said, 'And after that, if you want, we can find you a new preceptor. Someone local.'

Starting over from scratch. Her heart felt like a brick at the thought of it. Another thing soldiers did – Vita knew this now, from talk at the Soldiers' Home – was run from a battle. No matter how many deserters were hung by the neck, men facing a line of cannons and guns still weighed up their chances: which death was preferable? Strangely, though, she didn't feel defeated. She felt finished. She'd arrived at the terminus. She could pack up everything she owned in twenty minutes; less than that if she left her books behind.

'I'm so tired,' she said, startling herself; she hadn't meant to say that aloud.

Jacob looked at her sadly. 'I'm tired, too.'

CHAPTER TWENTY-FOUR

'The party . . . requested the woman to permit herself to be dressed in the Doctor's wig, gown, and canonicals; she consented; and in this disguise the resemblance was so striking, that it astonished all who were in on the secret, and would have deceived any who were not.'
(*Many Things in Few Words*,
Charles Caleb Cotton, 1820)

They made their way with one small black trunk, Jacob's leather carryall, and Vita's old maroon carpetbag to Cleveland's Union Station four days later, only to learn once they got there that their train was delayed.

They could see it sitting on the track while a car-knocker inspected the under machinery. A boy with a sooty face jumped up and down from the platform, handing him various tools from two open toolboxes.

It was a little past seven in the morning. They had tickets for the Express to Buffalo, and from there they would change to another line for Boston. After they saw their trunk loaded into the baggage car, they spent a few minutes walking around the new station. It was constructed out of huge slabs of chalk-colored stone, with high ceilings and long windows, like a cathedral. A monument to commerce and travel.

The ladies' waiting room was painted pearly white and reminded Vita of the inside of a hatbox. There was a separate washroom with private toilets, and a matron was on duty to help ladies with their dress buttons. Jacob went to have a shave and steam towel in the men's waiting room, but inside of ten minutes the conductor began walking through the station calling out, 'Express departure!' in a booming tenor voice.

She let Jacob carry her carpetbag for her. Apart from the medical instruments she'd accumulated – most of them hand-me-downs from Dr. Boutwell – she'd packed nothing much more than what she'd packed at the Lark's Eye Hotel. Of course, the instruments would be useless to her now, but perhaps she could sell them in Boston. One thing she had learned was how to be thrifty.

When she went to the office to say good-bye, she gave Dr. Boutwell the same story she had given Mrs. McDove and the Misses Pickens: a missing husband who had at last found her, the move to be with him in Boston. To Dr. Boutwell she added: 'I might as well, since the Cleveland Medical College won't admit women. I was thinking I might go to Mount Holyoke and study biology.' That was only a few miles west of Boston.

'But there's a medical college for women right there in the city,' Dr. Boutwell had said. He studied her face carefully. 'You might look into that.'

'Perhaps I will,' she said, though she didn't think she would.

What she really wanted was to sleep for a week. To wake up and pretend that she'd never wanted to study medicine in the first place. Attending a few biology classes would be a relief after all these arduous months. And to the world she could say: I have a husband and a home to take care of now. That answered all arguments. Of course, no one was asking.

After they watched a baggage man load their trunk into the baggage car, they took their hand luggage with them and looked for seats. The train was crowded. At last they found two empty seats in the middle of the last passenger car, and Jacob put their bags and coats on the rack above them. This was a modern, open train carriage, befitting the new modern train station. It had two rows of thickly upholstered seats going down the length of the coach, with an aisle between them. After they settled in, Jacob and Vita watched the other passengers arrange themselves and their belongings: men dressed like bankers or clerks, a few women traveling with children. There was one pregnant woman a few seats up. She was well dressed, and traveling alone.

'She seems close to her time,' Jacob said.

Vita nodded. 'A month. Maybe less.'

Even before they left the station some of the passengers began to uncover baskets of food, and the smell of fresh bread, sausages, and sauerkraut wafted through the car.

'Hungry?' he asked.

She wasn't, but he bought two oranges and a pint of milk anyway from a boy walking down the aisle with a cardboard box tied like a yoke around his neck. A few minutes later the train started to push itself forward like a clanking, clumsy worm. Slowly it picked up speed as they left the station and began passing commercial buildings, and then warehouses, and then wooden shacks. After the shacks ended, the stubbly unplowed fields began. Jacob peeled the orange and pulled off a section for her, the white threads of pulp like a sticky web woven into the fruit.

'They advertise gas fixtures, but do they use them?' he said. Unlit gas sconces were nailed at regular intervals along the train car walls, next to older boxes with thin wax tapers. A young boy with two missing fingers was lighting the tapers, ignoring the sconces. 'Half of these so-called improvements are only advertising ploys. The stoves in the middle of the coach make you think more of the car must get warm, but it doesn't. Too close and you broil; too far away and you freeze.'

'I'm comfortable where we are,' Vita said.

They had lost their easy banter; they were careful with each other. The scent of food faded and was replaced by a mix of train smoke, sweat, and tobacco juice. Although brass cuspidors had been strategically nailed down in the front and back of all the passenger cars, the floors and walls were still stained yellow with spittle. When Jacob passed Vita the milk with its little cardboard straw popping up from the neck, she smiled a thin smile of thanks.

Trying to be agreeable. They both were.

The train stopped briefly at two small depots in Ohio before passing through a corner of Pennsylvania and then into New York State. At a longer station stop outside Dunkirk, Jacob ordered a second breakfast for them: watery coffee and a dusty heel of bread spread with marmalade. The station café was papered with curling advertisements for carpets and oilcloths, seed warehouses, or billiards tables. Also a handwritten sign: 'No spitting out the window if the window is closed.' He wanted to laugh with her about that but she was looking down at her bread, spreading the marmalade.

We have to get used to each other again, he thought.

When they were finished he bought a newspaper and asked if she wanted a magazine. He bought two sticks of striped peppermint candy and gave her one. She bit off the tip right away.

'You don't try to make it last?'

'I always forget,' she said. 'Or maybe I'm greedy.'

Her jaw moved right and left as she sucked the candy. 'This is good,' she said. And then, 'Better than the marmalade,' as though she understood he wanted more from her and was trying to oblige.

It would take time, he knew that. They had both changed, but separately; and me, Jacob thought, probably for the worse. His hands were steady, but he couldn't trust them to remain so. Vita looked like her thoughts were a million miles away. She was always honest with me, he found himself thinking. She told me from the first what she wanted. I was the one who held myself back.

✽

When the train whistled to announce its departure, Vita followed Jacob back to their seats feeling, as she had all morning, as though she were wading against a slight but persistent current. She settled her cloak over her like a blanket and closed her eyes but couldn't fall asleep. Back in Cleveland, Dr. Boutwell would be seeing patients in his office. He'd be swabbing a bleeding wart with nitric acid or giving someone with heartburn a drink of water with salts of tartar. She had an unopened letter from him in her purse; she'd spotted the letter on Mrs. McDove's hall table this morning just as she was leaving. It must have come last night.

She didn't want to read it. Either he would express regret at her decision, which would pain her, or he would not, which would also pain her. The train rocked along with its clanking song of iron against iron as she opened her purse and pulled the letter out.

Jacob looked over from his paper.

'From Dr. Boutwell,' she told him. 'Just a final good-bye, I expect.'

But when she read it, she realized it was not a good-bye.

To the faculty of the Cleveland Medical College:

It is my great pleasure to recommend my student, Mrs. Vita Culhane, to your institution for the purpose of furthering her education in medicine and obtaining a medical degree. I have acted as preceptor to Mrs. Culhane for the better part of a year, and have found her, without exception, to be one of the quickest and brightest students I have ever had the good fortune to teach. A hard worker with an exceptional memory and commendable study skills, Mrs. Culhane has also excelled in assisting me with all the physical realms of doctoring, including diagnosis and prescriptions for cure, application of bandages, administration of medicines . . .

The glass window was smeared with exhaust, making the day seem darker, and Vita tilted the letter to get more light on it. She felt a weight on her heart as heavy as a sigh. She was touched, but also sad. Did she deserve this? She read it once through, and then read it again.

'Everything all right?' Jacob asked.

'Yes. It's not – it's a recommendation for medical college. The Cleveland Medical College. My interview is – was – tomorrow.'

'You have an interview at the college?'

'They're expecting a man. They don't admit women anymore. But I didn't know that when I wrote to them.'

There was a sharp jolt. Vita looked out the window. They were coming up to a little country station with a black line of crows perched on the roof.

Jacob asked, 'Did you want to go to it? The interview?'

'There wasn't any point.'

The train jolted again, and their car began to sway back and forth. Vita didn't ride trains regularly. Was this usual?

'What's happened?' she asked.

'I don't know. Skipper,' Jacob called out as the conductor passed their seats. 'Everything all right?'

'Probably picked up a stone in the wheels. It'll come loose after a few turns.'

'What's the name of this town?'

'Gillis, New York, but we don't stop here.'

He kept walking through to the next car, clearly not bothered by the train's movement.

After they passed the empty station, the train began going up a small rise toward a bridge. But the swaying only got worse as they climbed, and a new noise started up behind them: *chuck*; *chuck-chuck*. *Chuck*; *chuck-chuck*. By this time all the passengers were glancing at each other with anxious expressions. This didn't feel right. Jacob got up to look out from another window.

'What is it?' Vita asked when he came back.

'I can't see anything. But I'm wondering if the back of the train has jumped the track.'

'Wouldn't the engineer see it, and stop us?'

At that moment they heard the brakeman call out from the short platform at the end of the train, followed by the long cry of metal brakes. But even Vita could tell that at their current speed it would take some time to fully stop. The shaking had become violent now.

Jacob pulled her up. His face was white. 'We need to get out of this car.'

As they made their way unsteadily up the aisle, several other men stood too, but then they paused, clearly undecided about what to do. Jacob was in front, holding her hand, keeping her close behind him. They got to the next car, which shook a bit less but was also swaying like a pendulum. Boxes and bags began to tumble out of the overhead racks.

Jacob had to raise his voice. 'Don't let go of me!'

He kept walking as though he wanted to reach the very first car. The train, still trying to brake to a stop, was on the bridge now. Through the windows Vita could see a gully some twenty feet below. She and Jacob were almost at the front seats when she heard, or maybe felt, a popping noise, like a Christmas cracker being pulled apart. There was a loud screech of tearing metal, and she had to let go of Jacob to grab the nearest seat with both hands as the car pitched forward.

Jacob also fell, grabbing at the same seat with his arms around her, holding her in place. His mouth brushed her ear and she heard him inhale sharply.

'The pin broke. The last car –' he jerked his head back toward the car they'd just left – 'it's falling.'

Jacob could hear the cracking wood of the train car behind them as it started its free-fall over the rails, punctured by shrieks from the passengers – or was that the scream of twisting metal? Two small children and a young woman, who had been making their way up the aisle behind them, lost their balance and fell, sliding down the floorboards toward the potbellied stove. It was all Jacob could do to keep on his own feet. He fumbled, trying to get a better hold on the seat that Vita was also holding. Her back was to him; he could not see her face. Seconds later there was a deafening sound of wood snapping and splintering as the falling car hit the bridgework outside.

The force of it pitching off the rails pushed their own car forward, and Jacob, even while trying his best to stay upright, did what every other man and woman in the train car was doing – he locked eyes with another person; for him, the young woman on the floor who had grabbed a seat leg with one hand and with the other was grasping one of her children by his shirtsleeve. She stared at Jacob as she lay there on her side with the same naked stare he could feel on his own face, stripped of personality, knowing their turn was coming.

The sway of their car, which had never stopped, suddenly increased its arc dramatically. A couple of men managed to cross the aisle trying to balance out the swing with their weight. The train was still moving forward on the tracks even as it rocked back and forth over the gully. Jacob felt a depth to his fear which was also a kind of space, as though a tunnel had opened up within him. He knew there was little chance the swaying would right itself, despite the efforts of the men crossing the aisle and back again. All he could hope for was that their train car got past the ravine before it fell off the tracks.

It hung on for two more sways. On the third sway the car paused for a long moment in the air, and then, instead of arcing back, it continued its sideways fall, a graceless tumble that had within it, for Jacob, the briefest moment of relief. Anticipation was over. What he had feared had begun. There was a sharp crack as the car's iron pin broke, severing them from the train in front of them just as the car behind them had been severed.

Vita lost her grip and fell hard against him. They were both hurtled across the aisle as the car smashed onto its side, shooting out shards of window glass and wood splinters like a spray of bullets from a hundred guns. The car skittered over the scrubby ground next to the rails; they had made it over the bridge, but barely. A matter of inches. They began spinning on the ground like a toy top; for what seemed like hours Jacob could see nothing except a whirling panoply of arms and shoes and handbags and seat cushions. A few lit tapers fell to the floor. The smell of burning metal. As the car continued twirling, a loose piece of wood hurtled toward Jacob, striking him on his head, and he closed his eyes.

Vita's dress was twisted up beneath her, and although probably only a few seconds had elapsed since the train car stopped moving, it felt like much longer. She couldn't make out where she was among the clutter of seat cushions, straw baskets, a splintered walking stick, sheets of loose paper with musical notations, and tangles of dresses and coats and trousers, some of which were people. Why were the armrests so close to the ground? Her brain was working very slowly. The car, she realized, had landed on its side. There was a shattered window beneath her.

When she looked down at her dress she saw shiny sparkles; she was covered in shards of glass. That must be why her sleeves were torn. Her cheek stung, too, and there was something wrong with her shoulder. She noted these details distantly, as though she were examining someone else. A patient.

Carefully, she picked rhomboids of glass from her dress and shook the fabric free of smaller shards. Then she crawled over to where she could see Jacob – at first, only his arm. His eyes were closed and his scalp was bleeding furiously. She grabbed a striped blue cravat from the rubble and used it to tie up his head. He was breathing, thank God. As she knotted the bandage he blinked and opened his eyes. Outwardly she couldn't see any other injuries although, like herself, his clothes were all sliced up. His mouth worked once or twice as if words might be found among his upper teeth.

She leaned closer. 'What?'

He swallowed and tried again. 'Smoke.'

The potbellied stoves had overturned in the crash, and hot coals were strewn over the plush upholstery and mounds of loose clothing. A couple of women had picked up seat cushions and were hitting back a small fire at one end of the car, but there were several other flames flickering among the seats. A gust of wind came through a gaping hole, and one of the flames flickered higher.

'We have to get out of the car!' Vita shouted, while at the same time she crawled over to a nearby pile of glowing coals and began pounding them with a cushion.

Already a couple of men were dragging out the injured passengers. Jacob helped unpin a woman's leg from under a bent iron seat and started pulling her out. Vita could hear children crying. One was saying in a high, anxious voice, 'Mother, get up! Mother, get up now!'

There were two openings, front and back, with all the passengers crammed between. Thirty? Forty? At least ten were already dead from the crash. Vita crawled past a man sitting upright with blood spilling from a slice across his neck – a severed carotid artery – and another with a half-dented skull, his eyes blank with death. She found the boy she'd heard calling to his mother. He was holding onto a woman, whose face was so bruised that it was changing color before Vita's eyes.

'Let's get you out of this car,' Vita said to the boy, but he wouldn't let go of his mother's arm, shaking it and letting it fall and shaking it again.

An older man crawled over, his graying beard full of glass. 'I'll help your mother, son,' he said, and together he and Vita pulled both mother and son out. The mother was dead, but it was the only way to save the boy.

He was still crying, 'Mother, get up,' as he sat beside her on the ground when another woman, calling him Denny, crawled over and took him by the hand. He wrapped his arms around her neck and began to shake with scared sobs.

Vita went back to the train car. The wind was sweeping through it, keeping the fires alive and growing. She could see flames licking the varnished walls and devouring piles of clothes. She helped another woman out who was hugging an infant to her chest. The infant's head was thrown back and his mouth was open, with ashes like grimy cracker crumbs at the edges, but he blinked, so he was alive, too.

She found a long pleated cape and spread it on the ground. 'You'll be safe here,' she told the woman as she helped her sit down with her baby. But when Vita turned back she saw there was no going near the train car again. The smoke was too thick.

She felt her throat constrict. Where was Jacob? Flames were shooting out everywhere.

'Back! Back!' shouted the man who'd helped Vita with the young boy, Denny. His vest was covered in ashes and blood. 'It's a fire pit!'

The flames swooped up, bending and changing directions, a wily animal consuming every breath of air. The metal carriage seemed to glow, and the air was thick with the smell of smoke, wood varnish, singed cotton, and burnt flesh.

But there he was. He was standing a few yards from the back of the car, looking over the crowd. She tried to stand but all she could do was raise her arm. It was enough; he saw her. As he picked his way over he bent to retrieve a fringed black shawl that had blown from the train, and when he got to her he wrapped it around her shoulders.

'For a moment I thought you'd gone back in,' he said, kneeling beside her.

The smell of smoke on his clothes was so strong she thought there must be a live ember burning the cloth. She moved her hands over his arms and the front of his shirt, checking.

'I didn't go back in,' she told him.

He brought her hand up to his mouth. The gesture felt more like acknowledgment than a kiss: *We made it.*

Others were not so lucky. Vita could see the train car in the gully below them. It too had landed on its side; flames rose from a few of its windows. But there were survivors; they could hear shouts for help.

'We need to get to them. We can climb down over there,' Vita said. She pointed to a rough, half-overgrown path leading down to the gully.

Jacob looked at his hands. They were shaking violently. His leg was shaking, too. He tried to stand up, and immediately sat back down.

'Do you think you can get down there alone?' he asked her.

'What do you mean? Are you hurt somewhere else?'

He lifted his hands so she could see them.

'That's all right, that's the trauma. It will pass.'

'No, my heart, too. It feels – it's gotten wild all of a sudden.'

'It's beating hard?'

He nodded.

'Mine is, too. But we need to help those people. Try to, at least.'

He hesitated. She could see something convulse in his face. 'I don't think I can. I think I've – I don't think I can do any more. Help anymore. Look at me.'

'Jacob,' Vita said. She was scared, but she didn't want to show it. 'Come with me. I need you. You'll be all right. It doesn't matter if you're shaking. Even if you keep shaking. They need our help.'

Jacob looked at her, his eyes wet. He didn't know what was worse, staying up here, uselessly, or going down there and being useless. He might freeze, like he did when the wagon cart turned over his first day in Lark's Eye. And earlier, at Andersonville. The moment when he saw the guard lift his gun and point it at the back of Caleb's head. For half a second he couldn't find his voice to shout a warning. He was a half second too late.

Now looking down over the gully he could see a couple of men, railroad men by their uniforms, climbing down the embankment. Like Vita, they had blood all over their clothes. Vita reached out and Jacob let her take his hand. His leg still pulsed, but he found, once he got his balance, that he could walk. Making their way down the hill, though, the footing proved tricky, and twice he had to grab a scrub bush for balance.

At the gully floor they were met with open trunks and bags – hand luggage flung from the train car as it fell from the bridge. A jumble of shirts, ties, dresses, and vests littered the scrubby ground.

'If I can find my carpetbag,' Vita said, 'I might be able to find my instruments. You put it in the seat rack above us, remember? It might have been thrown from the train.'

'I'll look for it,' he told her.

Injured passengers were crawling away from the smashed train car, many on only three limbs as they cradled a broken arm or shielded their bleeding heads. Unlike Vita's car, this car had several ways out of it – holes torn open by the bridgework as it fell – and she thought some people might have been thrown out even as it was going down.

But the car was now engulfed in fire, feeding on the wood and upholstery. No one inside could escape anymore, nor was it possible to help them. The flames were too high and the heat too intense even to get near it. Pieces of charred clothing drifted by in the air.

But I can still help the wounded outside, Vita thought. The two railroad men – George and Orson, they told her – began herding people away from the flames and flying embers. Vita made a quick search for clean clothes to use as bandages, stepping over what she thought at first was a man's charred hat before she realized it was a dead rat. It must have been holed up in the train car and caught on fire as it ran out. Near it, two smaller rats – babies – lay dead on the ground, their tails just trails of ash.

'Vee! Your bag!' Jacob lifted it in the air to show her. It was ripped almost in two and scorched all over. To her dismay, the cloth envelope of instruments was gone. But the bottle of chlorine that she always carried with her, which she'd wrapped up in her old wool shawl, was still intact.

'Look,' Jacob said.

Vita followed his gaze. A heavyset man was half leaning and half sitting against a battered fence. She could see at a glance that he had a dislocated shoulder. But worse: his right leg had been shorn off below the knee. He was holding his coat, crimson with blood, against the wound.

'Can't feel it at all,' he told them, perhaps not quite understanding, in his shock, that the lower half of his leg was gone. Vita quickly made a tourniquet out of a child's pinafore she'd found in a suitcase.

'What's your name?'

'Charles Scaletti.'

'I'm Mrs. Culhane. My husband and I will bandage you up, Mr. Scaletti, and then we'll find someone to carry you up top. You'll have to make some adjustments, but you'll be fine. Make sure you see a doctor every couple of days or so to check the wound, just at the beginning.'

She found two seat cushions to shore up his leg. 'Now this will hurt a bit.' She positioned Jacob's hands on the man's dislocated shoulder and then cupped the elbow. She pulled his arm inward and up in one swift, firm motion, and felt the bone pop back into place.

'Put a blanket or anything you can find over Mr. Scaletti, and carry him up as quickly as you can,' she told Orson and George. 'Also, maybe you can find him some whiskey?'

'Is that part of your training?' Jacob asked, as George and Orson went off. 'Asking people their names?'

'I've learned that it helps them trust me. And it helps me, too.'

'How does it help you?'

But she was already rubbing chlorine over her hands again as she headed toward a man holding his arm. 'Fractured, I'm afraid,' she said as she examined it gently. 'I'll make a splint for it until a doctor can set it. That'll make you a little more comfortable, Mr. – ?'

But the man, with tears running down into his beard, said only, 'I need my wife. Who has her?'

'We'll look for your wife, don't worry, but I'm just going to see to you first. I'm Mrs. Culhane.'

She asked Jacob if he could find any wood she might use as a splint. 'A branch or a plank, something straight.'

Jacob found a scrap of fence railing and Vita tied his arm to the splint with a man's long silk tie.

'Where is she, then?' he asked again. 'Who has her?'

Jacob touched him carefully by the shoulders. 'Can you tell me her name? What she looks like?'

But the man could only keep repeating, 'Where is she? Who has her?' until George came to lead him away.

Vita tied two more tourniquets, bandaged a child's ear that had been half shorn off, and then knelt to examine a man's bleeding leg. He had a half-singed-off mustache and they found him sitting on the bare ground, shaking and whispering to himself. He didn't stop, even to tell them his name.

'Firm but not tight,' Vita told Jacob, who was wrapping the bandage. She touched the man's torn shirtsleeve. 'You'll be all right now, sir. You're out. You're safe. Orson here will find someone to lead you up to the town and to a nice, warm room. You would like that, wouldn't you? You're all right now.'

She put a blanket around him. The air was bitter with the smell of smoke and burning metal, and townspeople had begun climbing down to the gully with pails of water to put out the fires. As Jacob was helping Vita construct another splint out of a piece of the train's floorboard so she could set a boy's broken leg, they heard a shout. George and Orson had a woman between them, half carrying her. It was the heavily pregnant woman who'd been sitting across the aisle from them when they first boarded.

'You need to get her up the embankment,' she told the men.

'She won't go.'

'The pains are coming on too quickly,' the woman said. 'It hurts too much to move.'

Vita introduced herself, and explained that while she wasn't a nurse she'd been training with a doctor all this past year.

The woman nodded. 'I'm Mrs. Laura Randolph, but everyone calls me Mrs. Laura. My husband's mother and his aunts are all –' she broke off and inhaled sharply '– are all Mrs. Randolphs.'

She bent her head in pain. Another contraction had started.

When it was over she closed her eyes, marshaling her strength.

'Do you have any family with you?' Jacob asked.

She shook her head. 'I was coming back from a visit. I have two children at home. They were both fast births. But this one –' She looked at Vita squarely, one woman to another. 'The foot is out. I can feel it.'

A footling. Vita had heard of this but had never seen one. If a foot was out that meant the baby was in an upright position and would have to be pulled out by its feet. And *that* meant the head – the widest part – would be delivered last.

A painful birth, and a dangerous one. But at least she didn't have to turn this baby around, like poor Mary Eileen Doherty's baby.

'I have four of my own,' George said. 'The last one came quick, like this one.'

Vita tried to think. The depot was too far away, but hadn't there been a farmhouse near the bridge? And she could see wagons waiting on top of the gully; they could put a mattress in the back of one and drive her there. She pulled a handkerchief from her pocket, thankfully clean, and wiped Mrs. Laura's brow.

'Let's get you inside. I saw a farmhouse not too far from the tracks. And we can make you a comfortable litter to carry you up top.'

'No,' Laura said.

'We have to get you off this damp ground.'

Laura gasped. Another contraction had started. She was right; they were coming on fast.

Jacob said in a low voice, 'Can we carry her while she's having a pain?'

'I would like to,' Vita said, but Laura, although still in throes of it, heard them and shook her head back and forth.

'Do you see any doctors?' Vita asked Jacob. 'Someone from town should be here by now.'

Men were passing along buckets of water to throw on the fires, while four or five boys helped a line of injured men and women up the scrubby incline.

'There,' Jacob said.

Two men – one young and one old, both carrying the black bags of their profession – had just scrambled down the embankment and were looking around at all the bodies and torn-off limbs. Vita saw the younger one bend down, put his hands on his knees, and vomit.

'I'll go fetch them,' Jacob told her.

They introduced themselves as the Doctors Wheeler, father and son. The older one looked irritated when he learned what he'd been called over for.

'A baby! *That's* the emergency?'

'A footling breech,' Vita said. 'The labor is progressing too fast to get her up the embankment. But I can assist you.'

George returned with a bucket of water; he also carried, tucked under his arm, a man's square leather shaving kit that he'd spotted hanging from a bush.

'Bless you!' Vita said. She unzipped it and found, happily, soap and a bottle of oil strapped inside. Orson brought over a clean blanket and two clean shawls, and then he went off to help drag mattresses carrying people too injured to walk up the embankment. George stayed back in case they needed more help.

'What are you doing?' Dr. Wheeler asked as Vita began shaking out her bottle of chlorine into the bucket of water.

'Sterilizing the water. So we can wash in it.'

'Wash!' He made the word sound like a sin. 'Don't tell me you believe that claptrap.'

Vita was astonished. 'Haven't you read Dr. Semmelweis? Or Oliver Wendell Holmes?'

'Bosh. Doctors aren't a danger to their patients, we're the ones who heal them. You only need to oil your hands.' He turned to his son. 'Lubricant, that's all that's necessary. But first remove your ring, otherwise it might get tarnished.'

'Have you assisted a breech birth before?' Vita asked the boy. He had a long curly mustache and was doing his best to look anywhere except at Laura Randolph.

'Well, no, you see . . .'

His father cut him off. 'He only just joined me in practice.'

That accounted for his hangdog look, Vita supposed. She was thankful Jacob wasn't put off by the pregnant woman's condition. He was kneeling on the ground, holding Mrs. Laura's hand. Of course, Vita thought, in the war he had probably witnessed much worse.

'Let's take a look at how you're progressing,' the older Dr. Wheeler said, starting to pull up Laura's dress.

Vita tried to stop him. 'Dr. Wheeler. Please. You must wash your hands first. The bucket is all ready, it's right there.'

'Now don't coddle the young woman. It will only encourage her to believe other falsehoods in the future.'

'It's not a falsehood. It's a proven fact.'

'Oh you midwives! You read one newspaper headline and you think you know as much as a man.' Then, in a lower voice: 'If it's breech then she'll probably die anyway.'

Not low enough. Laura shot Vita a panicked look. A man began shouting for a doctor, and both the Wheelers looked across the field. Vita knelt down next to Laura. As she put her fingers over the inside of Laura's wrist to check her pulse, her eyes met Jacob's. He was on the other side of Laura, still holding her hand. He gave Vita a quick nod, maybe to mean he believed her, or maybe that she should trust the doctor – she wasn't sure which. Laura's pulse was slightly elevated, which she expected.

She squeezed Laura's fingers. Dr. Wheeler was wrong. The evidence was there. Washing hands saved lives, particularly the mothers'. The wind had picked up and was blowing downfield; they should make a windbreak. Maybe get a few boards from the train car, whatever had escaped the fire. Vita squeezed Laura's hand again and stood up.

'I've delivered babies before,' she told Dr. Wheeler. 'I can deliver this one. It seems as though you're needed over there.'

Jacob, crouching on the dry dirt next to Laura Randolph, was inclined at first to side with the doctor, although he didn't know anything about babies. There'd been an Irish couple at Andersonville, the Hunts, who'd had a baby – he was born right in camp. It was rumored that both husband and wife had been caught as spies conveying messages in hollowed-out eggs, although no one actually knew, and Mrs. Hunt was one of the few women prisoners at Andersonville. The Hunts were given proper housing (a tent on a wooden platform) once Mrs. Hunt's condition became known.

Harry, their baby, was a skinny hairless creature, but nearly everyone in camp made it a point to try to see him whenever they could, walking by the Hunts' little tent hoping for a glimpse. It must have been February or March before Jacob realized he hadn't seen baby Harry in weeks, only the parents. Had he died? The Hunts left in April and their little tent was immediately cannibalized. Just as well, since groups of Southern women began to visit the camp around that time to gawk and laugh at the prisoners, throwing bread or rocks from the guard towers. The bread, of course, the men would scramble to eat, which made the ladies laugh more. Would they have thrown rocks in the presence of a baby? Jacob wondered. Maybe. Nothing would surprise him.

But when Dr. Wheeler said, 'She'll probably die anyway,' Jacob felt a hot wave rise in his chest, and he wanted to chase both him and his son with his ridiculous mustache away. It was a miracle that Laura Randolph had got out of the train car at all. How could the man not want to do everything in his power to help her?

'I'm glad they're gone,' Jacob said as the doctors walked off.

'I'll need your help,' Vita told him. 'Can you do it?'

Her face was stiff and pale.

'Yes,' he said, not at all sure, and for a moment half wishing he could call the doctors back. He couldn't help but think of his mother and his sister Gracie, both of whom had died giving birth. But Laura Randolph was nothing like Gracie. Jacob still thought of Gracie as a small barefoot child, whereas Laura Randolph was tall and spoke with a posh, New England accent.

They were sitting at the far end of the field; further than anyone had been thrown, and further than injured passengers should have walked to, although some had out of confusion and shock. The flat expanse reminded Jacob of a field after a battle: bodies like torn paper dolls, corpses still bleeding. The denuded scrub plants that grew along the dry creekbed looked like skeletons waving their stubby little fingers in the wind.

They washed their hands again in the chlorinated water. George hauled a few jagged pieces of the train car wall to make a pallet, covered it with blankets and shawls, and helped Laura onto it. Vita greased her knuckles and the topside of her fingers with the oil from the shaving kit.

'Lubricant, like Dr. Wheeler said. He was right about that. But I'm not going to lubricate the palm of my hand because I don't want to lose my grip.' She knelt beside Laura. 'Do you mind if I talk out what I'm doing? It helps me concentrate.'

'I like your voice,' Laura said.

Vita smiled at that. 'You're in the minority, then.'

She asked George to find dishcloths or towels – 'Check the closed trunks, we want them clean' – and to moisten them with water. Newborns were slippery; she would need the towels for traction.

'Can you find something to wedge Laura's hips up?' This to Jacob. 'Maybe a train cushion? Wrap it up in something clean first.'

She'd been afraid to look at the baby's foot, but when she did she was relieved to see that the skin was pinkish red, not blue; it was bright and alive with the blood moving beneath it. The difficulty would be bringing out the baby's shoulders and head; normally the head, delivered first, expands the birth canal for the rest of the body. In Mary Eileen Doherty's case, the first twin enlarged the birth canal for the second. Not so here.

George came back with towels and blankets.

'Jacob, you'll need to stay behind Mrs. Laura. You might need to hold her. Go on, you can lean against him if you want,' she said to Laura. She guessed that the contractions had moved the baby fairly far along by now. A fast and dangerous delivery.

Vita grasped the dangling foot just as the other foot was beginning to appear. Bits of whitish-gold membrane stuck to the baby's skin. Laura was groaning and Vita was concentrating so hard she bit down on her tongue and drew blood. Inch by inch, trying to draw on both tiny legs equally, she pulled the baby down using the moistened cloths like oven mitts. Small thighs, kneecaps like pink gooey nickels. Forgetting herself,

Vita almost lost her balance as she half guided half caught the baby, who, as his bottom emerged, twisted himself around; he was facing his mother's right side now, although at the start he was facing her left.

'A little boy!' Vita cried.

Laura wrenched with pain, gasping and moaning. Jacob said, 'Did you hear that, Mrs. Laura – you have a baby boy!'

Still using the towels, Vita grasped the baby's tiny bottom with her left hand as she encircled his waist with her right. Knowledge was like wooden steps nailed one against the other: do this, and then this, and then this. She moved her fingers, ready to reach up into the birth canal to assist the head. Later she would have cramps in the backs of her legs from squatting, then kneeling, then squatting again. She hoped with every breath she took that the baby's umbilical cord was floating freely, and not caught around his neck.

'Push!' she said.

Laura, grunting with effort, started to slide toward Vita.

'You'll have to hold her!' she told Jacob. Jacob grabbed Laura by the armpits – *axilla, from the Latin ala, wing* – the words recited themselves in Vita's brain as she waited for the next movement. But the baby, moving so fast before, was suddenly rock still.

Something was stuck. One slippery arm had come out but not the other. Sometimes a baby traveled the birth canal with his hand raised, and Vita had read about doctors who had to break the slender humerus bone in order to get the infant out. Amelia had been born sucking her thumb, according to Mitty. But when Vita gingerly explored with her fingers, she found that it was the baby's raised chin, not his arm, that was in the way. Free the chin, she told herself; then you can direct his head with your outside hand, and pull. This then this then this. She carefully unwedged his chin.

'Jacob, keep holding her tightly. And George, hold her hand. Now squeeze George's hand hard,' she said to Laura, 'and push.' Laura squeezed his hand. George nodded. 'That's right,' he told her, 'as hard as you're able. That's right, very good!'

'Keep going,' Vita said. 'We're nearly there.'

She had no instruments with her, no forceps. In any case the baby's head was at a difficult angle for forceps. A flock of crows chose that moment to start calling out – they sounded indignant. When they finished, another set took up the argument.

'At your next labor pain, push,' Vita said through gritted teeth. 'Give it all your strength.'

She could feel the baby's skull with her outside hand. Then she felt Laura's womb contract.

'Push, Laura. You can do it. Push.'

Laura grunted, grimaced, pushed; and then the miracle happened: the baby's head emerged. Vita felt an unexpected, shivery shock, and tears came into her eyes. She splayed her fingers against the back of the baby's gummy head, resting the fat wedge of his neck in the palm of her hand. He was out. He was breathing. His huge eyes were wet and open.

Laura gasped. 'Is he all right?'

'He's wonderful!' Vita used the clean corner of a towel to check his nostrils. Her heart felt like a released balloon. 'A healthy baby boy. Let's get him warm. Then I'll cut the cord.'

He was greasy with vernix but healthy and whole. A miracle. I've come to medicine backwards, she thought; the miracle didn't inspire her, it surprised her. George wrapped the baby in a soft pink shawl, winding the fabric round and round, while Vita delivered the afterbirth, which slipped out a few minutes later like a postscript. The arguing crows rose up and, as if taking off to herald a new king, swooped left and right before soaring away.

'You did it!' Jacob said. He was looking at Vita. Then he looked at Laura. 'You too!'

They laughed. George wiped his eyes. 'A perfect baby boy,' he said.

The feeling of triumph stayed with Jacob as he helped cut the umbilical cord, washed the blood from his hands and wrists, and dried himself off with some poor fellow's shirt.

He had never felt like this before. Not even after a hard-won battle, although when he enlisted he thought this was exactly how he would feel. Trying on his uniform coat for the first time, bumbling with the armholes, he remembered thinking how jubilant he would feel in that coat after killing his enemies, the bastards. But he had been wrong. He had never felt jubilant.

A few thickset boys were pulling mattresses behind them in pairs, hauling up the last of the injured. The train car fires were finally out, though still smoldering. Vita stood and stretched. Then she scanned the field.

'I think everyone is taken care of by now,' Jacob told her.

He took her hand. She curled her fingers within his palm and stuck her thumb out on top of his knuckles. 'But shouldn't we make certain?' she asked.

We. The single short syllable made his heart fold over.

He could see cliff swallows beginning to descend from the mangled bridgework, looping their crazy loops; they were probably only hungry but seemed panicked and lost. He recognized the feeling, though he didn't feel it now. He felt useful and needed. George was bustling about like a mother hen, spreading a navy overcoat around Laura as she held her son to her chest. Soon Jacob would help George bring Laura and the baby up to the top of the embankment, and then he would climb back down and walk the field with Vita to make sure no one had been overlooked. After that they would climb up to the road again. An unofficial-looking man would help them into a wagon cart and drive them to a house in town, where they would wash, and eat, and sleep.

But for a moment Jacob just stood there, holding her hand.

'We should go back to Cleveland in the morning,' he said.

Vita looked up at him. Her face was smeared with sweat and dirt. 'Why?'

'Your interview tomorrow, at the medical college. You should go.'

CHAPTER TWENTY-FIVE

'But neither the advice to go to Paris nor the suggestion of a [male] disguise tempted me for a moment. It was to my mind a moral crusade on which I had entered, a course of justice and common sense, and it must be pursued in the light of the day.'
(*Pioneer Work in Opening the Medical Profession for Women*, Dr. Elizabeth Blackwell, M.D., 1895)

Cleveland Plain Dealer, *May 9, 1866*

Horrifying Railroad Accident on the Buffalo & Erie Railway

'A Passenger Car Thrown Down an Embankment! Twenty-Two Burned to Death! Sickening and Heart-Rending Scenes and Incidents!'

We are saddened to report a frightful railroad accident that occurred about one-half mile from the Gillis depot at approximately 12:00 noon this day.

After a sudden derailment and subsequent uncoupling on a bridge near the town of Gillis, New York, two train cars fell off their tracks, one falling nineteen feet to the ravine below. Most of those killed were in the last train car. Mrs. Eileen Weaver of Cleveland heroically helped a young Akron boy and his mother escape; the mother suffered a dreadful fracture of her left leg from which the bones protruded. Mrs. Atwater, of Castalia, with two children – a boy and girl – were unable to escape the flaming car and died therein. Another family, charred beyond recognition, were believed to be Catholic due to a crucifix found in their possession, and were taken to St. Mary's Catholic Church until their identities could be fixed.

Within a very short time after the accident, Gillis Mayor Mr. William Dudley Manning dispatched a horse and cart to the scene of the disaster, containing buckets, mattresses, bandages, and other needed materials. Mr. Manning himself helped rescue survivors. The Doctors Wheeler (father and son) also volunteered their services to the injured. With their assistance, and in the midst of this tragedy, a Mrs. Laura Randolph from Mayville, New York, gave birth to a healthy baby boy. Both mother and son are doing well.

The Relief Train – the special train for the survivors – was scheduled to arrive in Gillis by mid-morning using a sidetrack. Thirty-one corpses were laid out for the night in the freight house, while maintenance men from the Buffalo and Erie Railroad walked the length of the track with lanterns, examining the twisted rails that rose up, at the place of derailment, almost six feet from the ground.

Vita's black trunk – if it survived – would be loaded onto the Relief Train, bound for Buffalo, but she and Jacob took the Cincinnati Express at six in the morning. They'd been given beds for the night in a house in town, but Vita woke up still exhausted. Her bones felt like thin bendable twigs that could barely support her, and her throat was raspy from smoke.

'You'll be fine,' Jacob said.

'Except for the small fact that they don't admit women.'

'You'll have to convince them to make an exception.'

They changed trains at Dayton, and then again in Maryville. It was just past noon when they arrived back in Cleveland. Outside Union Station, bricklayers and masons were sitting on the curb or leaning on tethering posts, eating their lunches. Vita and Jacob took a cab to Mrs. McDove's, hoping that one of the Miss Pickens might lend Vita a coat to cover her blood-spattered dress.

The younger Miss Pickens, alone in the house, smiled when she saw them. 'Back so soon with your handsome husband?' But her face turned pale as Vita explained about the accident. And when she heard about Vita's interview, she said, 'We can do better than just a coat, surely.'

Vita tried on dresses while Jacob waited in the parlor. But all the dresses were too long for her and too tight in the shoulders. Finally Miss Pickens found a somber, charcoal-colored wool (her sister's, who was shorter) that would do. She knelt to tack the hem with a few stitches.

'This won't last but a day,' she warned.

'I only need a couple of hours.'

'But your voice, it sounds terrible! Can't you put off your appointment?'

'I'm afraid I can't.'

'Then how about a little tea with honey and lemon?'

She didn't have time for that, either. She simply had to pray that she wouldn't lose her voice entirely before the interview was over.

'At least let me get you a peppermint,' Miss Pickens said.

Vita looked at herself in the hall mirror. She felt as though she were in a disguise. Would she remember everything? *Elbow: olecranon. Outer bone: radius. Inner bone: ulna.* Jacob nodded at her reflection.

'You look like a doctor already,' he said. 'But without the bag.' She was too nervous to smile back.

Miss Pickens loaned her a small hat with a speckled feather in the band.

'It's a lark's feather,' Jacob said.

'Is it?'

'And larks bring luck. My mother used to say that. To the sick especially.'

Vita took the hatpin Miss Pickens held out and angled it expertly through the stiff cloth. 'I thought it was *bad* luck?'

'Well,' Jacob admitted, 'it can go either way.'

That sounds about right, Vita thought.

It was after one-thirty. The interview was scheduled for two. Although Jacob urged the cab driver to put the horse to a trot, they went as slow as a milk wagon through the streets.

❦

'It is a full three minutes past the hour,' the dean said, opening his office door. Then he took her in. 'Oh, excuse me, madam. I thought you were my afternoon appointment.'

'V. Culhane?' Vita asked.

He cocked his head. 'That's right.'

She held out her hand. 'So nice to meet you, Dr. Cassels. I'm Mrs. Vita Culhane.'

His eyes narrowed in surprise. She could see past him to his dark-paneled office, so like Dar's: the same thick carpet and long desk with its requisite animal skull paperweight. In place of Dar's framed beetles, a row of ink drawings – different views of the human heart – hung on the wall, glittering under glass.

'Your office reminds me of my father's office,' she heard herself say hoarsely. She tried to get her voice up. 'He's a physician in Lark's Eye, Massachusetts. May I come in?'

'A physician, is he? Where did he get his degree?'

'Yale.'

The magic word. He stepped aside.

'I suppose your father encouraged your interest in medicine?' he asked as she walked in.

'Yes, my father is very . . .' Very what? 'He has hopes for me.' Not entirely a lie. 'Though in truth it was my brother who was supposed to be the doctor. Sadly, he was killed in the war.'

'I'm so sorry.' Dr. Cassels shook his head. 'All these young men, so terrible. Which regiment was he in?'

'The 28th Massachusetts Infantry.' She swallowed again. 'And so, instead of him, here I am. Following in my father's footsteps.'

They were still standing near the door, and he did not ask her to sit. There was no noise beyond the thick walls of his office. She'd left Jacob on the ground floor, sitting on a cane chair by the door reading a newspaper. The dean wore a watch on a chain tucked into his waistcoat. He pulled it out to take a look at it.

'I'm afraid you've come to no purpose, my dear. If I'd have known you were a woman I would have answered your letter quite differently. We don't admit women to our lectures. Not anymore. Women are too sensitive for this kind of thing.'

She smiled. 'I'm hoping I can change your mind.'

'I rather think not. We did try it, female students, but it was unsuccessful.'

He began to outline their troubles with the women; how he learned that one woman had previously studied an alternative medicine – 'Grahamism, so ridiculous' – and was, 'naturally,' expelled immediately. Another was discovered to be pregnant. A third stopped coming to classes after the fourth week, the course being simply too difficult for her.

'And you've never had your male students stop attending, or study alternative courses on the sly?'

'There's also the fact that any woman in a lecture hall will be distracting to the male students. The sound of her skirts alone.'

He had an air of producing logical arguments one by one, regardless of their illogical nature. 'We decided that it was inexpedient to admit women just at this time. We took a vote.'

Inexpedient, like Dar's 'unnecessary,' was a useful word, Vita thought. No need to say that women were not worthy enough or intelligent enough, you only had to say that the time was not suitable. But suitable for what? For whom?

'There are some,' she argued, 'who believe that female patients might be more comfortable seeing a female doctor.' An argument she'd tried with her father.

'As to that, I am proud to say that I have seen quite the opposite – ladies who choose to suffer extreme pain rather than submit to an indelicate examination by a man.'

'You would rather see women remain in pain than be treated for it?'

'No, no; not I,' the dean answered, smiling. 'The women themselves choose it. Quite noble of them.'

Did the idea of women choosing pain make him happy?

'My dear, I can see you mean well, but you would not be able to endure the kind of horrors we doctors face every day – really you have no idea. Despite your father. A country doctor,' he added.

Vita started to tell him all the wounds and illnesses she'd seen as an apprentice – amputations, syphilis – but he turned his head.

'It is simply inexpedient right now.'

They were still standing. She could see that he expected her to make some polite comment expressing her disappointment and take her leave. Instead she said, 'Surely you must have some discretion in the matter. May I sit?'

She could move fast when she needed to. By the time he thought to put his hand to his waistcoat pocket again in prelude to checking the time, she was lowering herself in the leather-backed chair facing his desk.

'You admitted a woman two years ago, I believe.' Lucy had told her this, and although it was a small hole, the tiniest chink, she would try to crawl through it.

'Ah, Mary Bradford. Yes, well, Mrs. Bradford was married to one of the students, and she had her husband to assist her.' Instead of sitting behind his desk, Dr. Cassels pulled out the matching leather chair to Vita's, and sat facing her at a three-quarter turn, as though underscoring that this was a casual conversation and not an interview.

'Your husband is not a doctor, I presume?'

For a moment she was tempted to lie. 'No.'

'So there would be no man to help you with the more difficult work.'

She felt her chest burn. Her voice was getting worse but she had to keep pleading her case. 'I studied in the office of Dr. David Boutwell. Here is a letter of recommendation from him.' Dr. Cassels took the proffered letter but made no move to read it. 'I've read Quincy's *Dispensatory*, Haller's *Physiology*, as well as Jones, Boerhaave, and Vansweiten. I know Latin and Greek, and I've studied algebra since I was a young girl.'

She took a breath and was about to go on when she noticed that Dr. Cassels was looking not at her, but at her shoes. Glancing down, Vita saw that they were spattered with blood. She had forgotten to change them. She'd thought about the dress, but not the shoes. Maybe the stains could be taken for mud? But then he would think she was slovenly.

'I've just come from the train station. That's why I was late.' She took a chance. 'My husband and I were on the Express train that derailed yesterday near Gillis. You heard about that?'

'What, you mean that terrible train crash?'

'We had been sitting in the last car, but we were lucky enough to get to the car in front before it fell off the bridge. That car also derailed, but at least we got over the ravine. We had to crawl out of it while it burned up. Others were not so lucky.'

The dean leaned forward, all attention now.

'There were no doctors there at first, of course, so my husband and I did what we could for the injured. I had some supplies with me. Well, a bottle of chlorine to wash our hands. My instruments were lost when my bag was ripped open. We made bandages out of any clean clothes we could find.'

'Chlorine, that was fortunate.'

Inspired, she looked around the room. On a little square table near the bookshelves she spied an arrangement of wooden instruments and rolled bandages. She fetched the rolled bandages and a pair of scissors.

'For a sprained arm,' she began winding the bandages around Dr. Cassels's forearm. 'You must always apply the bandage in a right angle to prevent hyperextension. For the knee, I used the Duke of Simpson strapping to prevent a recurrent sprain.' She demonstrated on his left knee.

'A man's leg had been shorn off at the calf. I applied a tourniquet here,' she showed him her technique, 'tighter than this, of course. We stopped the blood flow and I believe there was enough saved skin for a sufficient flap. Another man's head was cleaved in two; nothing to be done about that. You talk about being sensitive, but there was no time to be sensitive. There were so many head wounds and fractured limbs, some with the bones protruding. And countless burns, which I doused in cold water. I attended them all. A boy and a young man both suffered broken arms; I splintered them like so.' She found a ruler to demonstrate. 'With planks of wood from the train car.'

The dean watched – first her face and then her hands – as she bandaged and splintered him; an eyebrow dressing here, a mastoid bandage there. 'At the very end I delivered a baby, a footling breech. The labor was progressing too fast to get her up to a farmhouse. The baby's chin got stuck in the birth canal, but I was able to unwedge it by hand. Both mother and son survived, and are doing well. Mrs. Laura Randolph. You might read about her.'

By now her throat was positively raw. She stopped and swallowed, trying to wet it. Was it enough? Had she demonstrated enough? The dean glanced down at himself: white strips of cloth streamed from his arms and head and one leg.

'I feel like a maypole,' he said with a hint of a smile, and her heart lifted.

'I suppose I will read all about your heroics in the newspapers tonight?'

'Eventually a couple of doctors came down from the village. Dr. Wheeler and his son. They were the ones talking to the newspapermen, not I.' A thought struck her. 'You don't believe me?'

'No, no. I believe you. Either that, or you're the best actress in Cleveland. These knots are quite well done. Dr. Boutwell trained you well.'

He was struggling to free himself from the bandages, and she knelt to help him. He had thick fingers with very square tips.

'We do have some discretion, it's true. The dean is allowed to nominate unusual candidates. As in the case of Mrs. Bradford. Well, I'll see what I can manage. No promises, you understand.' Rising from the chair, he said, 'You have a nice quiet voice, my dear. Nice and soothing.'

She was about to explain about the smoke, but stopped herself.

'Those passengers were lucky you were there. But why were you going to Buffalo if you had your interview with me today?'

It was not difficult to smile and, without answering, turn her attention to tidying the room. 'Goodness, haven't I made a mess here.' For a moment she felt like Amelia, who always knew how to get what she wanted. The dean still had a ruler splintered to his forearm.

'Let me help you remove that, Dr. Cassels,' she said.

CHAPTER TWENTY-SIX

'*The Lantern* is a woman's rights paper, and believes in allowing women to do anything that they can do as well as men, and is in favor of paying them as well as men are paid for the same work, taking all things into consideration. But it is opposed to their *trifling with human life* by trying to doctor a total stranger. That is why we are sternly opposed to the innovation; and, as we said before, we will set our face against female doctors until we are old and toothless.'

(*The London Lantern*, 1882)

September 1866, Cleveland, Ohio

Vita walked into the classroom three minutes before the start of the lecture. Although she did not want to cut it too fine, the few minutes before the professor arrived were always the worst. That was when the male students would all be joking with each other, telling anecdotes or relating personal news; like the women of stereotype, they loved to tell each other about sales they'd stumbled into, or clever purchases they'd made. They never spoke about medicine.

The lecture hall was on the second floor of the St. Clair building and smelled of dry wood, chalk, and cleaning ammonia. It had a high ceiling and long, leaded-glass windows on its east-facing wall, and in spite of the Gothic influence it felt bright and cheerful inside, at least in the morning. Vita sat near the windows behind a narrow oak table with a long, slightly uneven drawer in the middle. There were thirty such tables in the room, each accommodating two students who sat on high wooden stools. They faced the dais where a different professor lectured each day. Occasionally – and occasionally legibly – the professor chalked up something on the board behind him.

On her first day, arriving twenty minutes early out of nervousness, Vita felt the men glance her way and then turn to make low comments to each other. Waves of discomfort swept over her. 'A visit by a hot stream of ghosts,' Mrs. O. used to call it. Vita had dressed carefully in a plain dove-gray dress and a starched linen collar, with no adornments except her wedding ring. A man who introduced himself as Gravel came up to where she sat.

'We're doing a dissection today. A cockroach,' he said, watching her face.

'Yes, I know.' Notices about upcoming lectures were pinned up outside the classrooms.

'Won't those get in the way?'

'Won't what get in the way?'

'Your little apples,' Gravel said, looking at her breasts.

She stayed away from Gravel after that.

She also stayed away from Burgher, who rubbed against her arm whenever he slid by her, and Jefferson, who once asked if he could examine her calf muscle, and a few others who just had a look in their eyes. In this class, Anatomy, she knew all the men's names because Professor Horton admired the

Socratic method, and he constantly called on students to answer his questions, even the rhetorical ones. He never called on Vita, though.

Now, as she settled herself on the stool – only one more minute remaining – she half listened to the chatter around her; most of them were discussing the recent fire at Woolson's Foundry, with a rumble of guesses on what might have caused it. The stool beside her stood empty; a student named Finn used to sit there. He'd been one of the nicer ones. A couple of weeks into the class he asked her whether she was 'finding all this a bit tough-going.'

'A bit,' she admitted. 'You?'

'Not at all,' he answered breezily. 'My father's a doctor, you see.' But he stopped going to class after the first set of examinations.

When Vita dissected her first cadaver, everyone expected her to be sick. Instead it was Gravel who was sick. She worked steadily for over five hours separating and defining each nerve, each blood vessel, every tendon. The valves, the organs, the sinews. The human body was like a three-dimensional mathematical equation, she thought as she stood there in her rubber apron, beautiful in its machinery, most of it still mysterious. She wished she could discuss it with someone. She envied the men who went off together afterward; over lunch, she imagined, they might discuss the position of the intestinal folds, or the swelling of the mucous membrane. Later she learned – from Finn, before he disappeared – that they mostly talked about girls or the cost of meals.

It was their camaraderie that made her feel lonely, although it was worse when they sought her out ('your little apples'). When she came to class now, their eyes landed on her only briefly before turning back to their chats. They were getting used to her, but they did not like her. Their refusal to see her as a peer was like a wall that protected them, while she in turn saw them as skinny rabbits, shivering in the sun. They had ropy haunches and quick eyes, and although they were not afraid, they were vulnerable. They needed each other's friendship and approval in order to shore up their confidence. Meanwhile, she studied.

Just as the clock struck the hour Professor Horton strode in with his long black robe flapping behind him as if struggling to keep up. At the front of the room he took a moment to look over the students, while they quite correctly took that as a sign to quiet down. His eyes swept over Vita as they did over everyone else. At least she was no different in that.

'Today we'll be discussing the human eye,' Professor Horton began. 'I trust you've all read your Mackenzie. Who can list for me the three protective parts?'

Sclerotica, cornea, and choroid. Last night she had stayed up reading about the eye until her lamp oil ran out. When she got into bed, Jacob did not so much as roll over, although he made a small noise, almost a word, as she took his hand and kissed it.

'Burgher? What say you?' Professor Horton enjoyed posing as a Shakespearean actor when addressing his students.

'Sclerotica, cornea, and choroid,' Burgher said.

'Very good. And what is another name we use for *protective parts*?' He gave the words a theatrical emphasis with a roll of his tongue. *Tunics*, Vita thought, and Burgher said the same.

'Tunics. Correct. You may recall that injury to the tunic may lead to inflammation. That is all, Mr. Burgher.'

Burgher sat down, pleased with himself.

When he was in school, Dr. Boutwell told Vita, they were taught that placing leeches on a man's eyelids would cure eye inflammation. 'Foolish, we know now. I sometimes wonder what else we'll realize is foolish in the years to come. You'll have to get used to the notion that you'll be tested on facts that may later prove to be mistaken.'

'But why do some doctors persist in believing outdated ideas, even with mounting evidence?' She was thinking of old Dr. Wheeler at the train accident, who refused on principle to wash his hands. Or her father, for that matter.

'People want to believe that facts, some facts at least, never change,' Dr. Boutwell had said. 'A very human desire.'

The world was full of absurdities posing as truth, Vita thought, and not only in medicine. The problem, though, was that if you didn't move forward regardless, you'd have no chance of discovering the real truth. Which, of course, might also turn out to be false later on. How do you hold 'truth' both firmly and lightly at the same time?

Sunlight pierced the leaded glass windows as Professor Horton began lecturing on the blind spot in the eye, first discovered by Edme Mariotte in 1660. Vita had already read and taken notes on this phenomenon last night, while Jacob slept with a stocking tied over his eyes to block out the light. As the professor described Mariotte's findings there was a knock at the door. A man in a janitor's cap limped in, pushing a wooden cart before him.

'Ah, here we are, gentlemen,' Professor Horton said happily, addressing the students. 'Our cow eyes. Pair up, if you please.'

The dissection of the cows' eyes could now begin. The students stood and looked around for partners. Vita waited to see who would be the odd man out, the unlucky fellow who had to make his way over to her. Not for the first time she missed Finn, the only student who would willingly partner with her. But perhaps the difference between Finn and herself was that she expected 'all this' to be difficult. She felt a tingling kind of power standing there by her table, knowing that if no one paired with her, she was prepared to perform the dissection alone.

Jacob and Soot sat on a stone bench beneath a fruiting maidenhair tree near the St. Clair building, waiting for Vita. Soot swung his legs vigorously, his toes sometimes clipping the dirt. It was lunchtime, and for Soot a half-holiday from school. Jacob had announced he would take them all out for ice cream if he got the job he was interviewing for that morning.

'Do another,' Soot told him. They were sharing a bag of shelled peanuts. Jacob took a peanut, threw it in the air, and caught it in his open mouth. This had been their act for the past ten minutes.

'Now me,' Soot said, trying to do the same. This time he managed to catch his.

'Bravo!'

Jacob and Vita had set up residence in Mrs. McDove's adjoining rooms on the second floor, recently vacated by the Miss Pickens sisters. After the younger Miss Pickens, Anna, had married Mr. Nowicki, they all three decamped to a pale yellow brick house in Willoughby, Ohio – Jacob and Vita had visited them there twice. Reverend Simpers had started a school, The Ragged School, for poor factory workers' children, and was courting the rich daughter of a steel magnate who lived on Euclid Avenue, a Miss Augusta Gephard. Jacob had met her once, a silly creature in his view, who never took off her gloves and who declared that she 'liked nothing better than to help the poor unclean children at the reverend's little school.'

'Are you going to be hungry for ice cream after all those nuts?' Jacob asked Soot.

Soot scowled. 'You've aten more than half of them.'

Jacob's interview had been at a company called Standard Works, founded by John D. Rockefeller; the D was never left off his name, and Jacob fancied it stood for Determined. Vita's friend Lucy Frost had a husband who worked for Standard Works, and she told Vita about the job. It was on the cooper side of the operation under a man named George Hopper, who had been experimenting with a binding mixture that would keep Rockefeller's oil barrels leak-free. Jacob brought along his plans for barrel glue – Caleb's plans – to his interview, and Hopper was suitably impressed. He offered him the job on the spot.

So, not a lone inventor with a partner, but a man in a team. Collaboration, George Hopper declared, that's what the modern workforce would all be about. They would share the credit, although not, Jacob suspected, the profit. Still, the salary was a fine one, and he would be working in the heart of an up-and-coming city, a city of the new age, the modern age, the age of commerce. Or so George Hopper said. George Hopper said a lot of fine things that morning. And to be honest, Jacob found it thrilling just to walk into the new, stone building full of men in shiny dark suits running up and down the stairs, bursting into office rooms, and talking excitedly over sandwiches – a palpable atmosphere of innovation.

He looked forward to discussing his new work with Vita. A woman interested in the problem of glue! His father would never have believed it; he would have scoffed at what he considered her pretenses. Yet one more way, Jacob thought (hoped), that I'm different from him.

His nightmares and tremors still came on unexpectedly. But he warmed to their talk, and to, of course, the delicious feel of their damp skins kissing, the smells they brought up in Mrs.

McDove's old horsehair mattress. They were always careful about French letters, which they began to call the Simpers after Vita told him the story of that dinner conversation. 'Let me just get one of the Simpers.' He loved the cloud the two of them made together, heavy and light at the same time. He loved when their limbs were so entwined that it was hard to think of them as separate.

Vita gave him tonics and rubbed his temples with eucalyptus oil when the shaking was bad. Part of him liked that she went off to work or class every day, though part of him was nervous, too – what would she find out there in the world? But now, starting Monday, he would be out in the world, too. He would have his turn telling her stories about the men in his office, the work, even the great man himself, if he saw him – Mr. Rockefeller. Jacob could picture Vita's face as she listened, tightening her lips as she did when she was getting ready to ask him a question.

The campanile chimed the hour, and students began streaming down the steps of the building like rice scattering out of a tipped sack.

'There she is,' Soot announced. He crushed the empty peanut bag in his fist and hopped off the bench with some attempt at ceremony, followed by a slight stumble. Vita was walking down the steps, turning her head to look for them. A small oval of space surrounded her; all the other students walked in twos and threes but she was alone. Like an exotic species of plant, Jacob thought. He felt himself smile.

'You have the job?'

Jacob took her hand and kissed it. Her face flushed warm with pleasure.

'Beginning on Monday.'

They smiled at each other.

'Any dissections today?' Soot asked her.

'An eye. A cow's eye.'

Jacob winked at Soot. 'Illuminating, I'm sure.'

'Why a cow?' Soot asked.

They headed toward the street. Ice cream had been promised, and the warm day felt more like the beginning of summer than the end. They passed a flurry of circulars pasted on tree trunks advertising a 'Traveling Exhibition' of a giraffe, an ibex, and a Belgian giant. While they walked Vita told Soot about Mariotte's blind spot, the place in the retina that had no photoreceptors – no cells that are sensitive to light.

'He discovered this by dissection. By looking at the various parts of the eye. Just as we were doing today. And because he found no photoreceptors in that area, not even one, he deduced that there must be a blind spot there. A piece of the world that the eye can't see. Cows – cow eyes – are the same.'

'But I can see everything just fine.'

'That's the miracle: our brains use the surrounding details to fill in the gap. We don't see it, physically; we only believe that we see it.'

The mild wind felt soft on her face. She made a fist and tapped it against her mouth, covering a yawn. But wasn't it pleasant, she thought, to be tired and to walk slowly in the sun? She took Jacob's arm and squeezed it. As they crossed the road, she caught a whiff of sawdust from construction down the street. Another building going up.

'I'm going to be a doctor, too,' Soot announced.

'You already know more than half the students here, I'd wager,' Jacob said with a grin.

'Why do you want to?' Vita asked.

'If you're a doctor you know everything! You know things about somebody even they don't know. Also you get to cut up bodies and look at them.'

'Dissection is only a small part. Most of the time we're talking to people, to patients, trying to work out what's wrong.'

'Oh, well, that's easy,' Soot said. 'Talking to folks.'

Vita tilted her head. 'You might think.'

At the ice cream kiosk she asked for vanilla, while Soot and Jacob opted for chocolate. Freddy always preferred chocolate, too. Vita could picture him eating ice cream on a bench on the Lark's Eye town green, a smear of chocolate on his chin. She liked to remember him doing ordinary things like that. In the kitchen on his hands and knees with Riddle, when Riddle was a puppy. Or patiently teaching Sweetie a new trick. He'd always been more patient than she was. Dr. Boutwell said he'd wanted to work with animals, and sometimes she allowed herself a daydream in which Freddy had survived the war and did just that. But if Freddy had lived – and this was so hard to admit – she probably would have stayed in Lark's Eye despite all her dreams. She would have never married Jacob, never studied medicine. Her father, and the world in general, was so much against her. As a girl, dreaming, she didn't let that in. Probably for the best. Hope was the easy part.

'Should we find somewhere to sit?' Jacob asked, handing her the paper cup of vanilla ice cream. 'Or do you want to keep walking?'

'Let's keep walking.'

She loved the smell of all the trees that grew along the street, hickory and bur oak and maple; they were leafy and redolent, with leaves every shade of green. So different than the decimated fields in Lark's Eye. She'd not been back there yet, though she hoped to go between terms to see Amelia's new baby girl. Dar, who had been told of Vita's college admission, had so far not written to her, not even to answer her letter. However, Mitty had come to Cleveland for a week, and then left to visit an old school friend living in Boston, Mrs. Deborah DeLong, for a full month. Mitty loved going to all the museums and public lectures – 'Everything I wanted for you' – and now might stay even longer, as Mrs. O. was perfectly capable of looking after Dar and the house and really all of Lark's Eye if she had to.

I'm particularly enjoying the Geographical Society lectures, Mitty wrote, and have volunteered some of my time to copy correspondence for them. Such interesting expeditions! Sadly your father is still trapped in his own unchanging world. Six scrapbooks now on how the war could have been won in the first year, or the second, if this or that had been done – and his son would then still be alive. All these articles he's collected to prove a point that can't be proven! And yet he continues, trying to bolster his case.

Vita finished her ice cream and took Jacob's arm again. He and Soot had begun to talk about the cutter races on Euclid Avenue in the winter, and then about horses in general. The trees are greener here, Vita thought, but the stars are brighter in Lark's Eye. At least she remembered them that way. On clear summer nights Freddy used to take his telescope outside, and while Vita waited beside him – for hours and hours it felt like – he fiddled with the focusing knob.

'Now look through this,' he would say at last, 'and tell me what you see.'

To her the sky was just a jumble of winking lights. She pressed her eye closer to the eyepiece. Blinked. Focused.

'Really look,' Freddy said.

ACKNOWLEDGEMENTS

Profound thanks to my wonderful editor, Claire Johnson-Creek; your insightful suggestions made this story so much richer. Thank you for gently pushing my ideas even further, and for encouraging me to try variations. Huge thanks also to my agent, Susan Armstrong, for patiently reading the earliest versions (and later ones, too!). Your supportive feedback throughout kept this story on track.

I am greatly indebted to Dr. Nelson Branco and Dr. Linda Pope for advising me on medical details, and for reading multiple drafts of this novel. Your help was invaluable. Any errors in the rendering are solely my own.

Thank you to the folks at the Dittrick Museum of Medical History in Cleveland, especially Jennifer Nieves, for generously giving me your time and advice as well as access to invaluable research documents. The Duxbury Civil War website and the Duxbury Free Library in Massachusetts were also enormously helpful.

For reading my work-in-progress, helping me find my way through the rough spots, and giving wise counsel, I am tremendously grateful to Christine Acosta, Julie Ansell, Barbara Bos, John Henry Frankel, Lily Frankel, Kate Kennedy, Heather Lazare, Janice Maloney, Carolyn Peter, Conan Putnam,

Stephanie Reents, Dr. Thomas Thickett, Malena Watrous, and Xiaoyan Zhou. Also thanks to my sisters Maggie, Katie, Therese, and Bernadette, for always being pillars of support.

Miriam Sherin, you deserve a line of appreciation all on your own. Thank you so much for being my first, last, and many-times-in-between reader.

Special thanks also to my writing partner and comrade-in-arms, Alice Boatwright. I've been so fortunate to share this journey with you!

And finally, my most heartfelt thanks to my husband, Richard. I love that you'll discuss the same ideas and issues with me again and again. I couldn't have done this without you.

SOURCES

I consulted scores of books, articles, and memoirs as I researched the American Civil War, medical practices in the nineteenth century, American social and cultural history, and women's history. Some of these texts include:

American Physicians in the 19th Century, from Sects to Science, William G. Rothstein

Andersonville Diary, John L. Ransom

The Angola Horror, Charity Vogel

Aristotle's Masterpiece, Anonymous

Civil War Soldiers of Greater Cleveland: Letters Home to Cuyahoga County, Dale Thomas

Cleveland in the Gilded Age, Dan Ruminski and Alan Dutka

A Country Doctor's Notebook, Mikhail Bulgakov

Doctors Wanted: No Women Need Apply, Mary Roth Walsh

Ecstatic Nation: Confidence, Crisis, and Compromise, 1848–1877, Brenda Wineapple

Eternal Eve: The History of Gynecology and Obstetrics, Harvey Graham

Ghosts and Shadows of Andersonville, Robert S. Davis

Hospital Sketches, Louisa May Alcott

John D. Rockefeller, The Cleveland Years, Grace Goulder

Letters of a Civil War Surgeon, Paul Fatout, ed.

Lone Woman: The Story of Elizabeth Blackwell, Dorothy Clarke Wilson

The Married Woman's Private Medical Companion, A.M. Mauriceau

Military Medical and Surgical Essays, United States Sanitary Commission, 1865

Mould's Medical Anecdotes, Richard F. Mould

On Diseases Peculiar to Women, Hugh Lenox Hodge

Pioneer Work for Women, Dr. Elizabeth Blackwell

Practical Midwifery: An Account of 13,748 Deliveries in Dublin Lying-in Hospital 1847–1854, Edward B. Sinclair and George Johnston

Science and the Practice of Medicine in the Nineteenth Century, W.F. Bynum

Soldiers' Letters from Camp, Battlefield and Prison, Lydia Minturn Post, ed.

Tokology, A Book for Every Woman, Dr. Alice B. Stockham

The Victorian Homefront: American Thought and Culture 1860–1880, Louise L. Stevenson

A Woman's Quest: The Life of Marie Zakrzewska, MD, Marie Elizabeth Zakrzewska

We the Women: Career Firsts of 19th Century America, Madeleine B. Stern

Don't miss Martha Conway's engrossing, powerful read . . .

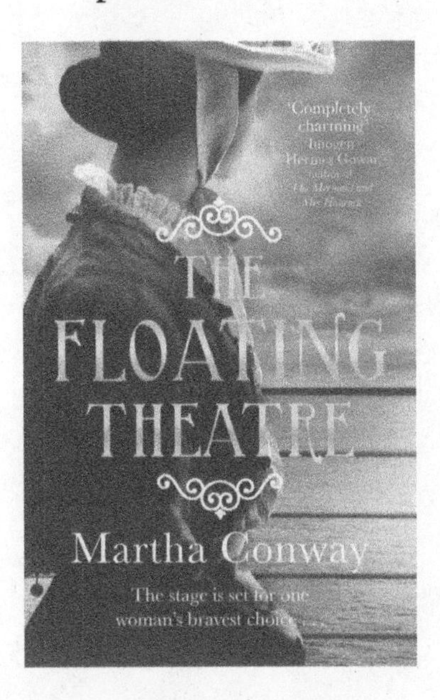

When young seamstress May Bedloe is left alone and penniless on the shore of the Ohio River, she finds work on the famous floating theatre that plies its trade along the banks. Her creativity and needlework skills quickly become invaluable and she settles in to life among the colourful troupe of actors.

But cruising the border between the Confederate South and the 'free' North is fraught with danger. May is forced to transport secret passengers, across the river and along the underground railroad.

But as May's secrets begin to endanger those now dear to her.

And to save the lives of others, she must risk her own . . .